To

Love
As Always
Ron & Margaret
xx
x

Also by Christine Thomas

Bridie

APRIL

Christine Thomas

HEADLINE

First published in Great Britain in 1990
by HEADLINE BOOK PUBLISHING PLC

10 9 8 7 6 5 4 3 2 1

British Library Cataloguing in Publication Data
Thomas, Christine
April.
I. Title
823.914 [F]

ISBN 0-7472-0267-2

Printed and bound in Great Britain by
Collins, Glasgow

HEADLINE BOOK PUBLISHING PLC
Headline House
79 Great Titchfield Street
London W1P 7FN

For my sister
Catherine Higgins

Acknowledgements

The author made extensive use of various non-fiction accounts of World War II in her research for the background to this novel, and would particularly like to acknowledge *Sheltered Days* by Derek Lambert (Deutsch, 1965), *The Incredible City* by Mrs Robert Henry (Dent 1944), *The Home Front* by Arthur Marwick (Thames and Hudson, 1976) and *My Sea Lady* by Graeme Ogden (Hutchinson, 1963).

Some of the incidents in the book were based on material in *The Home Front* by Norman Longmate (Chatto and Windus 1981), now available in paperback.

Prologue

George Dunbar blew a perfect smoke ring up towards his bedroom ceiling. It floated away from him and he squinted through it at the equally perfect curve of his wife's figure. He watched her contentedly, enjoying the double enchantment of her reflection in the wide mirror of her dressing table. She picked up a silver-backed brush and began to brush her waist-long, chestnut hair. George sighed with pleasure.

'Aren't pregnant women beautiful?' he remarked. April held the brush against her cheek for a moment and gently ran her other hand around the heavy curve of her belly. She smiled.

His eyes met his reflection in the mirror. He studied himself casually, sprawled, half dressed to go out, his dark, heavy set features already in his mid-thirties a touch florid from the fruits of success. He was little taller than his wife but wide shoulders and a forceful manner left people with an impression of a much bigger man. April caught his gaze in the glass and winked in amusement. She began brushing her hair again and, distracted from his self-absorption, George swung his legs off the bed and began putting cuff links into the starched white dinner shirt that would chafe him for the rest of the evening.

She gathered her hair into a thick knot and swept it

upwards, fastening it quickly and skilfully with long, bone pins.

'You've got the plans?' she asked, seeing him shrug into his evening jacket and pat his pockets. He opened it and showed her the slips of blue paper tucked into the breastpocket.

'Blueprints for our future. You're going to be a very rich woman, my darling.' He came and put his hands on her shoulders, bent, and kissed the nape of her neck. Her golden eyes gazed back at him, bronze in the lamplight that cast pools of shadow on to her face beneath its high, slanting cheekbones. She shrugged.

'I'm just proud of you,' she said. The baby kicked lazily. 'So is he.'

George straightened up. 'You and my son,' he said, laughing. 'It's all for you, you know. No point otherwise.'

April turned away, picked out a soft sable brush and, with quick little movements, began to stroke powder on to her flawless, milky skin. She thought of the long periods of withdrawal, the weeks of brooding and fretful silences; the shreds of paper scattered angrily in his study after nights when he did not come to bed. And at the end of it, the triumph, the exuberant delight of creation as he got it right at last. After five years of marriage, she knew that the true point was not her, not anyone at all, but the struggle itself; the long, creative battle between his own imaginative intellect and the limitations of his materials. Winning fired in him a kind of ecstasy, an exuberance for living that swept her up, too, only to drop her down again into loneliness when the next challenge possessed him. Sometimes it went on for months, and sometimes she fought her own hidden battles against despair and running away. George was the most exciting man she had ever met, but he frightened her. What if, one day, he didn't win? She patted rouge into the powder with light, deft fingers, leaving a tiny trace, a hint of colour.

'Nonsense, my darling,' she said lightly. 'You're too great an inventor to need a point. The baby and I just bask in your reflected glory. Like tonight.' She stood, dropped her robe in a heap at her feet and with one smooth movement stepped into a heavy red silk gown that left her shoulders bare and disguised her pregnancy almost completely.

'How do I look?' She turned before him.

'No one will notice me. They'll all be looking at you.'

'Nonsense! Once they've seen what you have in your pocket, you'll have them in the palm of your hand.' She laughed. 'Shall we go and enjoy your triumph?'

George's eyes glittered and he opened the door with a flourish. 'Lady Dunbar?' he teased, mocking his own excitement. 'Could be, you know, after this.'

'Lady Dunbar will do splendidly,' she answered, sweeping past him. 'It sounds very well indeed.'

His Lordship, she thought, descending the stairs to where a car waited to take them to the pomp and circumstance of dinner with the Institute of Civil Engineers at Westminster. It had a very pleasing ring.

Then the evil little voice whispered in her ear again: "What if, one day, he doesn't win?"

The after dinner speaker paused for the laughter to die down. He glanced round the opulent room, at flushed, well-fed faces gazing back at him through weaving trails of cigar smoke. Chandeliers burned brilliantly, outshone only by the startling blue flash of diamonds and the deeper gleam of other jewels. George reached inside his breast pocket and drew out the thin sheets of paper, waiting to regain their attention. He began speaking again, slowly unfolding the blueprints. The audience sat up in its chairs, all eyes on the papers he held loosely, almost carelessly, for them to see.

'You won't be able to make them out from there,' he assured them, 'which is just as well, since they are not yet under patent.' They laughed obediently. 'But here is the invention of the twentieth century.' He spread the blueprints out on the tablecloth in front of him, keeping them carefully turned so that his neighbours could not read them. He made a show of smoothing them.

'Limitless applications.' He tapped the papers and shook his head, as if in wonder.

'Hubris,' said a man's voice quietly from a table over to the side.

George ignored it.

'This will soon be in every home, every factory, every school, hospital, public building. In short, ladies and gentlemen, it will be as indispensible to our everyday lives as food and water. I am proud to announce that I have this week applied for the patent to the world's first two-way light switch.' He picked up the blueprints slowly and folded them with great care. 'That, ladies and gentlemen, is my new invention. Thank you.'

He sat down to a mounting buzz of excitement, and, after a few moments, a prolonged and mounting wave of applause. There was a kind of scuffle at the back of the room, and above the applause a voice called something that went unheard. At the top table, George leaned back, took April's hand in his, and began accepting a babble of congratulations. Shrewd-faced businessmen, designers, industrialists and academics;

the best in their field, every one of them, clamoured to shake his hand. It was intoxicating.

'Sir! Sir . . .' As the clapping died away, a man at the back of the room pushed back his chair and half rose in his effort to make himself heard.

George, grinning broadly, tilted his head back and tried to make out who it was.

'Harold!' he called, recognizing him and waving him forward. Harold struggled between the crowded tables towards the top table. 'Here you are.' George made to push chairs aside, so that Harold could join them. 'You can just squeeze in.'

'I'm frightfully sorry . . .' stammered Harold, trapped in the centre of attention. People began to stare and shuffle aside, trying to make way for him. Women pulled long evening gowns towards their ankles, clearing a path.

'Dr Dunbar . . .' Harold seemed to freeze, at a loss. The room fell silent. April suddenly caught Harold's eye, recognizing the sandy-haired man from the Patents Office who came to see George at home sometimes, and saw that he was appalled by something. Reluctantly he made his way through the attentive crowd, compelled now to explain his interruption in public.

He arrived at the dais, looking mournfully up at George behind the littered expanse of tablecloth.

'Go on, man,' George said quietly. 'What is it?'

The room strained to hear.

Harold swallowed.

'I granted an interim patent on that design two weeks ago.'

A sigh passed like a caress across the room.

'Impossible!'

Harold shook his head.

'I'm sorry, sir, but I did.'

George took the blueprints out of his pocket and calmly unfolded them on the tabletop. He spread them flat and turned them towards Harold.

'Take a look.'

Harold stepped forward and glanced at the drawings. Then he bent and looked more closely.

'I'm sorry, sir.' He straightened up, still staring at the papers.

'These plans?'

'Identical, sir, so far as I can tell.'

George went white. 'Someone has tricked me,' he announced quietly. 'Stolen them. Who?'

Harold shook his head. 'I can't remember offhand, sir. You'll have to look at the papers.'

April touched George's sleeve. 'Washington,' she murmured.

'Was that it?' demanded George.

Harold nodded.

'I sacked him two months ago.'

'He must've got hold of it,' said Harold sadly.

Slowly, George crumpled the prints. 'I'll sue him. I'll ruin that sly bastard for this.'

Harold's colourless eyelashes fluttered with interest. 'You can prove they're your invention, of course?'

George stared at him with unwinking scorn and barely noticed the murmur of speculation that began to swell through the dining room.

'Does anyone doubt it?' he demanded.

'No one here,' answered Harold hastily. 'But you'll have to fight it in court. It's no easy matter to prove possession of an idea, Dr Dunbar. Even someone as eminent as yourself will have to furnish proof. Can you?'

Harold's tactless professional curiosity brought George's fist crashing down on the table; glasses clinked and trembled and there was another brief, amazed silence.

'Prove it? Everyone in this room knows I invented that switch. Why *should* I prove it?'

'To get the patent back.'

April touched George's sleeve in alarm. 'Darling, leave it for now.'

He went very red, very white, and seemed to breathe with difficulty.

'George!' cried April shrilly. 'Oh, help him.' Hands reached out to catch him as his eyes bulged with pain and he fell heavily back into his chair.

The annual dinner of the Institute ended in scandal and disaster. The guests, excited and shocked, dispersed quickly, to let the doctor and the ambulance men in amongst the debris of what had turned out to be a most enthralling drama. April allowed herself to be taken home by the concerned and conciliatory President and his wife, where she took off the red silk gown, dressed in a warm, tweed suit and low shoes and, although it was by then the early hours, settled down to wait by the telephone for news of George's condition.

In the event, it was merely a mild stroke brought on by the stress of his sudden fit of rage. It left no trace but a tremor in his right hand that made drawing impossible, or at least the fine, precise technical drawing of his profession. Otherwise, George was fine. Only the heart had gone out of him.

'I won't give that bastard the satisfaction,' was all he

would say when urged to take the matter of ownership of the two-way switch to court.

'I think that's wise. More than I thought he had in him,' was Harold's opinion. 'If he didn't win – and there's every chance he might not – it would . . .'

"Kill him, you mean, only you daren't say so," thought April. 'It seems desperately unjust. Everyone knows it was his invention,' she complained, shifting uncomfortably on the drawing-room sofa under the weight of the baby, due any day. Harold had called on the pretext of advising George on the Patents Office's view of fraud but April suspected him of gloating.

'We do.' He shook his head in a way that belied his words. 'Proving it is a different kettle of fish altogether. It's not a just world. You can't bank on anything. I'd have advised him to be very careful, only he didn't ask for advice. What do his lawyers say?' he asked impertinently.

April stood. It was time for him to go. He'd done nothing to help George out of his inertia, any more than had the fork-tongued solicitors with their evasive words and sly, greedy eyes. She saw Harold out of the house and the air was somehow more breathable when he had gone. Standing in the cold, square hall of the big house, she put her hand to her side and felt her baby tap gently with one tiny foot.

'So long as you are all right, we'll come through,' she thought. 'Your father needs you, you know, to give him a point again, a meaning. Someone to inherit, you see. Otherwise . . .' The baby stirred, stretching against her lower ribs. 'I hope you're listening,' April told it sternly, and after that it lay quietly.

The baby lay very quietly for another two days and then

tried to make her way into the world feet first. April struggled until her strength was gone and when the doctor could not stem the sudden gush of blood, he knew he had lost them both.

George grieved immoderately. He closed himself up in the big, gloomy house and saw no one. He grew fat and unkempt, drinking the pain away until he hardly knew if it were day or night. Stained and shambling, he roamed the upper floor, keeping vigil over the room where they had died. Eileen, creeping uncertainly into the miserable place one day, found him sobbing incoherently, wild-eyed and trembling, his face buried in the pillow that had lain under April's head in death. Eileen stood in the doorway, repulsed and pitying. She mourned her sister, but vaguely; they had not been close.

For a long time George did not notice her. Then he raised his head and they stared at each other, horrified.

'You need someone to look after you,' she told him. 'It stinks in here.' She walked across the cluttered floor, and to George's consternation threw open the wide windows. Sunshine streamed in, making him blink painfully.

'You're a disgrace.' She picked up bottles and began to stack them to one side. 'And this isn't doing you any good, either.'

George, crouched by the bed, tears still wet on his face, watched her incredulously.

'Get out,' he snarled.

Eileen ignored him. She jerked the soiled silk coverlet off the bed and the sudden movement jolted him on to the floor.

'Look at this – ruined! Mother gave her this as a wedding present. Fancy spoiling it.'

George gaped.

'Come on, let's get you tidied up.' Gently she touched him on the shoulder, urging him up. It was the first human touch George had felt in more than six months and as she stood over him, waiting, he put up his hand and covered hers where it lay.

'Yes,' he said.

Eileen could not speak for joy.

They married the following year. Everyone said what a wonderful job she'd done. George began to work again and to pick up some of the old reins at his office. Eileen opened the house once more and they even ventured out into society in a modest kind of way. When their daughter was born, Eileen put her to her breast, helped by the midwife, and saw with all the clarity of those first moments after birth that she would be April, all over again.

'Dolores,' she said firmly, fending off the truth.

'April,' exclaimed George, gazing, entranced.

'No.' She knew she was weakened by loving him as he had loved her sister, helplessly, and that she could not protest for long.

George smiled, delighted and restored.

'April,' he breathed, touching the little face wonderingly, and Eileen knew she was lost. Now, once more, there would be only April.

April was not an easy baby. She cried, she screamed. At three months she got the croup and yelled Eileen's nerves to shreds. She turned night into day with a fine disregard for her mother's feelings, threw up her feeds and soiled her carefully starched and ironed baby dresses just, Eileen began to feel, to show her up and imply that she didn't look after her daughter properly. Eileen gritted her teeth; George doted and left all the work to her. Eileen wept, George smiled smugly at his pretty baby; she always smiled for him. Eileen, at the end of her tether, wanted to scream, but quietly, so George wouldn't hear, because she knew he judged her decidedly wanting as a mother.

One afternoon, watching her brilliant white sheets snapping on the line in a brisk east wind, edged with rows of equally brilliant white nappies, Eileen heard April wake and start to fret.

'You've only been down half an hour,' she cried, looking at the clock in despair. 'You can't have anything to cry about.'

April bawled, kicking off her blankets, her nappy round her knees. Eileen stood over the crib, tense and tired and, more than anything, frustrated.

'Please be quiet, April! Be quiet for Mummy, there's a good girl.'

The baby stopped yelling, opened tearless eyes, and squinted at her mother.

'There you are. It's not so bad. No need to carry on like that, is there? You going to be a good girl, now?'

April snapped her eyes tight shut, screwed up her face, and shrieked. Eileen's plain, regular features twitched and tears gathered, threatening to spill humiliatingly down her wan cheeks.

'Please, April,' she warned in a high, tight voice. 'I've had enough. I can't cope with any more yelling. Please stop.'

The baby's tiny, perfect bow of a mouth opened yet wider and she drew breath. Eileen watched as the exquisite infant turned purple, gathering steam, and her nerve gave way. April choked and never managed her next howl ás Eileen, distraught and hardly knowing what she was doing, snatched her from her cot and ran, bundling her in blankets as she went, into the wide, silent hall where her pram stood near the front door. 'Stop it,' she gasped, throwing the baby into the pram. 'Do you hear me? If you don't stop, I'll . . .'

She flung open the front door and bumped the pram ruthlessly down the two wide steps that led to the path, watching with satisfaction as April bounced, shocked and wide-eyed, all of a heap in her blankets. 'I'll show you who's in charge, young woman, and it isn't you,' hissed Eileen, pushing the pram at speed out of the gate, into the road and almost running off downhill in the direction of Wanstead Flats.

'You and I are going to settle this, Madam,' she panted, whirling round the corner into the great, flat expanse of grass that led into woods, lining the horizon. April rolled in the pram, frightened, fascinated, and at long last blessedly silent. Eileen marched savagely down the side of the grass, pushing the heavy carriage over a stony path. Her arms ached, her head ached, her eyes smarted and a big lump rose in the back of her throat until, with a final furious jerk, she pulled the pram to a stop, threw herself violently on to a mildewed wooden bench a little to one side of the path, on a slope, and burst into tears. April lay calmly watching clouds sail slowly past a hazy sun, her cheeks reddened by the cold, fresh wind that plucked at her disordered covers and blew Eileen's thin hair across her wet face.

'Why,' she sobbed at the side of the pram, April invisible inside, 'do you have to be so difficult? Why, why, why?' She thought of her sister, adored and admired and spoilt, and tears flooded again as self-pity overwhelmed her.

'I hate you,' she muttered, already half ashamed even before the words were out. But she repeated, for defiant good measure, 'I hate you.' She sat up straight and mopped at her face, chapped by wind and tears.

'I don't really mean you,' she said in the direction of the pram at last. April kicked, her feet waving in Eileen's line of vision.

'It's her, you know,' she said to the toes, whose bootees had long since come off. 'It's not really you. But he thinks it's her, and it's so cruel and you're too small . . . I know it's not your fault, but when you scream, I don't know what to do, and my head feels funny, and I can't bear it.'

April sucked her fingers and crowed. Eileen looked at her over the edge of the carriage.

'You see, you're just contrary. You yell when you're warm and fed and comfortable, but put you out here in the freezing cold with a wet nappy and you're happy as a sandboy. What do you expect me to do?'

April chuckled as Eileen scowled at her.

'You're a horrible baby, April. Sometimes I hate you. It isn't just my sister.' Saying it aloud made her feel very bad and guilty, but somehow better. She sighed.

'But I love you anyway. Isn't that queer?'

April merely went on sucking her fingers placidly and had nothing to say on the matter.

'Bother!' said Eileen, ten minutes later. A baby carriage came slowly along the same path, pushed by a flat, angular woman with a streak of grey in her dark brown hair. She was bent half double with the effort of pushing the pram, her face stern.

'Heavy going, isn't it?' She stopped when she came

level with Eileen and leant on the pram handle to get her breath.

'It's the stones,' said Eileen, crunching her handkerchief into a damp ball and hoping her face didn't give her away.

"She's been crying her eyes out, poor thing," thought the woman.

'Chilly, too,' she remarked, looking into her pram so as not to embarrass Eileen by staring at her. 'What a lovely baby,' she went on, peering at April, chortling though mottled with cold.

'Sometimes,' said Eileen non-committally.

'They can be awful, can't they?' The woman rocked her carriage gently. Her fourth child slept peacefully, hidden in a well-tucked pile of warm blankets. 'I'd watch she doesn't catch cold, she's kicked all her covers off. She's a bonny little one, isn't she?'

'Do you know,' said Eileen, throwing caution to the winds, 'sometimes I wish she would catch something, because it might wear her out and shut her up. Isn't that terrible.'

The older woman looked into the pram again, and felt April's frozen feet.

'Your first one, is she? I remember my first one nearly drove me mad. Up all night – I thought he'd never sleep. But they do. They settle eventually and then you wonder what made you so upset.' She spoke carefully, watching Eileen out of the corner of her eye as she began to pull covers over April and fished lost bootees out from down the side of the mattress. 'I know we aren't supposed to say so, but I think everyone feels like that sometimes. No one lets on, though, so we all think we're the only ones. I know I have.'

'Really?' sniffed Eileen. 'Have you?'

'Bless you, yes.'

'Oh.'

'I'm Rachael,' said the woman, whose face lost its
angularity in a wide, warm smile; deep grey eyes lit
with kindness studied Eileen shrewdly. 'Haven't I seen
you shopping down the Belgrave?'

'Yes. I'm Eileen Dunbar.'

'You're Dr Dunbar's wife?' Recognition dawned in
Rachael's face.

'Yes.'

'We're nearly neighbours, then. Can I sit down?' She
parked her carriage beside Eileen's and finished
tucking April in. April cooed, good as gold. Eileen
sniffed again and graciously indicated the end of the
bench.

'How old is she?' began Rachael. 'Mine's six
months.'

'Nearly the same. April's five months. She's had
croup for goodness knows how long.'

'Oh, croup. It's awful,' cried Rachael, warming
Eileen's heart as nothing had for a long, long time. 'My
dear, how do you manage? I got some wonderful stuff
from our doctor . . .'

The two carriages stood side by side with their
sleeping babies as their mothers leaned across the
bench towards each other, confiding. Cloud shadows
scudded across the flat expanse of grass and unconsciously they drew closer, pulling their coats around
them against the brisk spring wind. They talked and
talked, until the babies began to stir and it was time to
go home.

'Another lame duck?' said Rachael's husband toler-
antly.

'I rather liked her.'

'Well,' remarked Gordon, after a pause, 'perhaps you'll meet the famous George Dunbar. It'd be interesting to know what really happened. There was quite a scandal at the time.'

'I don't think she'd say anything about that,' said Rachael thoughtfully. 'I get the impression that family won't welcome prying. But she badly needs a friend.'

Gordon laughed.

'I liked her,' repeated Rachael. 'Don't you laugh like that.'

'If your wings are big enough to tuck another one under, Mrs Dunbar is lucky, is all I can say. You go on, love, with whatever makes you happy.'

'You won't mind if I invite her round, then?'

'What's one more?' answered Gordon, eyeing his crowded house, evidence of children everywhere.

'I'll ask her, then,' said Rachael.

So it began, the friendship which was to last the rest of their lives. Eileen had a friend, an ally, a shoulder to cry on; Rachael, seeing past her prickly, defensive manner, came to love her despite everything, and April, spending almost more time in Rachael's house than her own, came to have a second mum.

April turned out to have her father's brains. By the time she was eleven George was studying her school reports with satisfaction; Eileen read and re-read them with very mixed feelings. April's cleverness intimidated and bewildered her, though Rachael scolded and said she should be glad because women had a hard enough time in life and April would go far thanks to her academic gifts.

'Only if her father approves of what she wants to do,'

said Eileen unhappily. 'She talks about taking matriculation and going to Oxford, and sometimes I think she does it just to annoy him. She knows perfectly well how much he detests bluestockings and women getting above their place, as he calls it. But she answers him back and gets away with it, goodness knows how,' she added gloomily.

Rachael tended to be philosophical about George, which Eileen sometimes minded.

'Let them fight it out between them,' she said, her horsey features puckered thoughtfully. 'I'd stay out of it, if I was you.'

'I don't know that I can,' Eileen answered defensively. 'If I do, April thinks I don't care. Whatever I say, it's wrong, caught between the two of them. There's no getting it right.' She gave a martyred sniff. Rachael glanced at her sharply, detecting the hint of satisfaction betrayed by that twitching nose. She thought that if anyone needed defending, it was probably April.

'She's a lovely girl. She'll have plenty of young men around her later on. She'll be married before you know it, and then you won't have to worry.'

Eileen grunted non-committally. Shades of her sister rose at Rachael's words and she struggled to banish them as her friend reached down her mixing bowl.

'You want to share a batch of fairy cakes?'

'Where's your scales?' asked Eileen, looking on Rachael's shelves and rolling up her sleeves.

Rachael laughed.

'Gordon took them to school to demonstrate something or other. We'll have to use spoons.'

Eileen sniffed sadly. Gordon had the looks of a bluebeard and the nature of a lamb. He taught at a school in the City and took kitchen scales to school and did wonderfully ordinary things with his pupils, like measuring. On Saturday afternoons he would happily spend his precious free time train-spotting on the dusty platforms of Paddington station with his own three boys. Eileen sighed with envy. She fetched a set of tablespoons and began to count out the flour and sugar, while Rachael cut the fat.

'Just as well we can manage without gadgets. Men!' Eileen poured white flour angrily into a bowl and a small cloud rose above its rim. Rachael grinned understandingly.

'George plotting something new?'

Eileen shook her head. 'He gets ideas, but he doesn't do much about them. The heart went out of him long ago. It's just talk, these days.'

'It's sad to see a man give up.' Rachael dropped vanilla into the mixture and dabbed at it with a spoon. 'You want to take some of these back with you? April'll eat them.'

'If my daughter was half as sweet as her tooth, she'd be no trouble,' remarked Eileen dourly. Then she caught her friend's critical eye and smiled sheepishly across the mixing bowl.

'You leave her be and she'll do,' said Rachael sternly.

'I hope so,' sighed her mother.

The little family group marched across the Flats the following Sunday afternoon, their coats flapping in a bitter wind that had howled over the marshes all night and only seemed to let up as the day wore on.

'Fresh air,' said George, unmoved by their reluctance to stir from the fireside as the bleak March afternoon passed dully outside. 'Come on, it'll do you good.'

He strode ahead, Eileen and April dragging behind. Clouds raced across the sky, low and grey, and occasional flurries of sleet stung their cheeks, wet with tears from watering eyes.

'Let's turn back now,' begged Eileen. 'It's going to come down heavy soon, George.'

'It'll be sheltered under the trees.'

April narrowed her eyes against the stinging wind and the long, black line of the woods wavered in front of her, seeming miles away. 'I'm going back.'

Hopefully, Eileen trailed to a halt as well.

'We'll turn round, George,' she called. His over-coated figure didn't stop. April pulled her scarf tightly round her ears and began to walk back the way they had come. Eileen stood in the middle, uncertain.

'George!' she called again. April, hurrying, was already too far away to call to against the gale. Eileen saw her skirt round a solitary tree, with benches beneath it, to take a detour that would get her home by a shorter route. George stopped and looked back, his face a blur behind a thick muffler. Eileen half heard his call as April stopped and bent down to look at something under one of the benches. Then she straightened up and beckoned to her mother.

'Look!' Eileen heard, the words carried faintly on the shrieking wind. 'Look, come here and look.'

Eileen's numb feet took her first one way, to where George waited, poised for a last dash towards the woods, then towards April, who had crouched by the bench and seemed absorbed, her scarf flying, a bright blur against low, leafless branches.

'Eileen.' The wind carried George's voice away.

She made up her mind. Curiosity hurried her across the sparse, wet grass towards April, who looked round at her.

'Look!' she said once more, pointing underneath the mildewed old bench. Eileen bent and followed her pointing finger. A brown paper bag was caught by the wind, crumpled into the wintry mud against one leg of the seat. Just inside it, like a discarded scrap of something inedible, lay a minute kitten, hardly more than two or three weeks old. It bared its tiny teeth in mute fear, dragging itself backwards into its paper shelter on useless, scrabbling legs. Eileen looked at the back of her daughter's head and realized she was crying.

'It's going to die,' cried April, her lips blue. 'What shall I do?'

Eileen shook her head. 'Leave it.'

April touched the kitten's matted fur, distraught. 'We can take it home.'

The kitten gave one tiny miaow and slumped with closed eyes, exhausted.

'I think it's too young,' said Eileen gently. 'Its mother must have abandoned it, poor little thing. Leave it, April, it's probably covered in fleas.' She touched her daughter's shoulder, as if to take her away. April shrugged the hand away, pulling at the corners of the paper bag, which tore damply in her hand.

'It's a baby,' she cried desperately. 'Babies don't die. It doesn't want to die, Mum, it's a baby.' She picked up the little creature, cradling it in her hands. 'Look, it's shivering. Poor baby, poor baby . . .' she crooned, starting to put the dying animal inside her coat. 'You come here and get warm. I'll take you home.'

'April . . .' protested Eileen.

She flung herself away from her mother, holding the kitten fiercely. 'No!' she shouted. 'I'll look after it.'

'After what?' demanded George, looming over her against the blackening sky.

'This.' April opened her coat a fraction, glancing defiantly over his shoulder at her mother. 'I'm going to keep it.'

They stood, the cold wind bringing sheets of thin, half-frozen sleet in earnest, blotting out the distant trees. George moved closer and touched the kitten's head with one gloved finger. He pushed it.

'It's dead. Put it down,' he said abruptly.

April hugged the kitten closer. 'It's not dead.'

'It's dead,' he repeated. 'Put it down and leave it.'

She backed away from him. 'It's not dead,' she wailed. 'It's a baby. It isn't ready to die. Babies don't die, do they?' she appealed to Eileen, who watched George's face darken, afraid.

'Babies do die,' he said harshly, with no trace of pity. 'Put it down immediately, April.'

She began to sob.

He reached out, and in one quick movement the kitten was out of April's collar and on to the ground. It crawled painfully back towards its paper bag.

'Now leave it.' George grabbed her arm and began to pull her away, frogmarching her across the desolate flat grass, the wind howling at their backs.

'Stop it!' he roared, as she burst into tears. 'Stop your ridiculous fuss.'

'George . . .' whimpered Eileen, hurrying after them on frozen feet, almost running to keep up. 'George, she's only a child. She feels for the kitten.'

He jerked April to a stop and rounded on his wife.

They stood, confronting each other in the great, empty space, sad and angry and bewildered.

'We are going home,' he said, 'and you will leave that dead cat where it belongs. I don't want another word about it.'

'I don't think it was quite dead, George,' whispered Eileen. 'It'll upset April . . .'

He gripped her shoulder with a hand that hurt her.

'It is dead,' he said, his face grey and steely.

'Yes, dear.' Eileen recoiled. She watched him walk rapidly away, dragging April with him.

"It's you who can't face it," she thought, listening to the wind whistle through the bare branches of the tree behind her, blowing the paper bag shut, hiding the tiny death within.

'You've never faced April's dying and you never will, will you? She's never died, has she?' she cried aloud, full of bitter despair. The figures of her husband and daughter dwindled fast into the driving, icy rain sweeping the Flats, whirling on the storm. Eileen shuddered, chilled to the bone, and began to hurry after them. The kitten began already to stiffen, buffeted to and fro in its brown paper shroud.

Tearing free of George when they reached the edge of the Flats and the gate that led out on to the road home, April ran blindly, hurling herself into Rachael's warm kitchen, and Rachael's warm arms, sobbing incoherently until, seeing her calmer, Rachael warmed some milk and made thick, sweet cocoa and asked her in a way that said she didn't have to tell, what was the matter. April told her.

'Oh, dear,' murmured Rachael, fearing to say anything at all in case her tongue ran away with her. "Your poor mother," she thought, keeping her pity to herself.

'If I have a little girl,' cried April fervently, her cheeks brilliant with cold air, tears and passion, 'I'll let her do what she wants to. I'll let her have a kitten, and I'll never, never, never get angry because she loves it.' Tears flowed again and Rachael rocked her gently and wordlessly, waving Gordon away silently when he looked round the door to ask if she'd made tea. Eleven-year-old April looked up with red, swollen eyes.

'If I have a little girl, I'll love her,' she cried fiercely. 'I won't make her unhappy.'

'I know you will, my pet, I know you will,' murmured Rachael, suppressing her anger, which would do the child no good.

'Like you,' continued April. 'I want to be like you.'

'Then you shall,' promised Rachael. 'You're my own good girl. There now, you're my own good girl. Dry your eyes, my pet, and we'll put some cream on those chapped lips.'

'Can I stay here?'

'As long as you want. You can help me get tea.'

"And just you say a word," she thought furiously, "just you show your face in my door, George Dunbar, and I'll speak my mind about that child, regardless."

April stayed three days with Rachael. For a long time Eileen, embarrassed and mortified, wouldn't go round there. It was Rachael who made the effort for a reconciliation, wooing Eileen back, carefully, tactfully, a bit at a time.

'Because of the child. And because I don't suppose Eileen could help what happened. Her heart's in the right place, only you have to dig for it. And it doesn't do April any good if we fall out, does it?' she said, when Gordon asked her why she bothered. 'She needs us. You and me both.'

She looked at him with bright, challenging grey eyes.

'Who does? Mother or daughter?' he asked flippantly.

His wife frowned.

'Us? In loco parentis?'

Rachael nodded. 'Sort of.'

He thought about it for several minutes. 'Bless you,' he said, 'and why not?'

Rachael smiled. 'That's just what I thought you'd say.'

Chapter One

In 1929 George's business took a battering, like so many others, when Wall Street crashed. Not so very far away, in London's East End, Bridie DuCane, moneylender, sailor's wife and David Holmes's mother, lost her fortune. On the same day nine-year-old David, stubborn and disinclined to listen to advice, like his father who'd died when he was two, went tumbling into the canal that ran between their back garden and the black railings that enclosed the green spaces of Hackney's Victoria Park.

She'd warned him a hundred times: 'You be careful. And stay away from that lock. There was a boy drowned there last year, diving under the weir. He went down and couldn't come up again.'

'Yes, Mum.'

'Are you listening?'

'Yes, Mum.'

'I hope you are.' Bridie clapped the stiff, heavy covers of a ledger together and added it to a pile on her sideboard. 'I'm off. I'll be late this afternoon because I said I'd call round to see Lizzie when I've done at the office. There's bread and jam. There's enough for Ollie, too, if he comes back with you.'

Lizzie – Mrs Norris to him – was his mother's best friend, and Ollie, her son, had been David's best mate since they were both babies.

'Can I have some money for chips?' David watched his mother pick up her handbag.

'What's wrong with bread?'

'Nothing. I like chips.'

'I'll have to leave you enough money for Ollie as well.'

'He might not come,' said David cautiously.

'Well, I'll know he's here if he's not with Lizzie.'

'He might be.'

'You up to something?'

David shook his head.

'Here.' His mother took sixpence from her purse and put it on the table. David put the shining silver coin in his palm and turned it over. The King's head gleamed.

'It's a new one. Just minted.'

'I've got to run,' said Bridie. 'You be good.'

He smiled happily. She kissed the top of his head quickly and he heard the front door bang behind her and then the small clang of the gate. David slipped the sixpence into his pocket, grinning from ear to ear. The kitchen door swung slightly open and The Pope, followed by ginger Brother John, sidled round, looking for food.

'Hasn't she fed you?'

The cats looked up at him with dilated black eyes. The Pope bared small, vicious white teeth in a jet black face and swore softly. Brother John prowled where his bowl should be, tail high.

'All right.' David brought a bowl of boiled fish from the larder and filled their dish. They rubbed around his ankles, complaining, then bolted the food, dragging it on to the floor, snarling briefly.

'Out!' cried David when they had finished. Brother John licked his chops and stretched. David's boot edged near his tail and the cat trotted through to sit on the back doorstep in a patch of sun.

'And you.'

The Pope ambled away, unimpressed. David shut the door on them and felt in his pocket for the envelope he'd put there the night before, with a note for the teacher, its signature so beautifully forged that Bridie herself would have said it was hers.

'All set,' he said to himself, and picked up his schoolbag on his way through the hall, slamming the door as his mother had done on the empty house.

Sweet Seventeen idled by the lock, engines thrumming gently. Big Bert wiped his hands on his black-trousered backside and stared thoughtfully at his barge. 'Sits too high, unloaded. She's tricky,' he observed. 'I don't like goin' empty.' The lock-keeper, a tiny sparrow of a man, stood dwarfed, his braces hanging down and a damp Gold Flake glued to his lower lip.

'Might get shot of the rats,' he suggested, seeing something move at the edge of the tarpaulin which covered almost the whole length of the boat.

'Likely,' answered Bert, unmoved. ''ere comes trouble,' he added, as David came skidding round the corner of the lock-keeper's cottage. The little man picked the cigarette end off his lip and spat. He nodded at David, unsmiling.

''e's bunkin' off, ain't yer, pal?' Big Bert grinned and winked.

'Gawd 'elp yer if yer Mum finds out,' remarked the lock-keeper, with a ghost of a smile.

'She won't.' David tried not to think of Ollie's treacherous tongue. He wouldn't mean to but he'd blab if he didn't watch out, despite the best marbles out of David's collection and the sixpence.

'I'm only going as far as Regent's Park,' said the boy.

'Shank's pony back,' guessed the lock-keeper. David nodded, looking longingly at *Sweet Seventeen*. The lock-keeper shrugged.

'You lot comin'?' Fanny stuck her head out of her tiny, stinking cabin, wreathed in cigarette smoke and the fumes of frying fat.

'Come on, chum.' Bert jerked his thumb towards the barge and David clambered on to her low flat top. He sat on the tarpaulin and watched as Bert opened her engines and the barge pulled away from the lock side with a brief growl, then settled down to a steady rumbling. Above, Victoria Park began to slide by and a few minutes later they passed the end of David's garden, with its grass growing right down to the water's edge. He lay flat on the oily canvas, his face turned away and his heart in his mouth.

'Ain't no one going to bother,' called Bert. The boy stared at the back of his head and wondered how he always knew exactly what David was thinking. Bert whistled through his teeth, savouring the rich smell of bacon drifting from Fanny's cabin.

''ere, fetch this, love.' Fanny thrust a bacon sandwich and a mug of tea over the edge of her tiny companionway to David above. Fat dripped deliciously on his fingers and sugary tea steamed invisibly in morning sunshine. Bert looked round, sniffing.

'You'll get yours in a minute.' Fanny winked broadly and disappeared below decks again. David licked his fingers and wondered if he dared ask for more. His mother always said it was rude, but he was starving, and Fanny did bacon sandwiches like no one else anywhere.

'Can't steer and eat,' grumbled Bert laconically, without looking round. 'You takin' over, chum?'

Grinning with excitement, David slid off the tarpaulin.

Bert let the tiller swing wide as he stepped back. 'Come on then, look lively,' he said. 'You'll 'ave 'er in the bank.' David grabbed and hung on with both hands, his knuckles white. *Sweet Seventeen* ambled along placidly as the sun rose higher in a watery blue sky. Bert spat bacon bones into the canal's shining black water, then pulled his cap over his eyes and sat back contentedly.

'You're doin' just dandy, son. Keep 'er straight.'

Fanny watched them from the bottom of her companionway, smoke circling around and around her head.

"'e'd 'ave bin a good dad, if we'd 'ad any," she mused, watching her husband's black eyes steady on David under the cap's brim. "But some things ain't ter be." She sighed and lit another fag from the last one, tossing the empty packet over her head and into the water where it bobbed in their wake, gently up and down.

Bridie had hurried along the road to the bus stop, shifting her heavy ledgers from one arm to the other as she rounded the corner into the main road. Not looking, she tripped and nearly fell over the back of a man in overalls, squatting on the pavement, drawing arrows with a stub of chalk. A second workman, leaning on a pickaxe, said, 'Mind yourself, lady.' He pointed to their sign: Men At Work.

'I wasn't looking,' said Bridie. 'Sorry.' She looked over at him and her eye was caught by a folded newspaper lying on top of one of their toolbags. The headline was neatly displayed. WALL STREET CRASHES.

'Is that today's?' she blurted, shocked.

The workman followed her gaze. 'Yes.'

'I hadn't seen . . .' She looked up the road towards the bus stop. Men with sombre faces studied newspapers with headlines that all screamed the same catastrophe, black headlines two inches high.

The workman shrugged. 'Don't suppose it's much to do with us,' he remarked.

Bridie stared at him incredulously. 'Everything!' she cried. 'It has everything to do with us. You'll see.'

A number twenty-eight came into sight, far down the road. 'It has everything,' she said to the man again, and he wondered if she was going to cry. He watched her join the queue, weighed down by an armful of big books, and finally climb aboard her bus.

'Yes, ma'am,' he muttered, and his gaze wandered uneasily to the newspaper. 'Stop for tea?' he asked his mate, who was marking paving stones to be lifted. Suddenly he badly wanted to read the paper, to see if she was right.

Sam Saul, loanshark and Bridie's friend of many years, sat in his office above the junction of Mare Street and The Triangle and dialled a number. Engaged. He stared across the room, unseeing, listening in frustration. A newspaper lay before him, on top of a great pile of ledgers and bits of scribbled paper with figures all over them. The tall Jew, greying and slightly stooped with poring over the long columns of figures that once had meant wealth, hung up in exasperation, his lined, heavily handsome face sombre.

Instantly the telephone rang. 'I've been trying to get you,' said Bridie's voice.

'I was ringing you.'

'You've seen, then?'

'Yes.'

'You were right all along.'

'I've lost a fair bit, too.'

'How, if you knew?'

'I thought maybe I was the fool.'

'Oh, Sam!' cried Bridie, shaken. He had tried so hard to make her see; to warn her catastrophe was coming. She'd looked sceptical and asked him how on earth he could tell.

'It's in the air.' He'd tapped the side of his nose with gleaming, half-closed eyes, deliberately mocking the Shylock in himself. 'I can sense it. It's there between the lines in the news. By an ache in my bones, by the pricking of my thumbs,' he'd said, despairingly trying to make her listen, but she wouldn't. She'd stared at him doubtfully, instead, and then laughed and asked him how Ruthie was.

'My wife is well, thank you,' he had said stiffly, knowing there was no use in going on.

Now it had happened, just as he had predicted.

'My losses don't matter.' Sam spoke dryly. 'They will be small compared to yours, I imagine.'

'I haven't had time to think. I don't know yet. I haven't even got a paper. I came straight in to telephone you.' Beyond her desk Bridie could see the morning traffic passing her office window. It was a small window, for security, but it was not boarded with thick planks and barbed wire like Sam Saul's windows. His office was dim and stuffy. Hers was small and plain, always full of people. Bridie did not work in a fortress like other moneylenders in the East End.

'Perhaps I'll lose it all,' she said quietly, seeing in her

mind's eye the work of years brought to ruin because she wouldn't take a piece of advice from an old friend.

'Possibly.'

'Oh, damn!'

Sam heard the dialling tone and replaced his receiver. 'She would never listen,' he murmured to himself, not without a trace of unhappy satisfaction, and opened his safe, ready for the new day's business.

Sweet Seventeen chuffed steadily between the canal banks towards Regent's Park. David pricked his fingers painfully on the monstrous needle Bert had given him, and sucked them. His orders were to mend a tear in the tarpaulin with a patch and thread, but he wasn't getting very far. He stabbed at the leathery stuff again but the needle didn't go through.

'Bert,' he called, looking up to the front end of the boat. A shadow loomed crookedly ahead, coming nearer.

'Watch out, there!' shouted Bert, seeing the child kneel up, calling his name. 'Lie down, yer daft beggar.'

David looked up in confusion. The shadow raced nearer and he felt its chill on his face.

'Lie down,' yelled Bert, frightened.

The half-fallen tree scraped along the tarpaulin, shedding leaves and twigs. David scrambled backwards on hands and knees, trying to get out of the way, hearing Bert shouting and Fanny's hoarse voice calling. And then he was rolling and falling and sliding, rope tearing at his hands as he scrabbled to get a hold, and then he was in the water and something black hit him savagely on the side of his head and he gasped. Foul water filled his mouth and he hung for a long, long moment below the canal surface, knocked out cold by *Sweet Seventeen* as she passed by.

'Turn 'im over – quick, woman!' Bert put a large hand on David's back and began to push. Water spewed out of the boy's mouth and he coughed violently.

'That's it, you'll live,' Bert said gruffly.

David groaned and tried to lift his head.

'Stay put,' grunted Bert. He took a blanket from Fanny and put it round David's shoulders, helping him sit up.

'You stupid beggar, didn't you see it comin'?' he grumbled. 'You give us a proper fright.'

'No.' David's teeth began to chatter. 'I didn't see nothing.'

'Wasn't takin' no notice, more like. I said you could come along if you was careful. Call that careful?'

'I didn't see nothing,' insisted David, close to tears.

'Leave 'im be,' ordered Fanny from below. 'It's a miracle 'e ain't broke half his bones.' She leant out of her companionway with two mugs of tea. 'Hot and sweet. It'll bring the colour back to 'is cheeks.'

Bert felt carefully along David's arms and legs, asking him if he could move everything properly.

'You're lucky there's no damage,' he pronounced, sitting back on his haunches and sipping tea. *Sweet Seventeen* nudged the canal bank with no hand on her tiller. Fanny came to the top of her companionway again and looked David over seriously.

'That's goin' ter be the least of 'is troubles. You'll 'ave to tell your mum what you was doin' today, looking like that.'

'What?' he said, new terror gripping him.

'All black eyes and scrapes. And that woolly's

33

ruined. You'll have to tell 'er, duck. You look a proper mess.'

'She'll kill me.'

'I'll put some arnica on those bruises.' Fanny produced a small green bottle and began to uncork its top.

'Can I come with you?' begged David. 'Mum'll kill me.'

'You'd better get back home quick.' Bert glanced at Fanny, who nodded her head.

'If you get back now, you can scrub up and maybe not look so bad when she gets 'ome. Can you walk all right?'

'Yes,' said David dismally, emptying water out of his boots. Fanny patted arnica on to his face. It stung.

'You come again soon,' she whispered. ''e's not cross, but you give 'im such a fright 'e starts growling. Don't you worry. You just get along 'ome as fast as you can and get yourself all cleaned up.'

'I can come again? Promise?'

''course you can. But now you 'op it, there's a good boy.' Bert looked over Fanny's shoulder and David realized the barge had stopped. 'It won't take you long to get back.'

They helped him on to the bank and waved as the barge started moving once more, with that little roar of her engines. David turned and started along the towpath, his shoulders hunched.

'Oi!' Bert's voice boomed from further down, and David turned. ''ere's yer woolly.'

'Oh, I don't care.' David began to run awkwardly, hiding his tears.

Bert dropped the dripping jumper on to the deck.

'Next time, then,' he said, looking after the small

figure that was almost out of sight and didn't turn round.

Bridie went pale when she saw David's damaged face, but the storm he'd been dreading didn't burst. She seemed distracted. She asked about Bert, and Fanny, and where the devil he thought he'd been going, and how would he ever be a doctor if he bunked off school and failed his exams? But somehow her heart wasn't in it.

'Is Edward coming home?'

Bridie looked startled. Her husband was docked in Naples for a Royal Naval courtesy visit.

'Whatever makes you ask that? He's not back for another couple of months.'

'You look worried. Sometimes you look worried like that if you're thinking about Edward.'

'Do I, love?' Bridie put her arm round his shoulders and he winced. 'You got bruises everywhere, haven't you?'

David nodded.

'We've lost a lot of money today,' said his mother bleakly. 'That's what is making me worried. The world's stock markets have crashed and a great deal of the money your father left us was in stocks and shares. So I'm afraid we've lost a lot. You getting up to all this has just come on top of everything else. I'm sorry, Davey. And I'm sorry you had such a fright, even though you had no business being there in the first place and you deserved everything you got.'

'Will we be poor?'

Bridie smiled grimly.

'A lot of people will be, now. No, I don't think we'll be as badly off as them but yesterday we were quite rich. We won't be that any more.'

'Will I still be able to go to university?'

'I hope so. But we may have to scrimp and save.'

'You earn money, don't you, at your work?'

'I have lost my capital. I don't know how we'll go on.' She sighed. 'Sam tried to warn me. That's the worst bit.'

'Did he know?'

His mother nodded. 'I don't know how, but he did. But I didn't believe him, and so I lost much more than I need have. He's lost money, too, because I didn't believe him,' she added sadly.

'Edward says money isn't important.'

Bridie gave a short laugh. 'I know! It's important when you don't have enough, though. Ethel and Ted never saw Edward really go without when he was at home, and he's the kind of man who feels rich on enough.'

'I think money's important,' cried David passionately. 'I'm going to be rich.'

'Why?' she asked, surprised.

'If I'm rich I can do anything I want, can't I?'

'In a way. What do you want to do?'

'Go,' said David flatly. 'Away. And be a doctor.'

'Where will you go?' Bridie's green eyes narrowed and she studied his face as he spoke. David shrugged.

'Is what why you want to be a doctor? To be rich?'

He nodded. 'To help people, too.'

'You've a lot of your dad in you, haven't you?' she said thoughtfully. 'You think that way, you'd better go to school and no more truanting, or you won't be going nowhere except down the unemployment office.'

'I won't,' he said sulkily.

'Your dad always wanted you to have an education.

Maybe I should have done what he wanted and sent you away to school, after all.'

David knew she never meant it when said this. Bridie stroked the child's fair hair gently.

'Your dad would be proud of you,' she said softly. 'You're a good boy.'

He put his arms round her waist and buried his face in her skirt.

'I wish my dad hadn't died.'

'I know.' Bridie stood gazing down at her son, stroking the fine, tangled hair, so like the hair she had smoothed a thousand times when Francis had been weary. Then the spell broke.

'Bedtime,' she said firmly.

Chapter Two

'What on earth have you been doing?' demanded Miss Wilcox, looking across the heads of her unruly class to where David sat in the second row. 'And I don't suppose you've got a note, for whatever it was?'

'No, Miss.'

The class sniggered and Ollie looked over anxiously. David grinned, one eye almost closed by a magnificent bruise.

'No Miss, what?' enquired Miss, her grey head tilted to one side, shrewd eyes narrowed.

David averted his face.

'What were you doing?' she persisted. Ollie crossed his fingers and prayed that David wouldn't tell and get caned. The last time he'd copped it, Ollie remembered all too well, hadn't been nice for David's best friend. Caning made David so angry Ollie had been scared.

'I fell off a barge.'

Ollie held his breath.

'What were you doing on a barge when you should have been here?'

David looked at her with a bored expression.

'Playing truant, Miss.'

Miss Wilcox ignored the invitation to a fight.

'How did you manage to fall?'

'A branch knocked me off.'

'You didn't notice it?'

"Sarky," thought David, and didn't answer.

'I want to see you after school. Here, after dismissal.' Miss Wilcox turned to her blackboard and began to write, in long, looping letters.

'Now you've done it.' The tousle-haired boy who shared a battered, pitted desk with David dipped his pen in their joint inkwell and flicked it expertly towards Ollie, across the way. 'I bet you don't half get walloped,' he murmured with relish out of the corner of his mouth, sliding flat, wary grey eyes over David's face to see how he took the threat. David blinked rapidly and his fingers tightened on his pen.

'Gonna cane me, Miss?' The question rose clear and sudden above the scufflings and shufflings and breathings of the classroom. Miss Wilcox stopped writing on the blackboard but for a moment she didn't turn around. David's pen moved slowly across his book. Rows of boys stared at his bent head, such industrious concentration, and for once, thought Miss Wilcox, they all sat still. She put her hand to her thin cheek and felt it glow with a suppressed longing to laugh.

'I was going to give you a test,' she said, turning back to the class. David's pen carried on writing, his nose almost touching the page in front of him.

'But we could do it now, instead of waiting until after school.'

David's pen stopped in mid-sentence and the class leaned across their desks, all agog.

'Come here,' ordered Miss Wilcox, stepping down from her platform at the front of the room. 'And stand there.' She pointed to a spot by the blackboard. Little pools of chalk eddied round David's boots and he breathed lavender toilet water and the faint smell of mothballs from her black woollen dress.

'What for, Miss?'

She threaded her way through the rows of desks to the back and picked up someone's ruler.

'Look!' she called over the scraping of feet as everyone turned to watch. David began to go pink. Miss Wilcox pointed with the ruler. 'Can you read this notice for me?'

He stood quite still and stared towards the far wall of the room. Miss Wilcox put down her ruler and took drawing pins out of her noticeboard. She took down a stenciled sheet and held it out. 'Read this,' she said.

Half a dozen voices chorused, 'In event of fire . . .'

'Silence!' called Miss Wilcox. 'Now, David.'

At last he lowered his eyes.

'He can't, Miss,' said Ollie, in agony.

'I thought not,' said Miss Wilcox. She went halfway down the classroom.

'No, Miss.'

'Here?' She stood right at the front.

'Paper with letters on it,' said David sullenly.

Miss Wilcox took his shoulder and pushed him none too gently towards his seat. No one looked as he sat down.

'Anyone got any other questions before we get on?' She looked from face to face along the middle row of desks. 'My word, I wish you were always so quiet. We shall have to thank David for concentrating our minds, won't we?'

Sobered, the class got back to work but Ollie watched David's head droop lower and lower as a dull flush crept round to the back of his collar. It had only just begun to fade when the bell rang. Miss Wilcox gathered her books and stood up.

'David.'

'Come here,' hissed Ollie, pulling him back by the elbow as he went to barge out of the room. 'She wants you again.'

The class clattered and banged their way out to afternoon break in a dreary square of concrete underneath the headmaster's window. Miss Wilcox read the resentment in David's bright grey eyes and her bossy voice was suddenly gentle.

'Look,' she began, 'I think you need glasses. Ever since you came into my class I've wondered how much you were seeing. Not a lot, is it?'

David wouldn't look at her.

'I'm sorry we had to do it in front of everyone, but you asked for it,' she went on cheerfully. 'What shall we do about getting you to an optician?'

He scowled.

'I go past one on my way home. Shall I call in and get you an appointment? You'll have to tell your mother – perhaps you'd rather she did it?'

David shuffled and said, 'Will she have to pay for them?' in a very small voice.

'Good gracious, your mother can surely afford spectacles!' cried Miss. 'Some of them couldn't, but I'm quite sure yours can.'

'She ain't rich.'

'Isn't,' said Miss, patiently.

'She's lost it all, in a crash,' said David desperately.

Miss looked at him curiously. 'Oh,' she said, the thought striking her for the first time that the stock market collapse might have hit the moneylender. 'Oh, that's a shame, David. Is she worried?'

'Dunno, Miss.'
'Do you want to ask her about the glasses?'
David shook his head.
'Shall I?'
'Yes, Miss.'
'Go on, then.'
David fled.

'Can I come in?' asked Ollie, pressing his nose against the optician's window. Cupping his hands round his face, he could just make out the receptionist, sitting at a wooden table with her appointment book spread out in front of her. Four metal trays were piled high with papers and little parcels; spectacles in cases, frames for repair, and bundles of prescriptions, all fastened with elastic bands.

'Oh, go on,' he begged.

David kicked around two doors up, eyed by the greengrocer further up, wary for his oranges.

'Ain't sure I'm going.'

Ollie pressed his nose to the window again and the receptionist looked up. He hastily backed away.

'Why not?'

'I don't want to wear glasses.'

'Four eyes,' jeered Ollie, grinning and crossing his eyes horribly.

The door opened with a little rattle and a bell pinged above David's head as he slammed it behind him, leaving Ollie's contorted face outside.

'Yes, dear?' said the receptionist. Three fat women sat in a row on hard chairs. They paused in mid gossip, chins wobbling, to stare back at the boy's set, scared face with a greenish bruise round one wide, watchful eye.

43

'Come in, duck. We shan't eat you.' The woman in the middle clucked sympathetically and shook her head mournfully at the sight of him. The receptionist ran her finger down her page and said, 'David Holmes.'

'Yes?' he said, startled at hearing his name. He saw Ollie's face appear, squashed against the window glass.

'What do I have to do?' he asked, turning his back on the distorted vision.

'Just sit down, dear. Mr Hubbard will be out in a minute.' The lady wrote briefly in her book and said, 'Is your mother coming?'

'No.'

'We usually like a parent to accomany a child your age.' She glanced at him disapprovingly.

'My mother had to go to work,' he said stiffly, remembering the argument in the kitchen.

'I ought to come with you. Will you ask Miss Wilcox if we can change the appointment?' Bridie had said, peering at his face worriedly. 'I don't know he'll be able to test you with that bruise, anyway. I never realized you couldn't see. Why didn't you tell me? Oh dear, I've got to see the solicitor and I can't put that off. Any other time, but just now . . .'

Her words had tailed off into the worried frown that David saw more and more since the big crash she kept talking about. 'Can you manage on your own this time, Davey, if you can't change the time? I wish you'd told me before.'

"How could I have?" thought David furiously, sitting in Mr Hubbard's black chair in the dim light of an angled lamp hanging over the optician's desk.

'Is that better or worse?' murmured Mr Hubbard, slotting yet another round lens into the metal holder

44

perched on David's nose. The row of letters shifted and resolved themselves almost imperceptibly nearer to sharp black edges.

'Better.'

'Good, good.' The tiny man hopped down from his stool and noted something on a bit of paper. David squinted through the holder and could see the top of his head, covered in spiky, faded yellow hair, as he bent over to write.

'Are you a real dwarf?' he asked, fascinated. The optician spun round and nipped David sharply on one shin.

'Feel that?'

Astonished, David nodded, the holder slipping with the jerk of his head.

'That's how real I am. What did you think?'

Baffled, David stared myopically through his unlensed eye.

'Yes,' said Mr Hubbard briskly. 'Haven't you seen a small person before?'

'I don't think so,' said David cautiously, rubbing the pinch on his leg.

'Manikin, humunculus, micromorph and hop-o'-my-thumb,' recited Mr Hubbard rapidly, 'though personally I prefer plain speaking as in midget or, as you say, dwarf.' He pulled out a fresh rack of delicate, shining lenses and his thick, foreshortened fingers searched tenderly among the black-edged discs.

'I have always been small. You have always been myopic to the point of near blindness. The Lord of Light sends some suffering to each of us, only for you it is a mere matter of correction.' He clambered up on to the stool by David's chair and swung the rack of lenses closer. 'For me, it would take more of a miracle.' His breath on David's cheek smelled of peppermint and his bulbous eyes gleamed with amusement.

'Oh,' said David.

'What do you think, young man?' went on Mr Hubbard, removing lenses from the eye he'd been working on and tightening the holder for the next set. 'Does the good Lord send us only what we can bear? Or is He a monster? Or perhaps a little of both, eh? Read the Book of Job, young man, and consider. The Book of Job. Not that you will.'

David squirmed anxiously, his heart pounding at the nearness of this unpredictable imp. The dwarf laughed.

'Making you worried, am I? It's only my way. Take no notice, Master Holmes, I'll look after your eyes as if they were my own. I knew your dad, young man. What do you think of that, eh?' He spoke so abruptly that David was frightened.

'Hold still,' said the dwarf more gently, and slid a fresh lens in front of David's left eye. 'Better or worse?'

'Worse.'

'Good, good,' beamed the little man.

'Why?'

'Why what?' He took out the worse lens and put in another one.

'Why is it good whether it's better or worse?'

'A figure of speech. If you believe everything you hear, you won't go far,' said the dwarf severely.

'I don't know what you're talking about. Did you really know my dad?' asked David bravely.

'He looked after my mother,' explained Mr Hubbard, after a pause in which David could hear his breath whistling in his nose as he leaned over to adjust the holder. 'A finer man than your dad never lived. When I was born my mother never really got over it.

Me being born, that is. I went to her chest, so to speak. Midgets are inclined to chestiness, you know. Better or worse?'

'Neither.'

'Bother! Try this, then . . . I was talking about my mother. She suffered all sorts and your dad told her once she shouldn't have had a child in the first place. Hardly built for it, you see. But when she got bad, your dad arranged for her to go to the hospital and he paid for me to stay with my aunty out of his own pocket. She had eight of her own, you see, and she couldn't have taken me otherwise. And he took an interest, you see. It helped. He never lost interest.'

'Didn't you have a dad?'

The dwarf's breath stopped whistling abruptly. He pushed away the rack of lenses and stood looking at David, the two heads on a level.

'Oh, yes,' sighed the dwarf. 'In a manner of speaking.'

'What?'

'How does that seem?' Mr Hubbard twitched the holder and pulled David's head round to look at the letters. 'Can you read them all now?'

'Down to the bottom line.' The optician leaned across and lifted the holder full of lenses off David's face. He stood watching. A cry of disappointment burst from the boy's lips.

'I know,' the optician said calmly.

David's head swam and the room almost vanished into a dull haze of half light and shadow; objects blurred and trembled.

'It gives you a shock, the first time. Leastways, it does anyone blind as a bat, like you,' said the dwarf.

'I didn't know.'

47

'How could you? You had nothing to compare with.'

'I thought I could see,' cried David frantically.

'You could, a bit. Not half enough, though. It's a wonder you haven't walked under a tram yet.'

Blindly, David turned to the midget. 'Can I have glasses today? Please?' he begged.

'They'll take about ten days,' said the optician calmly. 'You'll have to wait.'

'I can't!'

'You have no choice.' The man had his back to David. 'Besides, it is a small thing to wait ten days. Some have to wait a lifetime without hope.'

'I don't understand anything you say,' cried David angrily.

'No. And it doesn't matter. Ask my receptionist to give you an appointment to have your spectacles fitted in ten days. Just let me measure for frames.' He held a measuring tool against David's face. 'That's all.' He opened the door to his windowless little sanctum. 'No charge,' he said abruptly to the receptionist. 'I'll see to it.'

Impassively she made a mark in her book.

'Yes, Mr Hubbard,' she said.

'You was long enough,' complained Ollie, who had grown bored outside the optician's and had pinched two apples from the greengrocer when he wasn't looking, to pass the time.

'He talked all the time. Really funny. Funny peculiar, not funny ha-ha.'

'Hasn't he given you any glasses?'

'You have to wait, stupid. You can't just get them. You don't know much, do you?'

In revenge Ollie polished his second apple and didn't

hand it over like he'd meant to. They drifted down towards Broadway Market, kicking pebbles in the dust.

'What did he do?' asked Ollie, curiosity getting the better of him.

'He said he knew my dad.'

'Your dad's dead.'

'Before.'

'Does he know your mum?'

'I don't think so. He's a dwarf.'

'Go on!' cried Ollie incredulously.

'It's true,' insisted David.

'A real dwarf?'

David lunged over and pinched him hard. 'That real?' he shouted, pinching again. Ollie dropped his apple, his light, brown eyes round with surprise.

'Lay off.' He pushed back and went to fetch his apple from the gutter.

'I don't want to go to the market,' David told him. 'I'm going home.'

'I'll come,' agreed Ollie obligingly.

They turned down the road that led to the park.

'Give us a bite,' demanded David as Ollie bit into his fruit, and then wouldn't give it back.

'Pig!' shouted Ollie furiously, grabbing at it, and suddenly the two of them were running hard to the park entrance, through the wrought iron gates and across the grass to the canal. David threw the apple in a wide arc into the water, laughing breathlessly. 'Go on then,' he jeered, as Ollie clenched his fists. They tumbled, kicking and punching, down to the towpath. Ollie had blood on his hands.

'Stop it!' yelled someone. 'Stop it!'

Gasping, Ollie looked up and saw Bridget standing

on the bridge, her mouth wide open with screaming at them.

'Mum's coming.' She hung over the side of the bridge and dangled her feet out over the water. 'You'd better stop that, quick.'

Ollie reluctantly sat up, straddling David in a patch of dried horse dung and dock leaves.

'She'll kill you,' warned his twin sister from above. 'Look what you've done to his face.'

David's nose bled thinly down his cheek. He wiped it on his hand and looked at his fingers.

'Ain't much,' he said, pushing Ollie off and sitting up.

'Whatever are you doing?' asked Lizzie, carrying shopping bags and coming up behind Bridget. 'Oh, my word!'

'Fighting again,' said Bridget virtuously.

'Nothing,' said Ollie.

'You can't be trusted five minutes.'

'Can I stay?' asked Bridget, starting to make her way along the bridge, hand over hand, with her feet still dangling.

'Not girls,' said David in disgust.

'I'm not girls.'

'You're worse,' said Ollie gloomily. 'Come on.' He and David scrambled up the slope away from the bridge, hands and knees slipping on grass.

'Wait for me,' cried Bridget. 'I'm coming.' She dropped off the metal parapet and ran after them, crying, 'Wait for me.'

Lizzie stood above the slow, gleaming water and watched her children disappear with Bridie's son towards the great band of horse chestnut trees that were beginning to fade as autumn approached. She picked up her shopping bags and walked slowly round to Bridie's house, whose garden sloped down to the same stretch of water. As she walked she caught the echo of three young voices fading into the distance.

Chapter Three

It was hard to imagine, thought Bridie, that the East End could look even poorer and bleaker than before the stock market crash. She walked slowly down the Roman Road to the street market, watching out of the corner of her eye groups of sullen men, smoking thin cigarettes held in the palm of their hand. They stood on street corners, quietly. She made a small detour into a back street, to walk past the main entrance of the labour exchange, and stared at the great queue that wound its way down the road and round a corner. Men, terribly quiet, very patient. There were long queues in the public library, too, for the newspapers, though there were few jobs there for the unskilled.

'They are completely without hope,' cried Bridie, meeting Sam Saul later in the day. 'It's frightening.'

'There's always been a lot of unemployment,' said Sam.

'This is different,' said Bridie, distressed by his indifference. 'You should go and look. Go and walk down the street for once. You'd soon see for yourself.'

'I do. And I read the newspapers. My conscience doesn't prick so hard. I've lost enough, and so have you.'

'Not like them. We've got Edward's wages and that's secure. But they're desperate.'

Sam tapped the side of his long nose and grinned.

'No,' shouted Bridie, outraged.

'Why not?'

She shook her head. 'I can't start all over again.'

'Why not? They need you more than ever now,' he persisted.

She got up and wandered over to Sam's office window, gazing unseeingly over the roof tops towards the tips of the trees, just visible where the park began.

'It's nicer here since you had all that boarding taken down.'

'Things carry on the way they are and it'll all go back up again,' growled Sam. 'People aren't nice when they're starving, Bridie.'

She said nothing. Sam scratched his chin and ran his hands through his thick, greying hair.

'You'll have to do something,' he pointed out. 'You can't just sit at home and mope. Isn't like you.'

'I'm not moping,' she said crossly. 'I'm trying to understand what is happening. They talk about revolution, you know. That if we get poor enough, it'll start people off and we'll have turmoil. If you go down the Roman Road and listen outside the pubs, you hear men talking like that. It's not all of them, but when I hear them, I wonder what might be coming and it frightens me. That,' she thumped her fist on the window sill, 'isn't moping.'

'My word,' he said mockingly, 'we'll have you political next. Edward won't care for that, will he? A political wife for a Navy officer. Tut tut, won't do.'

'You are detestable,' said Bridie coldly.

'No, I'm not. I'm a realist. You've lent money ever since I've known you, and you love it. Then you got a bit flashy and started sitting in an office all day and it all looked very nice. But you were still lending money, Bridie, and you'll do yourself no favour if you start forgetting it.'

He saw her fingers clench on the window sill. She still stood with her back to him, but she was silent so he went on, 'You made a lot, and you lost a lot. I won't say anything about how if you'd listened to my advice you could have avoided it, because regrets don't help.' He paused.

'I feel scared and I feel sorry for them.'

'I know,' replied Sam gently, 'which is why someone like you, who insists on the luxury of a conscience, has a duty to get back out there and help them.'

'Make profits, you mean.'

'All right!' he roared, thoroughly exasperated. 'Go and lend for nothing. See how far that gets you. See how long you can bail them out for next week's coal, or whatever else, by giving it away. Perhaps when you've beggared yourself, and Edward, and got well and truly down to their level, you'll be satisfied. And then you'll be off looking for someone to lend *you* money. Go and do your bit for the poor by becoming one of them.' He snorted derisively. 'Very fine, Bridie, very fine.'

'You remind me of Francis,' she said sulkily.

'Good!' snapped Sam. 'Because for all his faults, your husband had his head screwed on when it came to money. He wouldn't have listened to your nonsense. He knew that someone has to make money for there to be any to go round, or we're all in a mess. Time you grew up and learned that too.' He was jabbing an angry finger at her to make his point as she spun round to face him. The light from the window caught her hair and for the first time he noticed the threads of grey that were scattered in the dark, glossy red curls.

'Oh, well,' he muttered, distracted by an abrupt ache in his heart, 'I suppose it's up to you. Not my business to bully you.'

'No,' said Bridie, 'you're not bullying me. You're right. I just don't like seeing it that way.'

'You'll think about it?' Sam stopped staring at her hair and came round his desk hopefully.

'No.'

His face fell. Bridie shook with quick laughter and he saw, despite the silvery threads, the young girl who had stolen his heart in this ugly, barricaded room, seven years earlier.

'No?'

'I won't think about it. I'll do it!' she said cheerfully.

'Back to work?'

'Back to work. New beginnings.'

'You'll be all right? I mean, the street's a rough place.' Sam was suddenly anxious.

'Don't start that. You've spent all this afternoon bullying me into it, don't start trying to frighten me out of it again.' Bridie spoke sharply because in the crash she'd lost her dream, her office, and to go back to the streets called for courage she wasn't sure she had.

'I'll get you a new moneybelt,' he offered heartily.

'All right.' Bridie's voice sounded dismal. 'It's fine for you, sitting up here. But out there . . .'

'You've turned down going into partnership with me more times than I can count, so don't whine.'

She screwed up her face as if reconsidering. Sam shook his head.

'It wouldn't be a good idea if you did, not this way.'

'You can read my mind, can you?'

'More your face. It was tempting only as a way out. No good.'

'No,' she sighed. 'You're right.'

'You'll love being back.'

'I don't know what Edward's going to say.'

'You don't have to tell him, yet. See how it goes.'

'I don't lie to him,' she said stiffly.

Sam shrugged.

'And there's David. He'll be mortified.'

'Why?'

'You know how he is. He likes us to be nice. The streets ain't exactly respectable, are they?'

'He'll like the money, though,' remarked Sam shrewdly.

Bridie sighed. Then she giggled. 'I went up the other day and I could hear him talking. I didn't think there was anyone else with him so I opened the door to see what he was doing. He was giving himself elocution lessons! He'd got this book, and he was goin': "How Now, Brown Cow" in such a posh voice, I nearly burst not to laugh. I don't know what he'll think of next.'

'Nor do I,' said Sam grimly.

'Oh, it's only a game,' she cried, seeing the look on his face. 'He don't mean nothing by it.'

Sam smiled. 'I expect so,' he said, not wanting to blunder in where angels feared to tread.

'He wants to better himself, that's all. Anyone as intelligent as him would.'

Sam gazed at her under his bushy eyebrows.

'Wouldn't they?' she said defiantly.

'I'll see you get that moneybelt.'

'You don't think that's it, do you?'

'I'm a Jew, Bridie. Not a good Jew, I grant you, but I live like a Jew, though not so strictly as my wife would like. I play the Shylock without complaining and I stroke my fine nose and think what a splendid Jewish nose it is. But there are places, these days, where to be a Jew is not a good thing. I have to ask myself, if I were in one of those places, what would I do? How would it be if my windows were boarded again, against pogroms instead of my debtors?' He smiled thinly and glanced at his unboarded windows.

Absorbed, for he had never spoken like this before, Bridie watched his face harden and his sharp black eyes grow bleak.

'I'd be a Jew. Nothing would change. Whatever being a Jew meant at the time, that's what I'd be. And proud of it. Pretending otherwise would be the greater shame. The Nazis would have me then, if they could make me deny myself. Do you see?' Sam heaved a deep sigh and thrust his hands into his pockets, staring at her hard. Bridie pressed her lips together and smoothed the skirt of her coat carefully.

'Yes, I take your meaning. But David's only young and they all get these ideas. I think he'll follow in his father's footsteps, and Francis was what you'd call posh. David's just got that in him. He ain't pretending.'

'I merely meant that one cannot deny one's roots without paying a price.'

'I'd best get back to the cow pats and the pigsty, then,' suggested Bridie, half angry, half amused, her memory of the tiny Irish cottage she'd fled undimmed by time.

Sam opened his mouth to say something serious and decided he'd gone far enough.

'You'd better get home,' he told her, peering out at heavy grey clouds moving slowly from the east, bringing the promise of steady, cold, driving rain. He walked down the narrow flight of stairs with her, and into the road outside his office. He stood and rubbed his hands against the chill.

'Take care,' he said.

He watched her walk away. A restless wind picked at her hair. As she turned the corner it blew across her face. She turned to wave. Silver threads, thought Sam, so many, and I never noticed before. Then he went back upstairs to his stuffy little room with its huge old safe in the corner and sat with his eyes closed, trying to imagine her with white hair.

'Huh!' he exclaimed suddenly, and sat up very straight, drawing a heap of ledgers towards him. 'Enough of that,' he muttered, and settled down to work, undisturbed by the steady drumming of rain against his windowpanes, driving slantwise on the wind from the steel grey sky above.

Chapter Four

By the time Edward's first worried letters reached her from his last port of call, at the other side of the world, Bridie had been back at work for weeks. She closed down her shiny little office, dismissed the girl who had helped behind the counter, and fastened Sam's new moneybelt around her waist. Rumour sped like lightning through the streets that Mrs DuCane was back on her old rounds. People who had been ashamed to go to the office in Well Street opened their front doors eagerly and said they were glad she was back. Bridie's notebook once more filled with long lists of names and debts, and business took off almost faster than she could manage. As the Depression bit deeper and deeper into the East End, Bridie's customers grew into many hundreds.

'I can hardly cope,' she cried in exhaustion one evening, sitting in Sam's dingy premises. 'I wish I'd kept the office!'

'They wouldn't have come,' said Sam. 'They spend all day in offices, waiting for jobs, handouts, food, and anything else the poor fellows need to beg for. You won't catch them standing in a queue they don't by rights have to. You'll do better this way, going to where the business is. Moneylenders always flourish in adversity.'

'Edward's coming home.'

'Oh? I thought there must be something. Suppose he won't be pleased,' said Sam maliciously.

'And I heard last night Ted's lost his job.' Bridie bit her lip. Her father-in-law's gaunt face had haunted her as she did her rounds.

Calm, steady Ted had come home closed in on himself, and nothing she or his wife Ethel could say would bring him out of it. He'd sign on in the morning, he'd said, and that was it. He left the agitated women in Ethel's tiny scullery and went out, up the road to the corner, where Bridie saw him standing talking with several others, under a street lamp, when she finally went home late in the evening.

'Ethel's more worried about him than about the money. But I suppose Edward will want us to look after them. We can't see them go without.'

'Good,' said Sam.

Bridie's eyes widened in astonishment. 'What's good . . . ?' she began shrilly, when Sam cut across her.

'I merely meant that now Edward can't complain about your going back. If he's going to expect you to help support his parents, you have to work.' He said it so flatly, it took the wind out of her sails.

'I hope he sees it that way,' was all she said.

'He'll have to,' retorted Sam.

Edward arrived home three weeks later, suntanned and cheerful. He found his family grey-faced with worry and Ethel in tears.

'I don't know how we're going to manage,' she whispered to him, shutting the door on the sight of Ted dozing by the fire in the other room. ''e's so ashamed it's terrible. 'e's worked steady all his life, and now it's come to this.' She put her hand on Edward's sleeve and mopped her eyes with the hem of her apron.

'It's very bad, isn't it?' said Edward gruffly, clearing his throat and patting his mother's hand.

She nodded. 'There's so many out of work. They spend all week waiting at the labour exchange, but then there's nothing for 'em and it kills 'em,' she whispered fiercely.

He squeezed her hand. 'Come on, Mum,' he told her firmly, 'don't take on. We'll look after you. You and Dad don't have to worry.'

'I can't let you.' She shook her head. 'And your dad's pride won't let 'im, neither.'

'Just 'til he gets a job. I can't let you go without.'

''e wouldn't take it no other way. But there ain't no jobs, not at his age. 'e don't admit it, but I know,' she said bleakly.

'Then we'll just have to go along with him, eh?'

'I suppose so.' Ethel dried her eyes and picked up the steaming kettle with the corner of a tea towel. 'Bridie's doin' well, by all accounts,' she said hesitantly.

Edward frowned. 'I wish she didn't have to do it,' he said at last.

'She's got to fill her time, son.' Ethel reached into a small cupboard beside her sink and began putting white cups and saucers, edged with blue flowers, on a wooden tray. 'It ain't my business, but if she'd had more kiddies she'd be a lot better off than running round those streets again. And she ain't as young as she was.' She poured boiling water into her big brown teapot and stirred the tea leaves vigorously. 'Where did I put the lid . . . ?'

Edward reached behind her to the draining board

and handed it to her. 'Don't start that again, Mum. It just hasn't happened, that's all.'

'Well,' grumbled his mother, 'with you away all the time, what do you expect? Maybe if you was to get a shore job . . . ?' She filled a jug with milk and put it on the tray beside the cups and saucers.

Edward shook his head. 'I don't think it would make any difference,' he said. 'She's seen Dr Hamilton and I think his advice was for her to make herself busy with other things. So that's what she does.'

Ethel opened her mouth to argue.

'Mum,' said Edward warningly, 'she's a money-lender. She was when she lived here and I don't think she'll ever do any different. Whether I like it or not,' he added ruefully.

'A man ought ter wear the trousers in 'is own 'ouse,' grumbled Ethel.

Edward laughed out loud. 'You know Bridie better than that!'

'Don't you wish you had kiddies of your own?' she persisted.

'Yes,' said Edward reluctantly. 'But there you are.'

'I wish I had some grandchildren, that's all,' she mumbled. 'It'd be grand to have some kiddies round the place now, to cheer your dad up. It'd give him something to do. Susan don't seem to want to get married, and you and Bridie haven't got none. Sometimes I wonder what's wrong with us,' she added fretfully.

Edward picked up the tray. 'Susan will get married one day,' he said cheerfully. 'Let's wake Dad up and have tea.'

'Just the same . . .'

'No,' he said. 'Let it alone, Mum.'

Ethel turned off the dripping tap above her sink, twisting it hard. 'And that tap needs seeing to, when you've got a moment,' she called, twisting it again for good measure, having the last word.

'Where's Bridie and Nipper?' asked Ted, waking up.

'She's at work and he's at school,' Edward said heartily.

''ere's yer tea, Dad.' Ethel leaned across and put Ted's cup and saucer before him with a small clatter. He poured a bit of tea into his saucer and blew on it gently. He sipped noisily.

'Rum carry on,' he remarked, 'woman working like she does.'

Edward watched his father slurp tea. Ted's rough hands, calloused and blackened by years of portering at Billingsgate, held the saucer delicately.

'When she don't need to,' he added softly, when nobody spoke.

'I'm sorry, Dad.'

'It ain't your fault, son.'

Their gaze met over the rim of Ted's saucer.

'I'm sorry,' repeated Edward, for want of anything else to say.

'Might as well think of retiring,' remarked Ted after a long pause. 'There's not a lot going.'

Ethel tried to catch Edward's eye but he was staring at Ted.

'Come and live with us,' he suggested.

'No.' Ted sat forward and reached into his back pocket for his tobacco. 'Thanks for asking, son, but we'll stay here.'

Edward nodded. 'Then you'll let us help out.'

Ethel held her breath. Ted rolled a tiny slip of

liquorice paper and a few shreds of tobacco slowly between his fingers. He made a thin spill from a bit of newspaper and lit one end in the fire, holding it to the end of the little brown roll up in the corner of his mouth. He blew a stream of sweet-smelling smoke towards the fireplace.

'I was thinking more of helping you out,' he pronounced calmly.

Ethel's face dropped in utter dismay. Edward reached over and held out his cup, shaking his head urgently.

'I'll have another,' he said.

Ted took the roll up out of his mouth and held it between finger and thumb.

'I was looking at your house when I came round the other day,' he began, 'and it badly needs a coat of paint . . .'

Edward winked reassuringly at Ethel. 'It does. I was thinking the same thing myself this morning.'

'. . . and Bridie being out so much,' Ted went on, as though he hadn't been interrupted, 'she hasn't time to get that old fool Hemmingway round every time a small job needs doing. He needs more supervising than a baby. Look at what he did to your gas! Can't keep leaving your wife on her own with idiots.' Ted turned to face Edward severely. 'She needs proper looking after while she's out earnin' more than you or me ever did.'

'I think so too,' said Edward delightedly, squeezing Ethel's hand across the table.

'So, seeing as you're away so much, I thought I could see to things as they come up.'

Take or leave it. Ted leaned back and drew in a great lungful of smoke, rubbing his hands together. Edward's eyes met Ethel's cautiously.

'Hemmingway works on an hourly rate,' he said thoughtfully, 'and he doesn't like small jobs. Says it's untidy for the books and not worth while. What we really need is someone who will keep a general eye on the house and do what needs doing. A flat rate arrangement would suit me better, for general maintenance.'

Ted looked at him sharply.

'It would give me peace of mind if you'd do me a favour and take it on, Dad. I never liked to ask before, you being so busy. But if you could see your way to taking over, could we come to some arrangement like that?'

Ethel's breath hissed.

'Bound to be better than that fool Hemmingway,' said Ted, as if weighing the pros and cons.

Edward grinned. 'His loss. So that's settled, then. Thanks, Dad.'

Ethel snatched up the cooled teapot and shot out into the scullery to relieve her pent up feelings. She turned the tap on full.

'And while you're at it, Ted DuCane,' she called happily, 'you can change the washer on this tap.' She banged the overfilled kettle on to the draining board and looked for the lid.

'That stubborn old begger is going to do it,' she whispered to herself joyfully. 'Oh I never thought he would.' A newspaper lay on the side, a smudged photograph of the Minister of Labour, solemn but not downcast, staring out from the front page.

'You can get lost, an' all,' said Ethel savagely, plonking the blackened base of her kettle down on him. 'We're independent now.' She found the lid in the sink.

'I'll do 'er tap later,' said Ted to his son. They both grinned.

Years of Depression gnawed at the East End, planing faces into sharp angles and hollows, bending children's bones with rickets. Bridie wrote to Edward who was staying in Singapore for several weeks.

> Hardly anyone has enough to eat and women look so tired. They walk all day to find cheap food for the children, and they are worn out. I notice how men shuffle. It's so much standing waiting and waiting and waiting. No one has enough any more, so they borrow from me and I have a lot of bad debts. I walk and walk and walk. Only I have good shoes and good food, and they do not. That is a great difference, much more than I ever realized before. It hurts me very much.
>
> Ted has just done the garden ready for winter and he is well. So is Ethel. David's voice seems to have finished breaking and it is queer to hear his deep voice, a man's, instead of a little boy's.
>
> He needs to have new glasses since he complains again that he cannot read well and his head aches. I wish his eyes would settle down because it is more expense. But he must have them.

David accidentally echoed the same thought to Mr Hubbard as the dwarf breathed heavily next to his ear, shining a tiny light into David's right pupil.

'They should stop changing so much once you've finished growing,' muttered the optician. 'Let's have a look in the other one.'

David turned his head slightly so that Mr Hubbard could reach.

'Look at a point over my head,' instructed the midget. 'I don't charge you. Why does your mother worry about the expense?'

In the silence that followed all they could hear was their own breath.

'Well?' demanded Mr Hubbard, hopping off his stool and going to his desk with a pen in his hand.

'Dunno.' David wished desperately that he'd kept his mouth shut. It was hard not to say something when the little bloke was two inches away from your face all the time. He had simply blabbed. Mr Hubbard turned from his old mahogany desk with its angled lamp and walked round David's chair. He climbed up on his stool, standing eyeball to eyeball with his patient, arms akimbo.

'I asked you why your mother worries about paying for your new glasses, since she never has. I am waiting for an answer.'

David coughed with embarrassment and it came out a squeak.

'I'm still waiting,' pointed out the midget.

David stared into the gloom and wished he'd disappear in a puff of smoke, this pantomime person whose bulging eyes glared at him only inches away. David glared back.

'Very well,' said Mr Hubbard patiently. 'We will go through it a step at a time.'

David shifted in his chair, wondering whether the midget could stop him getting out and racing for the door. Mr Hubbard clenched one small fist under his patient's nose and growled, 'Don't think about it. Small, yes. Weak, no.'

The leather chair creaked as David lay back, helpless.

'You have had at least a dozen pairs of spectacles from me, over the last few years?'

'You know I have.'

'Don't take that tone with me. You have not been asked to pay for them?'

'And that's something I wanted to ask you . . .'

'Yes or no?' roared Mr Hubbard.

'No.'

'But your mother has paid for them? Or thought she was paying for them?'

'Yes.'

'How? I gave you no bills.'

'I saw some of those forms you use, on Mrs Partridge's desk. I made some.'

'Bills?' cried Mr Hubbard angrily.

'Yes.'

'Which your mother paid.'

'Yes.'

'Why?'

'Because I gave them to her.'

Mr Hubbard raised his fist and snarled.

David cowered. 'I needed the money.'

'What for?'

David went brilliant red in the darkened room. The dwarf felt the heat from his cheek.

'Go on,' he threatened.

'For lessons,' stammered David, looking desperately past the midget to the door.

'Lessons. What kind of lessons?'

He hesitated, wretched.

'I'll teach you a lesson you'll never forget if you don't tell me,' yelled the dwarf, dancing on his stool with fury.

'Elocution.'

Mr Hubbard paused with his fists in mid air, frozen. Then he gave a great shout of laughter.

'Elocution?' he shrieked incredulously. 'Oh, if that don't beat all!' He clutched at the arm of the chair for support, rolling with mirth and spluttering, 'Oh, I never did! Elocution. Oh, my word.' He wiped tears from his eyes. David cringed, wondering if he was demented after all. But after a bit Mr Hubbard pulled himself together, stood up straight on the stool again, leaned over and hissed venomously: 'What for?'

David swallowed hard. 'To speak better.'

Mr Hubbard balanced firmly on his stool and considered.

'It's true,' he decided finally. 'You do talk better. Less cockney, definitely. When I think back, yes—' He folded his arms, wobbled and caught at the chair again. 'But you haven't said why.' His full pink lips framed the word with spittle that flew past David's cheek. 'Why lie and cheat and defraud for it?'

David struggled upright, grasping for dignity.

'I want to talk well to go to medical school. I won't get in if I speak cockney. You've been to college. You know they won't have people like me; who talk like I did. They'd laugh.'

'Couldn't you ask your mother? Did you have to lie?'

'No. Yes,' said David.

Mr Hubbard rubbed his chin and climbed down off his stool. He marched up and down the small room.

'Mum wouldn't understand a thing like that. She ain't ever even been to school properly, let alone a university. She don't know what it's like.' David half got out of the chair and leaned urgently towards the dwarf. 'She don't, I mean, doesn't, know what they are like,' he repeated. 'She'd say, "Oh, snobs," and take no notice. But that's beside the point. I still need to get in.'

'Hmm. You still have a way to go, certainly,' remarked the dwarf dryly.

'I practise,' said David sullenly.

'You must want to go to medical school frightfully badly,' observed Mr Hubbard.

'I do.'

'What's so attractive about it?'

'I want to be like my father.'

'How well do you remember him?' asked Mr Hubbard curiously.

'Not as much as you,' answered David enviously. 'I wish I had been as old as you when he died.'

The dwarf grunted non-committally.

'And we didn't live with him after I was about two years old,' David went on. 'So I only saw him sometimes. Weekends. Things like that. I remember him dying, though.'

They kept a reflective silence.

'I envy you,' said David. The dwarf turned sharp grey eyes on him and stared.

'Don't be absurd!'

'I do. I think about you a lot,' David burst out passionately. 'You have all this, and it's your own. And I wish I'd known my dad like you knew him. You tell me how he was always interested in what you and your mother did. Well, if he hadn't died, I wouldn't have this awful problem about doing things. I'd get into medical school automatically if my mother was still married to my father, and he was still alive.' He gripped the optician's arm in his eagerness. 'Automatically,' he cried again, almost in tears.

'Well, I'm not sure . . .'

'As good as. It's so unfair.' A tear of pure bitterness

trickled down David's flushed cheek and the dwarf watched it fall with narrowed eyes.

'It's an unfair world,' he remarked at last. 'For everyone. Look at me, for instance. How can you talk about envying me?'

'You never seem to mind,' said David defensively.

'If you are to be a doctor one day, I hope you first of all learn something about tact,' observed Mr Hubbard quietly. 'For your patients' sakes, never mind your own.'

David gasped, taken quite unawares.

'Yes,' said Mr Hubbard. 'I'm glad you take my point. Now, consider your poor mother and what you've done to her. And how you've insulted me. And that's just the things I know about.' Mr Hubbard watched him carefully. 'Your dad was a kind man. Mostly.'

'Mostly?' David looked bewildered and pale.

"He won't take much more," thought the dwarf. "I'd better go carefully."

'You lost him because he died,' Hubbard went on, and then the old injustice loosened his tongue. 'He left us.'

David stared unwaveringly back into the bulging grey eyes. The dwarf's lantern-jawed face split in a malicious smile.

'You speak of envy,' he said, gently sliding in the knife, never a one, with his background, for coarse stabbings. 'But, you see, *I* am the envious one. He left us for you. Well, at the time, for your mother. You, of course, came somewhat later, though not, one has to say, quite as much later as would have been strictly proper.'

'I don't know . . .' David found he stumbled over his words because of the fear rising and mounting and piling up in his chest so he could hardly breathe.

'You don't know what?' demanded the dwarf. 'Your brother?'

Something roared in David's ears.

'Brother.' Mr Hubbard grinned horribly.

David wanted to run but his legs buckled with shock and still he sat in the dreadful chair, in the tiny room, in the half darkness.

'I never charged you because you are family,' explained Mr Hubbard, all trace of humour gone. 'But you have let me down.'

'You are my brother?' squeaked David.

'Your father and my mother adored each other. He thought the world of her but he never married her, not even when I was born, because a dwarf – a midget, my dear – would not have been a suitable wife for a doctor. She would have hindered his career, you see. So he kept her very quiet. Very quiet indeed. And then he kept me quiet. And except for paying her doctor's bills and my fees, that was all we knew of him after he met your mother.

'His first wife was respectable. Your mum was more or less respectable, at least after he married her, but a dwarf . . . No, definitely not respectable. So he left us.'

David sat with his hand to his mouth, white and pinched and staring. His lips barely moved as he whispered, 'It's not true.'

'Every word,' Mr Hubbard assured him. 'I never would have told you if I hadn't caught you out in all this cheating. I thought, "I can't keep quiet. Not this time." I did the last because he was my father, and I had no chance to speak my mind, and it would have hurt my mother beyond bearing for there to have been unpleasantness. She'd have gone along with anything,

she would, even if it did break her heart. But with you –
oh, no.' He shook his head vehemently, as though
winning an argument with himself.

'I want to go.'

'Please do.' Mr Hubbard stood aside and indicated
the door. 'Would you like some water first?' He
seemed just to have noticed David's pallor.

'No. I just want to go.'

'Your prescription then. You may take it elsewhere if
you'd rather. I'd understand.' He thrust it into the
boy's trembling fingers. 'I never meant to tell you.
You'll get over it.'

David looked at him blankly. 'I won't,' he muttered.

'I did. You will. Fathers are a tricky kettle of fish,
aren't they? Can't always go by appearances. You had
to know sooner or later, or grow up in fairyland.'

A wail broke from David. He threw open the door
on a waiting room full of faces all wearing spectacles that glinted weirdly at him in the bright light
of day.

'Noooo,' he howled. They shrank back on their hard
wooden chairs, astonished. Up the road he ran,
through the gates of the park, headlong across the grass
and into his mother's house, crashing and banging
every door behind him until he collapsed in the
sanctuary of his bedroom.

'Blimey,' breathed Ollie, left unnoticed outside the
optician's. 'What's the matter with him?'

'Next, please,' said Mr Hubbard. 'I'm sorry you have
had such a wait.'

'Must you be always proving you're the best?' asked
Bridie.

'It isn't that,' said David, taking his cup from her and

helping himself to ginger biscuits from a plate on the tray.

'Then I'd like to know what it is.'

'Obviously, it's money.' He shrugged. 'How else am I going to pay?'

Bridie shook her head, half proud, half alarmed. 'You haven't got in yet. I'm sure we'll manage.'

'Johnathan thinks applying for the scholarship is a good idea.'

'Oh, does he?' said Bridie weakly.

'Definitely.'

'Then you'd better go in for it, I suppose.'

'I'm going to.'

'I hope you get it, if you want it so badly.'

'I will, Mum, you'll see.' And to her surprise he got up and put both arms around her and hugged her close. 'Don't worry so.'

Bridie turned her face to his and kissed his cheek, feeling soft, golden stubble against her lips.

'Go on with you,' she said, and smiled to cover a sudden aching sense of loss.

Chapter Five

David began to worry his mother.

'He spends all his time up there,' she said to Lizzie one day, looking up at the ceiling. 'Studying.'

'What's wrong with that? He wants to do well. I wish Ollie would work a bit harder. You don't know how lucky you are.'

'But he doesn't do anything else.'

'Give him time. He'll have plenty to do when he gets to college.'

'That's just it,' cried Bridie, wagging her finger at Lizzie as if making a point.

'What is?' asked Lizzie, puzzled.

'All this talk of college. It bothers me. You'd think that was all there was, to hear him. I'm glad he's got ambitions, Lizzie, but I don't know that I like the singlemindedness of it. It's like there's never been anything else, not since he was quite small. There's other things in life besides studying, isn't there?'

Lizzie, shelling peas at the big scrubbed table in Bridie's kitchen, picked out a small white maggot and frowned.

'I hate them,' she said, shaking the maggot into the waste pail by her feet. It landed on top of a pile of shelled pods and wriggled frantically until it was out of sight. Lizzie watched it, her face screwed up in distaste.

'They make me go squeamish, too.' Bridie picked up a pod and began to slip it open with her thumb.

'When is Edward home next?' asked Lizzie.

'Not for ages. Why?'

'I wondered if he might draw David out of himself a bit, if you're worried.'

'I'm not worried exactly,' Bridie answered slowly. 'More at a loss. When I look at him I see Francis, and it seems like the clock has gone back in a peculiar sort of way. They are so alike. There's probably no more to it than that.'

'I think you once told me that Angus called Francis a fanatic.'

Bridie half smiled and nodded. 'He used to say there was none worse. But I think he was more than half joking.'

'Well, there you are, then. Like father, like son.' Lizzie popped a little cluster of tiny peas into her mouth. 'These are delicious raw,' she said. 'Seems a shame to cook them.' She held out her palm to Bridie, with a little pool of peas in the middle of it. 'Try some.'

Bridie took the baby peas in her hand. 'There was a funny thing, too.'

Lizzie peered at the vegetables.

'No, not them.' Bridie paused for thought. 'I forget when it was exactly; a while ago. David had some new glasses and when I asked him for the bill, as usual, he went all vague and odd and said there wasn't one. Apparently the optician gave him a free pair. David couldn't say why. Don't you think that's strange? It struck me at the time, but David was so offhand about it, it was one of those things you can't keep asking about, if you know what I mean. I felt I was making a mountain out of a molehill because he said there was nothing to it.'

'Maybe little Mr Hubbard was feeling generous. He's a dear man. He and David get on, don't they? It was probably just friendliness.'

'Maybe,' said Bridie doubtfully.

'It must be nice for him, anyway, to have someone he can talk to over his lenses, and not just get the same old gossip every time from the same old bunch of blind biddies.' Lizzie tossed the last pods into the pail.

'I have a feeling . . .' Bridie shook her head. 'Never mind. It doesn't matter.'

'Come over to us for Sunday. Perhaps Johnathan can put his finger on it.'

'If David'll come. As likely as not he'll want to stay in his room and swot.'

'Well,' said Lizzie, seeing no way out, 'you can only ask him. If he won't, he won't. We certainly shan't take offence.' She stood and swept pea fragments from her skirt. 'Every mark shows on beige,' she grumbled.

'It's pretty, though.' Bridie looked Lizzie's dumpy little figure up and down affectionately. 'And it suits you. Almost matches your hair.'

'Just what Johnathan said when he saw it,' cried Lizzie, pleased.

'I'll try to get his lordship to leave his books on Sunday, then.' Bridie kissed her in the kitchen doorway; she'd find her own way out.

'Stop fretting,' said her friend, and hurried up the stairs to the hall, pulling the front door to behind her with a bang.

Bridie sighed and began to wash the peas in the colander. Her fingers were darkened and stained with the handling of money. So much money. She thought of

79

it all: the miserable streets she walked daily, the pale defeated faces and listless men, the heavy coins around her waist. Then in her mind's eye she saw Edward, tanned and strong and sure in his tall, beautiful ship, on the far side of the world. She felt suddenly, achingly, lonely.

Upstairs David lay on his bed, listening to the faint murmur of women's voices below, the bang of the front door and the silence that followed. He rolled over on to his stomach and picked up the physics textbook that had fallen to the floor earlier. The formulae he'd been memorizing made no more sense than they had before. He closed his eyes and the distorted face of the dwarf hung before his eyelids. Nothing exorcised it, not even sleep. Nothing except hard work. David groaned softly. He balled his hand into a fist and beat gently on the coverlet. 'Go away, go away.'

"They adored each other." The words haunted him afresh each day and night, and disgusting images teased him. She'd been a dwarf. Things about it both puzzled and fascinated him, made him writhe in the depths of shame, prey to filthy thoughts that agonized and eluded him. Even going back, heart pounding and dry-mouthed, to see Mr Hubbard again hadn't taken away the depth of betrayal he felt. They sat after surgery had ended in the little back room. Mrs Partridge had made them a cup of tea and departed, her desk tidied for the evening.

'After all, it wasn't me who betrayed you,' the small man had said mournfully, perched on his stool, the angled lamp throwing his shadow huge on the wall behind him. 'It was your dad. I only told you. I never meant to, but I have and I can't undo it. You'll just have to get used to it.'

"Get used to it." Sitting on his bed, David ground his teeth with frustration but the dwarf's words came remorselessly back and back and back until he thought that if he couldn't turn them off, he'd go mad.

'He married your mother because she had you,' Mr Hubbard had continued. 'He was always one to do the correct thing. Except when it come to dwarves,' said the tiny creature acidly. 'Propriety came first then, naturally, him being a doctor.' He stressed the word savagely and looked sideways at David's stricken face.

'Propriety is doing the correct thing.'

'You've learned something at school. Self-interest, then.'

'I thought you said you loved him,' David burst out despairingly, letting go the tight reins of his misery.

Mr Hubbard's misshapen face softened so quickly it was magical to see. David watched the transformation with wonder.

'Oh, I did. I do.'

'Then how can you tell me these awful things?'

'Because they are true. It's not a judgement, you understand, simply the facts. I loved him even though I knew things about him that were deplorable.' Hubbard's rubbery lips grimaced at his own pomposity. 'From our point of view, of course. From others, he was admirable. It just depends how you look at it, see?'

'I don't think I do,' said David, downcast.

'You are too young,' said his half-brother kindly, blowing on a lens and polishing it on a bit of chamois.

'I don't think you look like him, except for your hair, but you talk a bit like him, don't you?' David said warily, in case he offended.

'Big words,' said the dwarf sarcastically. 'I wouldn't exactly say he had much of a way with children, but yes, he loved to talk. It was other things he wasn't so hot on. But my mother more than made up for that, and of course she was on my level.' The dwarf gave a short laugh. 'It can be tricky noticing things about people when they're three feet or so above your nose.' He continued to shake with quiet amusement. His shadow wavered on the wall.

'My mother's always worked so hard, she notices me but she doesn't always have time to go on noticing, if you know what I mean.'

Mr Hubbard nodded.

'And Dad died and Edward's always at sea. There've always been people around me but I sometimes feel as if there's no one there for me.' David sounded surprised. 'I never told anyone that before.'

'Hm.' Mr Hubbard slid his lens into its wooden case and selected another. 'Do you think she knows anything about this?'

'Who, Mum?' cried David, astonished. 'Oh no, I shouldn't think so.'

'It's our secret then.' Mr Hubbard glared at him sternly.

'Why are you angry?' asked David. 'What have I done now?'

'I'm not. It's just crossing my mind that I have opened a Pandora's box and I have to trust you now to keep the contents from flying out all over the place, and making the most appalling mess.'

'I shan't tell.'

'I hope not,' said Mr Hubbard, wishing David were twenty years older and wiser.

'I can keep a secret.'

'Good.'

'What was your mother's name?' David tried to imagine a woman as tiny as this side by side with his father. It made him feel quite odd.

'Penelope,' said Mr Hubbard in a short sort of voice, as if he didn't want to go into that just now. 'How old are you?'

'Nearly seventeen.'

'Is it that long ago?' murmured the dwarf. 'All those years and I still miss him, even though we never saw much of him after you and your mum came along.'

'I'm sorry about that. I still miss him, too,' said David, determined not to be left out, and the words took an amazing amount of the pain away. For the first time the brothers' eyes met with understanding.

"Next time," thought David, "I'll ask him what his first name is."

Shaking off the memory, he got up from his crumpled counterpane and went to the table in the corner of his room, under the window overlooking the road at the front of the house. Outside a dull, overcast sky would bring an early nightfall. He picked up the envelope that had come that morning and lain opened, then resealed, avoided until now. He pulled out the cluster of papers and stared once more at the single sheet that lay on the top.

"The applicant will submit a copy of the following documents," it said. There followed a list of examination certificates, and at the very end it said they wanted to see his birth certificate. Holding the papers, David sat on the end of his bed and thought about Mr Hubbard's dates yet again, hoping to find a mistake. But the dates were remorseless. However he worked it out, his parents could not have got married before he was born.

More of his brother's dreadful words fell into place.

'I'm illegitimate,' he murmured, 'and I never knew.'

There was absolutely no chance in the world, not the smallest most infinitesmial chance that any medical school would admit David if they knew. It was a more absolute barrier than stupidity or cupidity. It was the one thing that there was no way round. David took a deep breath and got up. He went downstairs to find Bridie.

Chapter Six

She read the application form in silence.

'You see, I need my birth certificate, and I realized I've never seen it.' David watched her closely as she looked up from the sheaf of papers, wondering what on earth she would say. It was only: 'Yes, you do. I'll have to find it for you.'

"How can she stay so calm?" wondered David, watching her prevaricate.

'Do you need it right away?' asked his mother.

'I want to send this lot off in a couple of weeks. No, not right now.'

'I'll look it out for you.'

And that was that. She picked up her darning and threaded her needle with steady fingers. David sat opposite her and began to fill in some of the papers, resting them on the wide arm of his chair. Glancing at her untroubled face, he began to wonder uneasily if Mr Hubbard hadn't been taking him for the worst ride imaginable. He went hot and cold at the thought of the things they had said, at the shame of it if none of it were true. Bridie noticed his fidgeting.

'Is something wrong?'

David flushed. 'No,' he lied.

It was on the tip of his tongue to ask her outright, to throw caution and secrets to the wind. But what to say if it weren't true? If it had all been besmirching, grubby lies? A dreadful, unforgivable betrayal? And he'd believed in it; that would be the worst betrayal of all. Saying anything was impossible. He gathered together the papers and made as if to get up. 'I just wondered if it was lost or something? It would take some time to get another one, and it would mean I couldn't send these off so soon although I expect it's all right to wait.' Hearing himself gabbling, he began to panic. 'There's plenty of time . . .'

'No,' his mother's soft voice broke in. 'I don't believe it's lost. I'll just have to look it out. I'm not sure whether it is here with my papers, or whether Mr Brown has it. I'll have to look. If Mr Brown has it, it'll take a day or two to get, that's all.' Her steady eyes studied him thoughtfully in the lamplight. Next to her on the shiny horsehair sofa, The Pope stirred and uncurled. He yawned, stretched, and jumped down. David patted his knee and The Pope hesitated, then trotted over and jumped up, settling down again with his black paws tucked neatly under him. David stroked the cat, silent on his knee. Its slanting yellow eyes closed complacently.

'Silly animal,' said David affectionately. 'You're mean with your purrs, you are.'

The Pope nodded off, whiskers twitching in his sleep.

'You could always be a vet,' suggested Bridie, watching the way David's hand curled so carefully around the little black shape on his knee. 'You might find animals easier than people.'

'People are more interesting,' he answered with all the wisdom of nearly seventeen years. 'People are more complicated. There's more scope with them.'

'Johnathan says it's harder to get into veterinary college than into medical school.'

'Perhaps.' David pulled The Pope's ears and the cat shook its head, disturbed.

'What would you want to do if you didn't get in?' asked Bridie casually. 'Have you thought?'

David glanced at his mother keenly, wondering again what she was hiding from him behind that straightforward, open gaze.

'I've thought I wouldn't have a future,' he said dramatically. Bridie stifled a great urge to laugh because she knew all too well he couldn't be laughed out of it. It would only make things worse.

'You should have other strings to your bow,' she said instead.

'I have. Chemistry. I could go into that, like Ollie. But he's a test tube chap and I'm not. Physics. Probably mathematics. I could do any of them, but they don't appeal.'

'Oh my, aren't you the clever one?' Bridie's Irish voice raised itself in mock wonder. 'You get any sharper, young man, and you'll cut yourself.'

'You don't understand,' he cried. 'You never went to school, and you think these things are simple when they're not.'

Bridie saw his long, thin inkstained fingers against the shiny black fur of The Pope's flank, and they brought back memories of Francis's touch on the nape of her neck. He'd stand at the back of her chair and look over the top of her head at whatever she was doing, his hand resting lightly on her skin. Her own fingers, blackened and broken-nailed, caught on the darning thread and she put the mushroom down in her lap. Maybe all she understood was money, but was that so bad? Sometimes, she knew, it embarrassed David.

'Maybe not,' she sighed. 'There's a lot of things I don't understand. Like the terrible things they are doing in Berlin. Did you see a newspaper today?'

'No. Why?'

'I saw Sam this afternoon and he was so upset. It gets worse and worse for the Jews in Germany. He had a *Picture Post* and someone had photographed Jewish men scrubbing a pavement in Berlin. The poor souls had buckets and brushes and they were crouched there, scrubbing paving stones, in the middle of a circle of Nazis, standing round, all grinning their evil heads off. God knows what makes those animals behave that way.'

'Don't insult animals!'

'Well, I can tell you, the only ones with any dignity in that picture were the Jews,' Bridie's Irish accent deepened in indignation, 'for all they were being made fools of. But the worst thing was that there were little German children standing in the front row watching, like you'd see kiddies watching at a circus, all laughing and happy. There was a little girl smiling to see this awful thing. What can the Germans think they're doing?'

'It's called reprisals,' said David. 'The Nazis do something beastly to some Jews, like throwing stones through their shop windows, and then they make the Jews grovel and clear up the mess.'

'Sam is beside himself. He says there's worse to come and we shall have war soon, whatever Chamberlain says.'

'Do you think it will come to that?'

'I don't know. Ted thinks so. He was talking about it all this morning. You know how he goes on. But I don't know what to think.' She picked up her porcelain mushroom and jabbed at David's heavy grey sock with a needle.

'I wouldn't be called up, I don't think, if I'm a medical student.' He stroked The Pope, and from his place on the carpet by the window Brother John opened one eye to check what was going on. Nothing interesting. He went back to sleep.

'No, I suppose not. They need a lot of doctors in wartime, don't they?' Her reproach was so soft David hardly heard it. 'Edward will fight at sea, of course.'

'Are you sure you haven't got the family papers here?'

David bundled The Pope on to the end of the settee by his mother and wandered restlessly around the room. The cat, his fur on end, shook himself and began to wash behind his ears.

'Would you like to make us some tea?' asked Bridie.

'No. Would you have a look now? Please, Mum.'

'Can't you wait until tomorrow?'

'Please.' David's anxiety made deep furrows on his smooth forehead.

"You are only a child," thought Bridie sadly, "and now we are about to change everything and there will be no going back." She pushed The Pope away and laid her darning down carefully.

'I'll go upstairs and look,' she said, knowing he could be put off no longer. David sat in a silence broken only by the rush of blood in his ears as he thought of what they might say to each other when she came back into the room. He closed his eyes and leaned against the back of the chair he had just left.

'Just let it be there, so I can know,' he asked the empty room. 'Please let her find it.'

* * *

Bridie went straight to her bed and drew out a strongbox from underneath. She took a key from her neck, unlocked the box and took out some papers.

'If you must, you must,' she murmured under her breath. She unfolded a thick sheet of paper and held it up to the light. David's birth certificate was like every other birth certificate, except for the word ILLEGITI-MATE printed across it in bold, black letters. She took it downstairs and handed it wordlessly to her son.

He rubbed the bridge of his nose until the giddy feeling passed.

'I'm sorry,' said his mother, standing behind the old sofa as if defending herself from him.

'I'd already worked it out.'

'You knew?'

'I wanted to be sure.'

'What will you do?'

'Do?'

'About your application?'

'They won't take me. Not with this.'

'I thought not. Johnathan said something a long time ago.'

'So we'll have to change it.'

Bridie's eyes widened. 'You can't!'

'*I* can't, but someone else might. Sam Saul should be able to fix a thing like this. He's got fingers in all the right pies.'

'Whatever gave you the idea Sam would do a thing like that?' demanded Bridie in a voice thready with nerves. David came round his armchair and slumped into it, his head on one side, staring at his mother.

'Because he's a crook,' he said drearily.

She shook her head. 'Not that kind. He's sailed close

to the wind sometimes, but he's legit these days.'

David said angrily, 'I wish you wouldn't talk that way. "Legit." It's embarrassing.'

'Very well, if it offends you, I meant that he does nothing illegal. I know he used to, but for years now – since Ruthie had David, really – he's been honest. He wants a business to leave to his son, not a prison record.'

'Will you ask him anyway?'

'I can't.'

'Yes, you can.'

'He'd never do it. He feels real strongly about things like that, and even more so at the moment, with the Jews being persecuted so badly. He thinks people should stand up for what they are. He'd say that it's not worth being a doctor if you can only do it at the price of pretending you're something you're not.'

David lost his temper.

'For God's sake, Mum, I didn't choose whether you and Dad got married or not before I was born!' he yelled. 'That is nothing to do with who or what I am. That was something *you* did and it's *your* fault, not mine. Why should I have it hanging over me all my life?'

'I don't know.'

'Well, then. Will you ask Sam Saul to fix it?'

'Asking isn't the point. He'd never do it and I'd feel so bad . . .'

'*You'd* feel bad?' shouted David. 'How do you think *I* feel?'

Bridie put her hand to her mouth. David was ashen and his wide grey eyes glittered with rage.

'I'll have nothing,' he clenched his fist and slammed it on to the arm of the chair, 'unless you do this for me.'

'I'll ask Sam in the morning.'

David's fist relaxed.

'Really?'

'Really,' she said coldly.

'Thanks.'

'Don't thank me,' she said. 'You may regret this later.'

'Never.'

She folded the papers and felt her hands tremble. 'I hope not,' she said, looking him straight in the eye, 'but I fear you may.'

'Well, that won't be your problem, will it?'

'My conscience will,' said his mother sadly.

'I should have thought that would trouble you anyway.'

Bridie wondered if this was her son, whom she loved more than her own life. It seemed that he was, and he was becoming a stranger.

'No!' yelped Sam Saul. 'Absolutely not. I'm surprised you ask.'

He stood holding the birth certificate in one hand, waving angrily at the ceiling with the other. 'What do you take me for?'

'Someone who's good at arranging things,' said Bridie meekly, trying to ride the storm, which was no worse than she had expected.

'But this,' cried Sam furiously, 'this I don't arrange. This is identity and I don't meddle with it.'

'I told David you'd say that,' she sighed.

'What do you want?' Sam narrowed his black eyes and glared at her. 'You want to start this lie?'

'I feel it is my fault,' she answered quietly. 'I do know it isn't David's. Why should he suffer because I married his father after he was born? He doesn't deserve to suffer for that and it seems to matter more than I ever thought it would. He says it'll bar him from doing what he wants, everywhere he goes.'

Sam looked as if he would have a paroxysm. He turned to his great untidy desk and rummaged angrily among the ledgers and papers that lay strewn in all directions. He dragged a newspaper out and opened it at an inside page. He thrust it underneath Bridie's nose and shouted:

'Look at that. You talk about being barred from things. Well?' The paper shook in front of Bridie so that she put a hand on to his to steady it.

'Where?'

'There. Third column. The photo.'

A gate in Berlin leading to a park, leafy and broad-lawned, a place of tranquillity where old people and lovers would stroll in the cool of a summer evening. The gate had a notice nailed to it.

'That,' shouted Sam, 'is what I mean.'

'What does it say?'

'*Juden verboten*. No Jews.'

'What does that have to do with . . . ?'

'Everything!' bellowed Sam. 'Simply everything. Once you start discriminating between people about things they can't help, whether it's their race or the colour of them or whether their parents were married or not, you give rise, in the end, to this.' He struck the paper with the flat of his hand. 'How do you think Hitler does it,' he demanded, 'if Germans don't go along with it? He'd get short shrift if they didn't.'

'The Depression . . .'

'*We've* got a Depression. It hasn't turned us into Nazis.'

'I still don't see . . .'

'Scapegoats,' cried Sam. 'The Jews are scapegoats and they come in very handy because people think they're different. Hitler is accusing them of anything he feels like and people believe him because they're a bit mystified about Jews at the best of times. So David's different – he's got a word on his birth certificate that certain people don't like. Are you going to let him go along and start lying to some ass at the medical school who cares more about that word than what sort of man David really is? I don't see much difference between that and saying a man is a criminal because his birth certificate says "Jewish". You start that and you're halfway down the road to being no better than Hitler.'

Bridie rose from her seat in Sam's office, flushed with anger. 'That's enough! I won't be told I'm no better than Hitler. I didn't come to see you to listen to you carrying on like a maniac. I know what's happening to your people is awful but it don't give you no right to go abusing others.'

'Am I?' he asked, perplexed.

''course you are. How can you say those kinds of things to me?'

'I feel strongly about this business with David. I can't have a hand in it, Bridie.'

'I never thought you would, only he wanted so badly for me to ask that I couldn't say no. I'm sorry I did. And I think I sort of understand what you mean about the Jews, but no one else would have the nerve to say it quite like you do.'

To her relief, Sam laughed.

'It's the thin end of a wedge. I don't like to see your son going that way.'

'Well, we'll have to see. It looks like doctoring is out. I don't know what he'll do next.'

David went pale when Bridie told him of Sam's refusal.

'I'm going for a walk,' he said. Bridie put her hand on his arm but he shook her off.

'I just want to get out,' he said bitterly, turning away furiously so that she wouldn't see tears in his eyes.

'Be careful, David,' she cried. 'It will pass. There are other things.'

'Not for me,' he muttered.

He walked very fast round the park, beneath the cherry trees in full blossom, past the rose garden at the far end and out on to the canal path that led to the River Lee. Eventually he turned down the towpath where years before he had run home after Bert dragged him out of the canal. He went through the gate, not far from his own back garden, that took him out into the main road, just up from Bethnal Green, and began to stride rapidly down towards the new tube station being built on the Green itself. He could see the building works in the distance, marking the turn off that would lead him home again in a full circle.

Workmen sat on a pile of pipes, smoking and drinking tea. Just as he drew level with them a boy ran in front of him, giving out handbills to passers by, who shook their heads and walked on faster.

''ere, 'olmes.' The youth shoved a small crudely printed handbill into David's hand. 'You comin'?'

He took in the ferrety little face with its unruly mop of mousy hair and remembered the boy who used to sit next to him at school. David stopped in his tracks.

'Mackie?'

He puffed out his hollow chest proudly. 'Yeah. Look!' he said.

'You've never joined the blackshirts?' said David in disgust.

'What you got against us, then?' Mackie drew himself up to his full height and David stared down at his rawboned, hungry face and felt sorry for him. Mackie pushed the handbill at him.

'Go on, take it,' he whined. David took it, glancing at the crude print.

'Rallies!' he snorted. 'Bunch of idiots strutting around in an old hall somewhere, more like, with that berk Moseley shouting his stupid head off. Don't be so daft.'

Mackie watched David pick his way around the workmen's pipes, eyes flat with hatred.

'You always did think you was better than anyone else, David 'olmes. You wait, we'll get yer one day.'

David turned and began walking backwards, laughing.

'You'll laugh the other side 'o your stinkin' face,' yelled Mackie, starting to run. David screwed up the handbill and tossed it contemptuously at him, still laughing. Mackie charged, head butting, and both boys went flying.

'Watch yerself,' shouted a man, coming out of the half-built station, carrying a hod of used bricks. Punching and kicking, the two of them rolled over and under his feet, the three of them tumbling in a flailing mass of arms and legs and flying bricks, into a pipe hole, one on top of the other, gasping and swearing and heaving to get out again.

'Bloody idiots,' roared the man, dragging himself upright in the dry, stony hole, spitting brickdust so that it just missed Mackie's face, jammed against the side of the dugout. David struggled upright, breathing hard.

'Blame him, little runt!' he said savagely. 'He started it.'

Mackie bridled and the brickie casually pushed his face into the side of the hole.

'Shut up and keep still or I'll stick your 'ead in a pipe what it won't come out of,' he said in a not unkind voice. 'See?'

Mackie scowled, his lip bloody and beginning to swell. The bricklayer ran his finger along the boy's arm.

'Nice shirt,' he remarked, shifting to sit more easily in the pipehole.

Mackie tried to draw back his arm but the bricklayer held it in a grip of iron. 'Blackshirts, eh?' he said softly. 'Well, what about that? I thought I spotted you earlier on giving aggravation to people what was minding their own business. You're a bloody public nuisance, son.'

'I ain't. I've as much right as you to stand on the pavement.' Mackie dragged his arm away bravely and started to wriggle upright.

'Is that so.' The brickie spoke almost tenderly.

'Yes,' said Mackie, getting braver.

'He givin' you bother, son?' asked the bricklayer, turning to David.

'Passing handbills about their rotten rallies,' said David, nodding.

'I thought so.' The bricklayer heaved himself to his feet, his head sticking up above the sides of the dugout. Pushing to get a purchase on its dry sides, he hauled himself out and sat on the side. He reached down and picked Mackie out like a child, by the scruff of his neck. He held the boy up, eyeball to eyeball, and spoke quietly.

'I never want to see you round 'ere again. And if you know what's good for you, you'll throw that stupid getup in the canal and stop messing about with evil little perverts like Moseley. Does your mum know what you're up to?'

'Yes,' squeaked Mackie defiantly.

The bricklayer shook his head sadly. 'Stone the crows, there's one born every minute,' he said disbelievingly. 'And she don't mind?'

'She comes with me.'

'Ugh.' The bricklayer gave up. 'Get out.' He raised one enormous, sunburned fist and slung Mackie effortlessly out of the hole. The little fascist flew in an arc over his tormentor's head and landed with a bonejolting crash several yards away.

'Scum,' remarked the bricklayer with disgust.

David gazed up at him from his seat in the pipeline.

'You don't mess around arguing, do you?' he said admiringly. The man dusted off his hands and leaned down to help David out.

'Nah,' he said shortly, 'not with the likes of them. They ain't worth it.'

'Jew lovers!' wept Mackie, lying on the ground too winded to move. It was his worst insult. They didn't hear him.

The bricklayer went over to the pipes and came back with two cups of strong, sweet tea.

'Fag?' he asked, shaking out a packet of Players. David hesitated, then took one from the paper packet and held it awkwardly. They lit up. The brickie sat in quiet amusement while David choked his way through half the cigarette.

'Need a bit 'o practice, don't you?' he observed.

David shuddered and held his cigarette away from his face until his eyes stopped watering.

'Uh,' he coughed.

'Try a sip of tea,' suggested the brickie.

The cigarette burned between David's fingers, sending smoke coiling around them.

'I used to go to school with him,' he said when he had his breath back properly, looking to see if Mackie was still around, 'and he never joined in anything. The teachers used to complain about it. Fancy him getting in with that lot.'

'Misfits and queers. Off their trolleys, the 'ole lot.' The brickie dismissed the British Fascists with a derisive sniff.

'You know about them?' said David, curious.

'I'm a Commie, son.'

'Really?' David was impressed and intrigued. 'I've thought about that, too, only I don't think my mother would like it.'

'Man has to make up his own mind about his politics. You think for yourself, lad. Ain't for yer mum to tell you what to think.'

'She doesn't exactly do that.' David felt guilty. 'It's just she thinks I'm still a child, not old enough to know what's what.'

'How old are you, then?'

'Eighteen in May.'

'I was married at sixteen,' said the brickie, puffing out his dark, stubbled cheeks dismissively. A whistle pierced the air.

'Gaffer,' he said. 'Got to get back. All the best, mate.'

They scrambled to their feet, throwing tea dregs at the dry grey soil and stamping out ends of cigarettes, smoked right down to their fingers.

One of the labourers wiped his hands on a bit of waste and called over, 'Any more of Moseley's lot, you just bring 'em along to us. We'll sort the beggars out.'

Laughing loudly, they disappeared into their half-built station, picking their way round cluttered bricks and pipes and heaps of heavy London clay.

The birth certificate forgotten, David walked excitedly back the way he had come. Twenty minutes later he disappeared into a dingy hallway halfway down the Hackney Road, in the bottom of a redbrick house whose sagging windows were boarded. Peeling paint hung from its windowsills. The house looked derelict, the door open to the early evening air.

'Yes?' said a young woman with dark curls and a bright red jumper. 'Can I help you?'

'I want to join,' said David, 'please.'

The dark girl looked at him and smiled. She handed him a form. 'You can start by filling this in,' she said in tones that came from Hampstead or Hounslow or somewhere else far to the west of Bethnal Green.

He leant on the edge of her table, opened his pen and began to write.

'You did what?' squawked Bridie, astonished and horrified.

'I joined the Communist Party on my way home.'

'You haven't!'

'Why shouldn't I?'

'They mean trouble,' keened his mother, wringing her hands.

'Everything I do means trouble. I can't do nothing right, can I?'

'Don't whine.'

'I'm not whining,' he yelled. 'There's just no pleasing you, is there?'

'It's not that.'

'What do you want, then? You're keen to censure me, but how would you like if it you'd wanted something all your life and couldn't have it just because of someone else's mistake?'

'It wasn't no mistake,' snapped Bridie. 'I wanted it that way. And I'm sorry you can't see that no one gets everything they want. Just because you want something badly doesn't mean you're entitled to it. I never said you had to please anyone, but you could be more reasonable.'

'It's reasonable, now, is it?' David shouted, hating her.

Bridie lost her temper.

'Grow up!' she shouted back. 'You've wallowed in self-pity long enough. There's nothing to be done about it, so the sooner you get on with looking for something else to do when you leave school, the better. Shut up, go and wash, and I'll get you your supper.'

'You don't care, do you? You don't care.'

Bridie glared.

David stormed upstairs and slammed his bedroom door with a crash which shook the house. Bridie ran after him and stood at the foot of the stairs, staring into the shadows after him, trembling with rage until all of a sudden her shoulders dropped and she went back to her kitchen, shaking her head indignantly.

"Knock some sense into his head, if You please," she implored, gazing upwards with an air of exasperation. A second crash came from the bathroom, followed by the sound of water running in the pipes. "Praise be to Heaven, he's impossible." Bridie lifted her indignant face. "Would You tell me what I'm to be doing with him?"

She picked up the breadknife and swiped savagely at a loaf freshly bought that morning. It buckled, soft in her grasp, so the knife slipped and grazed her finger.

'Fat lot of good You are,' she muttered, sucking her finger, listening to the silence upstairs. Fifteen minutes later David skulked back to the kitchen and found his mother spooning stew on to warm plates.

'Here,' she said, pushing his in front of him. 'Eat up and let's be having no more nonsense.'

Brother John, born a scavenger, curled his long body round the leg of David's chair and inhaled delicious smells. He miaowed officiously, squawking as David shoved him away with his foot. The cat crouched, motionless, watching David's shoes warily.

'Do they get enough to eat, the way they beg?' he mumbled, not averse to starting another argument.

'They're pigs. He's had fish already, only he scoffed it so fast I shouldn't think he noticed. He'd eat himself sick.'

'Cats don't.'

'That one does. The Pope doesn't.'

'Mum, do you think if I asked Sam myself, he'd change his mind?'

'What I think, David, is that if you bring this up one more time you and I are going to fall out. Badly. I have had enough of it.'

David put down his knife and fork and stared at his mother across the scrubbed deal table. She ate steadily, unperturbed by his gaze. He saw her red hair, shot through with silvery grey, falling from its pins around a tired face lined by hard work and laughter. Her square jaw had softened with passing years, but the lovely, wide mouth still curved as readily as ever, the same, radiantly open smile lighting candid green eyes, sparkling with good nature.

'I'm sorry,' he muttered ungraciously, half wanting her not to hear it even though he really was, in a way.

'So am I,' she said readily, 'but we'll find you something. It's no good being possessed by ideas you can't do anything about.'

'Possessed?'

'That's the word, isn't it?' Bridie helped them both to apple pie and looked over the table inquiringly. 'You can get possessed by ideas, can't you?' She poured custard, holding back the skin with a spoon.

'I thought it was more the Devil. But I suppose you can.'

'The Devil has more than one face,' said Bridie darkly. 'Don't underestimate him.'

'Oh, Mum, that's sheer superstition.'

'Is it?' asked Bridie, thinking back to eggs placed in barns, in secret places; odd little ceremonies behind hedges, glimpsed as a child. They prayed in church, the Irish countryfolk, and did something else to keep the other side happy when the priest wasn't looking. Or was obligingly looking the other way, thought Bridie, the memories suddenly sharp and clear.

'It may be superstition, but it's better safe than sorry.'

'What on earth's that meant to mean?'

Even Bridie couldn't quite say, but when she took the dishes to be washed, with her back to David, she crossed herself quickly because for no reason at all she was afraid for him.

Chapter Seven

The evening was flushed with red as the sun sank towards the horizon. David lay on his back, watching the oblong of his window turn from pale blue to green, to silver and pink. He could hear Bridie's wireless intermittently from downstairs. Several times she went up and down between her sitting room and the kitchen, but she did not come up to disturb him after their truce.

He pulled his pillows into a comfortable pile behind him, reached down by the side of the bed and picked up a textbook and a copy of a matriculation paper of the kind he would take in the summer. He worked until the room was too dark for him to see. Putting down his books, something caught his eye and made him look again. Past the end of his feet the mirrored door of his heavy mahogany wardrobe stood open and he could see his own reflection, lying in deep shadow. He scratched his cheek, puzzled by something, and the figure in the mirror did the same. But there was something else, standing in the mirror, but at the same time, out of sight. Something waited. David's skin prickled.

"Put the light on, open the door," his thoughts buzzed uselessly. He could not take his eyes from the dark reflection of the room. His limbs would not move, held fast by some presence in the glass opposite. Some invisible movement, perceptible beyond the edge of perception, came again and the fine, soft hair on the nape of David's neck stood straight up on end.

Downstairs he faintly heard the ten o'clock news begin on the BBC. Fainter than Alvar Liddel's voice came a whisper.

'David.'

His eyes popped and strained. The unseen presence broke its bonds of time and place and substance and flowed into the mirror triumphantly.

'Hullo, there.' Mr Hubbard stood before him, reflected in the mirror. And yet how could it be a reflection when he was not present in the flesh? Glass gleamed between them like the shining surface of water over the face of a drowned man. The midget beamed.

'Takes a lot of persuasion to make them let me do this,' he said chattily.

David moaned.

'Surprised, eh?' chuckled the dwarf.

David's eyes bulged.

'Ah, don't panic,' said the small creature brightly. 'It's a shock the first time, but you get used to it.'

David stared, witless.

'Cat got your tongue?' enquired the apparition. 'Here.' Mr Hubbard raised one short arm and spread his fingers towards the bed. The shock of his ice cold touch shot David a foot into the air and he landed with a soft blow to his back as the bedsprings squeaked and groaned.

'That's better,' said Mr Hubbard, 'but we can always do it again if you have any more trouble.'

'No,' he yelped.

'Nice and loud and clear. Good. Now, where were we?'

'How did you get in there?'

'Takes a lot of practice, I can tell you,' said Mr Hubbard, preening.

'I mean, you can't be . . .' David struggled with pure unreality, '. . . you cannot possibly be standing in a mirror.'

'Alice did. It's not that unusual,' said Mr Hubbard calmly.

'Fairy tales.'

'As you like,' said the dwarf offhandedly.

'You're an illusion. I'm dreaming.'

'Try and wake up then,' suggested the midget imperturbably.

'You're a nightmare, that's all.'

'If you like. Perhaps it's all in your mind,' agreed the creature accommodatingly. 'You can always think that, if it helps. But I'm still here, aren't I?'

'Are you?' squeaked David.

'Well, in a manner of speaking. Either way, you and I are having a chat, and I'm in the mirror on this side and you are over there. Now, we can spend our time marvelling at people in mirrors or we can get down to business. I haven't got all night.'

'What business?' wheezed David, feeling as if he had swallowed a bucket of sawdust.

'The certificate,' he said briskly.

'How do you know about that? I haven't seen you since . . .'

'It's obvious I would know, isn't it? Seeing what else I know, that is.'

'Oh.'

'Quite.' Mr Hubbard crossed the mirror and disappeared for a moment. There were scraping sounds and the overstuffed chair that stood by the window vanished slowly as if pushed unsteadily behind an invisible screen. It reappeared under its own steam in the mirror and a flushed, panting dwarf emerged from behind it, jumped into it and crossed his legs with a pleased look. 'That's the trouble with being small. Makes hard work of shifting things.' He settled back with a satisfied smile.

David trembled uncontrollably.

'You aren't a dream, are you?' he whispered, glancing terror-stricken at the empty space beneath his window.

'No. Which is just as well.' The small man drew out a vast white linen handkerchief and blew his nose loudly. 'A dream couldn't do much about getting you a new certificate. Wouldn't be much use at all.'

'Can you do that?' David's eyes narrowed against the dense shadows of the room.

'Certainly. I can fix anything,' he boasted. 'Fixing is our speciality.'

'Who is "our"?' asked David.

A wary look came over the mannikin's nutcracker face.

'Later,' he said snappishly. 'Possibly later on. For now, do you want the job done or am I wasting my time?'

'Is this something to do with being an optician?' asked David foolishly.

'No,' snapped the dwarf, getting cross. 'Nothing to do with the office at all. This is a favour, a sideline. Though I'd better be careful, saying that.' He looked uneasily over his shoulder into the depths of the mirror, now densely black with the coming of night. 'Come on, get a move on,' he muttered rapidly.

'What do you want me to do?' asked David, bewildered by the dwarf's sudden changes of mood.

'Make a bargain. New certificate in return for certain payments.'

'Oh,' cried David, horribly disappointed, 'you know I've got no money. Why have you done all this just to say that?'

'Money isn't everything,' said the dwarf peevishly. 'I never mentioned it.'

The surface of the mirror shimmered across his features in tiny distorting waves.

'Come on, hurry up. I'll guarantee you get into medical school – certificates, scholarships, the works – in exchange for something of value belonging to you.'

'What?'

The dwarf hurried on: 'You don't have to pay now, but the debt will become due in time. You must understand, though, that your obligation when the time does come is absolute. You will repay. No possibility of renegotiation. No possibility at all.' The mirror quivered again.

'What do I pay with, then?' asked David, suddenly so full of excited hope that he swung his legs over the side of his bed and reached out.

'Stay back,' squealed the dwarf.

David shrank away. The mirror heaved once then settled down.

'Don't do that again.' Agitated, Mr Hubbard wriggled forwards and perched on the edge of his chair.

'What do I pay with?' repeated David.

'Your soul.' The dwarf's tongue touched his lips, savouring the word.

'What?' said David, disbelieving. 'Excuse me, but I thought you said my soul.' He laughed nervously, embarrassed.

'You heard me aright.'

'That's nonsense,' cried David.

'A good Catholic boy like you, saying your soul is nonsense? Oh dear me,' jeered the dwarf.

'I mean your silly offer is nonsense. That sort of thing only happens in stories. If I turn my back and look again, you'll have gone. I've had enough of this.' He began to turn away angrily. The jolt of cold was so violent he doubled up in agony. 'What did you do that for?' he howled.

'I'm running out of patience, brother, that's why,' snarled the midget, drumming his fists on David's chair.

'You're not real,' David whimpered hopelessly.

'Little brother, don't you ever learn?' Mr Hubbard raised his hand menacingly.

David gabbled: 'All right, my soul. I don't know what you're going to do with it, but you'd better take it.'

'Sure?' the dwarf's eyes pierced the gloom like silver beams.

'If that's what you want.'

The hunched narrow shoulders convulsed with laughter, then the little man sobered. He fingered his lower lip thoughtfully. 'Then there's only the contract to sign.' He reached into his breast pocket and pulled out a single folded sheet of paper. 'I've got it all here. You can get it signed and let me have it at the shop. Soon as you can.'

David reached out for it but the dwarf hissed violently, 'I told you not to do that. You cannot cross the boundary to me, nor I to you; it would kill you. I'll leave it on the chair. All you have to do is sign it.'

'I can do that now,' said David.

'There is a form to be observed,' rebuked the dwarf. 'You don't just do things any old how.'

110

'What sort of form?'

'You must sign in blood. Not your own. There must be a sacrifice. Find an animal, slit its throat and dip your pen in the first blood to flow. Then bring me the document and your future is sure. I can't change what you are, nor give you personal qualities you haven't got, but I can fix things.' He chuckled and grinned, winking one eye rapidly through the gloom. 'Oh, yes, I can fix things.' He began to roll in the armchair, laughing uncontrollably.

'Are you the devil?' asked David solemnly.

The dwarf gasped and sobered up instantly. 'Dear me, no. Not the Devil,' he said, glancing over his shoulder again. 'I'm as human as you.'

'You really are my brother, then?'

'Oh, yes. I am what you see, only I have extended my range a little. I call on the Powers, you see. It takes years to learn. I have an aptitude, though. Showed itself quite young.' He spoke eagerly, his face alight with enthusiasm.

'Can you give me anything I want?'

'Haven't you got enough?' the apparition demanded waspishly.

'I mean, will you come back like this? As well as in your shop. You are frightfully confusing,' David complained.

'Oh, I know what this is.' The tubby little legs crossed and uncrossed several times. He seemed alarmed. 'You're thinking of Faust. Well, don't bother.'

'He had Mephistopheles there when he wanted something, didn't he?'

'Don't get greedy,' snarled the midget. 'I don't dance attention and you'd never warrant that kind of thing.

Try being grateful instead of demanding more than you deserve. Anyway, Mephisto was a devil and had the time; I've a shop to run. I can't do everything.'

'I didn't mean . . .'

'I don't suppose you did. You don't *think* enough to mean anything,' he interrupted spitefully. 'Some people would be pleased with a certificate and a scholarship thrown in. But I suppose perfectionism runs in the family, so I don't altogether blame you for it.'

The mirror gave out a rumbling growl and shivered warningly.

'Oh, oh, time to go,' cried Mr Hubbard. 'See you do your bit properly and we'll have you fixed right as ninepence.'

The mirror's surface heaved and swelled outwards and the air roared. David flung himself down on the bed, away from the explosion. After a long time he took his hands off his ears and looked fearfully for the mess of glass. The room was icy cold. Night and the pale strip of light that came from under the door were reflected in the wardrobe mirror. It was whole. The chair stood where it always did, under the window, a white shape glimmering on its seat. David got unsteadily to his feet, picked up the stiff sheet of parchment and thrust it hastily under his pillows.

'Are you coming down, David?' called his mother, from the foot of the stairs.

'In a minute.'

"His voice sounds hoarse," thought Bridie. "How odd."

The following morning dawned dull and bitter. A raw east wind blew Bridie's dressing gown around her ankles when she opened the back door to let in the cats, miaowing urgently on the step for their breakfast. The Pope bolted in, his tail fluffed out and the hair on his back standing high. David woke to his mother's shriek as she almost stood on the poor stiff little body on the concrete step. Brother John's glassy eyes stared up at her, very dead above the gashed throat, blood all around his little white bib.

'Oh my God,' cried Bridie. 'Whatever happened to him?'

She slammed the door on the cold wind and the colder corpse and sat down at her kitchen table, shaking.

The bargain was struck, and after Brother John, David knew there would be no going back.

Chapter Eight

The DuCane family usually weathered its major crises in Ethel's kitchen. The beginning of the Second World War was no exception. On 3 September 1939, less than a year since Mr Hubbard fixed David's future for him, they listened grim-faced to Mr Chamberlain's voice on the wireless. Edward was away at sea. Bridie thought of him, sitting in the cramped officer's quarters, waiting to hear the same deadly news. Susan was with the Andersons, already in the country, anticipating the war. Ethel, chattering with nerves, said it was worse than waiting for the Abdication and the marriage to that dreadful Mrs Simpson all put together. No one smiled.

'. . . unless we heard from them by eleven o'clock that they were prepared at once to withdraw their troops from Poland, a state of war would exist between us. I have to tell you now that no such undertaking has been received and that consequently this country is at war with Germany.'

'That's that, then,' said Ted gruffly.

Ethel put a hand over her eyes.

Bridie took the tea cosy off to feel the lukewarm pot. 'I'll make some more,' she said, getting up.

'What's going to happen now?' asked Ethel.

'The university will be moved to the country,' said

David, sitting over in the corner where Edward usually sat when he was at home. 'The move's been planned for ages.'

Ted flicked a glance at him but kept his thoughts to himself.

'That must mean they believe London really will get the worst, then, doesn't it?' Ethel asked anxiously.

'Must do.'

'What shall we do if they use gas?' She turned to Ted.

'Wear our masks.'

They all turned as one to look at the row of gas masks hanging in their boxes from nails in the wall.

'Oh dear,' wailed Ethel.

'They'll probably just bomb us out of existence,' called Bridie from the scullery.

'That's cheerful talk, I must say.' Ted tried hard to keep his spirits up despite his own dread that both of them were right. In the scullery the kettle began to whistle and for a moment it seemed that the monstrous wailing came from its spout. They all stared, wide-eyed, at the scullery doorway.

'It's sirens,' shrieked Ethel. 'They're here already! Oh, dear God, save us.'

She reached up and tore the gas masks from the wall.

'Here, put 'em on, quick. Oh, be quick.'

She fumbled with the straps and pulled on the black rubber snout so that it hung round one ear.

'I can't get the blithering thing on,' she cried, as the straps caught on her curlers. Bridie put her mask down among the teacups and helped poor Ethel untangle the muddle on her head.

'There,' she said calmly. 'Now breathe normally.'

Inside the mask Ethel gulped and turned puce. The wailing suddenly grew louder as Ted opened their front door and looked out, holding his mask over his nose and peering around the top of it. Ethel and Bridie heard a strange noise, glanced at each other over their snouts, and ran out to see Ted, scarlet from lack of oxygen, drop his mask and lean weakly against the wall, choking with laughter.

'Look!' he gasped, pointing outside. Wide-eyed, terrified that death would rain from the sky any second, Bridie stuck her head out and looked in the direction of his pointing finger.

'Willie,' stuttered Ted in a fresh outbreak of mirth. Bridie began to giggle and Ethel pushed from behind to see. Willie the local bobbie rode up and down at full speed on his bicycle, wobbling dangerously as he blew with all his might and main on a whistle and tried to point to the poster pinned on his chest at the same time: TAKE COVER.

'Get inside,' he roared, steering wildly past Ted, blowing lustily.

'Oh dear, Oh Lor', would you look at that!' Ted wiped his eyes and fell into further convulsions.

In the street, though, panic-stricken people ran in all directions. Women screamed for their children, looking, terrified, into the sky which stayed innocent and empty.

'Come on in, you silly beggar. If those Germans come over now, you'll cop the first one, carrying on like that.' Ethel pulled Ted inside and slammed the door firmly.

'Fancy making fun,' she scolded, pushing him back to the kitchen. 'Put your mask on proper. You don't want the Luftwaffe catching you like that.'

Ted guffawed again.

'Are they coming?' asked Bridie in a small voice.

'I'm scared.' She sat down quite suddenly in Ted's chair.

Outside sirens howled, Willie blasted frantically on his whistle as men and women ran into doorways, and strangers clutched each other, waiting for death to fall on them from the bright autumn sky.

David edged over to his mother and put his arm around her shoudlers, trying to see her through the tiny misted up window in his gas mask. 'I'm sorry, Mum.' The black rubber snout wobbled up and down and the glass misted up completely with his words.

'All right, love.' Bridie couldn't hear him. She was listening to the din outside, for the roar of planes and the end of the world.

'I said, I'm sorry, Mum,' David tried again desperately. Ethel had her hands over her ears, to shut out the dreadful noise and so she wouldn't hear the bombs falling.

'I'm sorry about Brother John.' David's heart banged against his ribs from the fear of divulging his frightful secret. Bridie took his hand and held it, nodding.

'At least we're all together, if we've got to go,' she shouted inaudibly, looking at their grotesque animal-like silhouettes. 'What a way to go, though.'

'Brother John . . .' David mouthed hopelessly, blinded by his own sweat and tears. 'Please . . .' Through the pandemonium a familiar voice spoke clearly to him.

'Little brother, it is no good. I warned you.'

'Then I might as well die,' he shouted into his dead rubber snout, tears rolling down his young face.

'Oh, dear me, no. Not yet, surely.' The voice sounded amused. Then there was a kind of crackling sound, like static, and the screaming of the sirens all over London. David fought for air and tore off the mask, white with horror. The grotesque little circle around Ethel's table stared at him mutely.

'Bleedin' coward,' Ted muttered into the privacy of his own clammy snout.

Bridie, her heart tight with fear, pulled a hanky from her pocket and mopped at David's distraught face. Her own breathing whistled in her ears so it was some moments before she realized the din had stopped.

An ear-numbing silence hung over the empty streets. Willie put on his brakes and skidded to a halt, scanning the sky. In sheer relief he blew one last immense blast on his whistle and pedalled straight for his own house where he found his young wife hysterical with fright, and admiration of his performance. She clung to his neck, sobbing with relief and excitement. He pushed her away, embarrassed.

'Men like you, 'itler can go boil 'is head!' she cried, kissing him again. ' 'e don't know what 'e's up against.' They both jumped violently as the sirens sounded again.

'It's the all clear,' cried Willie. 'I should've stayed out there. I came back too soon.'

His wife glanced at her hero. 'You done just the right thing,' she said tenderly, and put their gas marks back in their boxes. 'That'll show that Luftwaffe what's what.'

'The Luftwaffe never come,' Willie pointed out.

'So?' demanded his wife, hands on hips, daring him. Willie had no answer to that.

'Well, now we know what it feels like,' said Ted. ' 'itler's reign of terror 'as started on Willie Barker's beat.' He began to laugh again.

'I don't see what's so funny,' snapped Ethel, frightened silly and having had enough of Ted's irresponsibility.

'He did look silly,' said Bridie. 'Poor Willie! But he's awfully brave.'

'More than you can say of some,' said Ted.

'Now then, Dad.' Ethel fixed him with a steely eye and shook her head warningly.

'I'm sorry,' mumbled David hopelessly.

''ow do you think it feels in the front line?' started Ted, but Ethel said, 'That'll do,' in such a sharp voice, he stopped.

'We was all scared,' she said firmly, 'and when you're young you've got all your life in front of you. It's bound to be worse.'

David shook his head miserably.

Bridie threw her mask into its box and went out to the scullery, fetching in a fresh pot of tea and putting it in front of Ethel.

'Only a fool wouldn't be frightened of what we're going to go through,' she said quietly, looking straight at Ted. 'Poor Willie looking funny doesn't take the fear away. We laughed so much because we were all wound up. It isn't fair to go on at David.'

Ethel poured tea in silence.

'I meet a lot of refugees on my rounds,' Bridie went on, 'and they say the Nazis aren't like anything we've ever known before. They say they're different. Much, much worse than you can imagine.'

'How?' asked David.

'Organized. Ruthless. Ferocious. They say it's not ordinary war, between soldiers. It's ordinary people against armies. Look at us today. It's us against the Luftwaffe, isn't it? Not just the Air Force and people who do the fighting, but ordinary people like us.'

'Civilians always get caught up. What about all the usual stories of rape and pillage and soldiers on the rampage? It's always been the same,' said David.

'No, this is different,' argued his mother. 'This will be deliberate killing. They'll try to destroy London, to destroy the British. Killing us is strategy, and that's not like rape and pillage in the heat of the battle.'

'France'll stop 'em,' said Ted. 'They won't get past the French.'

Ethel grasped at straws. 'Then perhaps Edward won't see much action.'

Ted rubbed his ear and looked unhappy. 'Can't say about that, duck, I really can't. We'll just have to see.'

'Anyroad, you'd better get that door set up smartish, so we got somewhere to shelter,' she snapped, ready to criticize because he offered no comfort. 'If that'd bin the Luftwaffe, they'd 'ave caught us napping and no mistake.'

'Door?' said Bridie.

'Ted's goin' to put a door against the wall, so we have something over our heads in case the ceiling comes down. 'ow about David lending 'im an 'and?'

'Go on, David,' said Bridie.

'I can give you a hand tomorrow,' they heard David say.

'That's better,' murmured Ethel as the two men went out the back. 'It don't do no good to start bickering.'

'He doesn't mean it,' said Bridie.

'Nor does Ted, but you have to make allowances. 'e fought in the last one and 'e ain't never forgot it. 'e's a bit bitter that it's all 'appening again.'

'"They won't get past the French",' murmured Bridie, and the two women giggled.

* * *

They were all together again on the Monday, the first full day of the war. 'I said I'd meet Ollie and go to the pictures this evening,' said David, dusting off his hands after he and Ted had piled all Ethel's tables and chairs on top of each other and leant a sturdy door against the kitchen wall, making it impossible to move in the cramped little room. 'Would you mind if I went now?'

'You go on,' said Bridie.

Ethel stood on her scullery step, a look of disbelief on her broad plain face and her hands planted squarely on her stout hips.

'Just 'ow am I supposed to manage in this, then?' she demanded, looking the door up and down. 'Where do I put me kitchen?'

'Ask 'itler,' suggested Ted, feeling misunderstood.

'If it gets real bad, you'd best come and stay with me. I've put things down in the cellar so we can stop down there for the bombing. There's room for all of us and it'll be safer than this,' said Bridie, eyeing the arrangement with dismay.

'Ta, duck, but I'd rather stay in me own place, if I can,' answered Ethel. 'It might not be as bad as they say.'

'I think it may be worse. You'd better do what Mum says,' said David quietly. He bent to kiss his mother's cheek. 'I'm off.'

'What does he know?' cried Ethel indignantly.

'He's right,' said Bridie. 'And if Edward was here you'd be down in our cellar without an argument. He'd never let you stay here. David's right.'

'Right even when 'e's wrong, that one,' grumbled Ted. 'Like politicians. One day he'll get on the wrong side of the wrong person, and then there'll be trouble.'

'What do you mean? He's just young,' cried Bridie.

'I don't mean to hurt you, love,' said Ted, fishing in his pocket for his tobacco tin, 'but if you want to know, I think he should do his duty and join up. Not go mollycoddlin' about in some school.'

'We'll need doctors,' said Ethel.

'We need good soldiers,' growled Ted.

'He'll have to fight his war in his own way. I don't think it will stop him going to university. It's hardly his fault that it's come just when he's going to do his training.'

''e won't be fighting no war at all,' Ted grumbled angrily. 'That's exactly what I'm saying. It'll be us what fights, when it comes to it. Us and the ones what don't manage to wriggle out of joining up. 'e won't even be in London, looking after 'is mother, will 'e?' He stuck a thin roll-up in his mouth and his faded blue eyes held Bridie's.

'She's right, though,' said Ethel, breaking the tension. 'The war ain't David's fault. 'e didn't ask for it to come just when he was goin' off to university. If it 'ad come another time, I'm sure 'e'd 'ave joined up.'

'I never said it was his fault,' he conceded, 'but it don't do him no credit to go running off, leaving you at a time like this. And 'e ought to fight for 'is country, same as everyone else.'

Ethel sighed.

'Well, I don't like to see it, one of my family dodging out.'

'There's Edward,' Bridie said gently. 'The men of this family will do their bit, Ted, in their own way. You don't need to worry so.'

He struck a match. 'Come to that, I thought I'd go along to the ARP and see what they need. I'm still fit enough to do my bit.'

'You get along, then, and do it. What are you waiting for?' cried Ethel.

'You don't mind?'

'Mind?' she said. 'You silly beggar, I think it's the best thing you could do.' She grinned at Bridie triumphantly.

'I wouldn't be able to be over every day,' he said to Bridie, who shook her head dismissively.

'Then I might go down and 'ave a word with them now.' He pinched out his cigarette and put it carefully in his tin. He edged around the door, treading on Ethel's great feet so that she squawked crossly and clutched at him to keep her balance.

'I don't know what we're goin' to do about all this.' She waved a fat arm at the chaos and Ted slipped out of the room, heading for the street door.

'Suppose we might go to Bridie's,' she remarked loudly enough for him to hear, 'can't be doing with all this nonsense. 'im and 'is doors.' She sniffed and peered in the teapot to see if anything drinkable was left. 'If that's what you want, anyroad, ducks,' she added to Bridie.

'It is, when the planes come.'

'I suppose they will,' said Ethel, hopefully thinking they might not, after the false alarm.

'I'm afraid so.'

The two women looked at each other across the old door propped between them.

''e does 'is best,' said Ethel, and they both began to laugh.

Chapter Nine

David hurried along the Mile End towards the Odeon, keeping an eye out for Ollie's lanky figure. There was no queue to get in; most of London was still trying to get used to being at war. Ollie leant against the wall outside the entrance. On catching sight of David he bounded forward and put up his fists, pulling imaginary punches and grinning all over his face.

'You heard Chamberlain then,' said David, coming up and dodging the blows. Ollie quietened down and stood still.

'Yes. About time someone stood up to 'em. I'm glad,' he said soberly.

'What did you do when the sirens went off?'

'Ran like hell to get my stamp collection from upstairs and then we all sat in the cellar with Mum flapping and panicking because we had no blankets or food. She was all put out because the Germans hadn't been sporting and given more notice. Then nothing happened and we felt idiots and came up again. And then I came here. What did your lot do?'

'Laughed, mostly,' said David glumly, pushing open the doors to the foyer. 'Let's go in.'

They sat near the front of an almost empty cinema, feet up on the seats in front of them, faces tilted towards the flickering black and white screen. David's thoughts wandered.

'Ollie,' he said, 'did you ever have something you had to keep secret – forever?'

A grin spread from ear to ear on Ollie's clever, bony face.

'Oh yes,' he said happily under his breath, glancing sideways in the dancing light from the screen.

'I don't mean something like that.'

'You asked,' answered Ollie amiably.

'That's just Bessie, isn't it? I mean a real secret.'

Ollie chuckled.

'Bessie said she'd murder me if I told. *That's* a secret. Well, it was, until you started poking your nose in.'

'That doesn't count, whatever it is,' said David wretchedly.

'I can't think of anything else.' Ollie turned back to the picture. 'Why?' he asked five minutes later, when it occurred to him.

'Nothing.'

'All right.'

David sat with his arms folded across his chest to ease the numb, empty feeling inside him.

More than halfway through the picture they heard the usherette say 'Anywhere you like', and four girls banged down the seats behind Ollie and David. Ollie, irritated, turned to scowl at the interruption and didn't turn back – for so long that David noticed and turned to look for himself.

'Cor!' growled Ollie, turning away again from four pairs of challenging eyes. 'Look at the one in the middle.'

David glanced over his shoulder again. All four of them were unwrapping toffees, staring at the screen.

'Which middle one? There's two.'

'Don't be daft,' hissed Ollie. 'It's obvious.'

'Just let Bessie hear you.' David shifted in his seat and peered at her again. She sat gazing steadily at the screen, chewing her toffee so that her cheek bulged round full, perfect lips. Her delicate oval face, porcelain pale in the dancing grey light, was framed by long, dark, shining curls. David stared, fascinated. Deep-set wide brown eyes travelled slowly down the screen and on to David's rapt face. She moved the toffee to her other cheek and tossed her head.

'See what I mean?' murmured Ollie.

The picture dragged. David tried a dozen different imaginary ways of getting into a conversation with her. Ollie sat back in his seat, enjoying himself.

'We could do with another air raid,' he whispered, stifling a laugh.

David remembered the last and his spirits fell.

'Ask her for a toffee, then,' suggested Ollie.

David ignored him. They sat, ears attuned to the rustle of sweet papers and giggles behind them. David sank lower in his seat and tried to watch the end of the picture, to blot out the memories that kept coming back. The dwarf's voice saying: "It's no good." The hot gush of Brother John's blood on his hand and the ghastly journey the little cat must have made, dragging himself home after he should have been dead.

'No good,' murmured David, echoing his half-brother in despair.

'What?' said Ollie above a crescendo of music, signalling the end.

'Would you like a toffee?'

David turned, shocked out of his misery. The beautiful girl leaned down with an open paper bag in her hand.

'Go on. I saw you looking. We haven't quite eaten them all.' She put a slim hand into her bag and picked out two sweets. 'Butter ones,' she offered. 'Go on.'

Ollie nudged David sharply.

'Thanks.'

Dazed, David took the toffee and sat holding it, staring at her. The lights came up and he saw she had red lights in her dark brown hair, but her eyes were golden, not brown. They smiled at him.

'He's an oaf,' said Ollie to the girl. The other three fidgeted with handbags and coats and decided to stay and see the beginning of the picture up to where they came in.

'What did you think of the broadcast yesterday?' the pretty girl asked Ollie. 'Did you hear it?'

'I expect everyone did. What do you think?'

'I don't want to die,' she said unexpectedly. 'They all say Hitler's going to bomb us and gas us. I'm scared stiff.' Her eyes lost their liveliness and she looked suddenly lost and vulnerable and afraid. David's heart lurched. The group stopped chattering and listened.

'Shall you join up?' asked the girl.

'He won't,' Ollie answered for David,

'He's too young,' said David, getting his own back.

'Oh.' The four girls stared in open disapproval.

'He's going off next month to do his pre-clinical.' They all kept on staring at David, who felt himself go redder and redder. He unwrapped the toffee the girl had given him, for something to do.

'What's that, then?' demanded one of the girls.

'Pre-clinical. He's going to be a doctor. Medical students don't join up.'

'Really?' They seemed impressed now.

'What do you do, then?' one of them asked Ollie.

'I want to be a chemist. I don't know whether I shall fight.'

'Don't take infants,' jeered David meanly.

The girls considered him silently, four mouths pausing, toffee melting sweetly on their sugary breath.

'Shall we go?' asked Ollie, picking up his jacket.

'You're stopping to see it again then?' David asked the dark girl boldly. Ollie grinned.

'Yes.'

The others stared from her to David and back again.

'I didn't see it properly either.' David sat back in his chair. Ollie chucked his jacket down again and threw himself heavily into the seat next to David. The pianist plunged into her opening bars and the projectionist opened the shutters and switched on the reel.

'Here we go,' sighed Ollie in mock resignation. 'If she stops for a third time round, you can stay by yourself.'

'You can go if you want,' hissed David. 'I don't mind.'

'There's gratitude,' growled Ollie, much too curious to budge until David and the girl left.

'Go and get some sweets.'

Ollie looked indignant. 'Who, me? It's only just started again.'

'Go on.'

'Go yourself.'

'Got no money,' muttered David.

'Ah ha,' cried Ollie out loud, drawing glares from all round. 'I thought not.' He took a shilling from his pocket. 'Go and buy some sweeties then.'

David marched out to the foyer, bought half a pound of the same butter toffees the girls had had, and slid back beside Ollie.

'Here,' he said, handing the bag over the back of the seats.

'I'll never touch butter toffees again,' moaned April later, 'but he was so sweet, I couldn't say no.'

So she helped herself, looking back at him through dark lashes with enormous golden eyes, and David was lost.

'Oh,' he groaned.

'Yes,' said Ollie. 'She is.'

He was the only one who really watched the picture twice.

It was very dark when they emerged from the foyer doors to stand uncertainly on the pavement.

'Oh, look,' cried one of the girls, 'there's no lights at all.' The road stretched away with not a glimmer from windows and doors. The Odeon, behind them, closed its doors and dowsed its dimmed lamps as soon as the last of the audience left.

'Bleedin' blackout.' The manager, busy locking doors, stood with a great bunch of keys in his hand, surveying the pavement. 'They're already playing hell about it, and after yesterday it'll be no light at all. It'll kill business,' he added gloomily, locking the last door and disappearing inside the darkened building.

'Not even streetlamps?' asked the girl, turning to David.

'Especially not streetlamps, ninny,' said her friend, glancing at David sideways in the darkness, as if to say: "Just listen to her."

The girl with the golden eyes saw the look and stood a little closer to him. 'How are we supposed to find things?' she asked.

'We can walk.' Two of her friends linked arms.

'You can, but I can't. Not all that way, in the dark.'

'Where have you got to get to?' asked David.

'Ilford,' she said. 'It's miles and miles.'

'You can get the bus as usual. Things will still run, only in the dark.'

He pointed down the road where traffic was just visible, moving at a crawl.

'Uh!' She put her hand to her mouth. 'You must think me so silly.'

'I don't think you're silly at all.'

They stood awkwardly, each wondering what to say next.

'I'm off then,' said Ollie, feeling like a gooseberry. 'Nice to meet you.' He doffed his cap to the four girls and darkness swallowed him up in moments. All they heard were the metal tips of his shoes ringing away towards the crossroads at Mile End.

'You go on,' the dark-haired girl told the other three. 'I'll find the bus all right.' She gazed with trepidation through the gloom, over to where she had caught the bus a hundred times before.

'They haven't moved the stops, dear, just put the lights out.'

'Stop trying to show me up.'

David gathered his courage and said, 'Shall I see you over?'

'We'll get run over. They can't see a thing,' she said doubtfully, watching the traffic.

'I'll take you across.'

'All right.' She turned from the kerb and smiled at him.

'You sure?' asked one of the others.

'Yes.'

'See you tomorrow, then. Ta'ra.' The other three

linked arms and set off after Ollie, threading their way cautiously, like the rest of London, through dark streets, tripping and swearing and blundering into lamp posts and falling over sandbags. A car hooted wildly further up the road, avoiding another which had wandered too far on to the wrong side of the unlit road. Indignant shouts drifted clearly to the pair.

'Come on.' David grabbed her hand and they ran helter skelter through the ragged line of traffic. 'Watch the kerb, now.'

They stumbled on to the pavement and April giggled, leaning against the post marked 'Bus Stop' with her hands clasped round it. 'It's rather romantic, really, isn't it?'

'It's going to be a blasted nuisance, I should think,' answered David prosaically. 'There'll be no end of accidents if we keep on like this, and it's supposed to keep people safe.'

'I'd rather be blacked out than bombed, wouldn't you?'

'It won't stop them.'

'Don't you think so?' she asked anxiously. 'They've put up barrage balloons all over the place, and all those guns and searchlights. We'll be safe, won't we?'

'Nothing's safe.'

She seemed to consider what he had said, running her finger up and down the rough surface of the post.

'Don't you think we should fight, then?' She looked up at him, truly wanting to know what he thought.

David nodded earnestly. 'Of course I do. Someone's got to stop Hitler invading Russia.'

'Is that why we're going to war? I thought it was because of Poland.' She sounded puzzled.

'Are you a socialist?' asked David.

'No, I don't think so. I'm against the Fascists,' she said uncertainly, 'but I'm not really very political.'

'You should be, you know. Politics is what it's all about.'

'We're not a very political family, except for Daddy. He's very Tory.'

She giggled again, and David, hearing the high, gurgling sound, thought, "I bet he is, if he talks like you."

Then he risked spoiling it all by defiantly blurting, 'I'm a communist.'

One in the eye for Daddy.

'Oh. Are you?' Her eyes widened.

'Yes. Hitler will do us a favour if he knocks this lot down,' said David recklessly. 'It needs rebuilding. We could make the East End somewhere fit to live if we started again, from scratch. But first of all the Luftwaffe will have to knock it flat.'

He sensed her draw back, startled, and could have bitten his tongue for running away with him like that.

'Good thing my father can't hear you talk.' She sounded breathless.

'Why? It's logical.'

She smiled nervously, ill at ease. 'I think he'd think it was treasonable.'

'That's stupid.'

'I don't think my father's stupid,' she said stiffly.

'Sorry.'

'What if they kill us all? There'll be no one left to live here. It'd do no good rebuilding then, would it?'

'That's exaggerating.'

'Maybe, but that's what I'm scared of. I don't think it's stupid.' In the gloom, her golden eyes studied him wonderingly. No one had ever called George's ideas stupid before. She turned the suggestion over and over in her mind, fascinated by its unfamiliarity; fascinated by David, who had voiced it.

'I'm sorry,' he said again miserably, sure that he had ruined everything.

They stood. No bus came.

'What do you do?' asked David, to break the silence.

'I'm a secretary. I work for a lawyer in Whitehall.'

'Do you?' David looked her up and down. 'No wonder you look so nice.'

She blushed. 'The others are from my office too. We all live at home with our parents, so we decided to leave the war to them and go to the pictures instead. Selfish, I suppose, but you only live once, and it sounds as though it might not be for long,' she added gloomily.

'I just wanted to get away from it for a bit. I'd said I'd meet Ollie at the pictures and I couldn't see why not. I don't think it's selfish to do what you want to.'

'Daddy says I am – selfish,' she told him wistfully. 'He's awfully hard to please.'

'My father's dead.'

'Oh.' She was startled. 'Already?'

'Not in the war, silly. It's only just started. No, years ago. When I was a kid.'

'It's coming. The bus.'

'Can I see you home?' he asked.

'All that way? Oh, no. My father wouldn't like it.'

'Why? I'll see you safe, in this.'

'No.' She shook her head definitely. 'I'd rather go on my own, thank you.'

'Can I see you again, then?'

The bus drew closer.

She began looking for her purse in her handbag.

'Tomorrow? Here? We could go to the pictures

again?' David asked urgently, the dim blue lights of the bus coming ever closer. She hesitated and the bus drew up.

'Please,' he begged.

'Six o'clock?' she asked shyly.

'Six o'clock, here,' he cried.

'Yes. Goodbye.'

She climbed into the bus, went to sit down, then ran back to the platform. She clung to the rail and hung out, looking backwards.

'What's your name?' she called.

'What?' he shouted.

'Your name?'

'David Holmes. And you?' he yelled back.

Her voice carried, clear and high, above the sound of the engine and the driver grinding his gears abruptly.

'April Dunbar. My name's April Dunbar. Goodnight, David.'

Chapter Ten

One late May evening in 1940 Lord Haw Haw's braying voice crackled over the air waves from Germany, fervently reassuring all Londoners that they could rely on Hitler's sincerity. We'll invade just as soon as the moment was right, he promised, he had it from the Führer himself that it wouldn't be long now. They had no need to feel neglected.

'Hitler is coming, never fear,' he whinnied from millions of brown bakelite wirelesses the length and breadth of Britain.

Londoners in particular listened avidly to German broadcasts in a vain attempt to find out what was what in their city, where censorship and rumour fed each other to the point where no one believed a word they were told by their own side.

'Turn that creature off,' called Ethel from her tiny scullery, 'I can't stand him.' She came in, arms covered in soapsuds, as Bridie did as she was told. 'What shall we do for tea?' she went on, mopping her hands on her pinafore. 'I got no butter, no bacon, no sugar, and Ted's grumbling because 'e can't get 'is tobacco no more. Rations!' She sniffed eloquently, round face glum.

'We'll make do with a bit of bread and cheese,' said Bridie. 'And if Ted can't get tobacco, I could ask Sam

Saul if he can find any over in Golders Green. His wife shops around by car, so she's not that much bothered by the rationing.'

'Huh! Someone should do something about it. We can't all go swanning around in motor cars, collecting other people's shares from other people's shops,' answered Ethel crossly. 'It's time they put a stop to that.'

'I expect they will. But do you want me to ask him?'

'Yes,' said Ethel grudgingly.

'I'll see if he can find us some bacon, too.'

'I'll walk for that myself, ta very much. I wouldn't want to go encouragin' Mrs Saul to take what's rightfully someone else's. I don't think you should, neither.'

Bridie leant down wearily and fished out her shopping basket from by her feet. She began to unpack two small parcels of cheese and laid them out on Ethel's table.

'We'd all better start to help each other, otherwise the Germans have us half beaten before they even get here.'

'D'you think they'll come soon then?' asked Ethel anxiously.

Bridie shrugged. 'Who knows?' she said. 'Maybe they won't come at all, after all this time. They've been threatening to for so long everyone's got tired of waiting.'

'Mr Churchill don't talk that way.'

'No, but the people do.' Bridie sniffed at the rind on her cheese. 'And this isn't as fresh as it could be. They get away with selling real rubbish because everyone's fighting over what little there is.'

'There's plenty. It's only here we're short. You

should hear some of 'em carrying on about when they was evacuated. So much food and fresh vegetables they didn't know whether they was comin' or goin'.'

Ethel's grim expression softened into laughter 'I was chattin' to next door and she said 'er kiddies wouldn't touch it. They wanted their pieces, same as usual, an' the woman didn't know what ter do. Tried to make 'em sit at the table, knives, forks, an' all, and the kiddies wouldn't 'ave any of it. Stole from the kitchen instead. Next thing she knows, the kiddies send a telegram saying Missus has thrown them out and can they come home right now, because they're already on their way.'

'It must be a shock, being evacuated,' murmured Bridie, remembering how she'd come, long ago, frightened and alone, from Ireland to London, and how strange and huge and foreign the city had been to her country eyes.

'Most of 'em's back now, anyroad. They don't think 'itler's comin'. Mr Churchill can speechify all 'e likes, but those kiddies won't stay away from home. Next door's ended up walking most of the way from Dorset, can you believe? They was that desperate to come 'ome. I'm glad they're back. It wasn't right, no kiddies in the street. I didn't like the quiet.'

'"I have nothing to offer but blood, sweat, toil and tears,"' intoned Bridie gloomily. 'But all we really want is the sound of children in the streets, and blow the war! Oh, Ethel, no wonder Mr Churchill looks worried.'

'I ain't unpatriotic,' cried Ethel. 'And Ted's joined the 'ome Guard. You can't say we're not ready to do our bit.'

'I never meant that,' said Bridie quietly, tearing the

wrapping paper on her cheese into tiny shapes and scattering them on the table cloth.

''e 'as to keep a sharp eye out for fifth columnists dressed as nuns, droppin' by parachute over 'ackney Marshes,' explained Ethel seriously.

Bridie looked up, baffled. 'Nuns? Why nuns?'

'I don't rightly know. The Germans favour dropping in as nuns. It's what 'e's bin told to look for.'

'Good gracious.'

'Or priests. That's the other thing. They might come as priests.'

Bridie began to smile. 'I can just see the Marshes flapping with pretend nuns in all that black and white, trying to make out they're out for a stroll, however many of them drop in. Surely no one believes that?'

'It's what the 'ome Guard 'ave ter look for, so it must be right,' said Ethel huffily.

Bridie chuckled and shook her head.

'And they're hammering stakes into the marshes, to stop the Luftwaffe landing. Rows and rows of 'em, far as you can see.'

'I know, I've seen them. Lorryloads of trees going down there. I thought the Luftwaffe were going to bomb us and gas us, not land on us.'

'P'raps they'll do both, for the invasion,' suggested Ethel nervously.

Bridie leaned back in her chair and burst out laughing.

'I don't see what's funny about that!'

'I can just see all those German nuns dangling off their parachutes and landing on those rows of stakes, like witches. Uh, how grisly! It's so horrible, it's funny. It'd just serve 'em right if it happened like that.'

Ethel frowned and then suddenly brightened up. 'Anyroad, Ted says . . .'

'"They'll never get past the French,"' they chorused wildly, giggling helplessly. Ethel swept up the little pile of cheese paper on to a plate and began to lay the table.

'Let's just hope he's right,' murmured Bridie to herself, getting up to help.

'It's Dunkirk. He says it's awful,' whispered Lizzie to Bridie a few days later. She drew her friend inside by the hand and pointed upwards with a finger to her lips, to the room above where her husband slept like a dead man.

'Is Johnathan all right?' asked Bridie, keeping her voice low.

'Oh, yes. He's asleep now. Hasn't been home 'til first thing this morning. He's been on duty at Waterloo for two days solid and he's half dead. They're sending wounded up to London hospitals in thousands. The trains dump them off and turn round to go back again for more. He says it never stops. Soldiers are coming off the trains faster than ambulances can pick them up, and the doctors have to do what they can with them in the station. He's going back in a couple of hours and I'm going to volunteer to go, too.'

'Are they short?'

'Of course they are,' whispered Lizzie. 'Can you imagine it, Bridie? Johnathan says we've evacuated more than three hundred thousand men from Dunkirk, and it feels as if every one of them is ending up in Waterloo station. They need every pair of hands they can get.'

'Tell Bridget to come to me.'

'She won't be home for several days. She's training for this Home intelligence thing.'

They sat face to face, each afraid of alarming the other by admitting her fear.

'Lizzie,' said Bridie, breaking the tense silence in a very low voice, 'I'm scared. I try not to be, but I am.'

Lizzie folded her hands together and pressed them into her lap. 'Yes,' she said simply.

'Belgium and Holland gone,' whispered Bridie. 'The Germans are so close now.'

'And I'm frightened of going to Waterloo because it upsets me so, and I'm afraid for Ollie, wanting to go up in air planes, and you're afraid for Edward in his ship, and we're all afraid for ourselves,' Lizzie whispered back bravely. 'But it's like Mr Churchill says – you can't let the fear get a hold of you or you end up being afraid of it instead of the Germans.'

Bridie put her hands over Lizzie's clenched fists and held them tightly.

'I know. I'm sorry.'

'Don't you be sorry.'

'I don't know what to do, to help. You being a nurse, it's easy to see what you can do. All I could do is go into a factory but they don't want me.'

Lizzie gave a small smile. 'You can stay here and help us help the others.'

'It feels like cheating. That's not war work.'

'It is,' said Lizzie, quietly and firmly. 'For the time being, anyway.'

'Bless you,' whispered Bridie.

Lizzie curled her fingers around Bridie's and held them fast.

'We'll manage, just you see,' she promised. Bridie nodded, but the fear of even worse to come hung unspoken between them.

* * *

Mussolini joined Hitler on 10 June.

'Blast!' said Sam Saul, picking up *The Times* at breakfast the next morning. He peered closely at a photograph on the front page and studied a smudged picture of himself walking through Soho, caught in the darkness of the blackout by the photographer's flash.

'What?' asked Ruthie absently.

Sam glanced at her under his thick black brows and decided to put his proposition to her; mulling it over any further would be no use unless he could persuade her to help.

'There's something in the paper.'

Ruthie's plump arm, fingers heavy with gold rings, reached across the table.

'Here. They caught me yesterday.' He rustled the paper, folding it back.

'You never said you were caught in the riots!' cried Ruthie, staring at the photograph of her husband walking down Wardour Street. On the other side of the road, the photographer had caught a gang of men, throwing bricks at a window. The picture was murky, taken hurriedly.

'I just happened to be there.'

'What were you doing in Soho in the blackout? You could have been hurt,' shrilled Ruthie, her heavy sallow face paling at the thought. Her chin wobbled reproachfully.

'Yes, but I wasn't,' said Sam patiently.

'What were you doing there?'

Sam Saul sighed deeply, and began to tell her.

He strode carefully along the streets of Soho, avoiding lamp posts and people in the dark. Not a chink of yellow light showed from the strip clubs and restaurants, though he could see both were doing a roaring trade as clients and customers slipped in and out of shrouded doorways, faces ghostly under the feeble bulbs. Rounding the corner into Wardour Street he almost fell over two drunks squatting on the kerb in dense darkness, cigarettes hidden in the palms of their hands. Their cider bottle rolled and bounced noisily into the gutter and they swore at him. Sam kicked it angrily away, into the darkness, ignoring their curses.

'*Dreck*!' he roared, rounding on them. 'There's a war on. You sit there getting in everybody's way 'til sooner or later someone trips over you and breaks a leg and you're too sodden to notice. They should round you up and stick you on the Isle of Wight. Or just shoot you.'

The drunks leaned against each other, squinting after their bottle anxiously, waiting for him to go away.

'Ach, it's useless.' He turned on his heel and sensed their silent scramble to retrieve the cider. Glass exploded behind him. Sam swung round in alarm, thinking of the bottle, before he realized the magnitude of the sound. Running feet rounded the corner; men raced down the pavement with bricks in their hands. Windows shattered. Glass flew in great showers, shards smashing, shattering and tinkling, voices shouting. Blue lights winked dimly as doors opened hurriedly in the wake of the violence.

'Italian fascists!' screamed someone, and the little crowd took up the cry. Men slipped furtively out of doorways whose dim lamps had been suddenly dowsed, hurrying, hugging the walls for safety, afraid to be caught in the middle of it all. Somewhere in the mêlée a gun went off and more glass crashed and popped and crunched beneath boots as they ran, smashing the windows of every Italian restaurant.

'Cops!' shouted a man's voice above the din, answered by harsh laughter.

'Gonna round 'em up?' a guttural voice called, and the crowd quietened momentarily.

'There's no coppers,' shrieked a woman, and something in the sound chilled Sam Saul to the bone. A second shot came, a dull, unimpressive popping noise, and one of the tramps fell slowly forward as if imploring someone. Sam drew his breath in very sharply and looked round for shelter as the crowd snarled and hunted round the littered street for more stones to throw. Terrified Italians glanced out of their windows, fleeing upstairs or out over roofs and walls at the back, running for safety. Sam backed into a doorway and the door behind him gave to the pressure. He crept backwards, watching the entrance warily, then turned and bounded up a flight of narrow stairs.

It was pitch black in the building. As he stood listening on a small landing a door opened and a faint shaft of light spilled out.

'Papa?' squeaked a small voice, breathless with fright.

Sam Saul squinted into the doorway and his gaze travelled down until he saw a tiny girl in a torn red dress, looking up at him with great smudged eyes.

'I'm not your papa,' he said foolishly.

The child's lip quivered and she began to close the door.

'Here,' he cried hastily as another volley of bricks smashed into the building next door, 'are you by yourself? Where's your mother?'

The child put her thumb in her mouth and gazed at him expressionlessly.

'Can I come in?' asked Sam, bending down to look at her more closely. The child stared back. Slowly she lifted one tiny, grubby hand and scratched furiously at her head. There was a great crash from downstairs and Sam picked her with one long arm and pulled the door shut behind them in a single movement.

'Where are your parents, for heaven's sake?' he asked her.

She sat perfectly still in his arms, like a little doll, then her hand went back to her head and she scratched again, seeing hardly to notice what she did.

'You must be crawling,' remarked Sam, feeling his own scalp prickle warningly. He put the child down and began looking in doorways. One filthy room ran the length of the front of the building. Blackout curtains were nailed tightly over narrow windows and a low bulb burned over three mattresses side by side on the floor. Bundles of rags lay piled on one mattress and on another lay another child, a much older sister of the little one, who hung back by the door, sucking her thumb, one bare foot on top of the other.

'Hello,' said Sam. The young girl on the mattress stared at him with blank almond eyes. Wide, high cheekbones shadowed her thin, pinched face. Tangled, wheat-coloured hair clung, matted, to her head. Sam caught his breath and stared, then he went towards her and his nostrils pinched. A spreading stain soaked slowly into the mattress. The girl's face flickered momentarily, then was blank again.

'Christ!' muttered the tall Jew, appalled. The front windows overlooked the street and the sound of rampaging retreated as the mob moved on to Old Compton Street.

Soon he heard whistles blowing shrilly; shouts and panic-stricken voices as the police arrived.

'It's OK. You're safe now.'

It did no good. The girl on the mattress stared unblinkingly at something beyond Sam Saul.

'Doesn't she talk?' he asked the little girl by the door.

'No, sir,' said a deep voice.

Sam swung round, startled. A cadaverous man stood in the doorway. He was wearing what had once been a well-cut blue suit. He looked from the mattress to Sam and half bowed.

'Good evening, sir.'

'Are you their father?' demanded Sam belligerently.

'Yes. And you, sir?'

'What the devil do you think you're doing? There have been riots.'

'Yes. Always there are riots,' said the thin man simply. 'We did not think, in London, but . . .' He shrugged. He spoke slowly with a thick, unmusical accent.

'Where are you from?'

'Poland. We escaped from Warsaw, sir.'

'Oh. You're Jewish?'

The man in the blue suit inclined his head.

'Sir,' he answered with dignity.

'So am I,' growled Sam abruptly.

They faced each other across the shameful room, embarrassed.

'Sometimes I think it would have been better to die,' said the Pole apologetically, 'but the children . . . no . . . they are our future.'

Sam dropped his eyes and looked at the older girl. 'Your daughter? What happened to her?' Suddenly he badly needed to know.

147

The Pole's voice dropped to a murmur. Sam leaned closer to hear. 'The Nazis shoot my wife and her mother. They take some bread, you understand. The children cry in the night, they are hungry. My wife try to take bread but it was Nazi bread . . . so they shoot her and her mother. Christina, she try to stop them, but they laugh and hit her with their guns, so she run away with her mother's blood on her.' The words came slowly and he drew himself up. 'We are not thieves, sir.'

Sam could not speak.

'Now, my daughter, she is deep afraid. She is, how do you say, very shocked. She does not speak since then.'

Sam understood the spreading stain.

'Mortally afraid,' he said bleakly.

Her father nodded gravely. 'Mortally. You find the word for me, thank you. And the concierge say we must go in the morning. She call us animals and say get out.'

'Where will you go?' asked Sam after a long pause.

The Pole shrugged. 'I look for a place when English Nazis begin to stone us,' he explained.

'They're not Nazis,' said Sam wearily, 'just scared people. Fools. We are waiting for the Germans, you see, and we are scared too.'

The Pole dropped his eyes and nodded. 'What shall we do?' he asked softly.

The little child by the door clutched her father's knees and began a thin wailing, great wet tears spilling down her baby cheeks.

'We are dirty,' her father went on, lifting her up. 'These are all we save.' He gestured at the rags. 'The concierge say go because of this and I think others will not want such dirty people, too. And my daughter . . .'

'You speak good English. Did you have a profession?'

'I am teacher of physiology at medical school in Warsaw, sir,' said the thin man humbly.

Sam's breath whistled through his teeth. He knelt down suddenly by the girl on the floor and put his face close to hers. She shrank from him.

'We'll take care of you,' groaned Sam Saul, all of a sudden so sad and so angry and so helpless that veins stood out on his forehead. 'We'll see to you.'

The girl whimpered. Her father stepped forward, his hand outstretched. 'Please,' he protested.

Sam bounded to his feet. 'You stay here,' he said violently, 'until I come back. Until I come back, yes?' He mouthed the words slowly, to make the foreigner understand.

'Yes, sir.' The Pole spoke soothingly, as if to a child, seeing Sam's rage. 'We stay here.' He nodded vigorously to placate the Englishman.

'Just stay here.' Sam backed out of the dreadful place. The little family watched him with their fair, foreign, inscrutable faces.

'Stay there,' shouted Sam as he raced down the stairs and out into Wardour Street. Glass glittered like snow in the moonlight shining fitfully through shredded low clouds. Up and down the street no window stood unbroken.

'Animals!' snarled Sam Saul, echoing the Pole. Then he set off as fast as he could, his feet crunching glass, across moonlit London, to see what he could do.

It wasn't easy. He tried reason first.

'You can't evict them,' he said flatly, reining in his temper as best he could, having come all the way back to Wardour Street at five in the morning to catch the landlady when she emerged, holding broom and bucket, from her own squalid rooms somewhere in the back of the building. Down the street men swept up the ravages of the night, shovelling showers of glass and broken bricks into a lorry.

'I can, and I 'ave,' shouted the landlady, leaning on her broom and defying him to do anything about it.

'It's illegal.'

'No it ain't.'

'Children?' Sam Saul's voice dripped sarcasm but the landlady didn't flinch.

'It's their parents' fault. Should 'ave stayed where they belong, not come over 'ere spying and making trouble.'

'Their parents fled from the Nazis, who killed their mother and their grandmother and would have put them in a concentration camp,' he shouted back, wild-eyed. 'They're not spies. You're mad.'

'They ain't stoppin' 'ere,' said the landlady stubbornly.

'Please.' Sam tried to take a hold on his temper and wheedle her. 'I'll see your rent is paid. We could come to some arrangement.' He eagerly took out his pocket book and began to shuffle notes between his fingers.

'You'll get me shot,' muttered the woman, looking up and down the street in alarm. 'I told you, they can't stay. The CID come yesterday and questioned them, and so far as I know, that's as good as saying they're spies. They'll get took away anyway.'

'They are Jews!' cried Sam Saul in desperation. 'From Poland. Don't you understand? They had to get out. The Jews in Poland have been massacred by the Nazis. And you try to tell me that your lodgers are spies for the people who have been putting them down like animals?'

She leaned on her broom, unmoved.

'They can't be,' he groaned. 'Can't you see that?'

The landlady thought he looked as though he was going to cry and wished he'd push off quick.

'I don't know about that,' she said uncomfortably. 'You might be right, and then again, you might not. I can't take no chances. I'll 'ave more bricks through me windows and I can't chance it.'

Sam Saul wrung his hands. 'What are we coming to?' he mourned.

'It ain't my business,' snapped the woman, losing patience.

'No?' said Sam, looking up at her, his eyes piercing.

Her thin cheeks flushed.

'Then I'll have to take them myself.'

'Just as you like, dear,' said the landlady spitefully.

'Damn you!' he snarled.

She slammed the door in his face.

'No,' said Ruthie Saul.

'They have to come,' insisted her husband.

'Why here?' said Ruthie, dismayed.

'Because they have nowhere else. The whole of London believes that refugees are all fifth columnists and a hotbed of spies for the Nazis. They are being hounded and questioned by police, and last night they were being stoned. It's all in the paper.'

'How many did you say?' she asked reluctantly, twisting the rings on her fingers.

'Three. The father and two children. Their mother is dead.' Sam thought it best to keep a discreet silence about the state of them.

'Young?'

'One hardly more than a baby and one about eleven or twelve, I should think. It's hard to tell.'

'Why?' asked Ruthie sharply.

'At that age . . .' said Sam vaguely.

Ruthie twiddled her jewels unhappily.

'Please, Ruth. We have to do this.'

She looked up in surprise at the tone of his voice.

'You've changed,' she said, her face softening. 'I never saw you this concerned about people you didn't know 'til five minutes ago.'

Sam shook his head. 'I hardly recognize myself,' he admitted, shamefaced, 'but what's happening forces me to . . . well, I find myself looking at myself . . . knowing myself better. Or some such nonsense.'

'I love you, Samuel,' she said, surprising him. She reached across the table and put her hand on his. 'But I never thought I'd admire you.'

'And you think you're in danger of it?' he mocked her gently, trying to make light of things.

'Maybe,' she said, smiling her old, sweet smile, betraying behind her fat cheeks and painted mouth the shy, rosy-faced girl he'd married nearly thirty years earlier.

'Bless you,' he said, and kissed the plump hand that lay on his own long fingers.

'We're kosher,' she reminded him sharply.

He suppressed a smile and nodded seriously.

'Of course. I'll make a point of telling them.'

'I don't want foreign habits,' she began sharply.

'Ruth – don't spoil it.' Sam leaned forward and took her hand again solemnly. 'Let us give, this time, and be grateful.'

Ruth let her hand lie in his and felt the new strength in him. She stared at this stranger, at a loss.

'Go and get them, then,' she said.

France surrendered. People wept openly in the streets. Ted stood on the corner just up from his house, half-heartedly rolling a cigarette with Sam Saul's tobacco, feeling choked. He thrust the half-rolled cigarette back in the tin angrily and gave a kind of strangled sob. He put the lid back on with a despairing little snap.

'Curse them!' he cried aloud.

His nextdoor neighbour joined him on the corner. 'What's going to 'appen now?'

''ow should I know?' answered Ted testily. 'I never thought it'd come to this.'

'That's our alliance gone.' A man in a clerk's drab grey suit, unknown to either of them, came across the road and stood next to them, uninvited. 'We're on our own now.'

'I never thought they'd 'ave got past the French.' Ted stuck his hands in his pockets and glared at the pavement.

'They weren't supposed to get past the Maginot Line, were they? But they did,' answered the clerk.

'Bleedin' French weren't much cop when it came to it, were they?' A small, thin man whom Ted recognized from his days of standing in the labour exchange before the war came up behind them and spoke in a thin, brittle whine.

'I suppose you'd 'ave done better,' observed the clerk sarcastically.

'They say the Germans are invincible,' said Ted gloomily. 'You can't fight 'em like an ordinary army. It's new, this kind of war. It don't 'elp no one to start criticizing.'

'Someone's got ter get their bleedin' finger out,' said

the small man, ''cause the beggars will be over here before we know it. They must be just waiting to invade us now. What's to stop 'em after this?'

'Air Force?' muttered Ted. No one had the heart to answer.

'They say a lot of them's already here.' The clerk's beaky grey face looked from one to the other with narrowed, suspicious eyes. 'Hitler's been sending them over for years.'

'Fifth column,' said Ted's neighbour darkly.

'You can't tell, can you?' The clerk began to put the wind up them, enjoying himself. 'You never know who you're talking to, these days.'

'Spies,' said Ted's neighbour. 'They should shoot 'em.'

The clerk nodded thoughtfully.

'I think they do,' remarked Ted.

'Nah. That's the Nazis,' Ted's neighbour contradicted him with a scowl 'They got more sense than we have.'

'I'm sure we do,' said Ted.

'I go for internment myself,' said the clerk. 'They should put the whole lot away and stop messing around.'

'Who?' demanded Ted.

'All of 'em,' said the clerk eagerly. 'Foreigners. London's crawling with 'em. We won't be safe until they put 'em all on the Isle of Wight.'

'What's the Isle of Wight done?' murmured Ted's neighbour, grinning.

The clerk pulled at his lower lip importantly. 'Could even be you, couldn't it? Subversive talk like that.'

'Don't be daft! We was at school together,' said Ted contemptously. 'And anyway it don't make no sense to go interning people who've come 'ere to escape 'itler, because they're on our side.'

'How do you know?' demanded the clerk, feeling all eyes upon him.

There was a long, uneasy, pause.

'I suppose you don't. Not really,' admitted Ted's neighbour.

'Well then, there you are,' cried the clerk triumphantly. 'That's why we should put them all away. To be on the safe side, and never mind all this category A and category B. If they're not British, they should be locked up. And the Jews. We won't be safe until they lock up the lot.'

'The Nazis are putting all their Jews and foreigners in concentration camps. Why are we fighting them then?' asked the small man from the dole queue who had been following the talk intently, not saying much.

'I should report you. All of you!' cried the clerk, flushing with rage.

'Oh? Who to?' asked Ted, grinning.

The clerk looked sulky. 'Police,' he muttered.

Ted's grin vanished and he thrust his face into the clerk's with a nasty look. 'Bugger off,' he ordered him, 'afore I report you for talking like a collaborator. Way you're carrying on, maybe *you're* the one who can't wait for the invasion, so as you can shut up and shoot everyone you don't 'appen to like the sound of. Maybe you ain't 'eard it but this war is to stop that bloody 'itler doing exactly that, mate. So bleedin' well bugger off!'

Ted's blue eyes watched the clerk back away and turn on his heel, hurrying past men lingering on their doorsteps, their eyes bleak and angry and afraid. He looked back defiantly over his shoulder as he turned the corner quickly and disappeared from sight.

'They are talkin' about locking 'em all up. 'e's right, there,' mumbled the man from the dole.

'Bollocks!' exploded Ted, running out of patience.

'Now we know where we are. No more French. No more bloody Allies,' a man shouted down the street and every head turned to stare.

'Too right,' yelled back a voice from further down.

'We're on our own now. Know where we stand,' Ted's neighbour called dourly.

'Fifth columnists . . . I ask you!' Ted abruptly exploded in a great roar of rage and stamped off down his street to brood in Ethel's kitchen.

'I never believed they'd get past the French,' he said for the last time, 'but they 'ave, love, haven't they?'

'I'm afraid they have, duck. The French ain't going ter save us now,' she said sadly.

Over in Golders Green Ruthie opened her front door to Sam's impatient ring and gave a little cry. She retreated into her lavender-scented hall and watched him carry a stinking, emaciated body into her best room. A small man followed, carrying a child little more than a baby. Ruthie's hand flew to her mouth at the smell. Over Sam's shoulder she saw Christina's matted hair and beautiful, blank face.

'Oh!' she gasped.

Sam turned, the girl in his arms. 'Here. She needs you,' he said simply. Her father watched. Sam pushed the girl a little closer to Ruth, holding her easily. Her father smiled humbly, a smile of longing and begging and sorrow.

'Here,' Sam urged quietly.

Ruthie whirled round and flung out her plump arm, pointing at the stairs.

'Don't just stand there – take her up. She'll need cleaning up before anything else. And the baby.'

The two men looked bemused and Ruthie sighed with exasperation.

'The bathroom! Take them up,' she cried, 'so I can get started.'

Beckoning with a nod of his head to the professor, Sam began to climb the stairs, carrying Christina. The others followed him up.

Chapter Eleven

'It's been the best summer in years, never mind the war,' Bridie said into the telephone. 'But when are we going to see you?'

'I'm going to see some people near London next month,' David told her, 'and I thought I might drop in then.'

'Couldn't you do more than drop in?' asked his mother.

'I'm working hard, Mum. I haven't got much time.'

'Who is so important to you, you haven't got time for us?' persisted Bridie, hurt.

'Mum, it's not "who". I have to work. If I don't do well all the time I lose my scholarship. Then I'd be out, since we can't possibly pay the fees ourselves. I really have to stay here and work.'

'You think you're the only one?' retorted Bridie. 'You should see what it's like here. Everyone's at their war work all the hours God sends and still the factories are wanting more. I'm thinking about applying myself.'

'Turned you down last time, didn't they?'

'They wasn't so desperate, then.' Bridie stifled her irritation and explained, 'It's since Dunkirk. They have to replace all that stuff the army lost, so anyone who can hold a spanner is piling into the factories.'

'Good for them.'

Bridie's frustration sharpened her voice. 'Maybe I'll come up to see you.'

'Travelling isn't easy. The trains go where the troops want to, and they seem to do it awfully slowly. It takes ages to get to London from here. Last time I got stuck in Bishops Stortford for hours. Can you imagine travelling to London from Dorking via Bishops Stortford? They push you all over the place.'

'So you do come down then?' cried Bridie.

Caught, David lied carelessly. 'Just the once, a while ago.'

'You said "last time".'

'Did I?'

'I hardly ever hear from Edward, either. When he does write, it's either so short it doesn't say anything, or all crossed out with great black lines because the censor doesn't want me knowing where he is or what he's up to.'

'It's war. It can't be helped.'

"I want it to be helped. I'm frightened for Edward, and you and me," cried Bridie silently. The line crackled and hissed and somewhere voices spoke just too faint to hear. "Often I can't sleep for feeling the icy sea on my skin, and the tearing pain of salt water in my lungs. I imagine just what it might be like for Edward to drown. Or burn. Or just disappear so that I never know what happened to him."

Bridie's thoughts caught and tripped on the stone of her fear, pulling her back.

'You'll come for Christmas, anyway, won't you?'

'That's ages away. But, probably, if we aren't under the heel of the jackboot by then.'

'That isn't funny,' snapped his mother.

'Sorry.' She heard a grin in his voice and her hand

itched to smack him, just as it had years ago in Ethel's
kitchen when he wouldn't stop playing her up. She held
the black receiver loosely, wondering whether one day
she would lose him altogether. A small cloud drifted
across the morning sun, casting a passing shadow on the
coloured glass panes of her front door.

'It's quiet as can be here. Looks like Göring's
forgotten about us,' she said into a burst of static.

'Got better things to do, I suppose.' David yawned.
'Look, I've got to go.'

'Sounds like you've got better things to do than
spend time with your family,' snapped Bridie acidly.

'I'll do my best at Christmas. Will you write?'

'I always write.'

'Bye.'

She slammed down the receiver with a shaking hand.
The Pope trotted out of the kitchen and refused to look
up as she cried: 'Selfish child!' She snatched her money
belt off the hall table and wrenched it round her waist.
It was Saturday and she didn't usually work, but today
she strode over to Stepney to collect some debts. The
unfortunate women of the district got the rough side of
her tongue with a vengeance until the pain of David's
indifference wore off. When the afternoon sun began to
dip downwards, nearly all the debts were in.

As Bridie lingered in the warm streets of Stepney,
enjoying the feeling of a good day's work almost done,
Sam Saul was in Shaftesbury Avenue, skulking. Ruthie
had found an ally in Professor Nakiewicz. Each week
they watched in reproachful silence as Sam ignored the
Sabbath and went about his business just as usual.
Encouraged by the professor's hunger to observe them,
Ruthie began to bring back Sabbath rituals she had

been forced to abandon long since. When candlesticks and prayer shawls appeared beside the bowls of salt and hard boiled eggs, Sam felt stifled and fled.

On this particular Sabbath afternoon in early September he strolled down the Avenue, stopped, and put his nose close to the display of photographs outside the Shaftesbury Theatre. He made up his mind, pulled out his pocket book and was just rifling through it for the price of a stalls ticket when the sirens went. He looked up and down, seeing which way people went for the nearest shelter. Women ran, dragging children by their arms, protesting, feet dragging on the warm paving stones. Men ambled with dignity, not running. Too many false alarms had come to nothing except a few desultory bombs dropped nowhere in particular.

Sam began to walk rapidly towards the shelter, then heard shouts behind him and a faint, high, distant buzzing.

'Look at that,' said a voice quietly. Sam turned and found a man in a worn black coat standing at his shoulder, his horrified face raised to the clear sky in the East. Sam's gaze followed and his mouth dropped open. Far, far away, high in the sky like tiny silver geese migrating in exquisite formation, the first of a great, shining wave of planes broke away, leaving gossamer trails blossoming in the thin air. As the enemy bombers wheeled round the sun caught them in its brilliance, specks of glitter threading a sparkling circle. Before the watchers' eyes the Luftwaffe began to play follow-my-leader.

'Oh, my,' breathed the man behind Sam.

'They're ours,' puffed an elderly fellow, waiting in dinner jacket and faded black tie to go into the theatre behind them. 'No need to worry.'

Sam stared fixedly at the circling planes.

'Why are they doing that, then?' he demanded. The silver specks went round and round and round, then flew off. Before they had vanished from sight the next formation had appeared, nose to tail in the terrible game of follow-my-leader.

'Why?' demanded Sam again, unable to take his eyes away, but the old chap had gone. Up and down Shaftesbury Avenue people stood stock still and stared into the sky. Another formation wheeled in, beginning to circle, while the second lot, delivered of the weight of a bellyful of bombs, rose sharply above the oncoming hordes and flashed away with all the precise delicacy of a perfect manoeuvre.

'Dear God,' cried a woman, putting her hand to her eyes against a sudden shaft of late afternoon sun, 'it's the East End. They're bombing the Docks.'

People murmured reassuringly. The Docks. Just the Docks. The Germans were only interested in the Docks. They'd expected it. They were bound to get it, weren't they? The watchers began to drift into their shelters, chivvied and scolded by wardens, grumbling and scared now that the Germans were really here.

'They don't look real, do they?' said a frightened woman with a small boy on her knee, sitting next to Sam on the brick bench of the street shelter. 'They don't look as though they could do any damage.'

'No,' he said grimly, trying to blot out the picture of what must be happening underneath the pretty fair-ground chair o' planes dancing in the sky only five or six miles away. He sat with his face in his hands, ignoring the fussing women and fretful children around him, until his long legs grew so cramped he got up, pushed past the protesting warden and stood in Shaftesbury

Avenue again. He gazed eastwards while the warden glared, hands on hips, muttering that some people ought to be shot, setting a selfish example to others.

A great white cloud filled the eastern sky. Several men from the shelter crept out to join him. They looked up and gasped. The cloud swelled, higher and higher, tinged pink by early evening sunlight. Fire engines raced by, clanging frenziedly, skidding around corners, engines roaring, their clamour joining the deafening uproar of the great guns firing incessantly and uselessly at the silver invaders. The vast cloud reddened, its edges blackening, blooming ever higher as the sun began to sink, setting the barrage balloons blazing with a kind of awful beauty. Sam watched, holding his breath with the wonder and the horror of it. At a quarter past six the all clear sounded.

'That's that, then,' Sam heard on all sides as shelterers crowded into the road, making for home or theatres or restaurants or wherever else they had been going when the planes interrupted them. 'The Docks must be flattened.' Guiltily, no one said anything about the people underneath the departed merry-go-round. Just the Docks. The Germans probably won't even be back, they told each other, now the Docks are gone. And they hurried off, relieved.

Sam came to life and ran down the Avenue, waving furiously at a passing taxi.

'Hackney,' he shouted at the driver's enquiring face.

'No, mate.'

Sam shook the cab's door handle impatiently. 'You have to.'

'Can't do it, mate. Nothing can get through. Roads are full of emergency services. Every bleedin' fire engine in London's over there. They don't want us cluttering up the place, they got enough on their hands.'

The red cloud billowed upwards, a stupendous column of smoke, darkening the street.

'I have to,' cried Sam desperately.

'You could think of those poor beggars, getting it,' snapped the taxi driver angrily. 'Have a bit of thought.'

'I can't think of anything else,' groaned Sam.

The cabbie wound his window down as far as it would go and stuck his head out, gazing up, awed, at the pillar of flame.

'Sorry, mate,' he said. 'I'd take you if I could, but I'd never get through. You want to go there, you'll have to walk.'

Sam tried to smile but what the cabbie saw was a grimace of pure fear.

'Someone you know?' he asked, catching on.

'Someone I love. Sure you can't get through?'

'Not a chance. Good luck to you,' said the driver shortly.

Sam let go of the cab window and straightened up. His face caught the red glare of the sky and shone livid.

'I'll walk then,' he said.

The driver nodded and put his cab into gear. 'Hope you find her,' he called gruffly, and watched the tall figure hurry away towards The Strand and Ludgate Hill, into the shadow of the cloud, as fast as Sam's long legs would carry him.

When the sirens went again barely an hour later, he hurried on, ignoring them. A furious warden dragged him, protesting, into a street shelter just off Bishopsgate.

'Sit down or I'll 'ave the police in,' roared the warden. 'You're a bleedin' nuisance. Whatcher think this is, a kiddie's picnic?'

Sam subsided, cowed by the hostility.

'Sorry,' he muttered ungraciously.

He sat, offended and helpless, jostled and nudged by a cramped, bad-tempered crowd that gave off the sour smell of fear as they listened to the planes coming over, a deep, unending roar just to the east. Round and round and round they flew while fire engulfed the narrow, crowded streets of the East End, throwing into the darkening sky a blaze so bright men read their papers by the light of it five miles away. The evening passed and still the planes came.

'They'd better be done by closing time,' joked the warden lugubriously, popping in to see they were all right. The air thrummed in their ears as a bomber roared close overhead, and out of the thunderclap of its engine came a rushing whine and a detonation that split their eardrums. A child shrieked and a woman at the back of the shelter was held back by several hands as she sprang up in terror and tried to flee. The shelter was full of people who sat, holding their breath, listening to a wind as hot as the fire of hell rage up and down Bishopsgate, whirling dancing dervishes of shattered glass in its wake that glittered and sparkled in the ruby light.

'Sweet Jesus,' whispered the warden, standing bravely by the doorway in case anyone panicked badly and tried to run out, keeping an eye on the woman at the far end who sat with her head in her arms, sobbing.

'They're coming over here then,' said a man's shaky voice. He held a little boy in the crook of his arm, rocking him to and fro. 'It isn't just the Docks, is it?'

They avoided each other's eyes in the near darkness and a fresh wave of blast pulled at their shelter. It trembled and bricks shifted above them. The air swirled, heavy, full of hot grit and terrible smells.

'They must have hit a spice warehouse,' remarked the warden, spitting noisily out of the doorway. 'I could swear I can taste something spicy, like burnt Christmas cake.' He grinned encouragingly at his flock but no one smiled back.

'That'll be one of the wharves gone up. There's all sorts of stuff down there: oil cake, whisky, rubber, tar . . . jam, even. Burn like anything, that lot will,' said the man with the child after a bit, catching the warden's eye and trying hard to copy his courage.

'It's burnin' all right,' answered the warden, his voice drowned as another bomber went over, scattering a stick of bombs in a straight line half a mile from where they sat.

'It's all of London. It's not just the Docks at all. It's the whole of London they're after.' Sam spoke clearly into the din and everyone heard, lifting their heads to peer at him. 'We aren't safe. We've been kidding ourselves.'

All round the shelter heads nodded slowly, without bitterness, only a kind of dreadful wonder that they could all have so completely, and so self-servingly, misunderstood what the Germans were planning to do.

The baby that had been yelling stopped abruptly. Its young mother shyly opened her blouse and began to feed it. The men on the brick seats opposite considerately looked away, their profiles lit by the fires that began to gobble buildings not far away.

'It ain't that bad 'ere. Not like the poor souls gettin' it over there. I'll get along for a bit. You lot stay put and you'll do.' The ARP warden eased a finger underneath the strap of his hat and scratched his chin.

'You're going out?' asked Sam in astonishment.

'It's my job, mate.'

Sam watched with deep respect as the wiry little man in his round tin hat clambered over several arms and legs and ducked out of the shelter entrance.

'Where's he going, for God's sake?' he asked.

'He looks after more than one shelter. Goes the rounds making sure everyone's all right,' said a cultured voice, its owner invisible in the crowd.

'How do you know?' asked Sam in amazement. 'How do you know it all when this is the first time we've been bombed?'

The voice held a hint of amusement at his naivety. 'I'm a warden, too. I should be over in Hampstead only this is my night off. I wish I was over there, now they've come.'

Sam sat deep in thought. 'You do a lot of training?' he asked, picking out the other man in the gloom as someone moved from in front of him.

'Yes. Not that we were all that serious lately. We had got to thinking this would never happen. Just goes to show, doesn't it?' The man laughed wryly.

'Think they'd take me on?'

'Man,' said his friend, 'if it carries on like this they'll need everyone they can get.'

"I'll go along tomorrow," Sam promised himself, and it was comforting to plan for tomorrow, because there were moments that night when he began to think the world was ending in one gigantic firestorm and that all his tomorrows were gone.

Closing time came and went unnoticed; midnight passed, and while no more bombs dropped near Sam's shelter, the planes continued to circle the Docks and the streets of the East End until just after six in the morning. Just before four the woman next to him had put her head on his shoulder and began to snore softly, into his ear. He could hear her slow breathing below the numbing roar of planes; the whine, rising and falling, of their escorting fighters, twisting and turning in the searchlights like swarms of midges; the staccato thundering of anti-aircraft guns, and the appalling clamour raging from the distant disintegration of the East End. Around him, people dozed, exhausted by shock and fear.

At five o'clock a new warden put her head round the shelter entrance and cracked a few jokes with the wakeful ones. Sam smiled dutifully and shifted carefully to ease his numb shoulder. The woman groaned faintly and slept on until sirens wailed the all clear and Londoners everywhere, deeply shocked, pale-faced with strain, crept from their burrows and cellars, street shelters and every kind of bolt hole, to gaze, aghast, at the fantastic dust cloud blotting out the bright early morning sun and reflecting back the flames that engulfed the whole eastern horizon.

Sam stood outside the shelter, coughing and choking in dust and fumes, looking in horror up and down the glass-strewn road; shrapnel lay everywhere.

'Is there anywhere I'd find a telephone?' he asked a woman in a familiar tin hat.

She pointed a finger. 'Warden's post down there has one. Ask nicely and they might let you use it if the lines aren't down.' She smiled wearily and he saw that her face was rimmed with dirt and what looked as though it might be blood.

Sam swallowed hard, his throat dry, his eyes burning in the foul air. 'Thank you,' he said hoarsely.

'Cheer up,' called the ARP woman as she turned to go, 'it may never happen.'

Sam eyed the cloud steadily engulfing the city, the brilliant glow of flames licking its edges. 'I fear it already has,' he said, marvelling at her optimism.

He used the warden's telephone to tell Ruthie he was delayed in town and she was not to worry. Ruthie, who in Golders Green had heard nothing, was merely annoyed that he had been out all night. Then he dialled Bridie's number. It rang.

'Thank God! She can't have been hit,' he cried to the warden, who raised his eyebrows. The telephone rang and rang.

'There's no answer,' muttered Sam, unable to make himself put it down. He wiped grime from his mouth with the back of his hand and noted with disgust that he kept wanting to spit. A hand thrust a mug of thick, stewed tea into his.

'Here,' said the warden. 'Sorry, mate, but we need it.' He nodded at the telephone.

Sam put down the receiver obediently, taking the tea absently. The telephone instantly began to ring. He stood to one side, embarrassed by his uselessness, watching their drawn, grim faces, pale in the glare of an unshaded bulb.

'Is it very bad over there?' he asked diffidently, in a brief lull in their busyness.

'Bad?' The warden took off his tin hat and ran his fingers exhaustedly through thinning grey hair. He gave a long, braying laugh. 'Is hell hot?' he asked, and picking up his gas mask in its worn cardboard holder, went away without another word.

If she hadn't got all upset about David's refusal to come home more often, Bridie would never have been caught in the middle of it. The sirens went at tea time as she was walking briskly along Stepney High Street, thinking of dropping in to see Mrs MacDonald, the old midwife who had delivered David, if she was at home on such a fine afternoon. Hearing the rising wail, she sighed with annoyance; they were always calling false alerts. Once or twice there had even been a few bombs but it didn't look as though the saturation bombing they had so feared at first was going to happen. She quickened her step but didn't hurry.

Panicky, frightened women and children ran past her on their way to the street shelter down the road. A mother snatched at her toddler and carried him, kicking and squirming with rage, into the dark mouth of the shelter. A row of prams collected outside it and the place seemed full to bursting with yelling babies and shouting, terrified mothers. Men, carefully casual, ambled in behind them and everyone pushed and shoved and fought over spaces on the benches, their arguments drowned by screaming sirens. Two harassed women in warden's hats shouted and gesticulated at the entrance, imploring people to calm down and get inside in an orderly way. Bridie stood in the entrance, avoiding the pleading women, and saw that the benches were packed full. People crouched on the floor, holding children, blankets, a loaf of bread.

'It's full,' she said, wondering where to go.

'Come on, ducks, get in. Never mind us,' cried a hugely fat woman, who had been trying on a new corset when the alert sounded. Pink flesh rolled in smooth abundance over the tight, pinkish elastic with its stiff, ungiving bones, and fat purple legs stuck straight out in front of her. She put her hands on her knees to lean forwards, the better to see Bridie. Bosoms, thighs and suspenders strained against each other, for all the world to see. She pulled a faded robe ineffectually around herself.

'Come on, love,' she cried again, 'if they can fit me in, there's room for three of you.' She chuckled cheerfully and wriggled to try and make room. Her neighbours fought back, silently and grimly resisting giving another precious inch away. Bridie heard the sirens behind her and saw a sea of tightly packed legs in front of her. There wasn't room to put her feet, much less sit down.

'I'll find somewhere else,' she shouted to Corset. 'All right, duck,' the woman mouthed back, and winked incongruously at a young boy who sat with eyes round as saucers, staring at her undress. 'That Luftwaffe don't give a girl much notice.' She screamed with laughter and dug her neighbour in the ribs with a plump elbow. The youth blushed brilliantly and as Bridie turned away she heard the laughter rise again, pealing over the sirens as if mocking all the might of the Third Reich from the safety of a creaking salmon-coloured corset.

'Where's the next shelter?' she called, above the din. Ack-ack guns started up nearby, trying their range with an appalling series of vicious, ear-rending bursts of fire, drowning out the warden's answer. Tracer bloomed palely against the bright empty sky. Suddenly horribly afraid, she began to run, leaving the packed shelter behind and running and running, panting with fear, on down towards Saint Dunstans, where Mrs MacDonald lived, and safety. She flew round the corner by the end of the churchyard and gasped as more anti-aircraft batteries got into their stride close by. Blood drummed in her ears. She staggered to a halt, leaning on the grey stone gateposts at the entrance to the churchyard as what might have been a cloud passed over the sun.

Bridie looked up and stood paralyzed in the roaring, droning sledgehammer of sound announcing the arrival of the long awaited shadow. She stared upwards, head tilted right back, forgetting her danger, staring and staring at the beautiful, deadly planes, flying so orderly and so low, right over her.

'Oh,' she gasped.

Her feet were rooted to the ground. Above her, German hands reached for controls that would open the bomb doors. A few moments more. The leading planes peeled away and began to circle. Bridie's eyes followed them, mesmerized.

'They're ours,' she breathed, unable to take in the reality of the swastika insignias and what they must mean. 'Oh, how wonderful they look.'

Directly overhead, the first bomb doors eased open.

Chapter Twelve

Still staring, she saw their bellies open. Sticks of blunt black bombs rushed towards the ground at unthinkable speed, pulled as if by some giant magnet. Compression gripped Bridie with a fist that squeezed the breath out of her, then the air exploded and flung her headlong, tumbling head over heels and screaming, dragged her through a gap where it had plucked out the bent old iron railings and flung her across the churchyard where gravestones flew on the wind as if in some ghastly Hallowe'en, whirling and twirling, dancing on tidal waves of scorched air. A second blow lifted Bridie off her feet, spun her round and slammed her against the stone wall of the ancient church where she hung spreadeagled. Then, as viciously as it had picked her up, it dropped her.

She lay, eyes staring from her head. Above her another formation of planes broke and began to circle the church tower, shedding bombs which hurtled towards her, howling through the superheated air, exploding in the inferno below, sending up gigantic gouts of dust, rubble and human bodies. Fire leaped, orange and red, high into the scorched air, lighting the devastation around her with macabre brilliance, brighter than the sunlit day it had been earlier.

Bridie whimpered, a peculiar wave of movement

advancing on her as shrapnel danced and sang and bounced down towards the church door, veering off at the last moment into the grass. The path undulated with dancing steel splinters, itself rising and heaving and snaking with compression. Bridie gave a dry sob and tried to huddle further into the stone wall for shelter, but the stones grew hot. Turbulence tore at her with solid, scorching fingers, sending her dress flying over the church roof into the great boiling cloud that raged upwards. The fingers tried to pluck her eyes from their sockets then beat on her with a rain of scorching blows. Long churchyard grass crackled very softly, shrivelled and died. Bridie lay quite still, smelling singeing hair distinctly, over all the other smells. Lying, helpless, against the church wall, she began to burn.

Inside Saint Dunstan's a young woman raised her head, hearing, through her own, the thin screaming of another's terror. She took her hands away from her ears and listened intently. At first all she heard was a deafening roar, joined now by the fierce sound of fire as it raced along the narrow terraces of back to backs, bringing down walls and roofs in showers of sparks that were carried on the blast to start new fires. Fire engines screamed down roads that melted beneath their wheels. The clanging bells sounded with strange clarity above the frightful din. Then she heard it again: a thin screaming, like an animal caught in a trap; like one of dad's rabbits trapped by a ferret. A sound she knew. Agony.

The heavy church door tore itself from her fingers as soon as she drew the bolt and flung itself with a frightful crash against the wall of the porch.

'I can't,' she gasped, the words torn from her mouth by the maelstrom beyond the church door. Her baby turned in her belly, alarmed, and she fled back into the church. The door banged viciously to and fro as burning air sucked and boiled in the ancient porchway. Behind thick planks, well-boarded stained-glass windows cracked and buckled as lead casings began to soften. She moistened her lips, scoured bloody by flailing grit, and looked despairingly at the whirling tumult beyond the doorway. Her baby lurched again uneasily. She crossed herself.

'Dear Lord, I can't,' she muttered.

It came again, a low moan, beneath the noise of the storm.

'Shh,' she whispered, putting her hand to the baby's kicking. The great door banged fit to tear itself to pieces and she saw in terror that its planks were beginning to loosen. Searing air howled into the cool recesses of the church and sent a shower of hymnbooks flying over the altar steps, glowing and sparking in the darkness. The ancient walls, many feet thick, would withstand the blast and the heat, if she could close the door again. She edged her way closer to the porch, clinging to the carved, heavy pews whose polished varnish ran in raised blisters, scorched.

'I know,' she cried aloud and ran back to the vestry. Vestments hung in tidy rows on hooks in a big cupboard, carefully starched and ironed despite wartime shortages. Hurriedly tearing them down, she stuffed them into the small sink and turned the tap. As they soaked, she dragged them out, and struggled into them, sodden cloth clinging and resistant, until she dripped from head to foot.

'That should do it,' she said, crossing herself hastily by way of apology. Not daring to stop and think, she picked up her drenched skirts, waddled down the nave, darted clumsily past the crazily swinging door, and out into the storm.

The turbulent atmosphere sucked at her, the pressure threatening to pull her eyes from her skull.

Through the pain, the path to the church gate seemed to heave, rising and falling like the cakewalk in some insane funfair. Gravestones whirled and cartwheeled into a ruined roof a quarter of a mile down the road. Glancing, terrified, at the planes circling above, she ran as fast as she could round the side wall of the church, into a whirlwind that lifted her from her feet and sent her spinning, rolling and tumbling over the stones like a rag doll. It threw her with careless savagery against the body of the woman who lay, almost naked, curled like a foetus against the hot stones. She lay, gasping acid air, wet robes tangled round her limbs, feeling the water in them begin to boil . . .

"We're both burning," she thought, suddenly furious. She scrabbled to her feet and dragged at the inert body angrily, tripping and stumbling over her trailing finery.

'Come on,' she mouthed frantically, jerking Bridie fiercely half upright, the easier to drag her out of the way of the shrapnel littering the ground. She threw a look of sheer hatred up at the planes.

'Pigs!' she screamed, the word torn from her mouth as she hitched Bridie's lolling body firmly in her arms and flung them both with all her strength past the demonic door and slid across the polished surface of a brass floor plaque into safety. Then she leaped with the strength of pure terror, and throwing her weight against the door, she travelled with it on one of its maniacal swings and shot the bolts home.

They held and her nerves went. She slid down to the stone floor, holding her belly, and sat with her back to the door, shaking uncontrollably. After a while, calmer, she got to her feet unsteadily and went over to the body on the floor.

'Hey,' she hissed, 'you all right?'

"You'd better be," she thought furiously, "after all that."

The body, feeling the cool of the stone flags, stirred and tried to lift its head.

'Oh,' groaned Bridie in anguish.

'Keep still.' The young woman looked around her. 'I'll see if there's any water left. Wait a moment.' She rubbed her belly gently to soothe the baby and stumbled over the hem of her robes, back to the vestry. She turned the tap and a clear stream of water still ran out.

'Thank You kindly,' she said, looking upwards at the ceiling. She went back to the cupboard full of surplices and dragged them down. Some dusty cups lay in a cardboard box in a corner, leftovers from some long forgotten parish tea. She took the garments and two cups of water back into the church. Bridie struggled to sit up and the younger woman pushed her gently back.

'You stay still,' she ordered.

Bridie lay back obediently, peering up at the grotesque figure bending over her. It saw her expression and grinned.

'It's only me, don't panic,' it ordered, and pushed back its cowl of wet embroidered cloth to reveal a young, brown-haired woman with a drawn, frightened face. Then her eyes softened and twinkled.

'There,' she said, amused.

'Am I dead?' whispered Bridie faintly.

The figure gave a strained laugh. 'I think you weren't far off. But you're alive just now.'

'Oh.'

'Holy Mother, though, you're in a state, to be sure.'

She tore strips from the choirboys' robes and, dipping them in water, began to mop gently at Bridie's cuts and bruises.

'Hurt much?'

Bridie shook her head. Her rescuer worked busily until, after many trips to the tap, Bridie's wounds were washed and bound in holy linen. 'That should help 'em heal quick,' said the Good Samaritan irreverently. She raised Bridie's head on to her knees and began to wrap one of the priest's gowns around her.

'What are you doing?' asked Bridie, drawing away.

'I'm going to cover you with this, and then soak you. That way, the cold will help draw the heat from your body and you won't burn so badly.'

'You a nurse?'

'No. I did some first aid before the war.'

'I thought you put butter on burns,' gasped Bridie as the heavy cloth touched her.

'We're a bit short on butter just now, thanks to those pigs up there. If this was holy water it'd be even better, but Protestant water will have to do.' The girl chattered as she drew the folds over the whole of Bridie's body, seeing how it hurt.

'Now the annointing,' she joked. As she stood up, Bridie saw the big belly on her and tears filled her eyes.

'You saved my life, even though . . .'

The girl nodded. She picked up the cups and disappeared, coming back with a trayful. She poured them carefully over Bridie, soaking her. 'I heard you crying. I couldn't leave you out there.'

'But the baby?'

'Never mind.'

Bridie closed her eyes and lay quiet.

'I'd only popped in here to have a quiet half hour to take the weight off my feet after shopping, and say a small prayer for my husband. I go to mass over the High Street but I often pop in here other times. It's usually so peaceful, and now look what's happened. Talk about trouble.'

'How will I ever thank you?' Bridie sounded fretful. The strong smell of wet burned paper got up her nose and made her sneeze painfully.

'Stinks, doesn't it? The hymnbooks started to burn. Sorry, but I had to wet them and put them out or we'd have been on fire in here as well.'

They leaned against the back of the pew, lost in their own thoughts.

'How long was it?' asked Bridie after a while.

'Out there? Oh, not long. Hard to say, really.'

'Awful. Out there.'

'We've waited long enough for the stinking Germans. Now they're here with a vengeance.' She smoothed back Bridie's half-burned hair and felt the curls spring over her fingers in the near darkness. 'You've pretty hair, haven't you? Here, try this. It'll moisten your mouth.' The girl dipped a rag into a cup of clean water and gave it to Bridie to suck.

A bomb whistled straight overhead and they both stiffened until it exploded not far off and percussion shook the ground beneath their feet. Air danced in shock waves, ruffling the fringes of their robes, and ancient stones groaned and shifted.

'What's your name?' asked Bridie, to cover the moment of terror. 'I'm Bridie.'

'Winnie,' said the girl, wringing out another rag in a tea cup.

'Winifred?'

'Yes.'

'Not Winston.'

Neither of them laughed at the feeble joke.

'I couldn't leave you out there,' she said abruptly. 'So don't go fretting about it.'

Bridie saw that her truculence covered embarrassment and merely said: 'Do you live round here?'

'I've lived around here three years. My husband's a merchant seaman and when we got married I came down from Grimsby to live with his family. He's always lived here and he won't go anywhere else. It was a case of love me, love my family, so I knew if I wanted him, I had to take them as well.'

'It's like that round here,' murmured Bridie, thinking of Ethel for the first time. 'My in-laws live just up the way. I hope they're all right.'

'And mine.'

Talk lapsed once more.

'I'm drying out,' said Bridie eventually. 'I'm hot and wet and I'd rather be cold and wet, if you wouldn't mind too much, Winnie.'

The girl lumbered to her feet. She fetched another tray of water and dropped it carefully over Bridie, who shuddered as it seeped through to her burned skin.

'I'm sorry it hurts,' Winnie said apologetically, 'but I can't think what else to do. I'm pretty sure it's for the best.'

'What about you? How far gone are you, underneath all that stuff?' Bridie gasped, to take her mind off the pain.

'Nine months,' admitted Winnie reluctantly.

'Oh, my God!'

'It doesn't always happen right on time, does it? Not to the day, or anything?'

'Let's hope not. Are you all right?'

'Right as rain.' She patted her belly and smiled. When she looked over a few minutes later, Bridie had dozed off. Winnie settled her back against the pew, listening to the mayhem outside. Glass popped with sounds like gunshot inside its boards, but Bridie slept on. After a bit, Winnie's own eyes closed and she slept uncomfortably, shifting in her sleep with the pressing weight of the baby, dreamlessly surrounded by all the sound and fury of a living nightmare.

The planes' going wakened them. Then the all clear sounded. Bridie carefully tested her stiff, sore limbs and said she thought she might be able to move, just a little. Winnie jolted awake, having dreamed at last of an iron bar prodding her in the back as round and round a pile of burning stones she walked. Prod. Prod. She groaned in protest and squinted at Bridie.

'It's over.'

'Yes. What shall we do?'

They both turned to stare at the great door.

'Look outside, I suppose. Though I'm not sure I want to see. Do you?'

Bridie shivered under her robes. 'No,' she admitted. 'But I think we have to.'

'I'll go and look.' Winnie got to her feet, putting her hand in the small of her back, pulling a face.

'I'm so stiff,' she complained, stretching her arms. Then she put them down with a little squawk.

'Oh,' she cried again.

'What?' asked Bridie anxiously, trying to sit up hastily. 'What's the matter.'

Winnie looked down, hotly embarrassed and glad of the gloom that hid her face.

'I've started,' she said in a small voice. 'Here and now, in all this. Oh, did you ever?'

'How d'you know?' asked Bridie, struggling upright. She sensed Winnie blush in the darkness.

'My waters,' she whispered. 'I'm soaked.'

'Oh.'

'Quite,' said Winnie in a very subdued voice. 'It's just my kind of luck.'

'It is your first one, isn't it?' asked Bridie, realizing she didn't know.

'Yes,' said Winnie in an even smaller voice.

'Well, that's a blessing. The first one usually takes hours and hours and hours. Days, sometimes,' she exaggerated bravely, 'so we've bags of time. We'll manage, don't you worry,'

'How?' asked Winnie, gazing at the door again.

'Go and open it. That's a start.'

Winnie gathered her robes, hobbled across the flagstones, opened the door and screamed.

The Reverend Thomas nearly jumped out of his skin. As he reached for the door to his church, it grated open and in the doorway stood an hallucination, a substantial wraith, clad in an assortment of his own priestly robes and dripping all over. It was barely recognizable as a woman, but it shrieked like a woman, and had a woman's disconcerting habit of bursting into tears at the slightest shock. Reverend Thomas got over his own panic and demanded, 'What in God's name are you doing?'

'Oooh,' wailed Winnie, hopelessly unnerved by the unexpected sight of the curate, standing black as a bat in the porch, his outline shimmering and flickering by the light of fires raging in buildings nearby. A fire engine clanged its bell irritably somewhere nearby and at that moment a row of burning houses collapsed with a slow roar into an immense shower of sparks and flaming timber.

'Ooooh,' howled Winnie again, running backwards into the church until she tripped over her robes and fell in a heap at Bridie's feet. The curate rubbed his eyes and followed her into the gloom. He stood looking down at the two women with a baffled expression, his long nose twitching. Bridie clung hard to Winnie and stared up at him. ''tis the devil himself,' she whimpered.

'We are sorry to have made a mess,' Bridie said when she had recovered herself at last.

The curate blinked in amazement. Winnie sat up with dignity and pulled his ruined finery around her more tightly.

'We got trapped in here when the planes came. This lady is burned and I'm in labour. That's why we're wearing your clothes,' she said haughtily.

Thomas wondered if he were not more affected by the bombs than he had thought. He shook his head to clear it, but they were still there. Winnie clutched her belly and winced.

'It hurts, but only a bit. Do you think the baby will come soon?' she asked anxiously, turning to Bridie.

Thomas's appalled gaze shifted mutely, waiting for her answer.

'No. You've a long way to go if it only hurts a bit. I

wish I did.' She gave a little cry of pain and lay back against the pew. 'Will you help us, Father? We need an ambulance.'

Reverend Thomas found his voice at last. He cleared his throat.

'Yes. Yes. An ambulance.' He looked regretfully round his undamaged church with its cool whole interior. It was more inviting than what was outside, he thought, but the ladies needed help.

'Yes,' he said more firmly. 'You wait here.'

'We're goin' nowhere,' sighed Bridie, squinting wryly after his departing figure. Winnie twitched.

'Another one?'

'Yes.'

'They aren't comin' that often. I shouldn't worry. He'll get an ambulance and take you home.'

'You need to go to hospital,' said Winnie, thinking of her small room in her mother-in-law's house where all the baby things lay fresh and folded and ready. None of this shameful leaking into someone else's altar robes; she went scarlet and squirmed, just thinking about it.

'Soon,' murmured Bridie. 'I should think there's a lot goin' into hospital after last night. I don't suppose you and me are the only ones, not by a long chalk.'

'It's all on fire outside,' whispered Winnie uncertainly. The curate had closed the door behind him and the din of the fire and destruction left by the planes was muted after the numbing pandemonium of the night. They lay close together in their respective puddles, waiting for the curate to come back with help.

'Thank God David's out of this,' said Bridie, lying with her eyes closed.

'Who's David?'

Bridie thought of her fair-haired son and his enigmatic telephone call that had brought her here in the first place.

'My son.'

'You've just the one, then?'

'No.' Bridie let the word hang for so long Winnie leaned up on her elbow and looked at her curiously.

'There was Rosa,' Bridie said.

'You've got a daughter?'

'She died.'

'Ah.' Winnie's heart turned over at the thought of the baby about to be born.

'But you don't want to be thinking of that now.'

'No,' whispered Winnie. 'I don't think I do. D'you think he'll be long?'

'If it's as bad as you say, he may take a long time to get anything.'

'Oh dear,' said Winnie.

She was running the tap into another tray of cups when Reverend Thomas pushed open the warped door in a flurry of squeaks. She heard his voice saying something to Bridie. Another pain came and went. She bit her lip and leant on the edge of the sink; he'd bring help.

'They'll come when they can,' Thomas explained unhappily, dabbing at his long, thin nose with a snow white handkerchief. 'Oh, the smell. I did my best but you've no idea. There is such devastation, it goes beyond belief.'

'Ouch,' groaned Winnie from the background. Thomas winced.

'I'm sorry, but everywhere there are people much worse than you and everything – fire, ambulances, the lot – is stretched too thin. They will come, but I can't say when.' He coughed convulsively and a cloud of dust rose from his cropped brown hair. Behind his spectacles Bridie saw that his light, shifting eyes were afraid.

'We will wait, then.'

'I'm sorry.'

'I don't suppose the Germans'll be back at least. Do you?' she asked anxiously.

'I shouldn't think so. Not twice. The Docks are burning beyond control already. They've no reason to come back.'

'Is that the smell?'

He nodded. 'Spice warehouses – oil cake, biscuits, sugar, drink, God knows what – everything's gone up.' He ran his hands through his hair. 'Will you be all right there? I can't think how to make you more comfortable.'

Bridie beckoned him to kneel down beside her.

'It's not me,' she told him in a low voice. 'We must get help for her.'

'I can't . . .'

'No, listen. Would you kindly walk over to the midwife and ask her to come. Mrs MacDonald.'

Thomas leaped to his feet and clapped his hand to his forehead. 'Fool!' he cried, startling Winnie with her tray, just coming out of the vestry again. 'I was by there not ten minutes ago. I never thought.' He rushed out of the open door and they heard his boots crunch on broken glass as he sped through the churchyard to Mrs MacDonald's house, a few moments away.

'Someone's coming,' murmured Bridie, burning all over. Blisters began to form on her lips and Winnie held a cup of water to her, near to tears herself.

'Would you soak me again?' said Bridie hoarsely. 'I'm sorry, I know you hurt, too.'

'It keeps my mind off it,' Winnie said briskly, and she was crouched, spilling the last of the cool water over

188

Bridie's face, when Mrs MacDonald came noiselessly through the door, bag in hand and a great bundle under one arm. Bridie looked at the midwife's lined, beloved face and burst into tears. Winnie looked round in astonishment.

'I'm sorry. It's Winnie, here. She needs you. Don't mind me.' Bridie wept with relief and love. Mrs MacDonald took in the pair of them and dumped her bundles on a pew.

'Well, it's a good thing those Germans missed me,' she remarked, 'since it looks like someone needs lookin' after here. What a pickle!' She stood, arms akimbo, and calmly assessed the bizarre scene. Thomas arrived, dishevelled and disheartened.

'I've tried for an ambulance again. They are still busy digging people out of rubble who need transport more urgently, I'm afraid.'

His sparse figure bent over them anxiously. 'Will you be all right?'

'Never mind that,' said Mrs MacDonald briskly. 'Got a kettle?'

'Er—'

Mrs MacDonald didn't let him finish.

'Go and put it on. We'll need hot water. And collect everything you can by way of blankets or soft things. Some hassocks might do. We'll try to make her comfortable.'

He scuttled off to the back of the church to obey her orders and get out of her way. The midwife turned and grinned.

'That'll keep him busy for a bit,' she said cheerily. 'Let's be havin' a look at you, my duck.'

Winnie lay down on a narrow pew and raised the heavy robes.

189

'Whatever you been doin' in this getup?' demanded Mrs MacDonald, feeling gently across Winnie's belly and putting her little ear trumpet down to listen to the baby's heart. 'Lovely,' pronounced the midwife. 'Nice and strong and steady, and you've a long way to go yet. Not a worry in the world. Why don't you take that lot off? You'd feel better.'

Winnie dragged her ecclesiastical outfit off, leaving it a sodden heap on the floor, to Thomas's dismay when he came back. He'd never seen anyone look more pregnant.

'We'll just have to wait. Got any tea?' shouted Mrs MacDonald when he appeared.

'Tea?'

'Yes, please. tea,' said the midwife, glaring at him. He disappeared hastily back into his vestry.

'You have to keep them occupied,' said Mrs MacDonald firmly. Bridie forgot her pain and giggled.

'That's better, my duck.' Mrs MacDonald opened her bag and began to sort through, checking. 'Friend of yours?' she murmured to Bridie, nodding her head over towards Winnie, who sat on a pew, breathing hard.

'She saved my life. I'll tell you another time,' Bridie said weakly.

Mrs MacDonald nodded. 'We'll have you out of here in no time. Don't you worry about nothing.'

Thomas struggled with the teapot and cups and saucers, then realized he had neither milk nor sugar.

'I'm sorry, ladies. It's Russian tea without lemon.'

Mrs MacDonald gave him a withering look and the flustered curate almost dropped the tray.

'Shall I go and see if I can find an ambulance again?' he asked diffidently.

'Have your tea,' ordered Mrs MacDonald. He gazed uneasily at the back of Winnie's head.

'She won't, er, have anything here, will she?' he asked nervously.

'Not for ages. They'll be here long before that baby comes.'

He sipped his scalding tea and wished he'd not given in to the urge to see that his beloved church had stood unharmed. Beyond the open door they heard a bird sing mournfully in a blackened bush by the churchyard gate.

'They've done some damage, then,' observed Mrs MacDonald.

'Thank God it wasn't worse. No gas,' said the curate.

'I suppose it might have been worse,' agreed Mrs MacDonald doubtfully. 'But I'm not sure I can think how.'

'At least they've gone,' replied the curate, not wanting to argue with the fearsome old woman.

'Yes, they've gone. Thank God for that and good riddance,' cried Mrs MacDonald. 'We're safe now. We'll just wait quietly until a doctor comes.'

'You won't need me then,' said Thomas, seeing his chance.

'We might, to run messages,' snapped the midwife. 'So you stay here.'

Thomas subsided on to his pew, muttering inaudibly that this was his church. Mrs MacDonald sent him to boil more water, just in case.

'You can never rely on them,' she said to Winnie. 'Where's your husband, dearie?'

'Atlantic convoys,' said Winnie briefly.

'Ah.'

They settled down to wait.

'I think I have to go and see to other things,' said Thomas an hour or so later. 'They can't be much longer.'

'Go on, then.' Mrs MacDonald failed to hide her exasperation.

Thomas sidled towards the door apologetically, desperate to put some distance between himself and the baby he feared might be born right in front of him, on his own church floor.

'I'm frightfully sorry,' he stammered, 'but I should be seeing to my parishoners. Many have been hurt . . .'

He pushed the heavy door full open and they all jumped and froze in shock as the piercing wail of the sirens rose once more over London.

'But they've gone!' cried Winnie stupidly.

'They're back,' muttered Bridie from down on the floor.

And they were. Moments later the high drone of planes in the distance filled the evening sky, and the first sticks of bombs whistled and crumped three miles away, along the Thames. The ground shook.

'Shut the door,' screamed Winnie, remembering its living malevolence in the blast. Thomas ran to the big black oak timbers and pulled them shut as the first winds pushed at him like hands from hell. Above the church tower the black sky was lit with red.

'Ooooh,' whimpered Winnie, rocking back and forth, holding her belly.

Mrs MacDonald eyed her thoughtfully. 'The ambulance might not come, might it?' whispered Bridie, hearing the cacophany take hold outside. The old walls shivered as she spoke.

'They'll come,' said the midwife calmly. 'But we'll have to make do until they do.'

'God bless you,' murmured Bridie.

Mrs MacDonald smiled.

'I hope so, in all this. I truly do,' she said.

By three o'clock in the morning they had come to huddle together in the shelter of the tallest pew. Thomas cracked his knuckles miserably every time Winnie moaned. Mrs MacDonald had had him boil more water than they had anything to put it in. He got on her nerves.

'Tell you what,' she cried, seized by inspiration, 'give us some music.'

Reverend Thomas gaped. The woman was mad. Then he followed her gaze. 'Oh,' he gulped.

The small organ was nearby, at the back of the church; if a bomb took a direct hit on the door . . .

'Go on, you can play, can't you?'

'Yes.' Instantly he wished he had lied and just as instantly felt guilty.

"Sorry," he said silently, but God seemed to have deserted him and didn't help one way or the other.

'Go on, we'll sing,' begged Winnie, desperate for a diversion.

Thomas, harassed and terrified, leaped to his feet and into the organist's seat, pedalling furiously. The music rose, swelling and sweet, then thundered over their heads, drowning out the sounds of catastrophe beyond the church walls. One by one their ragged voices joined in song. Then they forgot their fear and danger and sang their hearts out, Winnie's soprano voice soaring above the rest, between her pains, and Bridie's hoarse throat miraculously soothed as she sang contralto.

'That's better,' muttered Mrs MacDonald with satisfaction, raising her white head to listen as Reverend Thomas's light tenor came bleating through the echoes as he soft pedalled for a quieter hymn. They sang and they sang and music poured from the old church so that the ARP man who came for them, while an ambulance with no lights waited outside, rubbed his eyes and stared with bleary disbelief at the great dark pile, its walls glowing in the firelight, filled with songs to the glory of God while the legions of hell roared overhead.

'Stone the crows,' he muttered to himself, pulling at the heavy door nervously, 'I must be off me chump!'

They had just started 'Onward Christian Soldiers' when the door swung open.

'Blimey!' he told everyone in the warden's post later. 'Dressed up as priests, they was. This old girl sittin' there brandishin' an ear trumpet, a geezer playin' 'is organ like a maniac, and one of 'em 'aving a baby. And all singin' their 'earts out! I thought I'd gorn orf me trolley, I tell yer.'

The ambulance drove at a snail's pace through rubble, round vast craters and beneath burning buildings hissing steam from firemen's hoses. It took Winnie to Mrs MacDonald's house, miraculously undamaged, and then went on to Bart's, where it left Bridie.

In a rain of bombs, Winnie gave birth to a baby girl.

'Clara,' she murmured as Mrs MacDonald bent down to put the baby in her arms. The small house shuddered, its walls bowing under the force of a nearby explosion.

'Best get under the table, if you can.'

When Winnie was able, the old midwife helped her and the baby into the tiny space underneath the kitchen table. The three of them huddled together, watching flakes of plaster drift from the ceiling.

'You've come into a right funny old world,' Mrs MacDonald told the baby, who dozed on her mother's breast in the cramped, makeshift bed, 'but you're a beauty, my love.' And she pinched Winnie's cheek, smiling. 'You'll do nicely.'

Winnie smiled back, closed her eyes and slept exhaustedly until long after the bombers flew away and the all clear sounded over the unrecognizable hell that had shortly before been London's very own slums. The East End was, as David had predicted to April on the first full day of the war, well on its way to being flattened.

Chapter Thirteen

Ted met Sam Saul standing on the pavement, looking up at the front of Bridie's house in Hackney.

'Thank God!' cried the moneylender. 'Where is she?'

'Ain't she here?' asked Ted, standing beside Sam, both of them staring hopefully at the house, as though it would tell them.

'No.'

Ted scratched his cheek worriedly. 'It's terrible a bit further down. I've been to see if I could help. They didn't get this far over.'

'Do you think that's where she's gone? Stepney?'

Ted shrugged.

'Can't say. She might of. Eth's going to go mad when I tell her Bridie's not here.'

He scuffed his feet uneasily, wondering how he'd break the news.

'I've been going mad all night, stuck in a shelter with a bunch of lunatics, worried to death about her,' Sam complained gruffly. Ted gave him a sideways glance, wondering, and his thoughts flickered to Edward, on the icy waters of the Atlantic somewhere.

'And shouldn't you be lookin' after what's yours?' he asked pointedly.

'Mine's safe and well, over in Golders Green, thank

you,' said Sam stiffly. 'They didn't come anywhere near us.'

'Well, ain't you lucky?' snapped Ted.

Sam noted for the first time how the older man's bright blue eyes were dull and red-rimmed by sleeplessness and shock.

'It doesn't help if we fight, you know,' he said more gently. 'I only want to make sure Bridie's all right. I watched the planes from in Town yesterday evening and was afraid for her, alone over here. That's all.'

'Huh.'

Sam nodded, as if Ted had agreed with him.

'And now she's not here, I'm more worried than ever.'

'You ain't the only one.'

'Where shall we start looking?'

Ted licked his dry lips and glanced up and down the road.

'There's the Town Hall. You ask there about missin' persons.'

Sam turned on his heel and strode off. He paused and looked back. 'Aren't you coming?'

Ted walked reluctantly after him. 'I don't know as Ethel would like it, you and me . . .' he began.

'Ethel will want her found as quick as we can, won't she?' demanded Sam patiently.

'Yes,' said Ted, making up his mind, and they hurried off towards Bethnal Green, hands in pockets, eyes fixed on the pavement beneath their feet, casting no shadows beneath the dense, dusty cloud that blotted out the bright morning sun.

They had to wait in a long queue while mothers searched for children, wives for husbands, the young for the old. At last the tired, unflappable woman behind the desk found Bridie's name on a list.

'She's in Bart's,' was all she could tell them.

'What for? What's happened?' asked Ted.

The woman shook her head and behind him a child cried monotonously in the arms of a pallid young girl.

'I can't say. You have to get in touch with the hospital yourself. I'm sorry.'

'Thank you,' said Sam, pulling Ted's arm. 'We'll go there now.'

'But . . .' Ted persisted. The woman sighed. 'I'd tell you, but I really don't know,' she told him more kindly, looking up at his gaunt face. 'They don't tell us what is wrong, only where people are.'

The white-faced girl shifted the baby on to her other hip and clucked her tongue.

'Now if you don't mind . . .' The woman looked past him at the queue. Ted turned away and the girl stepped forward and rested the baby on the edge of the table.

'Shut up a minute,' she told it, and looked at the woman. 'I can't find me mum,' Ted heard her say in a tight, frightened voice. He stood back and listened.

'Will you come on?' growled Sam impatiently.

Ted hurried after him, down the steps, out into the street again. They turned in the direction of the hospital and Sam suddenly turned and called over his shoulder.

'What?'

'There's a cab.' he shouted again, running after it with great long strides, waving his arms and calling. The cab driver slid to a stop and stuck his face out of his window.

'I'm acting ambulance,' he called.

'Then can you take us to Bart's?' cried Sam.

'Get in.'

They hopped in and the cab drew off with a jolt. Sam

sat back and hitched up his trouser leg with satisfaction, and stared. Ted's gaze followed his as he caught Sam's small, involuntary sound.

'That blood?' Ted stared at Sam's hand.

The cabbie watched them in his mirror.

Sam fumbled for a handkerchief with his left hand.

'I ain't had time to clean up. The last one made a mess of me cab. Leg blown off.'

In the mirror their faces tightened and Sam wiped his hand on his bloodied handkerchief, sickened.

The cabbie dropped them off in front of Bart's and wheeled in a tight circle to go back to the East End.

'Hope you find her,' he called from the other side of the road.

'How would he know?' said Ted, surprised, but Sam was already halfway into the entrance, looking around him for someone who might know where Bridie was.

'She's been sent away. We can't keep patients here who can be treated elsewhere. We are sending people all over the place, to wherever there are beds. Preferably out of London, like your daughter-in-law.'

Ted pulled at his ear, disappointed and confused. 'You mean she's not here?'

The nurse nodded, feeling sorry for all the anxious, bewildered people who could not take in the terrible things that were happening to them.

'She's not here,' the girl repeated kindly.

'Then where is she?' demanded Sam.

'Ipswich.' The nurse ran her finger down a list. 'Ipswich General. She came in burned but able to be moved. You'll be able to visit her there.' She smiled encouragingly, seeing their faces fall.

'That's an awful long way away, Ipswich,' muttered Ted.

'She'll be in for quite a while, with burns. They've sent her somewhere that's not too pushed. We couldn't possibly keep her here.'

'Thank you,' said Sam abruptly.

'I'm sorry,' the nurse repeated, running the list of names slowly between her fingers.

'Thank you,' repeated Sam automatically. She watched them go through the swing doors at the end of her ward, jostled aside by incoming porters, carrying something on a stretcher that screamed very quietly and rhymically, underneath a blanket. Ted went white as a sheet. Sam grabbed him savagely by the arm, hustled him down the grey hospital stairs and pushed him roughly through the front doors, out once again into the gritty, unbreathable air.

Ted coughed into his gnarled fingers. Sam watched him unsympathetically.

'Pull yourself together,' he ordered. Ted slowly straightened up.

'At least we know where she is. That's all that matters.'

Ted gazed up the road to the mêlée of ambulances and running, hurrying, purposeful people channelling an endless stream of wounded into the hospital and out again. He shook his head at Sam's words.

'No, it ain't all that matters,' he murmured, half to himself. 'It's well beyond that.'

'Getting sentimental won't help,' drawled Sam, deliberately refusing to be drawn in. He was taken aback by the dull flush of anger that suffused Ted's sunken cheeks.

'You ain't got no right,' began Ted bitterly. 'You

don't belong here and you ain't one of us. You get back to yours and leave us to look after our own. You ain't wanted here, with yer patronisin' and yer big talk. I'd get home, if I was you, and leave us be, Mr Saul.'

Ted emphasized the 'Mr' with contempt and turned away from the tall Jew with a dismissive shrug of his shoulders. Sam gazed at the back of his threadbare jacket with cool, surprised eyes.

'Forgive me,' he said finally. Ted stuck his hands further into his pockets and ignored him.

'I simply meant that for us, Bridie was what mattered. I didn't mean to suggest that no one else mattered. Or that this didn't matter.' He nodded in the direction of the frantic comings and goings at the far end of the road.

'Bugger off!' Ted swung round, furious. 'She ain't your business. She's ours. Our daughter-in-law. My son's wife. If you had any decency you'd remember that.'

'Oh, I do. Believe me, I do.' Sam's heavy irony was lost on Ted.

'Then leave her alone,' he snarled, clenching his fists in his pockets.

Sam stared at him reflectively. 'I have few friends,' he admitted, beginning to explain.

'I ain't exactly surprised,' Ted remarked pointedly and turned his attention back to the ambulance bay.

'But Bridie has been one of them for many years,' continued Sam. 'I am her friend, too. That's by her choice and I don't see why it makes you so angry.'

'It just don't seem right. Not with my son at sea, and all this.'

Ted's voice was oddly muffled and Sam realized with shock and shame that he was crying.

'Look, I'm sorry.' He stood helplessly, watching Ted's shoulders heave as anger, outrage and despair fought with shame across his bony features.

'It ain't you, really,' confessed Ted, blowing his nose loudly on a scrap of grey material and looking embarrassed.

Sam nodded. 'It gets to you,' he agreed.

A fire engine screeched past the end of the road, barely missing an ambulance that pulled out of its way just in time. They watched in silence.

'I have some refugees at home,' observed Sam, as if they had passed pleasantries for the last half hour.

'That so?'

'Jews. They got out of Poland when it got bad there. There's a little girl and her sister who doesn't speak since the Nazis shot her mother and her grandmother in front of her, and beat her with gun butts when she tried to help them.'

Ted looked at Sam, the anger in his eyes fading into reluctant respect.

'We shaved their heads, of course, to get rid of the lice, and washed them, and they eat like starving animals, so they're getting a bit of flesh on their bones now. The father is a doctor. He knows what to do. That is, after we shaved his head. My wife's given him a knitted hat to wear while his hair grows and I think it mortifies him more than the lice did,' added Sam neutrally, carefully looking anywhere except at Ted.

'Does it now?'

'They'll stay, naturally. Long as they need to.'

'Ah.' Ted was thoughtful.

'So it's different in Golders Green, you see. Not better or worse. Different.'

'Hmm.' Colour was coming back into Ted's cheeks.

'Better get going then,' suggested Sam. 'I'll telephone Ipswich, shall I? And let you know?'

'If you would,' said Ted gruffly, clearing his throat. 'Eth would be glad.'

'Yes. Anything else I can do?'

'You done enough.' Ted spoke exhaustedly. 'You like to drop by, Eth'll thank you. Just so long as we know she's all right.'

'Right away,' cried Sam, his voice drowned without warning by the rising wail of the sirens. They looked up at the sky with one movement and over the horizon heard the drone of oncoming planes.

'Good God, again?' cried Sam. Ted hawked violently and spat.

They walked as fast as pride would let them after the crowds hurrying panic-stricken to the nearest shelter. They settled on to benches just as the first bombs whistled and crumped over towards the Docks and the crowded streets where casualties from the last raid were still being dug out.

'That's the enemy,' remarked Sam, watching brick dust trickle down the walls as blast rattled them like a giant playing with a tin can.

Ted hesitantly stuck out his hand.

'Don't do for us to fight, does it?' he muttered.

Sam shook the proffered hand heartily.

'Certainly not,' he said.

Ruthie, hysterical with worry, was waiting for Sam in the hall when he returned hours later.

'Why do you go over there?' she shrieked. 'You've no need. You got all your business moved. Why do you go back there? You'll get yourself killed and you don't think of me, or your son, or that poor soul upstairs. No one except yourself, Samuel. You'll kill me with the worry of it, and then you'll kill yourself.'

'I went to help a friend.' Sam spoke very quietly, in a way that made Ruthie fall suddenly silent.

'What friend? This the same friend you stopped out for before?' she demanded resentfully, afraid of the answer. 'What kind of friend you got over in those slums?'

'Her name is Bridie DuCane. We've worked together for years.'

'Her?' screamed Ruthie.

'Her.'

Fat tears welled in her eyes and ran over her rouged cheeks. 'You got another woman,' she howled.

'I have a friend,' said Sam icily.

Ruthie rocked to and fro, wailing uncontrollably.

'Be quiet,' Sam ordered in a reasonable sort of tone. 'You'll scare Christina.'

Ruthie gulped and put her hand over her wide O of a mouth, holding back her shrieks of dismay.

'I went to see if she was all right, since she lives near the bombing. She's been badly burned, it turns out, so I helped her father-in-law to find out where they'd sent her. We got caught in a raid and I've sat in an uncomfortable shelter for hours and hours and I'm tired and I want no more hysterics.'

Ruthie seized on the most important fact.

'Father-in-law.'

'Her husband's in the Navy.'

'So she's married?'

'She must be, mustn't she, to have a husband in the Navy?'

Tears dried on her blotched red cheeks.

'It's enough, Ruth. I'm exhausted.'

She twisted her rings in an agony of uncertainty. 'She

your mistress?' she blurted out, angry with him for seeing that she absolutely had to ask.

'No.'

Every line and angle and plane of Sam's face went cold and hard and impenetrable, so that Ruthie knew he told the truth and that it made him suffer. She went over to the sideboard and took out a glass decanter and a brandy balloon.

'Here, make the most of it; there's no more in the shops.'

Sam reached out and held her wrist. The glass trembled in her hand. 'I've told you the truth.'

Their eyes locked, then Ruthie's dropped. 'I know,' she said bleakly.

He let go of her and flung the spirits down his throat. 'I don't want to hear another word about it then,' he told her, and walked out of the room.

Outside the door Professor Nakiewicz stood frozen, his hand on the doorknob. He listened impassively to their quarrel, following their quick, accented words with difficulty. Only a pulse that beat in his temple, exposed by the hated woollen cap, betrayed his anger. Silently he let himself out of the front door and went for a long, reflective walk in the streets of North London, wondering what it was in human nature that made a woman so exquisite of soul, so *sympathique* as Ruth, marry a man who patently did not appreciate her. No matter how far he walked, nor how seriously he addressed the question, the answer remained a mystery.

Chapter Fourteen

Lizzie's telegram about his mother's having been hospitalized in Ipswich crossed with David's journey to London to see April. They'd arranged to meet in Whitehall and when he arrived she was waiting, sitting with her chin in her hand on the steps of her office. Seeing him coming, she jumped up and ran to kiss him lightly on the corner of his mouth. David reached for her, to kiss her properly, but she pulled away, glancing up at the second floor windows of her office where she'd left her boss putting on his jacket to go round the corner for lunch.

'Come on. Mr Stephenson will be down in a moment and then I'll have to introduce you and it will be boring.'

She slid away from him and began to walk away quickly.

'Hey!' he called. 'What are you doing?'

She flicked her cardigan at him, her yellow eyes teasing. 'Running away from you,' she called.

He dropped his case on the path and raced after her, catching her by the arm.

'Don't pull,' she protested, giggling.

He swung her round and kissed her hard. 'Now run away,' he told her.

'Don't really want to,' she murmured.

David ran a finger along her high cheekbone and down the curve of her jaw to her chin.

'I think you must have Slav blood in you,' he said. 'Something fierce, anyway.'

April smiled over his shoulder. She saw Mr Stephenson stop at the top of the steps, look round without seeing them and set off for Lyons.

She shrugged. 'Have to ask Mum. She's always talking about what the family goes back to. You going to get your case?'

'I can't ask someone I've never met.'

'You'll get it stolen.' She pulled away from him and walked back towards the case.

'Don't. It's heavy. Why can't I, April?'

She stood over his case, her hand curled round the handle. 'You can, but not yet.'

'Why not?'

'Dad doesn't like me taking people home.'

'Why not? What's he got against you having friends?'

She shrugged. 'He's a bit jealous, I suppose.'

'That's stupid.'

'You said he was stupid the first time we ever met.'

'I've had no reason to change my mind, have I?'

April turned and gazed up at him, her heart racing. 'No,' she murmured, 'he hasn't made you do that.'

She knew David was the one person in the world whom George couldn't bully, and he was hers. The thought of the two men meeting filled her with dread in case, despite her faith in him, David gave in, cowed like everyone else by George's implacable will. Then she'd have lost him. Lost her love. The thought drained the blood from her cheeks. David saw her go pale and was instantly contrite.

'Don't let's quarrel. We've only got two days.' He

picked up his case and she slipped her hand into the crook of his arm.

'Where shall we go?' she asked, looking up into his eyes with such trust that he decided on the spot to take her home to Bridie. She didn't belong in the East End, but a girl like her wouldn't hold his background against him, David told himself stoutly, for the hundredth time. Then he quailed at the thought of April's elegance, her slim, manicured hands, next to Bridie's torn, discoloured fingers and blunt ways. April might after all think them beneath her . . .

'It's the devil,' he muttered.

'What did you say?'

'I said, I promised to see my mother while I'm here. Why don't you come and meet her? If I can't meet your family, you could at least meet mine.'

'Oh.' April took her hand away, suddenly downcast.

'Don't you want to?' She constantly puzzled him; it was part of her charm.

'Yes, of course I do.'

'What's the matter then?'

'Nothing.' She pouted prettily. 'I like it the way we are, that's all. Just us.'

'We can't keep on pretending our families don't exist, April. And, anyway, if we're going to get married, we have to tell them.'

April's eyes clouded. Tell George? So he could spoil it?

'Do we?'

'Don't be silly, of course we do.'

'I suppose so.' She sighed and he looked curiously into her face because she sounded so sad.

'What have you got against it? Why are you making it into a problem?'

'I'm not.'

'You are,' he took her arm firmly 'and there's absolutely no need.'

'You're hurting me.' Suddenly she was petulant and he felt guilty.

'Sorry, didn't mean to. I don't understand you.'

April frowned at him.

'Why don't you want to come and see my mother?'

She rubbed her arm sullenly. 'I did, until you started hurting me.'

David stared at her, bewildered. He snatched up his case. 'Let's go and get it over with.'

April trailed behind him to a bus-stop, dragging her feet. 'I only said I liked it by ourselves.'

'You didn't just say that.'

'That's all I meant.'

'It's not all you said by a long chalk.'

'You read things into things.'

'I don't.'

'You do.'

To April's fury. David began to grin. A bus drew up. They got on and found seats alongside each other but separated by the aisle.

'What are you laughing at?' she demanded, anger concealing how afraid she was that it might be her.

'Is this a lovers' tiff?' he whispered in her ear, leaning across the aisle, lurching as the bus rounded a corner.

April flushed. 'Don't be stupid!'

'I detest being called stupid.' David straightened up angrily.

'You're quick enough to call other people it, like my father.'

'Only when they are,' he retorted coldly.

They sat sulkily across from each other, not speaking

again, until the bus drew up at their stop in Bethnal Green.

As they got off the alert went, the sirens winding their long drawn out howl all across London. David took her hand anxiously, their quarrel forgotten.

'I can't see or hear any planes,' she shouted. 'Is your house far?'

'What?'

'Is your house far?'

'No.'

'Let's run.'

'We should find a shelter.' David, not used to the bombing, sounded frightened.

'Come on. If we're quick we won't have to stay in a smelly shelter. They're horrible.' She dragged at his hand urgently. 'Come on.'

Nearby, ack-ack guns in the park started up an ear-splitting barrage, shaking the ground beneath their feet. Tracer streamed high in the sky, delicate, harmless-looking.

'We should go to a shelter,' yelled David, but he began to run.

'Have you got a cellar?' April called breathlessly.

'Yes.'

'Down there, then. Look, they're here. Quick.' As they ran, the first planes appeared, tiny dark arrows shooting in high curves straight for them, over the east coast. David began to slow, holding a stitch.

'Come on,' urged April. 'David, quick.'

He could see his mother's gate. The oncoming bombers droned louder and louder, the drone become a great roar overhead as the first planes reached them. Swastika'd wings blackened the sky as they reached Bridie's porch. Pressed flat against the wall, David fumbled with shaking hands for his keys, his voice drowned as the first stick of bombs sent up the gas holders just off Stepney High Street with a bang like the end of the world.

'You've got a bloody death wish, April,' he screamed.

She leaned out of the porch, watching the planes go over, her hands over her ears.

'We're used to it,' she yelled, lips moving inaudibly in that terrible noise.

He flung open the door and they tumbled inside, the walls of the house bowing with blast.

'Mum?' David roared up the stairs, his hands to his ears.

'Feels empty,' shouted April.

'Cellar.'

He ran down a short passageway, flinging open a door under the stairs.

'Mum?'

It was pitch dark and a chill came up from below.

'Not there. Get down anyway,' shouted David.

They half ran, half fell, down the cellar steps. Above them, the house swayed and steadied itself, creaking and dribbling plaster in small, whitish trickles.

They stood in the dark.

'You there?' asked David shakily.

'Of course I am. Is there any light?'

He groped his way towards her and she felt him shake his head.

'What's down here?'

'Not much. You stay there.'

As his eyes got used to the dark, he could just make out the walls with their shelves that used to hold pickles and preserves. In one corner Bridie's tiny supply of coal was swept into a tidy pile. He tripped on the broom leaning against the wall and barked his knee, cursing. Then he trod on a pile of something rough and giving.

'There's sacks,' he cried with relief. 'A whole pile of them. Come over here.'

April felt her way across the cellar and almost fell on top of him.

'We can spread these out.' A fierce red glare seeped past the ill-fitting lid of the coal hole.

'We'll be able to see by the fires.' April sank on to the sacks and gazed at the bright round ring of flickering light.

'You're a cool one.'

David resented her calm courage; she wasn't an easy one to take care of.

'You don't panic, these days.'

They sat on the sacks, mesmerized by the orange and red glowing fitfully beyond the coalhole, feeling the heat of it.

'Is this what it's like, then, the Blitz?' David asked diffidently, feeling it was all the wrong way round; he should be telling her.

'All the time.' April sounded oddly indifferent.

'How do you stand it?'

'Don't get much choice.'

Glass exploded and shattered above.

'Sounds like Mum's windows gone.' He put his arm round her shoulders. 'You all right?'

'Scared stiff. I'm always scared stiff. Every night.'

He peered at her closely in the hellish glare. She didn't look scared stiff, she looked calm and composed. Her serious, thoughtful air reminded him of the statue of Our Lady in Mother Superior's office at The Falcon.

Schooldays . . . they seemed another era. The old school was probably already a heap of smoking rubble. April interrupted his dismal thoughts.

'What?'

'We might as well get comfortable. This'll go on all night.'

'Jesus!'

'You sort of get used to it. But not really.'

'When do you sleep?'

'Couple of hours in the morning.'

'I never realized . . .'

'People outside London don't.' A huge explosion shook the cellar floor and the coalhole brightened. Their ears rang and buzzed painfully.

'Sounds like another gas main's gone up.'

April saw he couldn't hear her. They sat, holding hands tightly, listening to fire crackling and roaring, and the long, rumbling crash of falling buildings. Dust seeped through the coalhole in little puffs. April coughed and David started to pat her back, then his arms were round her, pulling her down next to him on to the heap of sacks.

'We could die in this,' he said clearly, his lips against her ear. 'Tonight. Couldn't we?'

She shook her head, seeing his eyes glitter, so close to hers in the firelight.

'Or just one of us be killed.'

'Stop it.'

'I want to make love to you.'

She shivered.

'Now. In case we never have another chance.'

She lay inert in his arms.

'April?'

'I don't think . . .'

'I love you, and I want to marry you.'

'We shouldn't. What if . . . ?'

'What if we die, and we've never made love? I couldn't bear it.'

He buried his face in her neck, whispering things she could feel against her burning skin but could not hear. The house rocked above them, settling back, solid, withstanding the winds of war that raged round it. The cellar got hotter. From his secret corner under the preserves cupboard, The Pope crept out and sidled across the smooth earthen floor to the sacks, sniffing cautiously at David's sprawled legs. He moved between them, burrowing into their warm bodies, insistently.

'It's our cat,' said David, raising himself on one elbow.' 'Fancy him getting down here.'

April felt the small, furry body press against her own. She stroked his back, feeling the tiny vibration as The Pope began to purr, and her eyes stung with unexpected grief. For all of them. For everything. All the pain and destruction and death.

'I couldn't bear it either,' she whispered back. 'If you died, I'd die, too.'

'I love you so,' he groaned.

'I love you.'

He heard the words he had longed to hear and gathered her into his arms.

Mid-morning showed itself by a faint rim of daylight around the coal hole, waking them from the dead sleep that followed the all clear.

'They'll be back. We'd better get up.'

'How do you know?'

'They always come back,' she said matter-of-factly.

'April?'

She turned to look down at him, lying back, watching her.

'I love you.'

'I love you, too.'

'It's all right, then.' He spoke contentedly, smiling up at her.

'Yes, it's all right.'

They washed and looked to see if there was anything to eat in Bridie's kitchen while The Pope came in from the garden and stalked around as if no one had fed him for weeks.

'What's this?'

David put his head round the kitchen door and said, 'A money belt.'

'Do you wear it?' April picked it up and swung it in her hand. 'It's heavy.'

He watched from the doorway as the damned belt swung idly from the end of her fingers. It was the moment he'd dreaded.

'It's my mother's.'

He tried to sound casual but the words stuck in his throat, choking him.

April looked surprised. 'Is it so dangerous round here that she has to keep her money in this?'

David cleared his throat, swallowed and took the plunge. 'It's her business. She's a moneylender.'

He waited, holding his breath, for her outburst of disgust. April's gaze dropped to the belt again, simply nonplussed.

'Oh,' she said, at a loss. 'How interesting.'

'Not in the least.' He came into the room, snatched the belt from her finger and threw it into the bottom of the dresser, closing the door on it.

'I wonder where your mother is,' said April.

He leaned on the dresser, his back to her, his shoulders quivering with nervous laughter.

'What on earth's the matter?' she demanded. 'You're shaking.'

'I've been scared of this for months and months.'

'What? The bombs? You get used to them.'

David shook his head, almost crying with hysterical laughter.

'Your finding out we're not posh, like you. That my mother's a loanshark in the slums . . . I thought you'd ditch me.' He turned to face her, his face flushed. 'I've been terrified to tell you. You've no idea.' He began to laugh again. 'And all you said was "How interesting", because it didn't mean a damn thing to you, did it?'

'I do think it's interesting,' she began earnestly, and was brought up short by his great cry of mirth.

'Don't,' he gasped, 'you'll make it worse. Oh, April, you're priceless.'

Her lower lip went out ominously.

'No, I mean . . . oh, don't be cross. I can't help laughing. I'm not laughing *at* you, I promise. I've been the stupid one, April my love. You've no idea.'

'I don't know what you're on about,' she said stiffly, 'and I'm hungry and worried about your mother.'

The thought sobered him up.

'I'd better go and find out what's up. She's probably with Ethel. That's my grandmother.'

'What shall I do, then?'

'What about your parents?'

'I often stay in the shelter at work. They'll take it for granted I'm there. It's Mr Stephenson who'll fuss because I'm not in.'

'Then I suppose you'd better get back,' he said, hoping she'd say she didn't have to go.

'I think I had.'

'I wish you could stay.'

She came and slipped her arms round his waist, her head on his chest.

'Me too,' she sighed, 'but I can't.'

Next door had collapsed in a neat pile of rubble.

'That must have been that tremendous bang. We were fantastically lucky,' said David, awed.

He waited at the bus stop with her. 'You look like you spent the night in a cellar,' he murmured, teasing.

'Doesn't matter,' she said stoutly. 'Most of London spent last night in a cellar. You country bumpkins know nothing. You look pretty rough yourself.'

David grinned.

'Anyway, I hope you find your mother,' she said seriously.

'I'll give you a ring at the office.'

The bus, winding its way in a great detour through flattened streets full of craters, took an age to come. On the way into town, the sirens went again.

'Stops 'ere,' shouted the driver.

'At least he can't blame me,' sighed April, thinking of Mr Stephenson and her empty desk as she sat out the long, boring hours of another raid in a shelter not far from Bishopsgate.

'Your mum's in Ipswich,' Ethel told David, stewing tea on a little fire just outside her front door. She explained what had happened as best she could.

'And the gas is off again and we got no electric this afternoon. So we make do with this.' She poked her embers with a bit of stick and flames licked the blackened kettle. She perched her broad backside on a pile of bricks and rubbed her legs. 'Give me gyp,' she remarked sourly.

'You living all the time like this?' David tried to hide his horror.

Ethel pulled a resigned face and shrugged. 'Mostly.'

'Where's Ted?'

'Down the Post. 'e's on duty 'til tomorrer mornin'.'

'And leaves you here like this? By yourself?'

'I go down the shelter at night. It ain't very nice down there but Ted made me promise.'

'I should think so! Why don't you leave? Go to the country?'

'Don't you go sayin' that to Ted,' she cried scornfully. 'We ain't leavin'.'

'But you can't live like this for long.'

Ethel's face drew in on itself, suddenly hostile, an expression David had never seen on his grandmother's stout, good-natured features before. 'Don't you nag, David, 'cause I ain't goin'.'

He sighed. 'I have to go back tomorrow. Is there anything I can do to help?'

'Come an' keep me company down the shelter, if you like.'

David regretted his offer instantly, Ethel saw, and gave a short laugh. 'No, I thought not. You go on, I'll be all right.'

Sipping tea that tasted of sour smoke, David looked up at the leaning roof of Ted's small house and depression flooded over him.

'Landlord come round wanting rent the other day. I told him to sod off, greedy bugger,' remarked Ethel.

She'd never sworn in front of him, not as far back as he could remember. Hearing that depressed him more than the sight of all the bodies and rubble put together.

Ethel, who had once seemed to his child's eyes indestructible, was old and sick and worn out and no longer herself. Because of the war. David hated it.

Chapter Fifteen

'It's a grand life, if you don't weaken.' Mr Churchill's voice boomed across the garden from the wireless in the morning room. Down by the leafless blackcurrant bushes the elderly George struggled to make some kind of tolerable sleeping arrangement in the Anderson shelter. Eileen, in middle age a birdlike woman with thinning pepper and salt hair and a resigned expression, had tried to help but retreated to her kitchen after he had unleashed his impatience and ingratitude upon her.

'Grand life,' he muttered frustratedly over the planks of wood with which he planned to make some kind of bunk. It was a futile task. 'Have to get a carpenter,' he shouted in the direction of the kitchen.

'That might be rather difficult,' observed Eileen. 'They're all patching up houses.'

'What *can* you get?' he scowled irritably at the Anderson. 'Even at Christmas.'

'It isn't too bad actually,' called Eileen. 'I won't get a turkey, dear, you have to be royalty to get hold of one, but Lord Woolton says we should try rabbit instead.'

'Carrots!' snorted George irrelevantly. He continued to grumble inaudibly and then shouted: 'Rabbit – have a word with Jim. His grandson keeps rabbits. Ask if they'll fatten one up for us.'

'They're pets,' exclaimed Eileen, shocked. 'You can't fatten pets. Anyway, how fat does a rabbit get in ten days?'

'In the last war people ate rats and cats,' bellowed her husband. 'No use being sentimental over pets.'

Eileen paled. 'I couldn't eat a rat, George.'

He disappeared into the small humpbacked shelter and came out again, sucking his thumb.

'Splinters.' He stared longsightedly at his hand and tried to get out his spectacles from his jacket pocket, opening the case awkwardly with one hand. The liver-spotted flesh came into focus and he picked out the fragment of wood with care. 'Isn't April home yet, Mother?'

Eileen's lips tightened unconsciously and she sniffed. She had a wonderful repertoire of sniffs; they spoke louder than words.

'Not yet.'

'She should be.' George sounded fractious. Eileen watched his portly figure disappear once more into the interior of the Anderson before he came down the short path to the house. He frowned heavily and her heart sank. When April displeased him it could sour the atmosphere for days on end.

'She might have popped in to Rachael's. In any case, she's old enough to look after herself,' she said, getting out of his way so that he could wash his hands at the sink.

'Mr Shickelgruber is flattening London and my daughter works there. Taking care of herself is irrel-evant,' George said pompously, refusing to pay the respect due to Mr Shickelgruber's career change of name and call him Mr Hitler. He felt strongly that the former was more apt, and despite the affectation, stuck to it. Eileen sniffed again. 'She's been peaky just lately,' added George. 'Needs a holiday.'

'We all do,' Eileen told him crossly. 'What with one thing and another. But it's war and it's Christmas and we'll just have to make the best of it, like everyone else. Are you going to finish those bunks?'

'Thing's too small. It's no good.'

'I could have told you that, you old fool!' muttered Eileen when he'd taken his paper and gone to doze over it in the drawing room. She glanced vengefully up at the splendidly framed portrait of his first wife that hung – solely, she felt, to spite her – over the morning room chimney breast. The original April was, after all these years, still enshrined in the house and in George's heart. Her painted golden gaze stared complacently over all Eileen's doomed efforts to oust her. Eileen knew perfectly well that she was second best. Second best to both Aprils. Always had been. There was, she knew with gnawing certainty, nothing whatsoever to be done about it.

Sniffing, she began to lay the table for supper, tweaking the blackout straight when she noticed a chink of light glinting against the windowpane, showing the near darkness of the late December afternoon through which April should be picking her way home from work, stumbling through blacked out winter streets from the bus stop. No wonder she got home late; the old fusspot never went out in it, so how would he know? Eileen slapped silver spoons on to the table and carefully cut half an ounce of butter into three exactly equal portions. Then she sat down with a sigh by the small fire and waited.

April came in half an hour later. She did look peaky, thought Eileen, watching her take off her coat and warm her hands at the fire. Her cheeks were pink from cold air and brisk walking, but her great golden eyes looked dull. Brassy, thought her mother, with a certain satisfaction; even perfection could go off. She glanced spitefully up at the portrait which never aged, and sniffed.

'Are you all right, dear?' she asked, hiding her thoughts with the ease of long practice.

'Yes,' said April, not looking at her.

'Go and call your father, will you?'

April went to the morning room door and shouted: 'Daddy.'

Eileen winced. 'It's not very ladylike to yell,' she grumbled from the kitchen. 'I wish you wouldn't do it.'

'Who says I want to be a lady?'

'Well,' began Eileen, 'we've tried to bring you up as one . . .'

'All right, Mummy, I know.' April poured herself a glass of water and sipped it.

'. . . but you don't seem to care . . .'

'Mummy,' sighed her daughter.

Eileen sniffed righteously. 'You'll see,' she said, having the last word.

They sat around the heavy mahogany table, slippery beneath Eileen's starched white cloth. There was a pervasive scent of lavender polish, not quite smothered by the smell of cooking and food. April, exactly halfway between her mother at one end of the table and her father at the other, pushed potato around on her plate and pretended to eat. The clock ticked, deep tick tocks, tick tocks, that she remembered from her earliest years. George scraped his knife across his plate; Eileen pulled a pained face and sucked her teeth in disapproval. Silence hung like a pall.

April bowed her head lower and wished, as she did almost every evening, she'd never come home after leaving college. But war had threatened, comfortable rooms were hard to find and to afford, and the solid, faded luxury of home was there to be had. So she'd come back. George had been overjoyed and Eileen quietly furious. April speared a piece of potato savagely. Her parents gazes bored into the sides of her head and she felt the familiar throbbing ache of their invasion.

'Aren't you eating, April?' George stopped chewing with his mouth full, shunted the food to his cheek and spoke around the bulge.

'George,' said Eileen repressively. He ignored her.

'Something wrong at work? You haven't looked quite well lately.'

'No. Mr Stephenson says I can take on a junior if I can find one, we've got so much work. Otherwise it's all just the same as usual.'

'They can pick and choose these days, can't they?' remarked Eileen. 'Madge has just seen her maid off to do war work. Told Madge it was better pay and she'd be lucky to get anyone to replace her at the wages,' she added gleefully.

'They've been wondering in the paper whether Mr Bevin will call up women. If he does, Stephenson could find it hard to find a youngster.' George avoided any reference to maids, a sore point since he had dismissed their own when she'd demanded a rise in her wages or she'd go to join up. No rise, George had said, unmoved. She'd joined up.

'Might they call me up?' The idea appeared in April's head like a bolt of lightning.

'Yes, but Stephenson could get you exempted, I'm

sure, seeing as he handles war contracts . . . you're already doing war work, aren't you? This time round, anyway, it'll only be young girls, twenty or so. Not married women, of course, or anyone with children. Though you might have to do something in your time off if you don't sign up.'

'Or expecting,' added Eileen to complete the list of exemptions, intrigued by the idea of April disappearing into something useful. The WAAF, perhaps, where she might meet an eligible officer and get married at last. Eileen sniffed hopefully.

'That lets me out then.'

The remark went unnoticed for several very long moments. It hung, improbable, impossible, in the lavender-scented air above the supper table. Silver knives and forks caught the light and shone richly, then clattered heavily as George and Eileen put them down and stared at their daughter's bowed head.

'I beg your pardon?' said Eileen.

'I said, that let's me out then.'

'Are you thinking of getting married?' asked George, flatly refusing to understand.

'Yes. I'm pregnant.'

Eileen's breath hissed between clenched teeth. George glanced up at the April who hung on the chimney breast, his mouth half open as if to demand an explanation.

'You remember David?'

George pushed away his plate abruptly. David's one visit to Ilford had not been a success.

'I'm going to marry him.'

George lifted his head and slammed his fists down on the table; glasses jumped and cutlery rattled.

'No!' he roared.

'You can't stop me.'

In the sudden silence they listened to the faint roar of distant planes circling central London. Behind the blackout the red glow of the burning city lit the horizon from end to end. George looked as though he was holding his breath. Slowly he turned brick red. Eileen wondered with a kind of detached curiosity if he was about to have another stroke.

'It sounds bad tonight,' said April desperately. Her voice sounded shrill in her own ears.

Her parents stared at her, speechless.

'I heard an awful story,' she went on desperately, to fill the lengthening vacuum. 'You know they're shovelling rubble from the City into Hackney Marshes? Well, this little girl was out with her mother walking over to Walthamstow, and the next thing she knew, the child had a hand with a ring on it, trying to take it off. The mother had hysterics. The child had got it out of the rubble.'

'You're mad,' shouted George, going purple.

April suddenly put her hands over her ears, her elbows leaning heavily on either side of her plate of congealing food.

'Don't,' she whispered.

'Slut!' The word hissed round her like a whiplash. She shook her head. 'You marry that man and you'll get not a penny from me.' George breathed heavily, his jowls shaking with fury.

'I don't care,' April muttered, refusing to look up at him.

'You will, my girl,' murmured Eileen. 'You will. You'll care all right, when you find yourself on the street with his brat.'

'I won't be on the street. I have a good job and David will be a doctor when he's finished his training. We can manage.'

George laughed, a long, hoarse guffaw.

'Manage? How can he manage a wife and child on a student's money? And you'll not have a job when Stephenson finds out. It'll ruin both of you.'

April raised her head and stared at him with shadowed, defiant eyes. 'I don't know, but we'll find a way.'

'To think of all the money I've spent, giving you a good start,' he changed tack bitterly. 'You've had chances most would give anything for. Might as well not have bothered. Good money after bad. All I ever wanted for you was the best, and look how you repay me.'

April looked, and remembered otherwise. She remembered long, implacable silences with which he leant on her, longing for love, until she gave in; the months of monosyllabic confrontation over her determination to stay on at school after other girls left, to go to Oxford, to be a bluestocking. She chose to follow in his footsteps, to be an engineer. He adamantly refused her a livable income until she compromised and took languages. The other April had been a fine linguist.

'Women don't make engineers,' he'd stated as fact. George's facts could not be argued against.

'Women don't want to go tying themselves up with that treacherous profession. You go and learn French or something, girl. Something ladylike.' He'd spat savagely into the fire, dismissing her. And that had been George at his best.

Now a scowl crossed his face. He pushed his plate away and ordered curtly, 'Tea, Mother.'

Eileen pressed her lips together. 'You're being a bit hard,' she said surprisingly. April turned to her, amazed. Eileen smiled, pleased by George's anger at his fallen angel. Fallen indeed. She began to stack plates.

'Give her a chance. Let her make her mind up. If you carry on like this she'll run away and you'll likely never see her again.'

April's mouth dropped open in astonishment. 'I thought you'd be the one to throw me out,' she mumbled, the trap too subtly woven over the years to be recognized for what it was.

'My own daughter,' Eileen crooned reproachfully. 'I don't know how you could say such a thing, I'm sure.'

She sniffed forgivingly. 'You're all upset.' She got up. 'A nice cup of tea is what we all need.'

George, out-manoeuvred, glowered. 'Your mother's soft,' he said harshly. 'A fool to herself.'

'I'm sorry, Daddy.'

A spasm of grief and jealousy gripped George and he staggered with a short burst of pain. Eileen dropped the plates on the draining board and came to the kitchen door. He was staring openly at April's body, his expression unreadable.

'When I think of that fellow's filthy hands on you, I could . . .'

'What, George?' asked Eileen quietly.

'Kill him,' he shouted, and barged out of the room like a wounded bull.

The two women listened to him storm down the hallway, slamming his study door behind him.

'Good gracious,' said Eileen. 'Well, you'd better tell me all about it, young lady. It's a nice pickle, this is.'

The Aprils had got their comeuppance now, in a time-honoured way, and Eileen intended to relish every delicious moment.

* * *

The next day April telephoned David from her office.

'And?' he asked.

'Awful. He's furious.'

'Bad as you thought?'

'Worse. He says he'll disinherit me if I marry you.'

'Maybe you'd better listen, then. It's the only way you'll be rich . . .'

'One day you'll be a doctor.'

David cut across her.

'. . . so perhaps you had better listen,' he insisted. 'You're giving up an awful lot.'

'What about the baby?' she cried, dismayed.

'We don't have to get married.'

The line hummed and hissed.

'Don't you want to?' she whispered.

'I don't want you to miss out on a fortune, love. It's nothing to do with wanting to get married or not.'

'It's your baby. I thought you wanted it as much as I do.'

'I do.'

'Then why are you saying these things?'

'I'll never be rich, April. I know the kind of world you come from. You might wish you'd stayed in it.' David realized as the words came unbidden, words he hadn't even countenanced until this moment, how unsure he was of her despite the baby. 'Are you certain you want to marry me?'

'Do you think I'd have . . . let you . . . if I didn't?' she cried, frightened.

'I know.' Nevertheless he felt hemmed in by misgivings, paralyzed by doubt.

'I love you, and I really thought you loved me.'

'April, I do. I do! It's not that.'

'Well, what is it then?'

David rubbed his brow. 'I don't really know.'

'I do love you.'

'So do I. Let's just get married,' he said, cutting across all his doubt and confusion, impatient with himself, 'soon as I can get a licence.'

'Oh, yes! They can't say much if we do that, can they?'

'I really don't know.' He suppressed his anxiety, remembering George's sullen, hostile glances when they'd all sat round the table for tea; the heavy silences broken by April and Eileen's anxious chatter. 'I wouldn't like to think what he might do,' he admitted.

'Leave Daddy to me,' she said brightly. 'He'll come round.'

'I hope to God you're right.'

That evening George sat sullenly at the head of the table, eating steadily and ignoring their small talk. Eventually it dwindled into silence in the face of his baleful presence.

'I have made a decision,' he announced, making them jump.

'Have you, dear? What about?' asked Eileen blandly.

He shot her an irritated glance and laughter trembled on April's lips, betraying her nervousness.

'You'll live here,' he announced. They waited. Eileen folded her hands beneath the tablecloth and prepared to sit him out but April couldn't bear it.

'Who do you mean exactly?'

George gave a small, triumphant smile. 'I've been thinking that this house is too big for just the two of us, if you were to go. We've ample room to make a flat upstairs. You and your . . . husband . . . can live there, with the baby when it's born. You and the child will be safe while he finishes his studies. You will not leave here until he is in a position to support you properly.'

'But I'll never see him!' cried April. 'He can't live here. He has to stay in the college. He's miles and miles away and there are no trains. You know he can't come here. We can't do that.'

'Then you will have to tend for yourselves. If you want to be reckless, you'll have to take the consequences,' he went on, hoisting himself out of his chair. 'Don't expect me to subsidise you, now or later on.'

'Daddy . . .'

Eileen coughed to hide her dismay.

George held up his hand.

'Talk to him. Let me know by the end of the week.'

'I can't!' cried April.

'That's up to you.'

'Tell him where to put his help,' suggested David angrily. 'We'll manage. There's plenty of odds and ends of work I can do. There's a milk round going that would fit before and after lectures. And you could find something, even with a baby. Everyone's short of labour so you're sure to get something. Let's get married at once, and tell him to go to hell.'

'I thought you minded about the money?'

David thought of her fortune and stifled a deep sigh of regret. 'I do, for you. But I'll make my own, don't you worry.'

'David?'

'Yes.'

'There's one other thing that makes a difference.

232

He's offering to pay your fees if you agree to the arrangement.'

The prospect of having enough to live on in comfort sat seductively beside the freezing misery of the early morning milk round in January.

'He's offering to buy me off, is what he's offering.'

'I'm sure that's not it. He just wants to be sure you finish your training, so we have a secure future.'

A high whinny of laughter came down the line. 'Secure future?' he shouted incredulously. 'What are you talking about? Your father's addled your brains, April, if you think staying in London is secure. Or maybe you haven't noticed the Blitz?'

'He's trying to help. He wants to make it easy for us.'

'Is this what you want?'

The line sounded suddenly dead in the silence.

'The trouble is,' she admitted, ashamed, 'every time we go over it, I end up thinking he's right. It's not what I want, but I can't see how I can have what I want. I should have thought, only I didn't. Did we?'

'No,' said David drearily. 'At the time, thinking was not uppermost in my mind.'

'No,' she said in a very tiny voice, 'mine neither.'

'Well, Daddy wins,' he said stonily, capitulating.

'David? When you see him, please, please don't talk about communism.'

'I shall discuss the coming invasion, like everyone else. That do?'

'Perfectly. And getting married.'

'Of course.'

That evening he got very, very drunk.

The family doctor pulled April's dress down over her

knees and said, 'You can put your things back on now, Mrs Holmes.' He used to call her April, but now she was married he was more formal.

David sat waiting in the office, for once on the patient's side of the desk. He looked up as Dr Sheridan entered and washed his hands at a sink in the corner.

'Did you find anything wrong?' he asked nervously.

Dr Sheridan came round the side of his desk and perched on the end of it, folding his arms.

'You've been married two months?'

David nodded.

'And April was three months pregnant, so far as you knew?'

David nodded again. 'That's why we brought it forward.'

Dr Sheridan appeared to ruminate. 'I've known her since she was born. A lovely girl. Always was beautiful, even as a baby. Apple of her father's eye. Clever, too. Inclined to be a little excitable, though. Sometimes a little too much so. She needs a calming sort of environment, d'you see?'

'No,' said David, feeling confused about what the old doctor was getting at. 'I don't think I do.'

'Ah. Do any psychology, do you, these days?'

'A bit, later on. What has this to do with April's pregnancy, Doctor?'

The old man steepled his fingers 'Thought you might have done a bit of stuff on hysteria.'

David frowned.

'The absence of a heartbeat and April's minimal weight gain, Mr Holmes, is not due to anything wrong with her pregnancy . . .'

'But that's excellent news! Then what is it?'

'April isn't pregnant, you see,' said the doctor gently.

The room spun for a moment.

'You mean . . ?'

The old man nodded sympathetically. 'Family's inclined to it, you see. Eccentric, one might say. Father's a failed genius and mother's a sourpuss, if you'll pardon my frank speaking. April hasn't had an easy time between the two of them. Perhaps now she's married, she'll settle down; stabilize. Have a real baby, is my advice, and give her plenty to keep her busy.'

David sank his head into his hands.

'Come now, don't take it so hard,' Dr Sheridan said briskly. 'You've got a very beautiful wife; an intelligent, lovely girl. Nothing to worry about. You mustn't overreact, you know. Does no good.'

'No,' said David.

'What are you two talking about so earnestly?' April, fully dressed, came into the room. 'Do you know what's the matter, Dr Sheridan?'

'I'm advising your husband that the best thing the two of you can do is have a baby straight away.'

April looked baffled.

'But I am!' she cried. 'What do you mean?'

'No, my dear,' the doctor told her bluntly. 'You are not.'

April looked in consternation at David. His eyes met hers, full of accusation.

'I am. I was. I've had no monthly periods. I've got fatter. I must be.'

Dr Sheridan shook his head. 'Those signs were probably wishful thinking.'

April bit her thumbnail and looked from one to the other. 'What do you mean? David, what does it mean?'

'A phantom pregnancy. It wasn't real.'

She went white. David took a deep breath, stood up and held out his hand to the doctor. 'Thank you, sir. We'll try to follow your advice.'

'What was his advice?' asked April in a little girl voice, wary of her husband's mood. They walked down the street, not touching each other.

'To have a real baby, and in future try and keep a careful check on what's real and what's imaginary,' rasped David.

Her small, cold hand crept into his. 'I'm sorry,' she whispered, very low. 'I didn't know. I truly thought . . .'

He looked at her little porcelain face, pallid with shock and fear of him, great bronze eyes pleading.

'It's all right.' His anger suddenly drained away, leaving love and pity so entwined he no longer knew the difference. 'Home,' he said firmly, steering her towards the end of her parents' wide street.

Leafless trees stood black against dark, steel grey clouds. When the fires began to burn again that night, they pointed black fingers at the night raiders, picked out against the shifting beams of searchlights and the great red glow. David and April, hearing the guns thundering on Wanstead Flats half a mile away, crept closer under their warm blankets, timidly reaching for each other.

'I do need you,' she murmured, her breath warm on his cheek. 'I'm terribly sorry. Perhaps it happened because I need you.'

Need or love? he wondered sadly. Need, he thought, feeling her warmth seeping into him. George. Eileen. This dreadful, cold house, full of secrets and silences. My poor little needy love. His heart ached for himself and for her, because he knew now that what she said was true.

Chapter Sixteen

A dull end-of-January sky lay leaden over the city. Everywhere people looked battle weary. In between twice daily bombing raids, and mostly during them as well, trucks and lorries scooped up the smoking, steaming, stinking remains of the City of London and shot them into barges or dumped them in the Hackney marshes. The demolition trucks came roaring through what had been the streets of the East End in a never ending column, grating on people's tired nerves and keeping them awake if the bombing didn't because double summertime meant it was light unnaturally late of an evening, and the trucks kept running.

Mrs MacDonald wrote to Bridie:

There's a truck goes past my front door every four seconds. So much rubbish! They're shovelling London into those marshes at such a rate they'll be filled up and flat by the time they've finished. And when they tip a sweetshop in, you should see the kiddies scramble, grabbing everything they can find. And when they tipped Hatton Garden in, there were people looking for diamonds for days and days. I don't know that they found any, though.

The Luftwaffe seems to be leaving us in peace

these nights, but now we've got the clearing up from the daytime. I wonder, sometimes, how much more we can take. We're all just worn out.

Bridie read her letters and longed to see them all, often lying awake through her long nights, even when the pain was a mere whisper of its former self, dreading that she would not get back in time – that someone would be gone . . . maybe more than one. She brooded on her fear, hiding it from the nurses, sometimes seized by mounting panic that she'd never get home in time.

Visiting Bridie took an awful lot of fixing; people talked about nothing but the date of the invasion and wouldn't plan anything. 'What's the point?' they demanded, and looked apprehensively at the stormy winter skies.

'They're only waiting for three and a half days of good weather,' Lizzie told Sam when he called in one evening, frustrated by his failure to get to Bridie, hoping for sympathy.

'Who are?'

'German High Comand. Who else?' she snapped, her nerves frayed to shreds.

Sam thought about it. 'What's the half for?'

Lizzie shook her head. 'And you know what else they say?'

He waited.

'It was on the wireless,' she cried, full of indignation, 'that when they've settled in and taken everything over, they're going to sterilize all our own men, and make our young women have a German baby every year. I never heard anything so outrageous. Do you think it's true?' she asked fearfully.

Sam thought of some of the other unthinkable ideas the Germans had put into practice and shrugged uneasily.

'I hope not.' He pulled a pained face and tried to make light of it to cheer her up.

'I couldn't bear it if Bridget . . . and then there's the chemicals and gas and that. They are saying the most dreadful things are coming,' she tailed off miserably.

'At least it's quiet at night just now. Come on, Lizzie, don't grumble. Could be worse.'

'Could it?'

'Much,' said Sam, though his flesh crept at the warnings in the newspapers. 'Oh yes, indeed.'

'But that's just what I'm afraid of,' she sighed querulously.

'We all are,' said Sam Saul, taking a bundle of paper out of his pocket. 'And I'll just burn these, if you don't mind.' He screwed up the bundle and dropped it on the fire.

'Are those pamphlets?'

The Germans dropped tons and tons of leaflets as well as bombs.

'Yes. Telling us in detail what they'll do to the Jews when they get here,' said Sam calmly.

Lizzie's hand flew to her mouth. 'I'm sorry,' she cried contritely. 'I didn't think. It must be even worse . . .'

'Not worse. Merely a different twist of the screw.'

'I can tell you a story about that. It'll cheer you up,' said Lizzie, smiling gleefully. 'Johnathan was called to an incident the other day where there'd been a dogfight over a football match. There were about four thousand people watching, and a German came down in his plane. Well, this big cheer went up, and they all went rushing out to see it, because it only fell one street away from the pitch. Well, they called Johnathan because the pilot was badly wounded and by the time the ambulance got there, by all accounts, he'd worked himself into a right old state.'

'The German?'

'Yes,' Lizzie went on. 'So Johnathan tries to help him, and the German gets very abusive and shocked, and starts swearing and spitting at Johnathan. So they put him in an ambulance and Johnathan takes him to hospital and gives him a sedative and a blood transfusion. Well, he calms down for a while. Johnathan goes back to check on him after he's had a couple of pints of blood, and he's acting up again.' Lizzie began to giggle, pink and shaking with laughter. 'So Johnathan says: "Now, my boy, you must settle down. You've been over excited, but we've put a couple of pints of good Jewish blood inside you and I hope it will mend your manners." He said the German looked at him in sheer horror then burst into tears. Don't you think that's funny?'

'Not very,' said Sam Saul coldly.

'Oh dear, I'm sorry. You're getting very sensitive.' Lizzie wiped her eyes on her apron, trying not to laugh any more.

'Sensitive!' Sam exploded furiously.

The laughter died on Lizzie's face. 'I have to laugh,' she said, 'or I'd go mad.'

'I know,' Sam said icily. 'But somehow I can't, not any more. You're quite right. I've become sensitive.'

Several times Sam Saul thought he'd got his plan off the ground, but each time there was either a particularly terrible raid, so people couldn't get away on any pretext whatsoever, or his black market contacts let him down, or the new tyres the vehicle needed to be driveable simply weren't available. He began to think he'd never get going.

Some weeks after April discovered she wasn't pregnant, however, Sam picked up his telephone, which by some miracle was working, and triumphantly began to ring round. Then he called on Ted and Ethel, whom he found hammering boards over their sagging window frames.

'It's a charabanc,' cried Sam with one of his most winning smiles, pleased with himself fit to burst. 'It'll take all of us. And the petrol's in it. All you have to do is get away from whatever you should be doing next Saturday.'

Ethel and Ted stared at him as if he had dropped from the sky.

'How'd you do that, then? Where'd you get petrol?' demanded Ethel.

Sam tapped his nose and shook his head.

She looked up and the down the desolation of their street and broke into a great grin.

'I'm comin' fer sure,' she told him. 'I could do with a day out.' Her face clouded. 'But what I can take Bridie, I don't know, I'm sure. We've nothing left, have we, Ted?'

He stared at his leaning, windowless house, its small roof half blown off, patched with a bit of tarpaulin.

'Not a lot, duck.'

'I've got champagne,' announced Sam. 'It'll do from us all.'

Ted scowled but Ethel's eyes sparkled.

'Who else you takin', then?' Ethel thought champagne was best not argued about.

'Everyone!' announced Sam expansively. 'My Poles

are coming for the day out, and maybe my wife. David can get down by special leave and has got himself a lift, so he'll be here. April, of course.'

Ted's face darkened. He and Ethel glanced at each other, but nothing was said. Bridie had not been well enough to travel for the brief register office wedding and her letters had said little about her thoughts on the hasty marriage.

'Mrs MacDonald will come. She's said she'll make a collection of bits and pieces of rations and make us some sort of picnic for the journey. Lizzie, Johnathan if he can get someone to take his duty, Bridget, and . . . wait for it!' Sam drew a scrap of paper out of his pocket and eyed Ethel gleefully. 'I had a phone call: Edward's got three days in London while his ship's refitting up North. He's coming, too.'

She clapped her hands to her cheeks and whispered: 'Oh my Lor'.' Ted went a worrying purple colour, as though he'd had a stroke.

'He's safe, then?' cried Ethel, when she'd got over her surprise. 'Where is he?'

'One of the yards.' Sam consulted his bit of paper. 'Greenock. He'll be up there several weeks, overseeing work, and he can get away for three days. It was hearing from him made me bang one or two heads together – a charabanc this weekend or I had a debt or two that would suddenly get urgent.'

'Edward rang you?' she asked.

'Why not? Sensible fellow.' He picked up a couple of Ted's nails and tossed them around in his hand.

'Well, I never.'

'I don't suppose he knows much about what's goin' on here,' observed Ted. 'Don't let on, do they?'

'Only so the Germans don't know all the damage

they're doing,' said Ethel, anxious to avoid bitter recriminations against the government.

Ted opened his mouth to argue, then, catching her eye, shut it again morosely.

'Him and David see more eye to eye these days, don't you, duck?' Ethel wanted to keep the peace. Ted, disillusioned, inclined these days more to the left; David, shocked by human suffering, inclined more to the right side of the left. Their new accord had helped paper over the family's disappointment and mystification about the suddenness and secrecy of the wedding.

'If you all congregate here, seven o'clock Saturday morning, I'll pick you up,' Sam said heartily, to distract Ted from his gloom.

'And when's Edward comin' then?' asked Ethel. 'Does he say?'

Sam consulted his scrap of paper. 'Gets into Euston on the sleeper at six o'clock Friday morning and goes back by the same Sunday evening.'

'Oooh,' she keened with joy and shuffled out to make her fire in front of her doorway. A hopeful rat nosed round the remains of previous fires and scuttled off under the great piles of bricks that sprawled for as far as they could see. Ethel hissed angrily after it and threw a stone in its direction, bending to rub her aching legs.

'You'll stop for tea?' she called.

Sam winked at Ted as her slippers flip-flopped back in again. 'That would be very nice. Thank you kindly, Ethel.'

'Thank *you*, kindly,' she said firmly, pulling the top off her tea caddy to peer inside at how much was left. 'We've a lot to thank you for, Mr Saul.'

He grinned. Edward's arrival gave him the perfect excuse to go to Ipswich without in the least upsetting his newfound harmony with Bridie's family.

On the sleeper, Edward slept like a dead man, half woke to the sound of milk churns in Carlisle and then slept again until his train pulled into Euston, on time, at six o'clock. In weak morning sunlight the whole place was deserted and quiet, every platform piled high with mail sacks, vegetable crates, wooden boxes and milk cans. He found a washroom with hot water, shaved and tried to smarten up. Then he went outside.

For months on end he had seen only the sea; the wide, unending, restless sea. At moments, in the remorseless exhaustion of the Atlantic battle, there had been moments of unutterable beauty. On watch at first light, he had watched the fading stars in the dawn sky brightening over a milky sea, the whole picture bathed in the calm silence of a new day of clear weather. The sun would follow, creeping over the horizon, suffusing the whole atmosphere with luminous gold, tinting the pastel blue peaks of the ice edge with rose. At night the sea and sky were one vast darkness, illuminated fitfully by the northern lights flickering over the glossy surface of the heaving sea.

London came as a shock, oddly crowded and empty at the same time. Posters were everywhere. Edward studied them, bemused. 'Careless talk costs lives'; 'Is your journey really necessary?'; 'Don't be a Food Hog'; 'Give a woman your place in the shelter'. Round a corner he found; 'Britain can take it'.

'Take what?' Edward muttered, and by way of answer looked up at the long, elongated rows of barrage balloons, hanging low in the sky. He saw gun emplacements and their tired crews; the curious emptiness of the dusty, cluttering streets. He walked fast, keeping an eye open for a cab. None passed him as the sirens wailed, the sparsely poulated streets emptied altogether. He walked on, shouted at by a warden who ordered him into the nearest shelter and angrily told him he should be wearing a tin hat and carrying a gas mask.

'I've got neither,' growled Edward, and went to shelter in the nearest pub, which had its doors open for the publican to sweep the floor into the street. He passed the time looking at a map of Europe tacked on to the wall which showed the present state of Germany's conquering advance; it was a sinister picture and England looked terribly alone. The publican, blearily rubbing his eyes, chatted as he wiped his tables.

'Been away, then?'

'At sea.'

'Long?'

'Eight months.'

The publican grunted sympathetically. 'Changed a bit then.'

'Some,' said Edward.

'Where did you come in? St Pancras is gone. Victoria's a shambles, and most of the rest is pretty much of a mess,' he remarked thoughtfully. 'I keep waiting for this place to go. Do you know,' he went on more cheerfully, 'someone said there's a dinosaur hanging out of a window in the natural History Museum in Kensington, looking like it's climbing out. Makes the kiddies squeal, I should imagine.' He chuckled and turned his cloth around to a cleaner bit, leaning over to swab down another table. When he turned back, the closing door caught his eye; the sailor had gone.

The journey home depressed Edward and Ethel's tearful hugs did nothing to raise his spirits. A sense of disbelief weighed on him as he sat, trying to chat, in the half-ruined house he'd known all his life. He felt he no longer belonged.

'We're better off than many,' Ted said, misunderstanding his despair. 'You'll see, son. There's a lot have to live down the shelters, in only the clothes they got on when they was blown out. We ain't got it so bad.'

Ethel poured dried egg carefully into a bit of milk and water, stirred it and lit the gas under a blackened frying pan. 'Fried egg coming up,' she called cheerfully. Edward looked at the mixture without enthusiasm.

'But how can you live in this smell?' he asked, sickened by the sour odour of burning homes, furniture and bodies. The East End was one huge bonfire, he thought, constantly extinguished only to be just as constantly relit.

'It's the incendiaries that's a nuisance.' Ted lowered himself into a wooden chair on the doorstep and Edward saw with a pang how he had aged. 'Firestarters. You can put 'em out easy enough, if you can reach 'em. But they get in the gutters and that's a devil of a job.'

'King Canute,' muttered Edward. 'Why in God's name don't you and Mum get out? You can't go on living like this.'

'Don't you start now, Edward.' Ethel put a plateful of the something she called fried egg in front of him.

'What's it going to take for you to see sense?' he demanded.

Ted shook his head. 'I ain't goin' while I've got my roof over my head. We manage.'

Edward looked up at the cracked ceiling. 'You call this having a roof over your heads. It's been blown off.'

'We've got the gas back on,' Ethel pointed out.

Edward chewed on the dismal egg.

'And we've got our place in the shelter, nice and comfy. The men play cards and I help mind the kiddies. It's quite nice.'

Ted turned round unseen and stared disbelievingly at Ethel, but she had her elbows stubbornly on the table, watching Edward's every mouthful.

'It's company, anyroad,' she added defiantly, feeling Ted's silent laughter.

'He'll see for himself when the moaning minnies go, won't he? It's very cosy, son, very cosy.' He winked at Ethel, heaved himself out of the chair and took down an overall. 'I don't let her stay here at night. Raid or no raid, your mum goes down the shelter. You can see her down, son. I'm on duty.'

'That's something I'd better get clear,' said Edward, swallowing the greyish stuff on his plate with an effort.

'What?' demanded Ethel.

'I'm not going down the shelter, Mum. I'm going over to Hackney and, if I have to, I'll shelter in my own cellar. I'll be back first thing.'

'Oh,' she said, disappointed. 'There's lots of people I've told you're comin'.'

'You're not stoppin' with your mother?' asked Ted, taken aback.

'No, Dad.' Claustrophobia squeezed painfully in his chest. He couldn't go down a hole, like a rat. Too many people; a sweating jumble of bodies; airlessness. He saw the reproach in Ted's face and wished he hadn't come home to disappoint them so but stayed with the sea and the sky where Death, now more familiar than them, was dwarfed by the sheer vastness of Nature herself.

'Well, I'm blowed,' Ted muttered.

'I'll see you in the morning.'

'The world's a funny place when you don't stop with your mum.'

'Sorry, Dad. I can't.'

Wordlessly, Ted pleaded with him. Too much had changed. Edward shook his head and his father turned away.

Ethel held court down the shelter while up above the night was quiet. 'You'd think he'd want to spend time with us, comin' all this way,' she said, bewildered and hurt. 'I don't know him, no more. It's like a stranger comin' home.'

'It must be hard for him, having Bridie away. All that time at sea and then not to see her . . . it's rough, Ethel. He must have been so worried about her.'

'We're all so worried about each other, there's no choosin' between us,' answered Ethel dolefully. 'But you can't help it.'

'Don't do no good, though, does it. Oh, blow!' The woman dropped a stitch and turned the grey sock she was knitting round to pick it up again.

'I still think it's not right,' muttered Ethel. 'No matter how you look at it, it ain't right.'

Chapter Seventeen

'The King is still in London,' they sang at the tops of their voices as the charabanc bumped and lurched its way around cratered, potholed roads and made April feel sick. She listened to them all singing and joking with a sinking heart. Once out of London, Sam, who was driving, had to stop at every junction and crossroads to debate the way. Ruthie, wearing a martyred air and her best fox fur, sat just behind him, chaperoning the Poles, who watched the whole Rake's Progress with baffled fascination.

April, sitting across from her, studied the older girl's lovely, expressionless face, half hidden by glossy wheat-coloured hair that hung forwards across her hollow cheeks in a short bob. April wondered about the terrible experience Sam said she'd had. Christina looked as out of place as April felt; she wished she could talk to her but they said the girl didn't speak.

'They've taken all the signposts down so that the Germans don't know where they are,' David told her as Sam stopped and ruminated yet again.

'What Germans?' asked April obtusely, looking out of the window.

'As in invasion. And spies, parachutists, what have you.'

She looked irritable. 'I know that. They did it ages

ago,' she said snappily, her mouth puckered unhappily.

'What's making you so bad-tempered?'

She slipped her hand into his and he squeezed it. 'Meeting your mother. I'm scared to death.'

David pulled her to him, hidden from the others by the tall seatbacks, and kissed her.

'You'll like her.'

'Will she like me, though?' April twisted her wedding ring anxiously.

'Why ever shouldn't she?'

'Ted and Ethel don't,' she said wistfully.

'Yes, they do.'

She shook her head stubbornly.

'What makes you think that?'

'Nothing. Just the way they are when I'm there. Sort of formal. Look at them now – they're never all jolly like that with me.'

'It's just because they don't know you yet. They'll be all right eventually.'

April looked at him and he saw she really was miserable.

'They're East Enders.' He saw she didn't understand. 'They're very tight knit, don't take outsiders in easily. Family is everything. But now *you're* family, so you're part of us and they'll love you anyway. Once they accept you, they'll do anything for you. You'll see.'

'That's a bit like Rachael,' said April. She looked round at Bridget, leaning over the back of the very back seat, laughing at something. 'I think they'd rather you'd married someone like that,' she told him sadly.

'Me? Never,' David laughed.

'I bet they even had someone in mind.'

He confirmed her worst fears.

'I think my mother and Lizzie would have liked it if Bridget and I had got together, but we grew up like brother and sister and there was never any chance of it.'

'They'd have liked it all the same.' April craned her neck round again and briefly watched dumpy little Bridget, now conducting a raucous rendering of 'The Lambeth Walk' from the back seat, wispy fair hair pushed back behind her ears, her round, open little face rosy with excitement and laughter, brown eyes sparkling.

'She ought to be plain with those looks, but she isn't.' April sank back into her seat and sighed.

'You know something?' David offered.

'Go on, then.'

'I've always wanted to get away from it. All the get togethers and living in each other's pockets. It's nice in some ways, but I get stifled by it.

'I don't know why, but I always had this idea that one day I'd leave it, that somehow I didn't belong like they did. If you're content to live all your life in the same small place, it's fine. But I'm not, so you see I'd never have stayed anyway.'

'That's funny.'

'Is it?'

'No. I mean, what you've just described is what I always wanted. I used to dream that I was Rachael's child really, that there'd been a mix up and I really belonged to her and Gordon. Only when I was young, of course.' She wriggled with embarrassment at her confession and looked at him anxiously. 'Don't laugh.'

'I'm not. If I'd had your parents, I think I'd have dreamed the same sort of thing. Nothing funny about it.'

'Anyway, I think they blame me for taking you away,' continued April.

'Now that *is* silly. I'd already gone to medical school.'

'I didn't mean like that.'

'Why are you working yourself into a state? Just be yourself and you and Mum'll get on nicely. Stop fretting.'

'I just hope she likes me.'

'Shut up.'

David begn humming to the last verse of the song and then began to join in properly.

"You see," thought April, "you're one of them whether you like it or not." She thought of George's wordless sulk, ever since she'd got married, in the still house heavy with unspoken words, and tried to imagine her parents sitting, swaying through the Essex countryside, in a battered old coach. Suddenly she giggled. They'd think the whole thing awfully beneath their dignity. She felt for David's hand and he twined his fingers around hers and looked down at her, smiling encouragingly.

'Don't worry. Everything will be all right.'

Timidly, holding his hand tight, in a barely audible voice April began to sing.

'You can't all go in at once. Rules are two visitors to a bed.' Sister barred the doorway and eyed the horde with astonished disapproval.

'Oh, go on,' someone called. 'We've come such a long way.'

'If you'd told me so many were coming, Mr Saul, I could have warned you.' Sister stood unyielding, her hand firmly on the door jamb. 'I suggest Lieutenant DuCane goes in to see his wife, and you can all wait in the corridor. I'll send someone to find an extra chair or two.'

'Right you are, Sister.' Sam shooed them all back and let pass a couple of people who were obediently visiting their relatives two at a time. Edward disappeared through the swing doors.

'Give him a chance to see her on his own,' ordered Sam. Ted and Ethel bridled and he said hastily, 'I think I can get us all in, in a bit.'

Ethel sat down on a hard chair, looking extremely put out. 'Who does he think he is?' she hissed. Ted affected not to hear.

The swing doors swished again and Sam vanished. Christina, wide-eyed, held Ruthie's hand while her father looked around the British hospital with interest. David and April sat side by side further down the corridor, on a wooden bench.

'Just look at us all. We've probably got more doctors and nurses out here than they've got in there,' remarked Lizzie, laughing. The Professor smiled courteously.

'They let us in,' he agreed. 'Surely.'

Sister's gaze was steely and Sam's breezy confidence began to desert him.

'Are you trying to bribe me?'

'Yes,' he agreed readily. 'Please. It's taken me ages to manage this trip. London is such a mess, you've no idea out here in the country how impossible it is. We couldn't come before, we've been too tied up with trying to stay alive.'

'I'm sure you exaggerate.'

Sam put his paper packet of nylons on her desk gently and stood up. The little cubicle was stuffy and reeked of a whole lot of smells he hated: carbolic, bedpans and sweat.

'It would be impossible to exaggerate what is happening to London, especially the part these people come from,' he said in a quiet, measured tone. 'I would not have the words. They do not exist. We have never had to describe such things before.' He paused thoughtfully. 'No, perhaps the trenches in the last war were much the same; impossible to visualize if you hadn't been there.'

Sister regarded the bag of stockings expressionlessly.

'Mrs DuCane's relatives and friends would do her more good than all your medicines,' Sam suggested.

'I didn't say you couldn't see her,' Sister observed neutrally. 'I just wondered why you felt it necessary to bribe me.'

'To make sure we got in.'

Sister crackled with starch as she leant forwards to touch the little parcel.

'I would have let you in anyway, when I'd cleared enough space round her bed and seen that no one else was put out by so many visitors. I couldn't have you all rushing in like that. I've twenty-five patients to think of, Mr Saul.' She withdrew her hand. 'Take your stockings.'

He shook his head. 'Have 'em anyway,' he said cheerfully.

Sister pursed her lips and frowned. 'They're black . . .' The look in her eyes betrayed her.

'Oh, go on. What's a few stockings?'

'A lot when you can't get them for love nor money,' sighed Sister, looking down at her ankles longingly.

'It's a deal then,' he cried.

'No, Mr Saul, not a deal.' He heard suppressed amusement in her voice. 'I simply will allow you all to visit, when Mrs DuCane's husband has had a little time with her. I don't need a deal.' She smiled stiffly.

Sam winked cheerily. 'Anything you say, Sister.' He jumped up and was out of the cubicle in one bound, heading down the ward.

'Mr Saul.' Her voice froze him in mid stride. 'Outside.'

'Yes, ma'am.' Sam grinned guiltily and allowed her to direct him with her eyes back into the corridor.

'Yup. We can all go in when she says,' he announced to the row of enquiring faces.

"Who does he think he is?" thought Ethel again. "He's practically the only one here who isn't related to her and he's stagemanagin' the lot of us like he owned her."

'Oh,' whimpered April, wringing her hands.

'Don't be silly.' David looked up as the swing doors swished open again. Sister stood, a dark blue figure guarding her territory jealously.

'You can go in in a moment,' she said. 'And please be quiet so as to minimize disturbance to other patients. We don't usually allow this kind of thing, but Mr Saul has been very persuasive.'

Christina stared impassively at April, who had suddenly clasped her hands together as if praying. Her husband whispered something that made her half smile through the strain clearly written on her face. No one noticed how Christina's clear, blank eyes dilated each time they drifted over April's husband's face. His fair hair and pale blue eyes, behind their gold-rimmed lenses, the lean, predatory features and his slight, wiry build made him practically the spitting image of the young, jackbooted, leather-coated Nazi who had shot her mother in the face and laughed as he thrust his gun up the girl's dress in a jeering, obscene gesture of contempt, beating her brutally away from the dying woman. Christina did not so much remember as recognize a familiar nightmare, with deep, unconscious, perfect recognition. She looked away from the pair on the bench and gave a small, silent sigh.

'You can come in, now.' Edward stood in the doorway. 'I've told her you're all here and I don't think she knows whether to laugh or cry. Mum?'

Ethel led the procession down to the far end of the long ward. Faces on pillows turned to stare, and then with a cry of joy Ethel saw Bridie sitting, dressed, in a low armchair by the side of her bed and ran to hug her.

'Can I? Does it hurt, duck?' she asked, holding back in case it did.

'No, I'm nearly better.' Bridie held out her arms and Ethel hugged her carefully.

'Oh my, I've missed you,' she cried, sitting on the edge of the bed and mopping at her face with the corner of her cardigan. 'Just look at me.' She half laughed, tearful with joy.

Ted bent down and kissed Bridie's cheek.

'Glad to see you,' he said gruffly. Bridie looked past his shoulder at her son who stood hand in hand with an extraordinarily beautiful girl. She looked so frightened, thought Bridie, as if she was about to bolt. Over Ted's shoulder she said, 'This must be April.' He stood up and moved to make way.

'This is April, my wife, Mum.'

'Hello, Mrs DuCane,' whispered April.

Bridie gave her a quick, piercing look and then she was patting the bed beside her and saying in the kindest way, 'Come and sit here, April, and tell me about this shotgun wedding of yours.'

'Oh!' April perched nervously on the side of Sister's creaseless counterpane and gasped, 'Were you awfully disappointed? We are sorry. Are you terribly cross with us?' April felt her tongue run away with her from sheer terror of saying the wrong thing. She stopped herself with an heroic effort.

'I was more disappointed not to be there than cross.' The poor girl looked frantic. Bridie let her be for a moment, watching the subdued mêlée around her bed, everyone unpacking gifts and offering each other chairs and shuffling into a great semi-circle around the bed.

She smiled, having caught the eye of a woman she didn't know. She was short and stout and had dyed hair, elaborately pinned and tucked around a brightly painted face. She clasped the hand of a young girl who looked vacantly over Bridie's head.

'Mrs Saul,' hissed Ethel from her perch on the end of the bed, following Bridie's gaze.

Her eyes widened with amazement and she held out her hand to the woman.

Ruthie touched Bridie's dry, scar-smooth hand and the two women looked at each other with unconcealed curiosity.

'Pleased to meet you. My husband told me about your terrible accident,' said Ruthie. 'Glad to see you're better.'

'Yes, much,' said Bridie, looking at Christina.

'She's a Pole,' said Ruthie. 'A refugee. She doesn't talk.'

'I wonder if she will, one day.' David leaned forward curiously and looked into her eyes with clinical interest. Christina met his detached gaze and to their horror opened her mouth and screamed soundlessly. Ruthie hastily threw her arms around her, pulled Christina to her fur-clad bosom and rocked her to and fro. 'We don't know,' she mouthed over Christina's head, at their surprised faces. Then she was whispering rapidly in Yiddish and the terrified girl seemed to hear.

'Good Lord, what happened?' asked David.

'Sometimes I think she sees things, but they are in her mind only.' The Professor bowed apologetically to Bridie and touched his daughter's short hair.

'Christina?'

She burrowed herself deeper into Ruthie's arms.

'Is best to wait. She comes back to us soon.' Her father, thought Bridie, had the saddest eyes she had ever seen. 'She seems to trust Mrs Saul,' she said gently, wanting to comfort him.

The professor nodded. 'She is wonderful woman,' he breathed and all of a sudden his eyes were full of devotion and not so sad.

"Oh, my word," thought Bridie, and glanced at Sam who was busily unpacking a cardboard box that had appeared from nowhere. Lizzie put a basket of oranges on the arm of Bridie's chair and kissed her cheek.

'Smell these,' she grinned. 'Johnathan found them in the Portobello Road the other day. Don't know how he got them, and I didn't ask. He said they were for you and no one else could touch them. Sends his love and says get well quickly. And you do look well, doesn't she?' she appealed to the rest.

'She'll do, considering,' observed Ethel.

'Is there much scarring, Bridie, love? I can see hardly any.' Lizzie asked outright the question on all their minds. Bridie held up her hands and they saw the unnaturally shiny, purple flesh. She moved her fingers stiffly.

'They've stretched the tendons so I'm almost back to normal. Because I had my hands over my face, they burned but my face is hardly marked at all. My back is, where the stones were so hot and I lay against them.' She laughed tonelessly. 'But I haven't turned into a freak, thanks to Winnie.'

'She would have come, but she's left London, with the baby. She's had enough . . . bombs and what have you. She got herself evacuated somewhere safe in Northumberland. She said ever so sorry and she'll write.'

'Is it worse, then, in London?' asked Bridie.

Ted shook his head. 'Not worse, love. Just too much for someone with a baby; gone on so long it's too much for anyone, if you really want to know.'

Edward's gaze stayed steadily on his wife as they all claimed her. She said something else to April, who smiled nervously and turned to David in appeal; he felt rather than saw Ethel watch and stiffen. Then there was a loud pop, like a gunshot, and they all jumped in alarm.

'It's the invasion,' squawked Bridget.

Heads turned on pillows all down the ward, but Sister didn't appear.

'Only teasing!' Sam held up the frothing bottle and cries of amazement and 'Champagne! Oh, my goodness' covered April's words.

'We – I thought I was pregnant. In the end, I wasn't,' she blurted to Bridie. 'That's why we got married so quickly. David was cross, but awfully nice about it, when we found out I wasn't after all.'

'I thought it might be something like that.' Bridie spoke calmly.

April's heart banged against her ribs. 'My parents are

furious. I thought you would be, too,' she whispered under cover of the excited opening of several more bottles and handing round of glasses brought in in Ruthie's capacious black bag.

Bridie's shrewd grey gaze seemed to see right through her. 'I'm sorry about the baby, dear.'

'There never was one,' said April bravely. 'It was all a false alarm, the doctor says. I know he thinks I'm a bit neurotic, but I was so sure. I truly thought I was. I felt pregnant. Well, I've never been pregnant, but I felt like I thought it would be.' She picked at the counterpane, filled with shame.

'I knew I was having David and I'd never been pregnant, either. It's something a woman knows, isn't it? Maybe you had a very early miscarriage. I remember Mrs MacDonald – over there – telling me a woman could lose a baby early on and never even know it.'

'Dr Sheridan never said that,' cried April, feeling a great weight lift off her at her mother-in-law's suggestion. 'It could have been that, then, couldn't it? Perhaps I'm not neurotic after all.'

'That's a big word for a small mistake. It's a doctor's word. I'd take no notice, if I were you . . . unless you make a habit of it.'

Bridie smiled crookedly, watching her through half-closed eyes, wondering how much David had told her. She suspected that he was probably dissembling with his wife. Bridie had mused a hundred times on the mystery of the disappearance of the word ILLEGITIMATE from his birth certificate, never daring to ask for the truth. April seemed to know nothing about it.

Bridie pushed her gloomy thoughts away, adjusted her cushions behind her and sat up to take a glass of champagne from Mrs Saul's plump hand.

262

'Here's a toast,' cried Sam above the chatter. The other women in the row of white and blue beds watched, enviously scenting the wonderful smells of oranges and apples and wine.

'To you, Bridie, and to your coming home soon.'

'To your coming home.' They all raised their glasses and sipped. Ethel coughed and her eyes watered. Edward patted her on the back and she gasped, 'Oh my, it's strong.'

'Another toast.' They looked at Edward expectantly.

'To victory,' he offered, unhesitating.

'Victory!' cried David, taking April's hand.

'To the end of the bleedin' Blitz.' Ted held his glass out towards Sam for a refill. He'd rather have beer, but it was nice enough stuff.

'Amen,' cried Ethel and downed her glass determindly. Sister glanced at the clock in her cubby hole and remarked to Staff that they'd have to go as soon as they'd finished drinking and to make sure everything was cleared up the moment they'd left or Matron would find out, and then there'd be trouble.

'Yes, Sister,' said Staff, wondering where the old bat had hidden her sense of humour all this time; she was really quite human.

'Someone's left a parcel,' she said, picking it up.

'I know all about that. I'll deal with it.' Sister almost snatched it out of her hands and pushed it into her pocket, avoiding Staff's surprised eyes.

'Yes, Sister,' she said, giving a sideways glance at the bulge in the pocket, underneath the immaculate apron. 'I think I understand.'

'The sluice needs scrubbing,' remarked Sister repressively.

Staff sniffed champagne on her way to the sluice and

a grin spread over her face. So that was it! Even Sister had her price. Staff laughed and caught the orange someone threw her. She ate it, sitting with her feet up on the sink she was supposed to be scrubbing, knowing no one would come and check, and enjoyed herself no end.

The journey home was long and slow. Bridie had cried, despite herself, when the time came for them to go. Her tears dampened everyone's spirits. Then there was the dull glow on the horizon as they got nearer London; the Luftwaffe had called while they were away. Everyone felt heady after drinking champagne, and depressed at going back to the city. Edward sat alone at the very back of the charabanc, with his eyes shut.

'Are you asleep?' whispered Bridget, leaning over the empty seat next to him.

He half opened his eyes and shook his head. 'Just thinking.'

'Do you want to be left alone?'

He appeared to consider carefully, then said, 'No.'

She slipped into the empty seat and he closed his eyes again, seeming to doze off.

'I'm sorry we were all there, too,' she said.

Edward shook his head. 'It didn't matter.'

'Yes, it did.'

'It can't be helped.'

'Couldn't you have stayed with her?'

'Yes.'

Bridget waited patiently.

'But it would have made it worse. I might have said things to her . . . hurt her.'

Bridget sat quite still, her head bent attentively, her eyes fixed on his strong, sensitive, calloused hands, brown from exposure to the sun and wind. 'Things that are better not said . . . if you are about to leave, that is.'

'Things like being afraid?' asked Bridget. 'You'd have left her knowing how afraid you are?'

Edward ran a hand over his face and said, 'I'm ashamed of it. There's that, too.'

'It must be terrible, out there. We read the shipping losses, of course, but I suppose we try not to think about what it really means. Until you meet someone who is part of it.'

'It's extraordinarily lonely, you see, at the same time as being so crowded you could kill each other for a bit of space sometimes.' He leant his head back on the seat and she watched him try to find words. 'There isn't a private moment aboard ship. We practically live in each other's skins. We have to; that way we survive. There is the most incredible trust; we've all saved each other's lives, one way or another, and yet it makes you feel so alone, knowing you're going to die. The middle of the ocean is the loneliest place in the world. We sail and sail and it's like we're going to fall off the edge of eternity sometimes. It goes on and on, and there's not a soul . . . very Ancient Mariner!' He laughed apologetically.

'You feel very small, until the bloody Germans start flying over, dropping bombs on you, or something like the *Tirpitz* or the *Hipper* starts shooting at you, and then you feel like a sodding great target on the surface of the water that they can't possibly miss. A lot of the time they don't; we've lost a hell of a lot of ships. And that's without the U-boats shoving torpedoes up your backside. The Germans are frightfully good at it, sinking ships,' he finished gloomily. He thought of the asdic, going blip, blip, blip, day and night, until no one noticed – except when it stopped.

'They sink anything that floats. They don't discriminate. Supplies, refugees, warships . . . doesn't matter.'

'I've read that, too.'

'I have killed a lot of people.' He said it suddenly and matter-of-factly and Bridget sensed that it mattered appallingly to him that she should not judge him.

'Yes,' she said simply. 'How could you not?'

'When Sam gave me champagne this afternoon, it reminded me of something.'

Bridget waited again.

'"For dead men, deadly wine". Swinburne. You see, I read poetry these days,' he mocked himself gently. 'There's a superstition that a sailor dies if a wine glass is allowed to ring. I kept being tempted to run my finger around the rim until mine sang.'

'Challenging fate? Your fear?'

'In a way.'

'Something else?'

Edward closed his eyes again and then sighed deeply. 'The only other person I ever told is Bridie,' he began.

Bridget put her hand gently on his sleeve. 'Don't tell me unless you are sure.'

He nodded, as if agreeing something with himself. 'I used to have a dream. Quite often. I had it before I met Bridie, and it was the oddest thing, because she was in it. She was a kind of wraith, or spirit, and in the dream she called to me to cross a deep river. As I crossed, it turned to ice and my body was trapped in it, cut to pieces. Then I'd wake, very frightened, and I always went back to sleep and I always dreamed that my soul was high above the river, looking down on my trapped body. Then I'd get further and further away from the

Earth, up into space, led by this spirit. Led into the heavens, as it were.' He lay back, still with his eyes closed. 'After I met Bridie, the dream stopped. It was as though I was free of it.'

'It started again?'

'Yes.' The word was only a sigh.

'It is telling you . . .'

'That I am going to die.'

The charabanc swerved round a corner and jolted Ted awake. He'd been snoring with his mouth open and Ethel nudged him and told him to shut up.

'All right duck,' he mumbled, and promptly dropped off again. Halfway down the coach Christina stared unblinkingly at the back of David's head; he reached up once or twice and rubbed his hair, feeling her gaze as a kind of prickle, but he didn't turn round.

'Are you very sad?' Bridget whispered.

Edward looked at her gratefully. 'Yes. There is ice in the Atlantic. Sometimes we are very close to it. It's the ice I think about, you see.' He looked out of the window at the passing hedgerows. 'It should be dark. Double summertime makes things a bit strange, doesn't it? At sea, we are intensely aware of night and day, a bit like animals. We watch intently, too, like animals, even in the dark. The enemy come at all times, and so does the ice. It is very beautiful; blue and green and rose and gold.' He spoke dreamily, almost wistfully.

'I'm glad you didn't tell Bridie. I think you were quite right not to.'

Bridget held her hands loosely in her lap. She contemplated her fingers, with their short, square nails, and wondered what it would be like to touch him; how his lean, used body would feel under her hands.

'You see why I couldn't stay?'

'Yes, perfectly.'

Edward continued, as though beyond embarrassment, 'I want very badly to hold on to her. She would ease it, you know, the solitude.' He stumbled over his words. 'But if I did, I couldn't leave her. It wouldn't be fair to leave her, then, not with all my fear dumped on her. So I held my tongue.'

They watched with unseeing eyes as the flat countryside sped past, Sam remembering his way. Edward pulled himself up and pointed. 'It's so ugly, isn't it, yet look what we do to defend it.'

'It's more than that.'

'Of course.'

'Edward?'

He turned to her. His thick brown hair had been cut very short; to keep lice at bay, he'd said earlier, grinning. It made him look like a haggard youth, prematurely old, his wary blue eyes too full of memories.

'Would it be of any help to hold me?' Bridget spoke very low but very clearly, so that he would understand that there was no mistake. He heaved another sigh and closed his eyes for a long time. Then he put out his hand and took her fingers in his.

'Yes. I would like that.'

'It would be . . . I think Bridie would feel that it was all right.'

Their eyes met for the first time. Bridget lifted his big, rough hand and enclosed it in hers.

'You will come home with me?' he asked. 'Tonight?'

'Of course.'

'Bless you,' was all he said.

David endured his in-laws' hostile silence that evening,

staying there since Edward was tactiturn about him and April going back to the house in Hackney.

'Ye Gods, I don't know how you stand it,' he said loudly, half hoping they might hear. April leant on her elbow, watching him undress. She moved over in the single bed to let him get in.

'Won't that miserable old bugger even let us get a double bed? It's ridiculous; we're married. We can't go on like this every time I come up to town.'

'They've said we can make a flat of the top floor, but you can't get anyone to come and do the bit of work it needs.'

He shifted around, cramped, cross and uncomfortable.

'David?'

He propped himself against the headboard and began to play with her hair.

'Hmm?'

'I wish we hadn't gone today.'

'Why ever not? I thought it was fun.'

'I don't think it was very nice for your mother, having everyone there like that. Edward looked awfully sad and he hardly had a chance to talk to her at all.'

'It's wartime. Can't be helped.' He pulled her closer. 'She liked you, anyway.'

'How do you know?'

'I just do.'

'She's nice,' said April shyly. 'I expected to feel scared of her, but when I talked to her, I wasn't.'

David yawned and then laughed. 'She scares me sometimes. She's got a real Irish temper on her when she wants to. Then we all have to look out.'

'Does she get cross a lot, then?'

'No, not often. Not much bothers her, but just

occasionally it does.' He grinned. 'Then there's fire-works. Not like your lot, all down in the mouth and nobody speaking. With Mum, it's a bit wild but it's over quick.'

'I'm sorry,' whispered April. 'They are a couple of miseries, aren't they?'

'Not your fault.' He pulled her down beside him. 'Why are we talking about them, anyway?'

April gave a small smile and shook her head. 'I don't know.'

'Come here, love. You did all right today. I was proud of you.'

'Were you?' She breathed shyly.

''course I was.'

He reached over and switched off the light.

Chapter Eighteen

Bridie came home only a few weeks after the charabanc trip. Her train stopped and started, sat in a siding somewhere for two hours, went backwards for a short distance and finally drew into Liverpool Street in mid-afternoon. She stared out of the window as the remains of East London slid past and when they paused for ten minutes, waiting for a signal to change, a wet, acrid smell of smouldering drifted through the carriage. The train jolted forwards again and crept into the shambles of Liverpool Street where she gathered her small bag under her arm and walked out to try to find a bus. Coming out of the station, she drew in her breath and stood, numbed.

'The bus for Hackney, please?'

'Over there, duck.' A woman in porter's uniform pointed to a bus stop that two days before had been a mass of broken concrete, but was now neatly cleared. Bridie picked her way across what had once been a station forecourt, so absorbed in the bomb-ravaged scene around her that at first she didn't hear her name. Surprised, she turned.

'Mrs DuCane,' called April for the third time, hurrying around a pile of hastily dumped pipes waiting to be laid, to mend a shattered water mains. The water itself gushed and spattered into a spreading, oily pool, lapping at fallen masonry thrown into the road by bombed out buildings across the street. Two turncocks were fixing a metal bar into something in a crater that Bridie couldn't see, saying they'd soon have it off. April, out of breath, stopped beside her and they both surveyed the growing pool.

'I'm sorry to be late. I meant to meet your train but they're never on time, and anyway my boss wouldn't let me go. He wanted his dictation finished and there was nothing for it but to do shorthand at the speed of light and race him through it. How are you? Was your journey all right?' She stopped, putting her hand to her mouth. 'Oh, dear, I didn't say, did I? Mr Saul rang me at the office and said you'd be on this train, and he'd have come himself only he couldn't. So I said, did he think you'd mind if I came instead? And he said he thought it would be all right . . .'

Bridie smiled and started to speak.

'. . . you don't mind, do you?' cried April. 'I'm sure you'd much rather have had Mr Saul meet you, but since he really couldn't . . .'

Bridie put her hand on April's thin arm and kissed her cheek in mid sentence. She stopped chattering as if Bridie had struck her.

'Thank you, April,' said Bridie. 'I didn't expect anyone to meet me and it's very kind of you to come. I'm glad you did.'

'Oh!' April's breath caught nervously and she choked.

'You really mustn't worry so much,' said Bridie, waiting for her coughing fit to finish.

The girl nodded. 'That's what David says.' She said his name shyly, not looking at Bridie.

'He's right.'

They stood awkwardly. The station was very quiet

and the clink of the men's metal key sounded loud. Water gurgled in the drain near their feet. They could see it swilling around just below the broken cover.

'It's a mess, isn't it? It must be an awful shock for you.'

'I've seen the papers,' murmured Bridie.

'Yes, but the papers still don't say how bad it really is, do they? How could anyone imagine this if they hadn't seen it themselves?'

Broken, tumbled buildings, twisted humps and hillocks, craters where once roads and homes and gardens had been, stretched away as far as she could see, as if a monstrous child had played sandpit games here, digging holes and tossing its spade carelessly with boredom; knocking over its building bricks, singing . . . all fall down.

'Do you know if my house is still standing? The last time Lizzie Norris wrote to me, Ted had found it a bit damaged but livable. But that was a week or two back . . . I can see that things change.'

April nodded wearily. 'They do, don't they? I'm afraid I don't know about your house. I've only been there once.' She blushed scarlet and could have bitten her tongue off.

"So that's how it was," thought Bridie with amusement.

'It was at the beginning.' I'm making things worse, thought April desperately. 'Of the Blitz.'

Bridie's grey eyes watched her daughter-in-law's confusion with steady, veiled thoughtfulness. April caught her gaze, blushed beet red again and said, 'I wonder how long the bus will be? I mean, I expect you're tired. I've got the rest of the afternoon off, though, so it doesn't matter. I mean . . . oh dear, I'm sorry.'

"What a kind little rabbit," thought Bridie. But how queer for David to want a rabbit.

'Then why don't you come with me?' she suggested. 'And if my house is in one piece, and there's some gas, we could have a cup of tea.'

'The sirens generally go about teatime or a little bit after. A lot of people start queuing for the shelters well before then. Won't you want to go down?'

'With you?'

'I usually stay in the office. There's a bunker there for staff, where we can stay. Quite often we couldn't get home and back. I don't often go in a public shelter. They're not very nice. The smell's awful and you catch things.'

'Then we'd better go down my cellar.'

April nearly choked and was rescued by the bus, which came straight through the pool, sending up a great bow wave and spattering muddy water right up the front of their legs.

'Pig!' shouted April. She pointed to her splattered skirt and the driver leaned out of his window and laughed, giving the victory sign with two nicotine-stained fingers.

'With knobs on.' April held up two fingers angrily and the driver winked.

"Not such a rabbit after all," thought Bridie.

'Bloody men,' snapped April, turning her back as the bus drove in a large semicircle to pull up.

'Do you know,' Bridie told her confidentially, warming to her daughter-in-law, 'I think he's a woman.'

'Then she should know better,' cried April crossly. 'You can't get soap for anything, to wash them out.'

'Hello, darlin'. Sorry about yer dress.' The woman

looked down at them from her cab, guffawed and hitched her overalls up across her skinny shoulders. 'Nah, really,' she said. 'I didn't see yer until it was too late, too busy steering fer victory around that lot.' She jerked a thumb at the Water Board men, who were wiping their hands on a bit of rag and watching the flow of water stop. 'Wonderful, ain't they?' Real admiration and affection softened her coarse voice.

'Yes, they are,' April answered, climbing into the bus with Bridie's bag. The conductress punched their tickets and April sat pleating the little bits of pink paper between her fingers, biting her full lower lip.

'I didn't mean to be rude,' she said.

'Rude?' Bridie was astonished. 'It was a harmless bit of fun.'

April looked relieved. Bridie took the worn tickets out of her fingers.

'You'll have us payin' again, you shred them up like that.'

'My mother would say I'd been common,' April said brightly. 'I am, sometimes.'

'I wouldn't know what common was,' said Bridie firmly.

'It's . . .'

'Look at that! I hope we're not goin' to end up like that,' cried her mother-in-law.

The conductress leaned out of her platform and exclaimed, 'Good heavens!' in a very genteel voice. 'Oh, golly.'

'She's never from round here,' murmured Bridie, craning to see properly. A double decker bus rested resignedly on its nose in a massive crater that cut the road in half. April giggled.

'It's awful really, I know, but it makes me think of

Pooh Bear stuck in Rabbit's doorway for a week because he made such a pig of himself on the honey. It's the way the wheels are so helpless, stuck in the air like that.' She giggled again, and put her hand to her mouth in apology.

"If she'd stop sayin' she's sorry every time she opens her mouth, I could quite like her," Bridie decided.

They had to take a long way round to get past the obstruction and the sirens began to scream ten minutes away from their stop. The driver pulled over and climbed out of her cab.

'Shelters,' she called calmly. 'Terminus.'

'Come on. If we're quick we can get home.' Bridie forced back the panic that the sirens brought flooding to the surface and tried to hurry. April stopped guiltily.

'I don't think you're strong enough yet,' she shouted above the din.

Bridie stopped and turned. The rising wail held steady at fever pitch and April saw that her mother-in-law's face was white.

'It's a shock for you. We'll get in the shelter. Quick.'

'Get down there,' roared a warden, coming round the side of the parked bus.

April pulled at Bridie's sleeve. 'Come on,' she begged.

'I . . . I feel queer.'

Planes droned in the distance, getting louder every second.

'Yes. It's the noise.' April grabbed the bag and put her arm firmly round Bridie's waist. 'We've got to hurry. Can you manage?'

Bridie clung on to the girl, her legs trembling and refusing to move.

'D'you want a hand?' asked the warden sharply.

'Help me carry her. Quick!'

Between them they half carried Bridie into the underground shelter, already packed full with grey-faced people. Several of them moved up as best they could to make room and April knelt down by Bridie and rubbed her hands.

'We've got used to it,' she explained. 'You forget not everyone has. And we have to get in quick, because the first thing they drop is an absolute shower of incendiaries and then everything starts burning. The fire spotters put them out, but we're best off down here. You're not well enough to go putting out fires.'

'I should have learned, shouldn't I?' Bridie's voice shook. 'That other time, I didn't shelter when I should have and look where that got me. I'm sorry.'

'You are quite safe down here.' April sat beside her and put her arm gently round Bridie's trembling shoulders. 'Does it hurt?'

She shook her head. 'No, you can't feel scars. I think it's the sirens made me come over all queer.'

'Cuppa?' asked a small woman, her hair tightly wound round curlers flanked by a fearsome row of crocodile clips.

'Tea?' Bridie looked round in surprise.

'Yes, duck. Got bread and jam out the back, as well. I've popped a spoon of treacle in it, seein' as you look poorly,' she added kindly, then lowered her voice so that no one else could hear. 'But don't let on or they'll all want it.'

'She's just come home from convalescence. I don't think they should have sent her so soon,' said April worriedly.

'Oh, yes? Hurt, was you?'

'A bit,' murmured Bridie. April took the hot tea and stirred it until it cooled a bit.

'Well, at least you're all right now. There's a lot aren't. I've seen things these last months I'll never forget, not to my dyin' day. Things I wish I'd never seen. Terrible things.' The crocodile clips rattled as she shook her head glumly and went back to spreading thin layers of jam on grey bread.

April gave Bridie the tea. She sipped it and colour began to come back into her face. She wasn't much like David, April thought, he must take more after his father. She wondered if Bridie would have pictures of David as a little boy.

'Do you have to do war work?' asked Bridie, for something to break the silence between them.

'My job counts as war work, but I suppose I could do extra. I've always wanted to drive. If I learned, I could drive ambulances or something.'

'Why don't you then?'

April suddenly looked downcast. 'My parents wouldn't like it.'

'You're over twenty-one and a married woman, and you're needed. I shouldn't have thought your parents had any say; they won't if the government decides to conscript you. I never heard such nonsense!' answered Bridie brusquely.

'Oh,' April was startled into exclaiming, 'that's just the sort of thing David says.'

'I'm glad to hear it,' Bridie answered.

'You see, it's terribly hard to argue with them. They always seem to know what's best.' April sounded apologetic again and Bridie, fortified by tea and rest, felt impatient with her.

'Why argue? You just go and do it. Getting married, driving . . . if you want to do it enough, no one will stop you.' Bridie stopped, realizing April's eyes were filling with tears.

'You are angry. David said you weren't, but I knew you would be.' The beautiful golden eyes swam and April's voice rose in a wail. Bridie regarded her with consternation.

'Now look,' said her mother-in-law firmly, setting down her empty cup on the floor under the bench to take back later, 'I once worked for a housekeeper and we had a bit of a set to. I done something she disapproved of, and she told me so. I did just what you're doin'; I cried my eyes out, but it did no good. She told me to shut the waterworks because she wasn't impressed. Once we'd got that straight, we made it up and got on better than before. She took no nonsense from anyone, did Mrs Goode, and I'm a bit the same.'

April's tears stopped like magic and she watched Bridie warily.

'Now then, I can't have you burstin' into tears and apologizin' every five minutes. You and me will get along nicely without it. I wasn't angry with you for marrying my son, let's have that straight. And what you and David do now is your own business. I won't interfere.'

'I thought . . .' began April, but Bridie held out the teacup. 'Will you kindly take this back?' she asked, forbidding any more discussion.

'Yes,' said April meekly, scrubbing at her eyes with her sleeve.

'Your mum better now?' asked the little woman in the canteen.

'My mother-in-law.' April touched her wedding ring proudly, to show the woman who glanced and nodded. 'Yes, thank you. She's much better.'

'Good.'

April stood at the back of the shelter, listening to the dull, crumping thud of a bomb landing not far away. She could pick out Bridie's reddish hair in the half light and, watching her unseen, April felt an unfamiliar excitement and trepidation. Bridie had thrown out a challenge. Not the devious kind, that Eileen was good at, but a direct one, an open offer of respect, if she was up to it. April wasn't at all sure she was, but she knew, standing there, that she was going to try.

The raid lasted, as usual, until dark. Bridie, exhausted, lay aching on a wooden bunk that someone gave up for her, seeing she wasn't well. April hovered anxiously until Bridie told her sharply to sit down and read or something, if she could. Lying listening to the sounds from above – terrible, muffled and curiously unreal – she felt overwhelmed by homesickness for the quiet hospital ward and the little curtained space that had been hers for nearly five months. The convalescent home, perched by the cold grey sea, seemed like a distant dream.

Chapter Nineteen

An April breeze sighed through the tight buds on the chestnut trees in the park as ack-ack teams in their gun emplacements stacked shells with a series of loud metallic thuds, treading thick grey mud where once there had been green grass, and daisies in summer. Silver barrage balloons swayed and strained on long moorings. A little way away, over on Mare Street, a factory building sank gracefully to the ground with a subdued roar. At the far end of Bridie's street a gang of rescue workers dug cautiously into a pile of rubble, pausing every few moments to call, listening for a sound, a cry, that would mean the people buried in it might still be alive.

Bridie's house had been badly damaged in the night while she and April sheltered nearby. A side wall had slid in a heap on its own foundations, exposing the rooms inside like the open front of a doll's house. Her bedroom, that Edward had christened the whorehouse, long ago, with its gold walls and pale carpet that he tolerated because Bridie loved them so, was open for all to stare at. Everywhere was covered in a thick layer of red-brown brickdust.

"It's like one of those horrible dreams," she thought, trying to take it in, "where you're sitting on the front seat of the top of a bus with no clothes on." The sense of exposure distressed her and she opened the gate hastily, dragging April after her.

'I haven't got a key.' She pulled letters and a powder compact out of her bag, scattering them on the doorstep. 'I must have!'

April began to laugh.

'What's funny?'

'Looking for a key. We can walk straight in, through the side.'

Bridie let her bag fall on to the step. 'It's too much for me. I can't think at all.'

April scooped up the bits and pieces and handed them to her. 'Come on,' she said gently. 'Let's see what's left.'

'Do you think it's safe?' Bridie went back down the path and stood looking up. 'It might all come down on us.'

'I suppose it could.'

'Oh, damn! I'm going to cry. After what I said to you, that's rich, isn't it? But I can't help . . . Oh dear. Oh, look at it! And next door's gone . . . and all up there.'

'You're still not strong, Mrs DuCane. You're trying to do too much,' cried April. 'I wish there was someone to look after you properly.'

Bridie fumbled in her pocket for a handkerchief and blew her nose.

'I'll manage, thank you kindly,' she said ungratefully. 'Shouldn't you be getting back to your office?'

'Oh, blow the office.'

"There's no pleasing her," thought April, confused.

Bridie leapt in fright. 'Oh!' she gasped, clutching her chest. The Pope rubbed ecstatically round her ankles, looking up hungrily. 'That cat'll be the death of me,' she cried.

The Pope stopped purring and mewed.

'I don't suppose he's been fed in ages. Nothing to feed him on, anyway.'

'What shall we do?' April eyed the cat crossly; they had enough to do, looking after themselves. Cats could mouse for their living.

'I expect even the mice are on short rations, these days,' said Bridie, reading her face. She bent down and picked him up. 'We'll go to Ted and Ethel,' she told him. 'They'll have a drop of milk for you.' The Pope put his claws out and jumped down.

'I think if you're bombed out you have to go to the Town Hall, Mrs DuCane.'

'Oh, do I?'

'You have to fill in a lot of forms, to get your furniture moved and something put over the holes so it won't get all rained on and stolen. You have to tell them. And then there's damage claims. It's an awful lot of traipsing around.'

'Ted can see to that; he probably has already, he looks after the house. Come on.' Bridie pocketed her handkerchief, stowed her handbag under one arm and opened the gate imperiously. They passed the rescue workers down the road, standing in a little group, watching a man crawl into a gap in the debris.

'At least we're better off than the poor souls under there. No sense in weeping over spilt milk, April.'

April's jaw dropped. Mrs DuCane been the one crying, and now the old girl was skipping off down the road like nobody's business.

'Well, I'm blowed,' muttered April.

Bridie hurried on.

'Wait! Wait for me,' her daughter-in-law called, running to catch up.

A little cheer rang out behind them as the rescue workers heard a faint voice call from a cellar far beneath the debris.

'There's always someone worse off than yourself,' remarked Bridie briskly.

April thought better of trying to reply and decided to go back to work after all, so they parted at the corner.

'It was kind of you to come.' said Bridie. 'I'm sorry we're all at sixes and sevens – I was going to make you some tea. Another time, when I'm sorted out, though I expect I'll stay at Ethel's.'

'Another time,' said April. 'I'll look forward to that.'

Bridie watched her go. She's a nice girl, she thought. David's not done so badly after all.

April waited for a bus to come. She's all right, really, if you don't mind her tongue, she thought.

I think we'll get along quite nicely, the two women decided generously, each about the other, going their separate ways.

Chapter Twenty

The war dragged on and on and on and David got lonelier and lonelier. His work began to suffer. He kept telephoning.

'I need you. Why can't you come here?'

'Come to London.'

'I can't stand staying at your parents' house; they make me feel like a leper.'

'There isn't anywhere else. Your mum's house is bombed out.'

'Then come and live here.'

'I can't.'

'Why?' asked David for the hundredth time. 'Why not?'

'I've got my job,' she said patiently. 'And we can't do without the money.'

'Yes, we can. You can find something here. There's plenty of work; we could manage.'

'I'm already doing war work. If I leave, I'll be conscripted and have to do something like farmwork, and I don't want to. I like my job.'

'More than me,' David said sullenly.

'And anyway,' April pursued the familiar arguments, ignoring him, 'Dad says he'll only pay your fees if we live here. We can't afford to lose that and my job. We couldn't live.'

'Aha, now we get to the heart of the matter.'

'What do you mean?'

'Daddy.'

'No, it's not. That's horrid.'

'But true.' But David said it under his breath. 'I can get odd jobs and we'd manage somehow.'

'No.'

'We could,' he said stubbornly. 'You're my wife and I need you with me. Why don't you want me, too?'

'I do,' April answered softly. 'I miss you. But I can't come and live down there. We agreed that.'

'Your father told you,' he retorted bitterly. 'Having my arm twisted isn't an agreement. Not in my book.'

'You aren't practical,' sighed April.

'I'm bloody lonely and frustrated,' he shouted miserably.

'Don't swear at me,' she snapped.

'I give up!' yelled her husband, and slammed down the phone.

White-faced, David pocketed the rest of his change and banged out of the telephone box, almost knocking over a girl waiting to use it.

'Temper, temper,' she said, her cool voice mocking. 'Marital trouble, David dear?'

'Well, well, if it isn't Keyhole Kate,' he snapped.

'Ouch!' She pretended to pick something nasty out of one eye and laughed. 'Wifey not obliging, then? Tut, tut. Silly girl doesn't know what she's risking, does she?'

David flushed angrily.

'Oooh, you are cross, aren't you? Do you want to tell me about it?' Suddenly she was serious. 'Look, I'm sorry. I can see it's tough.'

David drew a very deep breath and let it out hard,

whistling through his teeth. 'I want her to come down. She won't,' he said succinctly.

'Oh dear. You've tried everything?'

'Everything I can think of, that's practical and possible over the telephone or in letters.'

'Limiting.'

'That doesn't work, either. I've tried.'

Cutie grinned. 'I'm sure you have,' she murmured. 'Lucky wifey.'

'Shut up,' he snarled.

'You'll go far with a bedside manner like that. Try psychiatry.'

David glared at her; she always mocked, and it always left him helpless.

'I gather your own bedside manner is a trifle overstated,' he snapped, trying to embarrass her, but she was unembarrassable. Her merry blue eyes looked straight into his and she drew down one painted eyelid in a slow, enormous wink.

'I practise,' she told him, with a perfectly straight face.

'So I hear.'

A heavy step made them look round – the cleaning woman who did David's room stood there.

'Oh, it is you, then. Could I ask you to clear up your room of a morning so I can get in there to clean, Mr Holmes?'

'What's wrong with it?'

Mrs Whitley pursed her lips and looked offended. 'It's a pig sty, young man. I don't know where you was brought up, I'm sure. Other young gentlemen don't make such a mess.'

Cutie hid a smile. 'Oh, they do, Mrs Whitley, they do.'

Mrs Whitley looked through her; young ladies were strictly forbidden in gentlemen's room, on pain of expulsion, but this one knew more than was good for her. Cutie, considered Mrs Whitley with acid disapproval, was fast.

'He'll clear up like a lamb tomorrow, won't you, David?' Cutie grinned. 'I'll lend him a hand.'

Mrs Whitley ignored the bait.

'I'd appreciate it, Mr Holmes, or I might have to stop doing for you, otherwise.'

'She's threatening me,' said David incredulously.

'Take no notice.'

'She can't do that.' David was furious.

'Leave it be, David.'

He raised his voice. 'I'll have you up in front of the bursar, Ma Whitley, if you don't look out,' he called after the cleaner. She paused, her back to them. 'Your job is to clean the rooms, not to threaten the occupants.'

'David, don't,' urged Cutie.

Mrs Whitley turned, her face a blur in the dark corridor. She gave them a look of pure venom, her coarse mouth clamped shut.

'Stupid old woman.'

'You shouldn't make an enemy of her,' said Cutie uneasily.

David snorted.

'Never mind, the harm's done now. Look, I'm going to ring my parents and then I'm going up to the common room to have a coffee. Why don't you come?'

'There's nothing else to do,' he muttered ungraciously. 'I can't work.' He thrust his hands down into his pockets and stared at her through the gold-rimmed spectacles. 'See you up there.'

Cutie backed into the telephone box, pushing the door open with her bottom.

'Your trouble is, you're too touchy by half,' she told him, turning round. The door shut itself heavily and he could hear the clunk of coins going into the box. She half turned back and grinned at him through the glass, starting to talk to someone. He began to wander down the high, gloomy corridor that led to the stairs and the common room on the first floor, dragging his heels in case she caught him up, but she must have chatted for a long time to her parents, if that was who she was really phoning, for she didn't turn up for a good half hour, by which time he had gone.

'You'll ruin my marriage. Is that what you want?' April faced George across his booklined study, hearing the words deadened by the overstuffed, heavily curtained room, where the smell of stale pipe smoke hung in corners.

'Don't be absurd.'

'I'm not absurd.' April stamped her foot with rage. George raised one thick eyebrow a fraction as if to say, 'Oh no?'

'You enter into an absurd relationship in an absurd manner and at an absurd time, and you say you are not foolish?'

'It isn't.' Colour crept up April's cheeks at his words. 'It's not absurd.'

'I'll be the judge of that.'

She stood silent.

'I'll protect you from the consequences of this foolishness, but only on condition you do nothing to make it worse. If you want to run off and prevent him finishing his medical training, so that the two of you live in poverty all your lives, by all means do so. But I warn you, I shall wash my hands of you, and no matter how you beg, you'll get not a penny from me.'

'I never beg,' April muttered resentfully.

'You've never had to, my dear. You've had everything you wanted and this is a fine way to reward us. You have disappointed me gravely, April. I hope you realize that.'

'What about David? Must I disappoint him as a wife, too? I have to disappoint one of you, don't I?'

George stared at her coldly.

'As to how you comport yourself as his wife, my dear, I have not the slightest wish to know.'

April sobbed with rage and fled from the room, banging the door behind her. Down the passage, in the kitchen, Eileen cocked her head on one side and listened. She heard the door bang and April's feet run upstairs and clucked her tongue.

'Temper, temper,' she said, echoing Cutie more than a hundred miles away. Upstairs another door slammed and the house was still.

April leant her hot cheek against the cool porcelain of the lavatory bowl, panting with rage. She pulled her feet under her and knelt up, pushed her fingers down her throat and vomited. Afterwards, washing her hands and face in cold water, she looked at her pallid face in the mirror above the bowl. A stranger stared out at her, with feverish yellow eyes and pinched nostrils.

'I hate him and I hate you,' she whispered viciously at the reflection, feeling her belly tenderly. It was flat and empty as ever. No baby. Nothing at all to fill her aching emptiness. Then she remembered Bridie and Ethel, talking about darning socks in the shelter and cracking jokes, cosily wrapping themselves in grey blankets on chilly evenings, sharing . . . Once Rachael had been there for April but now she was so worried and so busy with the war that even she didn't notice the girl properly any more. No one did. She put her hands to her face and cried, violently, angrily, until she had no tears left.

Chapter Twenty-One

On 10 May London burned from Dagenham to Hammersmith. The Luftwaffe kept up a shuttle service all night, to-ing and fro-ing across the Channel, bombing up in Northern France, returning to drop their loads on a city that burned ferociously beneath the light of a full moon. A low tide in the Thames meant the fire services ran out of water. At dawn the all clear rose, along with the barrage balloons, into a sky that was invisible behind a dense pall of smoke.

'Crumbs!' Ethel came up out of the tube and coughed.

Everything was red; fires raged down both sides of the street, hot embers showered down and the stifling smoke eddied, stoking the inferno. A pump operator was setting his hoses into a sewer, to try for water, and the firemen wearily waited for a trickle to stem the flames.

'There's buildings down on yer hoses. Again. A good 'alf mile,' shouted a short, fat fireman in a tin hat, appearing out of the smoke.

'I'm trying here,' called the pump operator, bent over the broken sewer.

The fat supervisor pushed his hat back and scratched his forehead gloomily. Ethel saw that his eyebrows had been burned off. He caught her staring and his filth-runnelled face split in a lugubrious grin.

'Twenty mile an hour they've bin layin' hoses, but we can't keep up. Everything's gone up. And what Jerry didn't start, the gas mains and the electrics and those bleedin' penetratin' bombs have. Boom! All over the bloody place. No gas, no electric, no water, no drains left – no nuffink,' he finished, with gloomy relish.

'I ain't had most of those in months, except on and off,' retorted Ethel folding her arms across her ample chest. 'What are you complainin' for?'

'We've generally had water.'

'That's true.'

The small man mopped his brow again with the back of his hand. 'Whew!' He puffed out his round cheeks and let out a long whistle. 'Hot as hell, ain't it?'

They contemplated the fires in silence. A steel lamp post bent at a strange angle, wilting in the heat, its paint running slowly into a dirty black puddle at its twisted base.

'All right?' called the supervisor to one of the crew, who stood examining the end of his hose with an air of resignation. The man shook it and let it drop, grinning at Ethel, teeth gleaming in his black face.

'Nicholson's Gin Distillery in Bromley,' he recited, 'then the tobacco warehouse in Victoria Dock, then we get sent to the Guinness bottling store at North Woolwich. Now here. Shame, really, isn't it?' He laughed and coughed. 'This Blitz is the biggest bloody rush what I've ever known.'

'Think that one needs a hand,' interrupted the little supervisor urgently. Ethel squinted against the smoke, trying to see where he pointed, towards a fireman with slickers covered in tar, his face black with bruises and oil. He tried to roll a hose but it slipped from his arms. Flames roared and popped, and behind him a wall tottered and began to slide. 'Watch yerself,' bellowed the supervisor, starting forwards at a run.

The fireman stood staring at the hose, lying across his path. Ethel put her hand to her mouth in horror. As the wall leant gracefully forwards, about to cascade in a great shower of sparks and red hot bricks, the little supervisor cannoned into the firefighter and they both went rolling and tumbling out of its way.

The fireman screamed.

'Bloody fool!' yelled his rescuer.

Clumsily, Ethel ran over, slipping and sliding in greasy, boiling mud.

'Get out of there,' she shouted, half choked by smoke and stung by flying, burning splinters. Fire reflected on the surfaces of a thousand rancid, oily puddles and a great, elongated crash reverberated in the ground under her feet as several houses fell into a crater. A broken piano fell on its back with a jangle of keys and snapping wires and lay, a sad mass of huge white splinters. The supervisor jumped to his feet but the fireman knelt where he had fallen, turning watering red eyes on Ethel.

'I can't 'ear nothing.' His voice was hoarse and cracked and burned.

'Come on,' Ethel yelled, her fat round face mottled with terror.

'Just this noise in me head.' His eyes bulged. 'They hit the bells, missus, the bells. It was two bombs, one either side on the church tower, and they hit the bells. The blimmin' bells.' He moaned and went to touch his head. 'Christ.'

'You want a doctor,' whimpered Ethel.

'Get 'im inside, Missus,' shouted someone from the pump. 'There's a doctor just up there.'

Ethel scrubbed at her eyes 'I can't see . . .'

'There!' the supervisor shouted impatiently, waving his arm. 'Come on, mate.' The fat little man pulled the fireman's shoulder.

'I see him,' cried Ethel.

They dragged the fireman to his feet. Smoke billowed and shifted and cleared. Prams and corrugated sheeting lay all entangled with bloodied heaps of bedclothes, torn pillows and gas masks, smashed food and lost toys, whose owners lay dead in a crater a little further away. A doctor crouched on the ground, flames glinting on steel as he cut trousers from a shape with a gaping red hole in it and began to operate.

''e's tied up for the minute.' Ethel swallowed hard, dry-mouthed. 'But I'll fetch him to you when 'e's finished.'

She helped sit the fireman down on the top of the escalator steps. People stopped talking and watched.

'Poor beggar,' said a woman holding a baby. The fireman moaned, a whining little sound that made the hair stand up on Ethel's neck. 'I'll go and tell that doctor to come, soon as he can.'

The fireman laid his head on his arms, on the wooden stair. Then, very quietly, he was gone.

It nearly finished Ethel; she went very pale and swayed. The woman with the baby handed it to a small girl.

'Hold him,' she ordered, 'Careful.' She put her arm round Ethel's fat, quivering shoulders.

'You get 'er a drink of water,' she shouted at another child, sucking its fingers with a bit of blanket held against its impassive face.

'Ta,' muttered Ethel, sipping water. 'Sorry to be a trouble, but I come over real queer.'

'Someone's covered 'im up, now, poor soul.'

Ethel was too upset to speak.

'You by yourself?' asked the woman.

Ethel shook her head. 'My daughter-in-law.'

'What's 'er name?'

'Bridie.'

The woman shouted to the child. 'Go and call "Bridie" up and down the platform, duck.'

They heard her above the chatter of voices as more and more people left the tube station, running for it through the burning streets.

'Why do they go?' Ethel asked childishly. 'Out there? There ain't nothing there to go to no more. The Germans are going to win.' A billow of smoke came through the station entrance and they coughed harshly, something acid catching their dry throats.

'Don't talk daft,' the woman gasped. 'You hear?'

Bridie came to the top of the escalator.

''ere's the lady, Mum,' said the child.

'She's 'ad a bit of a turn.' The woman wiped her streaming eyes and the baby choked and began to yell. She grabbed the little girl's hand. 'We'll be gettin' along.' They skirted round the body on the stairs, disappearing into the yellow smoke.

'They'll bring one of those cardboard coffins and take him away in a minute,' said Bridie, staring up the escalator. 'Don't take on so, Eth.'

'Why?' asked Ethel bleakly.

'Why what?'

'Everything,' said Ethel helplessly.

'God knows. I don't know how you can go out there. I can't.'

'That's your accident,' Ethel wheezed, becoming calmer.

Bridie glanced up at the corpse again, guessing what might have happened. 'But there's one blessing, if you want to look at it that way.' She sat down next to her mother-in-law, breathing in her sharp smell of sweat and fear.

'What's that?'

'He won't need no coupons.'

'Bridie!' said Ethel sharply. She put a hand to her legs and winced. They hurt her all the time, these days. 'That ain't nice.'

But shrouds weren't rationed. And it was the end of the Blitz.

Chapter Twenty-Two

Because of the pail, the scraps were saved,
Because of the scraps, the pigs were saved,
Because of the pigs, the rations were saved,
Because of the rations, the ships were saved,
Because of the ships, the island was saved,
Because of the island, the Empire was saved,
And all because of a housewife's pail.

April hummed the wartime nursery rhyme cheerily, dusting and wiping and polishing her tiny flat energetically. She paused to shake the duster out of the window and looked down into George's garden. The roses and lawns had gone, replaced by an allotment. A ramshackle assortment of runs and cages surrounded the corrugated roof of the Anderson, just sticking up above ground level. Hens clucked and squabbled and scratched alongside rabbit hutches and a modest pig pen, inhabited by Lord Woolton, the neighbourhood porker, affectionately and disrespectfully named after the former Minister for Food. Eileen had jibbed at pigs, to start with, but, viewing her empty larder, depressed by the prospect of living indefinitely on baked potatoes and cabbage and under pressure from George and April (for once on speaking terms and in cahoots because they both loved their food), she agreed to put up with a future supply of pork chops.

George had tried shooting pigeons and blackbirds but his erratic aim had promptly brought the neighbours bustling forth to point out with a good deal of shouting and arm waving that whereas Hitler's shooting at them they could put up with, George's was taking liberties. Enough, they said firmly, was enough. When the indignant shouting had died down, they had sympathized with each other over the longing for pigeon pie and agreed instead on a communal pig, to be housed in George's garden, for whom the whole street collected and delivered its peelings daily. Lord Woolton prospered and got fat and the street licked its collective lips hungrily, and waited.

April grinned at the memory, shook her duster thoroughly into the warm air, then turned to survey her room with pride. She knew it was a room that could only have been found in nineteen forty-two and she loved it. Instead of the heavy, ornate furnishing in her parents' part of the house, April had carefully arranged her flat with a sparse selection of utility furniture. Simple, practical and, she thought, stylish, without frills of any kind. Utility goods, she said firmly to Eileen, from clothes to settees, from sheets to pots and pans, meant less precious material in their making, fewer workers to make them and more people in the aircraft factories instead. David had patriotically refused Eileen's offer of what she called 'proper goods' as a wedding present and agreed with April, even though it strained their meagre budget.

'It feels like our flat now. It wouldn't if it was all filled with her stuff.' April's motives had not been particularly patriotic and she'd accepted with delight Rachael and Gordon's gift of a set of heavily embroidered linen sheets and pillowcases that owed nothing of their old-fashioned luxury to the utility drive.

She ran her duster over the tiny table they used for eating, and at which David worked for long hours when he came to stay. He never called it coming home, like she did. She picked up a textbook on general physiology and weighed it in her hand proudly.

'Dr and Mrs Holmes,' she murmured. It had a wonderful sound. She put the book back on a small pile and folded her duster.

The house was silent and motionless below her. Outside dusk began to gather and a light dew hung in the air. George was reading in his study and Eileen was down the road, drinking tea with Rachael, who was taking the Home Front with extreme seriousness and answered the call of the nation with zeal, application, ingenuity, and enough worry to give her a nervous breakdown. Stoical Eileen enjoyed listening to her ceaseless and imaginative chatter, making little sympathetic clucking noises and agreeable small nods of the head as Rachael expounded the dangers and worries of Gordon's fire watching and his shovelling incendiaries into buckets of sand; of her very youngest son dodging shrapnel as he cycled to school, of ration books, gas masks, Food Flashes, air raids, collecting cardboard and punctured saucepans for salvage, rents in her blackout material, feeding the budgerigars on grey national loaf and sawdust.

But mostly they fretted together about food; the crisis in the kitchen. Hearing Lord Woolton shuffle in his pen and grunt quietly to himself, April's lips twitched with amusement at it all even though her stomach rumbled louder than anyone's with constant hunger. The core of the crisis was complicated rations;

there were green books for babies, blue books for children, buff books for adults; different coloured books had different value coupons; tinned food and biscuits were rationed by points instead of coupons; the meat ration swelled or shrank according to the season, the convoys, and the temper of your butcher. If you wanted to worry, thought April, there was plenty to be going on with. The wonderful memory of Eileen's carrot marmalade rose in her mind and she giggled.

'Dig for victory,' she said aloud to herself. 'Oh dear, poor Rachael.'

Rachael assiduously collected the Ministry of Food's Kitchen Hints.

'Look,' she cried, arriving on the doorstep excitedly one day with a recipe for carrot marmalade.

One of Hitler's many crimes was the ruining of the British breakfast; they hadn't tasted marmalade for over a year, oranges being things of the past, and they missed it. George agreed to their digging up some of his less successful carrots, the poor soil in his garden being healthier for carrot fly than carrots. Rachael and Eileen energetically gathered their withered harvest and worked hard all morning; they boiled the carrots and sweetened them, then painstakingly skimmed off the scum, thick with carrot fly corpses, leaving a doubtful looking residue, which they sealed in jamjars.

'Do you think it'll taste all right?' asked Rachael, eyeing the gluey contents of her jars dubiously.

'It'd better, after all that work,' cried Eileen, undismayed by appearances. Nonchalantly, she put one of the precious jars on the breakfast table next morning, called up for April to come and have breakfast with them and waited, with exaggerated indifference, for their reaction. George spread the nectar on his toast and bit into it. He frowned.

'Good God, what is it?' he asked incredulously.

'Marmalade,' said Eileen proudly. 'Rachael and I made it with those carrots you gave us.'

'And do you know what he did?' demanded Eileen afterwards, telling Rachael the tale with compressed lips and slitted eyes. 'He got up and took the jar and poured the whole lot on his compost heap. It's the last time I make all that effort, just to please him. He needn't think I'll bother again.'

Much to April and George's relief, she didn't.

April closed the window and turned on the wireless. The news was depressing; more defeats in North Africa, explained away by bitter complaints from battalions there about the inferior nature of their equipment.

'That's enough of that.' She intended to enjoy herself, so she changed programmes until she found music, turned it down quite low and fetched a bag and a towel from her bedroom. Sitting at the little table, she put David's medical books in the middle and propped a mirror against them. She'd planned this for weeks and was excited now she was actually going to do it.

'Here we go,' she murmured to herself, taking a pair of scissors and a comb out of the bag. She draped the towel round her shoulders and, twisting to see as much as she could of the back of her head, began to cut her long, glossy hair. She worked, snipping carefully for ten minutes, cutting shorter and shorter until it just reached the tops of her ears. Satisfied, she ran her hands through it and leaned back to see. It was a ragged mess. Unruffled, she took the towel, shook out the hairs, and removed a hoarded bottle of precious shampoo from the bag. She boiled the kettle, filled the washing up bowl with warm water in the sink George had installed in one corner, rinsed in cold water and a drop of vinegar and rubbed her head briskly with the towel. Then she ran her comb through her hair, a strange sensation, it being so short, and shook her head. She looked in the mirror again, and smiled. Without the weight of its own length, the damp dark hair sprang up around her head in a halo of curls.

'That's better,' said April, turning this way and that, to see, humming to the tune of 'My Old Man', coming over the wireless.

Out of the bag came a candle and several used up lipsticks. Pulling the blackout over her window, she put on the light, lit the candle and began melting bits of lipstick. Most of it fell into the candle, which kept going out, but in the end she transferred enough melted lipstick into one of the holders to make a useable one. It was a disappointing orangy-brown colour, but April put it to go solid; it'd be better than nothing. Then she went down the steep flight of stairs to the bathroom. The house was still silent.

"Mum's late coming home from Rachael's," she thought.

The Government decreed one bath a week, and no more than five inches of water. April undressed and turned on the tap, watching water steam into the cold tub. She took the ruler Eileen had marked at five inches with a thick red line, and held it in the bath. Five inches of water, she thought resentfully, was an invitation to pneumonia, but she scrubbed herself thoroughly with her tiny ration of soap, dried quickly and ran back upstairs as the front door banged.

'Hello,' called Eileen, hearing footsteps.

'Hello, Mum.' April began to close her door, not ready to be seen. She had her dressing gown on and was plaiting the shorn off hair, so that she could use it as a false piece, when Eileen knocked.

'Go away,' muttered April.

'Rachael thought you'd like this . . .' Eileen came in without being asked, with a bit of cake on a plate. She nearly dropped it.

'Whatever have you gone and done?' she squeaked.

'Cut my hair.'

Eileen stared.

'It'll save on shampoo,' explained April. 'Do you like it?'

Eileen thought of the picture downstairs, of her beautiful sister with waist-length hair.

'Your dad isn't going to like it,' she said with gusto.

'I do.' Her daughter tossed her head and the loose chestnut curls shone.

'Look,' she added, and carefully stroked brown lipstick over her full lips. 'How's that?'

'It's a horrible colour,' answered Eileen critically, her head on one side.

'I mixed them all up.'

'What's all the titivating in aid of, anyway?'

'It isn't in aid of anything.'

'You're not up to something, are you?' Eileen's face narrowed suspiciously.

'What sort of something, Mum?'

'You remember you're a married woman, my girl.'

'Oh!' April's hand flew to her mouth. 'Don't say anything to Joe, will you?'

'Joe? Joe who?' squawked her mother, her eyes quite round.

'GI Joe.' April burst out laughing at the dismay on

Eileen's face. That'd teach her to pry! Eileen sniffed eloquently and retreated downstairs, to make weak tea for George's nightcap and gaze thoughtfully at the picture of April. She decided to let George find out for himself.

At half-past two in the morning there was a commotion. Hearing it even from the top of the big house, April lifted her head sleepily and listened, at first expecting to hear bombs or that the house was on fire, but it was only voices, shouting, and then a loud bang.

'I want to see my wife.'

April sat up.

'At this hour?' roared George's voice. 'You can't just come here disturbing everyone. Are you drunk?' he added contemptuously.

'No.'

'Well, you're blasted inconsiderate.'

'I am sorry to have woken you. I've been trying to get here all day; you know what transport's like. I've walked a good deal of it.'

'Bloody inconsiderate.' George ignored him. 'Damn you!'

David shot out a fist and pushed his father-in-law hard against the door jamb. George gasped, his face blotchy with rage; his fists clenched.

'You want a fight?' he shouted, dancing up and down heavily, his doughy cheeks wobbling ludicrously.

'No. I want my wife.' David slammed the front door behind him and moved like an eel, out of George's reach. 'I don't fight old men.'

He ran up the stairs, leaving George breathing stertorously, his fists still raised uselessly. Eileen appeared in a doorway on the landing, pulling a gown round herself and looking frightened.

'Whatever are you doing?' she quavered.

'Coming home,' called David with heavy sarcasm. She saw him disappear up the next flight of stairs and went to peer down into the hall. George banged his fist on the wall and swore with words she'd never heard him use before.

'Oh, dear,' she mumbled, and crept back to bed, feeling it would be wise to leave him until he had spent his rage as best he could.

David dropped on his knees by April's bed and buried his head in her warm blankets.

'What are you doing here?' asked his wife, amazed.

He raised his head again and looked up at her, barely able to make her out in the dark, and when he spoke his voice was full of anguish.

'I had to come. April, Edward's dead.'

Chapter Twenty-Three

April crept out early the next morning to go to work, leaving David in an exhausted sleep. Her shorn head gave her a shock when she looked in the bathroom mirror; she'd forgotten. Tip-toeing downstairs to the front door, hoping to avoid her parents, she had her hand on the door when Eileen poked her head out of the morning room door and hissed: 'April.'

"I could pretend not to hear," thought April, trapped, "but it wouldn't work; she'd only run after me."

Eileen, head spiky with crocodile clips, stood in the doorway and beckoned.

'I'll be late, Mum.'

'I want a word.'

'Can't you wait until I get home?'

'April.' Eileen sounded menacing.

She sighed and went into the morning room. Her mother confronted her, twisting her hands in her dressing gown belt, winding and re-winding the tassel round her fingers in agitation. 'Do you want to kill your father?' she blurted.

April stared at the floor by Eileen's feet; she noticed her mother's slippers were both worn right through on the same side, exposing blue-veined feet that should have been decently covered.

'You know he's got a weak heart,' Eileen continued, when April didn't answer. 'And what that man upstairs who calls himself your husband thinks he's doing, coming here at two in the morning and threatening decent people, I'm sure I don't know. I'm going to have to tell him he's not welcome in this house any more, April. Fancy carrying on like that. Aren't you ashamed?'

'Mum . . .'

'Your dad's been good to him,' Eileen continued. 'He's been good to you as well, young lady. A lot of girls would like to be in your shoes, believe me. And you've not got the grace to be grateful.'

'Mum, David's stepfather has been killed.'

'Oh. Oh dear. I suppose that does put a different light on it.'

'He'd been to see his mother and he came here afterwards because he wanted to tell me. He is terribly upset.'

Eileen cast about to save face. 'Well, it's still no excuse for violence.'

'Dad wouldn't let him in. Look, I have to go or Mr Stephenson gets really cross. I'll be home late because we'll have to go and see David's mother. Do try and be nice to him when he comes down, and tell Dad to let him be.'

'Well, I don't know . . .'

But April was gone. Eileen stood alone in the room, hearing her shut the front door gently behind her.

'Oh dear,' she said, and sat down at the cold, highly polished table, working and working the frayed tassel fretfully. 'Oh dear, oh dear, what are we going to do?'

April stood in front of Mr Stephenson's big mahogany desk and watched him steeple his fingers in the way he always did when he was about to say no. His sparse hair was combed back from a high, arrogant forehead and he had a Roman nose, down which he frequently looked at the world with contempt. Mr Stephenson did not suffer fools – which was how he classified the majority – gladly. April was not a fool. He trusted her, which was more than he could say for most of his staff. But he hid his approval behind a truculent, driving style, which made him a difficult boss to please.

He rested his chin on the tips of his fingers and considered. She was efficient, competent, discreet, reliable, very decorative, and he knew that she knew a good deal that she shouldn't. She knew, he reflected uneasily, where a good many wartime bodies were buried. Or, at least, he suspected that she suspected, which could amount to the same thing in the end. It was both her value and her danger to him which made up his mind.

'I understand how difficult it is for you, having to live apart, but many people do in wartime. Fact of life. Think of all the sailors' wives who don't even get letters for months on end. Many of them live with the same tragedy as your family, I'm afraid. I can't possibly let you go. I'd never replace you. I'm very sorry, April.'

'Can't I resign?'

Mr Stephenson shook his head. 'You know better than that, my dear,' he told her softly. 'We've never formally conscripted you, but if you'd rather . . . I have no doubt at all that we could get Government permission to keep you. We advise and liaise on so much of their tendering. Can't afford to lose someone who knows the ropes like you do. Would be a nuisance for both sides.'

April looked down to hide her disappointment and frustration.

'I am sorry,' repeated Mr Stephenson, his calculating grey eyes watching her closely.

'Couldn't I do something equally useful near the college, just so we could be together more? Can't I be useful somewhere else?'

'I think we've been over it enough,' he said blandly. He picked up a folder and April was dismissed.

Staring at the closed door, Stephenson heaved a sigh of relief. If she'd chosen to be awkward, it could have been quite tricky . . . very tricky, in fact. He wondered if he hadn't better offer her a raise. Deciding it would be a wise move, he bent back to his work.

April put away the papers she'd been working on and locked the filing cabinet, then stood looking out of her window at the fresh green of the trees in the courtyard below.

'Beastly old man,' she muttered furiously. Sparrows hopped busily under the trees, scavenging in the thin grass, bright eyes wary for the building's cat. In the far distance a plume of smoke rose into the low clouds, pinpointing a spot where there'd been an unexploded bomb, hidden for months until something suddenly set it off. April watched the smoke waver in the breeze without really seeing.

'I'd like to rat on him,' she thought, but the very thought scared her. She knew that Mr Stephenson knew that she knew his department traded with the enemy. She typed contracts that were odd and after a while had begun to understand and to be afraid. Britain bought German oil in exchange for industrial diamonds, or rubber for tin, or wheat for engine parts . . . so it went on, industry on both sides determined to flourish, irrespective of Axis, Allies or anything else. That, she reflected, catching sight of the cat crouching, tail twitching, just out of sight of the sparrows, was Mr Stephenson's power.

"By making me work in criminal dealings he's corrupted me," she thought bitterly, "and now he daren't let me go, and I daren't leave, and there is nothing I can do about it. War drags us all down, one way or another, whichever side is winning," she concluded sadly.

The Blitz was a distant memory. Tied up by the Eastern and Russian Fronts, the Luftwaffe made only sporadic attacks on British cities. Bombsites all over London were thickly overgrown with rosebay willowherb, golden rod and dandelions. Many were turned into allotments and pigsties to feed desperately hungry people.

'Digging for Victory released shipping space for battle equipment; tanks, guns, planes and soldiers,' explained Mr Churchill, urging them on to self-sacrifice.

'Bet he ain't starvin' hungry all the time,' grumbled Ted. Ethel had shot him a scandalized look.

Edward, David had explained when he began to be able to talk about it, had been killed during an attack on one of the convoys of merchant ships and their escorts, carrying war supplies to Russia. April was fascinated and chilled by stories in the newspapers of ships battling Arctic seas and frozen wastes to bring supplies to brave, mysterious, savage Russians in their fairytale towns with stirring, mystical names – Archangel, Murmansk, Polyarnoe – set in terrible, unimaginably strange places, white, frozen, ghostly.

David gave her Edward's letters and she read and re-read them by the hour, absorbed in Edward's words, seeing in her mind the wonderful, terrible pictures he'd tried to paint with them, trying to imagine the Arctic circle.

> There are no trees, no green fields, birds or flowers. Although now, nearly summer, the sun shines, it is rather as if a searchlight has been turned on, to light up a ghostly, volcanic land-scape. The people of Archangel and Murmansk seem like inhabitants from another planet. You can't tell the men from the women. Some have Mongolian faces, but others are fair and blue-eyed.

Below the window, the cat pounced fruitlessly. The sparrows flew up in a fright, twittered excitedly in the branches above the ground, then came back down again in a little flurry of brown wings. The cat retreated, feigning disinterest.

April read another page.

> I have vivid memories of the voyage we have just made to Archangel. We sailed round the snow-covered coast of the Arctic in terrifying silence. To seaward, we saw the pack ice and in the distance the blue ice wall itself. The sea was as still as a millpond and our ship's wake stretched behind us like a scratch on a piece of glass. Archangel turned out to be a ghost city, eerie under the great white arc of the sky . . . But since then our Arctic peace has been shattered with

terrible frequency by the drone of an approaching
shad. It circles us several times, then off it goes to
report our whereabouts and back come the dive
bombers. (I heard a good shad story in Murmansk. The C.O. of *Hyderabad* called up a shad,
that had been circling and circling, on his Aldis
lamp, and signalled in English: "For God's sake
go the other way, you're making me giddy."
Whereupon the shad replied: "Anything to
oblige," turned round and circled the other way.)
There is nothing half-hearted, though, about the
attacks. They come at us out of the sun, sup-
ported by high level bombers and low-flying
torpedo bombers. They come at us from all points
of the compass and do terrible, incalculable
damage . . . the sun is our enemy. I think of it as
an orange in a butcher's shop, on deep blue tiles,
and we look like being the meat on the slab if we
aren't very lucky.

April had been surprised the censor hadn't cut that
out, but no thick black ink had obscured Edward's
story.

On an earlier trip we had fog. Heavy snow was
falling and the ship was a mass of icicles and
drifts. We rigged a blue lamp as anchor light and
this shed a weird glimmer over the foredeck.
From time to time we could hear the moaning of
sirens as ships tried to grope their way down-
channel. At times I got the impression that we
might easily have strayed into another world – a
world which was lit only by a ghostly blue star,
where darkness reigned. I wondered if we had all

died in some unaccountable way and were serving our time in hell. I began to speculate whether we had been there for days or years. The crew moved like phantoms about the decks, swathed in bundles of clothing, the ship's bell clanged incessantly and the snow fell with the relentlessness of an advancing army.

I have plenty of time for reading; real self education. If this war is good for anything, it is good for that . . . and for thinking, and for writing to all of you. I have been thinking that if I survive, I might try my hand at writing.

'Goodnight, April.'

"I bet he'd have made a wonderful writer," she thought, shaken out of her reverie by Mr Stephenson's voice. He disappeared down the stairs, to reappear a moment later, walking briskly across the courtyard, his bulging briefcase under one arm. She wondered what he really knew about anything; if a relative's death to him would be merely another statistic in the frightening shipping losses; whether he had a heart, and if he had, she wondered wearily, what or who could touch it?

Bridie felt frozen as the Arctic ice in which Edward had died. She was aware of Ethel making endless pots of tea and of Ted, sitting in his chair by the door, rubbing his knuckles ceaselessly, until she itched to tell him to stop. She let Ethel's cups of tea go cold, unable to comfort her mother-in-law by drinking them. She wondered dully if she would ever know comfort again. She sat for a long time with her eyes closed, her head on one side, leaning on her open hand. Ted thought she was dozing, motioning at Ethel to leave the tea where it was when she went to move the cup.

But Bridie was thinking, trying to grasp it. She'd dreaded this moment so long, now it had come, it had no reality. Her mind went round and round in vague circles. He'd been gone so long, so far away, to such unimaginable places, that she'd imagined it might be easy to imagine him gone forever. Bridie, dry-eyed, discovered that the impossibility of his death was imagining him nowhere, when he had always been somewhere. How could a person be nowhere?

She opened her eyes and stared at the planks over the boarded-up window of Ethel's tiny scullery. She tried to remember Rosa, and her mother, but those deaths seemed too far away. Hearing Ethel fill the kettle yet again, her nerves snapped.

'Can't you sit down a minute and leave that blasted teapot alone?' she shouted.

Ethel leant her big, rough hands on the top of the running tap, leant her forehead on them and began to weep, her tears washed away down the drain by running water.

'Dear God, I'm sorry.' Bridie got up stiffly and held Ethel tight, wishing she could cry too, but no tears came.

David and April arrived in early evening. David patted Ethel diffidently on the shoulder and kissed his mother.

'How are you?' he asked.

No one answered.

'I'm so terribly sorry,' April said awkwardly, feeling the unbearable tension and at a loss what to do, fearful of making things worse.

'Not even a funeral,' said Ethel angrily, blowing her

nose while tears gathered in her eyes again. 'They can't even bring 'im home. They can't bring my son home.'

'Lost in ice. They never found him. We'll get a letter from 'is commanding officer but I don't know as they'll tell us the truth. They won't, if it don't suit 'em.'

'Ted,' shrilled Ethel warningly.

'We'll get a letter, duck.' He withdrew into his silent contemplation of the huge, weedy bombsite that stretched, pocked with craters and bits of wall, across from his battered home.

"My boy, my home; go on, 'elp yourselves and take the blimmin' lot," he thought savagely. "Why stop there?" He began rubbing his knuckles again. The movement eased the pain.

'I'd like to get out for a bit,' Bridie said. 'If you don't mind. I need some air.'

April looked at her anxiously.

'Shall we come with you?' she asked.

Bridie shook her head.

'I'd like to walk by myself for a little while. I hope you won't mind.'

'You don't want to be on your own at a time like this.'

'No, Gran.' David reached and took one of Ethel's red hands in his. 'Let Mum do what she wants.'

Ethel stood back reluctantly and watched Bridie take an old coat from the back of the door. Suddenly she looked tired and shrunken, worn out and grey as her threadbare coat, its hem turned down to make better use of it as a blanket when they sheltered rough during the early days of the Blitz.

"She feels destroyed," thought April. "Can't they all see it?"

'Let her go,' said David quietly.

* * *

Bridie walked, and after a long while she found herself standing in front of her house by the canal, its roof roughly repaired against rain and wind, its damaged side wall covered. Tarpaulin had been fixed against the bricks with long pieces of wood nailed across each other; two stout beams fastened in place, embedded deep in thick clay soil, braced it against falling down. Her cast iron railings and garden gate were long since taken for salvage, turned into tanks or guns, leaving open the weedy, overgrown little garden.

The Pope's favourite vantage point, beneath the lilac, was deserted. He'd gone wild, fending for himself, offended by their attempts to move him to Ethel's. Bridie brought food at first, until they needed it themselves. He hated cooked potato skins and ersatz gravy and one day after she'd called and called, and he didn't come, there seemed no reason to go back.

"It's as liveable as Ted and Ethel's place," she thought, wondering why she had stayed away so long. The front door scraped open, half jammed by thick drifts of grit and brick dust in which mice had made quick, scuttling tracks. The stairs had been knocked a bit sideways when the house was hit, but Ted had said they were safe enough. She left the door open, to let in light, and slowly climbed them, bringing down showers of dust and fragments of loose plaster. She smelled damp and the sour droppings of vermin. Crossing the undamaged landing, she turned to climb to the top floor, to the whorehouse. One wall was now tarpaulin, the floor sagging crazily towards it.

Most of her furniture was taken away, before it could be ruined or looted, but the big bed remained, its covers torn and twisted and stained by rain. She crept across the dangerous floor and sat on its edge. Timbers creaked, shifted, then settled again. She smoothed the cover with her hand, feeling it dreamily, slowly drew up her knees and crept underneath, pulling her coat around her. She pulled the bolster, where Edward's head had slept a thousand times, under her cheek, and closed her eyes with a sigh.

Sam Saul found her fast asleep in the light of a half moon whose meagre gleam shone through a gap in the partly mended roof. Frightened of bringing the whole room crashing down, he tiptoed cautiously across the boards and bent over, just able to make out her face on the pillow.

'Bridie,' he whispered, his hand out to stop her jumping up in fright, which could shake the floor. 'Bridie, my love.'

She sighed and turned her head on the pillow.

'Bridie, don't be frightened. It's me, Sam.'

She looked at him from half-closed, swollen eyes.

'Everyone is half crazy with worry, wondering where you'd gone. I didn't say; I just came over to make sure you're safe.'

'I don't think it is very safe,' she murmured drowsily. 'But it doesn't matter.'

Sam scratched his nose thoughtfully. 'You're right, it's not.'

'It's the only place I could bear to be,' she whispered.

He stroked dull grey hair back from her pale face.

'I know.'

'I can cry here, you see.'

'Yes.'

'Don't go, Sam.'

She felt him nod.

Then his weight was off the bed and she heard him

feel carefully round by the door leading to the landing. Satisfied it was safe enough, he carried in the old armchair that had once stood in David's bedroom.

'Are you warm enough?' he whispered. 'I've found some blankets. A bit damp.'

'Put them here,' she said.

Sam spread the blankets on the ruined bed and stretched himself out beneath them. Her hand crept out from under the coat and found his.

'I won't go away.'

She cried until she fell asleep again. Sam, with his head on his folded jacket, watched a mouse cleaning its whiskers contentedly in one of his smart leather shoes, and after a long time, he fell asleep, too.

When his mother and Sam woke in mid-morning – cramped, damp with dew, smelling of mildew and feeling headachy – David was striding up and down the courtyard beneath April's office, waiting for her to take her lunch break. Mr Stephenson said she could take two hours, in view of the situation, and at half-past eleven she ran down the steps. David looked drawn and red-eyed.

'You look awful,' April said sadly.

'I feel awful.'

'Haven't they found her?'

He shook his head. 'But she'll be all right, wherever she's gone, if people will just leave her alone.'

'Ethel?'

'Yes. She wants Mum there all the time. I'm not surprised Mum can't stand it.'

'Ted leans on her, too.'

'They can't help it, but they're going to have to manage, somehow. I've got to get back. Sounds heartless, doesn't it, but I don't mean it that way. It's just that I don't think I can do anything useful.'

'Poor David,' April said gently. 'It's hard for you not to be useful, isn't it?'

He seemed taken aback. 'What do you mean?'

'Only that you seem out of your depth where there aren't any answers. Just death, and living with it.'

He stared at her curiously. 'You keep surprising me, you know.'

'Do I?'

'Couldn't you surprise me and come back with me?'

'You know I can't. We keep going through it, David, but nothing has changed.'

'Can't or won't?' he asked bitterly.

'That's not fair!' she cried, and explained about asking to leave, and how Mr Stephenson had said he'd force her to stay because of the war. 'He says I have more of a duty to my country than to you. I haven't got any choice. Everyone else can see it, why can't you?'

He thought of his bare room in the big, isolated mansion in the country. The long, dark nights and lonely evenings.

'It's futile.'

'The war won't go on forever.'

'What if the Germans win? Do you ever think about that? We'll never have had time together.'

'No, I don't think like that, and I'm not starting now,' she said passionately. 'I can't, or I couldn't stand it.' She swept out her hand to the ruins, the implacable grey austerity that narrowed their lives day by day.

He began to button his raincoat. 'Well, there's no point in dragging this out, is there? I might as well go, and let you get back to your patriotic boss.'

'You're so full of self-pity,' she yelled furiously, 'I

can hardly believe it. Where's all that courage your mother's got?'

'In my mother.'

'Well, try and find some in yourself.'

David stood stock still, then nodded to himself. 'You make out you're a fragile little bird,' he said, 'but you're not. You're stronger than me.' He began to walk towards the tube station.

'David.'

He turned, but kept walking.

'I love you.'

'Can't think why,' he mumbled, but she didn't hear.

She waved and waved until he turned a corner and was lost to sight. Mr Stephenson drew back from the window as she retraced her steps slowly towards the office. He didn't want her to catch sight of him watching.

The moment she passed his door, he called her in and told her she had a salary increase, then just as abruptly dismissed her. It was the first time in his life that Mr Stephenson, smart lawyer who slid like a big, fat, invisible fish in and out of labyrinthine depths of legal nicety, had suffered from a bad conscience. He felt angry with her because he didn't like his weakness, not one little bit.

Chapter Twenty-Four

In the big lecture room on the ground floor, overlooking what had once been a magnificent park, Cutie took one look at David, further along the bench setting up some test tubes, and drew in a sharp breath of concern. He looked dreadful. She twisted the metal holder in front of her, making sure her own test tubes were secure, and sidled past the three students between them, peering over David's white-coated shoulder as he bent to adjust a screw.

'What have you been up to?' she murmured. 'You look like something the cat brought in.'

David squinted through his glasses at the blood in one of the glass tubes, and straightened up again.

'Is it supposed to coagulate like that?'

'No. Where have you been? Didn't they have razors, wherever it was?'

He ran his hand over the blond stubble on his chin and pulled a face. 'I spent the night sitting in a siding near Dorking, while they waited for some trucks. They stuck said trucks on the back of the train and evidently felt a need to put something in them. Bit like Eyeore and Pooh's honeypot. So we sat there for a few more hours, with everyone complaining and cursing and saying at least if there's an invasion the Germans could be depended on to run the railway efficiently, which nearly gave an old geezer in Air Force uniform apoplexy. And then, finally, they produced an extraordinary quantity of off-white lavatories. They stacked the lot in the trucks, looked very pleased with themselves, and eventually we got moving. I got a lift up from the station, so I just got here in time for this class. Have I missed much?'

'You can borrow my notes.'

'Thanks.'

'Come up afterwards and get them from my room.'

'Out of bounds.'

'Not for collecting a few notes. I think you'd better start that again.' She prodded the congealed mess of blood with the end of her pencil. 'Use that.' She pushed a tiny glass saucer containing a greyish powder towards him. 'That's the right stuff.'

'Don't know what I'd do without you,' whispered David, catching the lecturer's eye resting on the two of them.

'Miss Cuthell. Mr Holmes.'

'Thank you,' said Cutie aloud, grinning at the lecturer and making a show of consulting David's folder. 'I understand now.' She squeezed her way back to her own place and began practising routine tests on blood, her thoughts half on her work and half on the intriguing question of David. She smiled to herself, deftly adding three drops of a clear chemical to a test tube and shaking it. David Holmes, medical student and married man, was a very interesting quantity indeed.

At lunch time they climbed the three flights of stairs to the wing in which some of the women students had their rooms. David looked down the empty corridor and said, 'Are you sure?'

'There's no one up here usually at this time of day,' she said calmly, putting her key in the lock. 'They're all downstairs fighting for food.'

'It's better here than in London. Food's so scarce there they don't think of much else.'

Cutie opened her door and gestured him inside. It was a small, oblong attic room, with a sloping ceiling and a window that looked out over the roof of the great house. David could see the tops of the trees that lined the driveway, and steam coming from a kitchen vent rose past the chimney stacks.

'You are up in the Gods,' he remarked.

'I like it.'

'So do I.'

She had made it cosy by bringing from home a bright patchwork quilt that lay over her bed, scattered with small cushions. Warm apricot-coloured curtains framed the little window and two old armchairs had their sagging bottoms disguised by travel rugs and more fat cushions. A tiny gas fire stood in what had once been a servant's grate, and David watched her unfold a gas ring out of its top.

'I've never seen one of those before,' he observed.

'Sit down, and I'll make us some tea.' She took a miniature kettle from a cupboard, and a tea caddy. 'I have to get water from the bathroom.'

He sat back in one of the deep armchairs and stretched out his legs. He felt bone weary.

'This is nice,' he said when she came back.

She put the kettle on to heat and sat on the edge of the other chair. 'Where do you stay, when you go up to town?'

'With my in-laws. It's not town, really. They have a huge house in Ilford. That's Essex. My family live in

Hackney, though. Or used to. Mum's been bombed out and she's been living with my grandparents in what's left of their house. You can't call any of it living, really.'

'Has something happened, David?' she asked very gently. The little kettle began to sing. He gave a great, weary, resigned sigh, put his head back on the armchair and said with his eyes closed, 'My stepfather died.'

Cutie took the kettle off her tiny hob and poured water into a brown teapot.

'Do you want to tell me?'

He opened his eyes and looked at the top of her head as she bent to stir the tea. 'You are the first person who hasn't said you're sorry. Actually asked me what I feel.'

Cutie gazed into her teapot and waited.

'Everyone thinks of Mum and Ethel, of course. And for them it's frightful. Although no one says anything, and I know they don't mean it, there is a feeling that he was only my stepfather. I'm only entitled to a sort of second class grief; they've got the real thing.'

'Hm.'

'Sometimes I was so jealous of Edward, because Mum loved him more than me.'

There, it was out. He glanced away, shamefaced. 'I sound like a two year old, don't I?'

'Yes. A hurt two year old, who would like to cry but thinks he's too big for such babyish things. Who despises his own fine feelings while wallowing in them.'

David's blue eyes snapped open. 'Don't play the psychiatrist with me.'

Cutie ignored him. She poured two cups of tea, but left them standing in the fireplace.

'Was April very fond of him?'

'She barely knew him. He's been at sea all the time we've been married, except for one visit. That was when Mum was still in hospital.'

'Does April get on with your mum?'

David was silent.

'Your grandmother?'

'Not at first,' he said reluctantly. 'But they seem to have got a lot closer recently. I don't know what it is. I should be pleased, shouldn't I? Why aren't I?' He seemed genuinely puzzled.

'In-laws any good?'

He laughed, a short, humourless laugh that spoke volumes.

'Uh, dear.'

'They give paranoia a whole new meaning. She hovers in corners, watching with mean little eyes, always wanting a word. He bullies all of us in ways that are quite obvious until you try to do something about it, and then you find he's spun such a web, you're as trapped in it as he is. The harder you struggle, the tighter it pulls. I never met anyone like him before.'

'Nasty piece of work,' remarked Cutie, watching their tea go cold.

David laughed again and she saw the shame deep in his eyes. 'When I'm with April, I sometimes think they're hovering in the corner, by the ceiling somewhere. At any rate, I wouldn't put it past the old girl to have her ear to the keyhole.'

'Poor David. That must brighten up your love life.'

'Wrecks it.'

He wondered gloomily if confession really was good for the soul. The thought stirred a deep, uneasy memory.

'So there's no one there for you,' Cutie observed.

'How do you mean?'

'Your mum and stepfamily are all busy mourning your stepfather, April's being drawn into the conspiracy of womenfolk, and the in-laws go bump in the night. And I take it April isn't moving up here, or she'd be with you by now?'

David shook his head.

'To do with Mr Creepy?'

He nodded. 'I think so, although she has several irrefutable reaons for needing to stay in London. All roads seem to lead back to her dad, though, however tortuously.'

'How very sad.' She sat at his feet, clasping her knees in her arms. He felt a rush of affection for her; she seemed to care more than his family.

'I am sorry, David. About your stepfather and everything. It's one of the saddest stories I've heard.'

He coughed to dislodge the lump in his throat.

'I'll make us some more tea,' she said brightly.

When she came back from refilling the kettle, Cutie found him asleep, his spectacles skewed to one side, the fair stubble casting shadows on his cheeks. She stood holding the kettle, gazing at him consideringly, then lit the gas ring and made another journey to rinse the cups and empty the teapot. Pouring herself a fresh cup, she took it to her desk, shrugged out of her white lab coat, and settled down to work.

She worked steadily until footsteps along the corridor and several banged doors told her that afternoon lectures were over. David stirred in the armchair and stretched out his legs. Cutie got up and locked her door, then she went to the armchair and bent over him, her hand against his cheek.

'David,' she said softly.

He woke with a start, peering over the spectacles that hung awry from one ear.

'Oh,' he said. 'I've been asleep.'

'All afternoon.'

He found he was holding her hand without knowing how it got there.

'I would have put you to bed,' she said, 'Only you looked too comfortable to disturb.'

'I feel comfortable with you,' he said, realizing as he said it that it was truer of her than of anyone he knew.

'Good.'

He reached up – she was so close – and pulled the comb from her hair. It swung round her face like amber silk and her half-closed, well-mascaraed lashes dropped in mock confusion.

'I like the way you paint your face. How do you manage to get make-up when no one else can?'

'Here and there.'

'Cutie . . .'

Her eyes were so close he saw tiny flecks of black and silver in her irises.

'Would you . . .?'

'I thought you'd never ask.' She pulled gently on his hand and led him to the bed beneath the slope of the attic ceiling.

David stood for a long moment, feeling the warm curve of her neck under his hand and the steady beat of her heart against his. He thought of April and tried to pull away, but loneliness engulfed him with its familiar dull, heavy pain. She lifted her head and her eyes held his myopic gaze until he sighed and muttered, 'Come then.' And the loneliness and sadness were blotted out for just a little while.

* * *

Six weeks later Cutie saw him several evenings in a row on the telephone, apparently listening to someone talking nineteen to the dozen on the other end. She tried to get him to come out walking in the lovely May evenings of 1942 but he was preoccupied and distant. He seemed distracted and absorbed even when they were in bed together and since he didn't volunteer any information, she asked him bluntly what was going on.

'April's pregnant.'

'But that's wonderful news, isn't it? Why are you looking so sour?'

David leant on his elbow and looked down at her, still flushed from their lovemaking.

'Look at me. I'm lying in your bed, talking about my wife to another woman, while she's all on her own with those vultures in Essex. It's hardly the manly thing to do, is it?'

'Fit of the guilts, then.'

'Yes.'

'There's no need for it.' Cutie rolled restlessly on to her side and pulled a cigarette out of a packet.

'I wish you wouldn't smoke,' David told her, suddenly irritated.

'I know, but I fancy one.' She lit it calmly, indifferent to his distaste. 'You needn't feel guilty; I'm no threat to April. When the war is over you'll get together properly and pick up where you left off. All this,' she gestured to their bodies, 'is only a way of bearing it all. Nothing in our lives is certain any more. We have to get through the best we can. I don't feel guilty about that.'

David breathed in a cloud of cigarette smoke and coughed.

'I feel guilty, and then I see you every day and I want you even more. I like you so much, that's the trouble.

April and I are lovers, but we haven't had time to be friends. With you, there's the most wonderful feeling of friendship, and I don't want to lose you.'

'You needn't. We can be friends afterwards. Sex is neither here nor there, really. It doesn't matter very much compared to the rest.'

'I thought only men talked like that.'

'Goes to show how many women you really know.'

'Not many,' he admitted.

'Well, then. What are you fussing about?'

'Letting April down. I don't think she'd see it your way.'

'Then let her free herself from the Uglies and come here,' said Cutie quietly and, David realized, angrily. 'If she can't do that, then she has only herself to blame. She's as guilty as we are.'

'Oh, I say, that's not fair . . .'

'Who said anything about fair?' Cutie slid another cigarette out of the packet and David noticed with astonishment that her hands were shaking with anger. 'If life was fair we wouldn't be stuck here, in the middle of a war, half starved, bored, scared to death, and only kept safe in the middle of this Godforsaken countryside because they'll need us to patch up the bloody bodies they're busy maiming in ever more imaginative ways. And you want to wallow in guilt and self pity! You disgust me, you really do. If you don't like it, get out.'

She swept off the bed and banged her little kettle on to the gas ring. David watched her buttocks quivering with indignation and burst out laughing.

'You're quite right,' he cried. 'You always are, damn you.'

A thin stream of smoke trailed over her head from the cigarette in the corner of her mouth.

'I can't stand whingeing.'

'I promise I won't. Scout's honour.'

She whirled round with a freezing glare. 'Honour is an unfortunate concept to bring into it.' Smoke got into her eye and she seemed to wink, at odds with her anger.

'Now who's on their high horse?' David grinned.

Suddenly her shoulders slumped and she took the cigarette out of her mouth and threw herself into one of her chairs, one naked leg swinging over the arm.

'I'm a mite jealous and I'm not used to it. Take no notice.'

'You are?' cried David in astonishment.

'I want a baby, too. But it's out of the question. Your April has ruffled my feathers.' She gave a forced laugh. 'I don't ruffle easily and I'm not good at it.'

Well, I'm blowed.'

'Don't say any more. Not another word, or we'll fall out.' She stuck her head round the side of the chair. 'Agreed?'

'If you like,' nodded David, feeling all of a heap.

'I do,' she said firmly. 'Do you want some tea?'

He opened his mouth to say yes, when there was a heavy knock at the door and a key began to turn in the lock.

'Who the hell . . .?' David pulled the sheet across himself as the cleaner marched in, putting her mop and bucket down just inside the door with a clank and a thump. Cutie, stark naked, sprawled in her armchair with a cigarette hanging from her lips, met Mrs Whitley's narrowed little eyes, seeing them flicker to the bed then back to her, first surprised, then outraged, then coldly calculating.

'A love nest, eh? I suspected as much,' she observed in her flat tones.

'What are you doing here at this time?' demanded Cutie.

'Didn't get finished,' stated the cleaner laconically.

'Would you please get out and come back at a more convenient time?' Cutie asked, staring the woman down. She ground the cigarette out in her unused saucer, stood up nonchalantly and fetched a robe from the floor at the side of the bed. Knotting it round her waist, she turned to the cleaner, who stood unmoved by the door.

'Please?' she said sweetly. 'You can come back in ten minutes.'

'You're not fit to be a doctor. Strumpet!' hissed the cleaning woman, closing the door and leaning on it with her mop clutched to her breast.

'That's a bit strong,' protested David, but she cut straight across him.

'I knew it soon as I set eyes on you. A bad one if ever I saw one, I said.'

'Did you really?' said Cutie coolly.

'And him.' The woman pointed a yellow duster at David, jabbing it viciously. 'Him and his mouth.'

'Oh dear, I knew it,' muttered Cutie.

'Think you can treat people like dirt, don't you, just because you're going to be doctors? Think it gives you the right to walk over anyone you fancy. I'll show you whether you can walk over me.' She twisted the duster venomously in her red, raw hands and shuffled further into the room, towards David on the bed. He instinctively shrank from her. 'Get her out,' he begged Cutie.

'I'll go when I want to,' snapped the cleaner.

'Look, I know Mr Holmes didn't mean to offend you. I'm sure he'll apologize. Won't you?' she said meaningfully to David, who sat up.

'Yes. Of course. I'm frightfully sorry if I hurt your feelings. I didn't mean to.'

Mrs Whitley shook her head.

'Won't do.'

'Well, what will do?' snapped Cutie, exasperated.

'Don't take that tone with me, young woman. I could have you two expelled for this. I want compensation for the trouble and upset you've put me to, or I'll have to report you.'

'Compensation?' Cutie's voice rose incredulously. 'Whatever do you mean?'

'She means she wants money, for keeping her mouth shut,' said David.

The cleaner nodded vigorously.

'Good grief.' Cutie looked at her closely, as if she were a particularly ugly specimen in a jar in the path lab. 'Do you really.'

'Yes,' said the woman defiantly.

'Well, how much did you have in mind?'

The cleaner's greedy eyes screwed themselves up and she took her time about calculating.

'Pound a week. Between the two of you,' she added generously.

David gasped. 'I can't pay that. I haven't got it.'

'You'll have to find it, then, won't you? Ten minutes, you said?' She picked up her bucket and clanked aggressively out of the room, banging the door behind her.

'Oh, damn!' Cutie stared after her furiously. 'Now what do we do?'

'She'll keep her word. She'll report us if we don't pay,' David said, wishing that this would turn out to be a bad dream. He pinched himself; he was distressingly awake.

'They'll expel us,' Cutie said flatly.

'Yes.'

We can't let that happen.'

'You got any money?'

'Less than you, I should think.'

'We'll have to pay her, give ourselves time to think.'

'Never pay blackmailers,' said Cutie bleakly, 'is advice easier given than taken.'

They fell silent.

'I can't see any way out,' she admitted.

An idea came into David's mind. He shivered, but the alternative was certain expulsion and utter disgrace; the end of all his dreams. 'I think I know someone who might be able to help us. I don't know how, but he fixes things. I could ask him.'

'Fixes things. How are you going to fix that evil old woman?'

'I don't know, but I can find out if there's a way.'

Suddenly Cutie stopped looking haughty and looked young and crumpled and frightened.

'Well, you'd better do it quick,' she said, 'because otherwise we've had it.'

'You and me both,' agreed David darkly. He dressed rapidly and went downstairs to make some telephone calls. The problem would be how to track down Mr Hubbard if he'd been bombed out in the Blitz. At first he had no luck, pretending he needed new spectacles and wanted to find his optician.

'Can't you go locally, where you are?' asked a couple of people.

'No,' he said. 'Can't afford it. Hubbard is cheap.'

He dialled a couple more times, and then he struck lucky.

* * *

The dwarf welcomed him into his consulting room with a flourish and a beaming smile.

'Going to let me check you over while you're visiting home, eh?' He rubbed his gnarled fingers together and gestured David to the old black chair.

'What happened to the other place?' David surveyed the makeshift surgery as Mr Hubbard scrabbled in a filing cabinet for his records.

'Time bomb went right through the roof into the top floor. By the time they came to defuse it the place was a perishin' great hole in the ground. But I had a chance to get my stuff out, and this was empty, so here we are. I was only closed for a couple of days.'

The new surgery was on the ground floor of a tenement opposite the corner where Sam Saul used to have his office. David knew it well.

'And how are your studies?' enquired the dwarf, dragging his little stool over so that he could climb up to David's level. He grunted over the card on which he had David's prescription, then turned off the main light. In the warm glow of the desk lamp, David felt time slip back in an extraordinary, comforting way.

Hubbard held a black card over David's right eye. 'Start reading the card. Left eye first.'

He read the first two lines and hesitated.

'Actually, that's what I wanted to see you about,' he mumbled.

'Finish the card.'

David did as he was told.

'And the right eye.'

David began to wonder if he hadn't heard.

'Good,' said the dwarf, reaching for the lens holder and perching it on David's nose. 'Eyes troubling you with all that reading, are they?'

'No, it's not that.'

Pursing his thick lips, the dwarf put a masking lens in front of David's left eye and popped a clear lens in front of the other one. 'Now read the card.'

'I've got a problem,' David said desperately, fearing Mr Hubbard was going to refuse to help by ignoring him.

'Of course. Why else would you come here? You can get your eyes fixed anywhere. You must have made quite an effort to get here from where you are, so it must be a considerable problem, little brother.'

'It's a woman.'

Mr Hubbard said, 'Hold still, will you?' and dropped another lens into the holder. 'Your wife?'

'You know I'm married?' asked David, telling himself that he should know better than to be surprised at what the dwarf knew.

'I keep up,' he said vaguely. 'How's she doing?'

'Doing?'

'The baby,' said Mr Hubbard archly.

'Good grief, you really do keep up, as you put it.'

The dwarf whistled through his teeth while he put a third lens in the holder. The card became clearer almost right down to the bottom.

'Better or worse?'

'Much better.'

'Let's try the other one.' He reached across David's nose and whipped out the masking lens.

'Look . . .' said David.

'Woman trouble. It's not your wife, therefore it is most likely some adulterous association that threatens your peace of mind. Yes?'

'Not exactly. Yes.'

'Not exactly. Yes. You'll have to explain.'

David did.

'Ah,' said Mr Hubbard, having listened to the sorry tale without comment. 'And what do you expect me to do?'

David, embarrassed and fearful, was lost for words.

'You want another little favour, is that it?'

'Yes.' David sighed with relief.

'Read the card.'

He read the card.

The dwarf pulled at his long lower lip.

'Not much to choose between you and Dad, is there?'

'What do you mean?'

'He had an eye for the ladies, didn't he? Got carried along and never knew where he was going. Sounds like you're a bit of a chip off the old block, eh?'

'This is different.'

The dwarf gave a wheezing laugh and said sarcastically, 'It always is, dear boy, it always is.'

'It's not Cutie who's the problem. It's this other woman. She'll blackmail us and if we can't pay. She'll shop us.'

'And to think of the education you've had.' Mr Hubbard sounded pained.

'Tell on us, then.'

'Hardly better,' murmured the little man. 'But one can't expect miracles.'

'I was hoping for one,' admitted David. 'You did a miracle last time.'

'Don't "do" miracles. Perform them.'

'Stop picking holes in my grammar and tell me whether you can help. I don't know what we'll do if you can't.' David twisted round in the chair to look at him full face through the heavy lens holder.

'You look as though you've got a gas mask on,' remarked Mr Hubbard. 'Do please keep still.'

'Well, can you?'

Mr Hubbard became very still, his rubbery face only inches from David's.

'How could you pay?'

His heart began to race with fear.

'Another sacrifice or something?'

'What have you left?'

'Left?'

'You've already bargained away your soul. What else have you that could possibly be of sufficient value?'

Utter dismay chilled David to the bone. Suddenly it was no longer a dishonest game to be played with the dwarf, a bogus promise for real goods, but an awful, inexplicable reality.

'Your immortal soul is your most precious possession. You have mortgaged it already,' the dwarf pointed out relentlessly. 'You have no surety of comparable value to offer.'

'You mean I'm bankrupt?' David fell into the dwarf's terminology with a sense of terror.

'Pretty much so. Unless you have an asset we don't know about.'

David shook his head and the lens holder wobbled. Mr Hubbard lifted it off and looked at it thoughtfully, weighing it in his hand as he weighed something else in his mind.

'There is one thing . . .'

'What?' asked David eagerly.

'Your child.'

David paled. 'What about my child?'

'If you pledge us the child's soul, we'd accept that.'

David held his breath in horror.

'You mean, you want me to sell you the baby like I sold you myself? That's wicked!'

'All right, all right. Don't get righteous about it; no one's making you do anything. You go and sort your little problem out for yourself and I shan't say another word.'

'How is it possible? To sell someone else . . . How can that be possible?' Trembling, David watched him note the lens prescription on his card.

'It's not, strictly speaking. It merely weighs the odds in our favour. Call it lease lend, if you like. I'll take an IOU on the child, but if you don't think . . .' He shrugged.

'But I can't do anything else. I'll get expelled.'

'You should have thought of that before your libido got out of hand,' said the dwarf softly.

David's lips trembled uncontrollably as he tried to frame the words, but for a long time they wouldn't come. With his back to him, writing at his shaded desk, the dwarf felt his terrible struggle and sensed rather than heard his capitulation.

'You are unspeakably evil.'

'I'm afraid so. But I force you into nothing. These are choices you make of your own free will. You came to me for help; I did not invite you.'

'But I have no choice!'

The dwarf turned on him such a withering look of comtempt that David shrank away.

'All right,' he whispered. The words came out in an agonized voice. The dwarf shivered with ecstasy.

'The child?'

'Oh, God damn you, yes.'

"God has, long ago," thought the dwarf, "and you have damned yourself, little brother, a thousand times over today. I would not be in your shoes for all the delights of eternity." Aloud he said, 'There will be just the small matter of the sacrifice, then, as before. Will you see to that?'

Through stiff, white lips David said, 'Yes.'

'Righto, then. I'll have your spectacles made up and send them on, if you'll leave your address on that bit of paper.'

'What then?'

'That's all.'

'No, I mean, what will you do? About . . . you know . . .'

'Ah. It'll sort itself out. If you could just pop something in the post that belongs to her . . . you have no need to worry about further details. That's my part of the deal.'

David wrote out his address, his hand shaking so that he had to print in big letters. The dwarf clapped him on the back sympathetically.

'It passes,' he assured him. 'You'll find it fades away. I'd even warrant you don't believe a word of it in a day or two's time. Disbelief is a most merciful thing, little brother.' He shook this head with a peculiar kind of sadness. 'A most merciful thing,' he repeated.

David took a deep breath and was very afraid he was going to be sick. 'I have to go,' he mumbled.

Mr Hubbard let him, standing gazing at the scrap of paper with the address.

'I wish it hadn't come to this,' he said angrily, as though to an unseen presence. 'I feel rather bad about this one.' He cocked an ear as though listening for a reply, but nothing moved or spoke. Annoyed, he threw a handful of glistening lenses at the wall. They dropped to the floor in a glittering shower of broken glass and

Mr Hubbard thought somewhere he heard a laugh.

That night David went down to the Stepney pub which had escaped the bombing and got quietly and insensibly drunk. A week later Mrs Whitley slipped on a wet patch of her own cleaning liquid that she'd carelessly spilt and went head over heels down a flight of thirty stone steps. Her neck was broken. The students had a collection for her family and some went to the funeral service in the village church. David and Cutie avoided each other, unable to meet the fearful questions in each other's eyes. The affair was over.

Chapter Twenty-Five

'Well I never!' said Lizzie. 'Are you sure about this?'

Bridie glanced at the letter again and then nodded. 'It'll do me good to get away. Time goes so slowly with not much to do except stand in queues for food. I think if I was really busy, it would take my mind off . . . things.'

'You don't think you might be doing too much? After being ill and everything?'

'I've had an examination and I'm quite fit to do something like target plotting or driving. It's long hours, but I don't mind that. And it'll be better than sitting brooding. I need to do something, Lizzie, keep myself occupied, or sometimes I think I'll go mad. And I don't want to be cruel, but I'd like to get away from Ethel. I know she's unhappy, and only wants comfort, but if she goes on about Edward much more, I'll be at my wit's ends.'

Lizzie took the letter again and read it properly, then handed it back. 'It's a nice uniform. I've rather fancied it for myself,' she said, smiling. There was a knock at the door.

'It's on the latch,' called Lizzie.

Sam Saul walked in, looking unusually gloomy.

'Hello,' he growled, put out to find Lizzie in Bridie's kitchen when he wanted her to himself.

'Guess what?' cried Lizzie. 'The ATS has accepted Bridie. She starts next Monday.'

Sam's black brows drew together like thunder. 'You've actually gone and done it?' he demanded.

'Yes,' said Bridie.

He shook his head, as if to show he was beyond words. Lizzie hid a grin.

'We'll have to do without her,' she remarked.

Sam scraped a chair out from the table and sat down heavily without being asked. 'I'm fed up with doing without,' he said childishly.

Bridie gave a rare smile and pointed out that the ATS might put her on the guns in Victoria Park, and then they'd see as much of her as ever.

'It's Bridget and Oliver's birthday on July the fourteenth. That's the day after tomorrow. Ollie can't be here, but Bridget's at home. We were wondering how to make a cake – have a little party. Now we can celebrate my new job as well.'

'Cake? You'll be lucky,' scoffed Sam, glad to put a dampener on the idea of a celebration.

'Bridget went dancing down the palais with a GI the other evening,' said Lizzie, 'and came home with chocolate. What do they call those things?'

'Hershey bars,' said Sam.

Lizzie grinned. 'Trust you to know,' she said tartly. 'Well, it seems they've got everything. Soap, food, sweets . . . I told Bridget she'd better bring him and his goodies home, but she's all off jitter-bugging and that.' Lizzie sounded quite envious. 'I'd love some real stockings,' she went on wistfully. 'It's not the same, soaking in potassium permanganate dye, is it? Never really looks right.'

'It's chillier, that's for sure,' remarked Bridie. 'But I

suppose with uniform we'll get it all provided.'

Sam, blind to the grey in her hair and the long lines of pain and grief that marked her face, thought of predatory officers stalking pretty women and his eyes sparked jealousy.

'Bridget says they all go off to Madame Tussaud's; she says they call it the Wax Museum and they'd rather see that than Buckingham Palace. Funny, that, isn't it?'

'Blasted Yanks think they know it all,' growled Sam.

'Well, we have something here they never had at home, haven't we? That'll give them fresh experiences,' observed Lizzie quietly. They looked at her curiously.

'What's that, then?' asked Sam.

'Bombs,' answered Lizzie, her mouth compressed into a straight line. 'And if any of them come hoity toity with me, I shall tell them so.'

They stared at her, then Sam broke into a wide, sardonic smile. 'Quite right, too.'

Lizzie got up and went over to the dresser. 'She did bring one thing home that I thought was rather nice. You can't eat it, but it made me nearly cry to read it, seeing it written down like that. Here.'

She had a copy of the pamphlet given to GIs when they arrived in Britain. Leaning over Sam's shoulder, Bridie studied it.

'"Don't be misled," she read aloud, "by the British tendency to be soft spoken and polite."'

'Huh! They should try listening to ack-ack crews, they should,' remarked Bridie. 'The language is enough to make your hair curl, walking across the park.'

She read on.

If they need to be, they can be plenty tough. The

English language didn't spread across the oceans and over the mountains and jungles and swamps of the world because these people were pantywaists . . . Britain may look a little shop worn and grimy to you. The British people are anxious to have you know that you are not seeing their country at its best. The houses haven't been painted because factories are not making paint – they're making planes. The famous English gardens and parks are either unkempt because there are not men to take care of them, or they are being used to grow vegetables. British taxicabs look antique because Britian makes tanks for herself and Russia and hasn't time to make new cars. British trains are cold because power is needed for industry, not for heating. The trains are unwashed and grimy because men and women are needed for more important work than carwashing. The British people are anxious for you to know that in normal times Britain looks much prettier, cleaner, neater . . .

'They didn't take much of a look at pre-war Plaistow, did they, whoever wrote that?' said Bridie, after a lengthy silence.

'I thought it was lovely,' said Lizzie defensively.

'Well, I don't agree with all his ideas, but when David says one good thing about the war is that it's pulled down the slums and brought full employment, I have to say he's got a point. Remember what it was like before, Lizzie. We're puttin' on rose coloured spectacles if we think different. We did need shakin' up, and it seems it's taken this to do it. It's bringing all sorts of things Francis spent his life dreamin' about.'

'She's right,' said Sam.

Lizzie sighed. 'I know. It just seemed nice to have someone saying they appreciated us, for a change. It was nice to be reminded that life wasn't always this way. I didn't mean I don't remember the slums and the unemployment.'

'So long as the government remember too.' Bridie turned to look out of the window at the bright July day outside. 'And so long as we win.'

'So what are we going to do about cake?' asked Lizzie briskly, to dispel the air of seriousness before it turned to gloom.

'I've got a couple of bottles of champagne,' volunteered Sam.

Lizzie laughed out loud. 'I think champagne comes out of your taps, Sam. Well, I won't ask you where you get these things. I'll just say, yes please.'

'Let's see what you've got in your larder.' Lizzie went to the door of Bridie's pantry just as there was another knock at the door.

'That'll be April. She said she'd come after work because she was leavin' early. On the latch,' Bridie shouted up the stairs, before following Lizzie into the pantry. As April came in, the two women surveyed the shelves.

'Yes, well,' drawled Lizzie, 'fish paste isn't much help, never mind whale sausages – revolting things. Do you eat them?'

'Not much choice, is there?'

Lizzie pulled a face. 'I can't. I'm sick. They stink of fish.'

'I've got an egg I've been saving,' offered Bridie reluctantly.

'Kangaroo tail soup?' squawked Lizzie, grabbing a

tin off the shelf. 'Where on earth did you get that?'

'Up the street. One of the neighbours had a food parcel from Australia with that in it. I'm going to save it for Christmas,' she added firmly, snatching it out of Lizzie's hand, afraid it'd get eaten. 'It's a present. Special. Even you can't have it.'

'Prunes!' Lizzie pounced. 'And sultanas. Oh, we're away. Here, put them on the table. Got any flour?'

Bridie hesitated.

'I'll pay you back,' Lizzie said hastily. 'I don't mean to eat your rations.'

Bridie reached into the empty meat safe. 'Here. But I do need it back.' She had an ounce of butter, a twist of paper with a quarter of a pound of sugar and a couple of ounces of flour. 'We should be able to do nicely,' she said, carrying the precious stores through into the kitchen.

April looked round-eyed at the sugar, and moaned. 'I'd give anything to gobble that up,' she said. 'I'm hungry all the time, and I have this longing for sweets. It's torture. I lie in bed at night, thinking about them until my stomach rumbles and groans.' She laughed. 'Trust me to have cravings for something I can't have. Wouldn't be fish paste or boiled nettles, would it? We've got plenty of them.'

Bridie dipped her finger into the sugar.

'Here, lick,' she said, holding out her finger as if to a child.

April pulled an ecstatic face and took the tiny treat.

'I'm goin' off to the ATS, so we're trying to make a cake for that, and for Bridget's birthday,' Bridie told her without preamble. 'But it's a bit tricky because we're short.'

'A cake to eat?' asked April.

They looked at her.

'What I mean is, my friend Rachael made a cake out of a hat box. She iced it and everything and it looked really lovely, but the only bit you could eat was the icing,' she admitted mournfully.

'To eat,' said Lizzie firmly.

'I'm not havin' cardboard cake,' said Bridie stoutly. 'I wouldn't give Hitler the satisfaction.'

'Prunes or nothing,' Lizzie giggled, getting into the spirit of the thing. 'It'll be a lovely surprise for Bridget. She won't expect anything.'

'I'll bring the champagne over tomorrow, then.' Sam got up to go. 'In the evening. What time?'

'About eight do you and Bridget? April, can you get here?' They all nodded.

'Eight then, Sam, please.'

He let himself out without ever having said what it was that had brought him in the first place. He needed to have Bridie on her own, and it didn't look as though he'd have a chance before she left. He caught a bus at the end of Mare Street that was going more or less in his direction and sat as it picked its way slowly along through the ruins, lost in thought.

They soaked the prunes and mixed them with a few sultanas into the butter and flour and baked it into a solid lump.

'Looks nice and filling,' remarked April, her mouth watering. 'What about the sugar?' she added hopefully.

Bridie gave her another taste and then tipped it into a bowl with cocoa, the egg white and a drop of water. Mixed together, the result was a slightly gritty chocolate icing that spread only a little lumpily over the cooling cake.

'There,' cried Lizzie, standing back to view it, 'how's that?'

'It needs something written on it,' said April, scraping every last trace of icing off the bowl with her finger.

Bridie shook her head. 'That's the last of the sugar.'

April chased a smear of chocolate thoughtfully. 'I know. Got any condensed milk?'

'A small tin.'

'I could pipe some on to it with a toothpaste tube. Use it like a nozzle.'

They gazed at her respectfully. Bridie emptied her toothpaste on to a saucer and April cut open the end of the tube. They washed it thoroughly and watched with bated breath as she squeezed 'Happy Birthday Bridget' on to the cake.

'It doesn't run too much,' she remarked, seeing the milk congeal slowly. 'I think that looks really nice. It'll be a treat with champagne.'

'You haven't put Bridie's name on. It's her cake, too.'

Bridie saw her daughter-in-law's face fall, and saw her glance sadly at the bit of sweet milk left in the tube.

'Eat it up, love,' she said, smiling. 'I can do without.'

'Truly?'

'Truly,' said Bridie. 'You look after my grandchild and eat all you can. That's what matters.'

It was a sobering thought, a grandchild, born into the middle of all this. Bridie, without even really thinking about it, went to the pantry and took down the can of Kangaroo tail soup.

'And now a treat for supper, for pregnant ladies with cravings,' she said brightly, glaring at Lizzie and daring her to say anything.

Lizzie covered her mouth and spluttered.

'Shut up, Lizzie Norris.'

Lizzie, grinning, did as she was told.

They had a wonderful meal and sat round the old kitchen table, listening to the house creak and settle around them as the evening cooled and light dew covered the tarpaulin roof. Plaster trickled down the damaged walls with a sound like the rustling paws of a thousand mice. Away to the north searchlights swept the sky as an ack-ack unit practised manoeuvres in a serenely empty sky. April caught a late bus home, full of kangaroo tail soup and contentment, and with Bridget's champagne party still to come.

Closing her eyes, she held the moment; these were things she'd dreamed of, family all round her, people to love and laugh with, people who joked and cried and cared about each other. People who fought and made up again. People who died. People who grieved and who yet lived on in each other. Real people, thought April, with a deep, deep sigh, and I'm one of them, and my baby will belong to all of us. Folding her hands across the small swell of her belly she felt dreamily that at last, in the middle of all the war and the worry and the hunger and her loneliness for David, in spite of everything, today she really knew what happiness was.

Sam arrived in the house in Golder's Green to find his wife and the Professor sitting together in the drawing room in the dark, the blackout not up and the sky beyond the windows crisscrossed by searchlights.

'No planes,' said Ruthie, watching the window. 'I don't know why they've got all those lights going.'

'I would have taken everyone down to the cellar if there had been any danger,' the Professor told him.

Sam burned with annoyance. The Pole was beginning to talk as though he was head of the household and Ruthie had taken to deferring to him on all sorts of small questions that before she would have dealt with on her own. Christina, Ruthie said, now whispered half a dozen English words when close to her, though she'd never spoken in Sam's presence. He was beginning to think of the Pole as a sort of blasted poodle, with his anxious, respectful eyes that followed Ruthie everywhere. That was what Sam had wanted to talk to Bridie about.

'I have good news. We wait here until you come home, to tell you,' said the Professor.

Sam tapped his nails impatiently on the back of their sofa. 'Yes.'

'I have the job.'

'The one in Timbuctoo?' asked Sam under his breath.

'Please?'

'Excellent. The one in . . . ?'

'With the college that has moved to Surrey. The one from London.'

'There's probably several,' Sam muttered, refusing to be drawn into a long list of universities roosting in the provinces, well away from the bombs.

'The medical college. I teach physiology,' the Professor said proudly.

'Congratulations. When do you start?'

'In October. I am hoping you very kindly allow us to stay until I find a house. Then we go, but we never forget your kindness, Mr Saul. And this dear lady.'

Sam coughed irritably. 'Told the children?'

The little Pole beamed in the darkness. 'They are so happy.'

Sam startled them both by saying loudly, 'But they'll miss Ruth, won't they? Miss her badly.'

'Sam . . .' she warned.

'You are going to have to make your own decisions, Ruth. Our friend, too. Let me know, if you would be so kind, what the outcome is.'

'Sir . . .'

Sam turned away. 'Let us not waste words lying to each other. I can't be bothered,' he said, and instantly regretted the coarseness of his tone. 'I mean, I understand that there are serious questions to be considered. I hope I make myself clear.'

Left in the dark, Ruthie and the Professor turned to each other in consternation.

'Oh dear,' wailed Ruthie, her lipstick a purple gash in the searchlights' swinging beams. The Professor took her hand and held it tightly.

'He is a good man, your husband,' he said softly. 'He has – how you say it – a gold heart, but he hide it well. He give us permission, you know? You hear that like me?'

Ruthie clutched his thin, dry hand.

'He isn't a good Jew. I never could make him observe.'

The Professor murmured, 'Is a shame. But he is good. Maybe not good Jew, but a good man. You don't grieve to lose him?'

'Of course I do.' Ruthie held a handkerchief to her eyes. 'But what's to hold us together? Him and his business, day and night. I never know where he is, and I'm always worrying he's in trouble.' She sniffed and dabbed damply at her cheeks with the tiny embroidered handkerchief.

'And your son? What will he say?'

'I hardly ever see him. That's Sam's fault, too. The boy was always scared of him and his sharp tongue. Now he's in the Air Force we don't see him, but he stops away anyway. They want to break my heart.'

'Hush,' said the Professor, worried that her wailing would bring Sam back downstairs again. Eventually, Ruthie subsided and, seeing her tears shining in the lights that flashed across her face, he took her in his arms and kissed her.

'We tell him tomorrow, yes?'

'Yes,' sniffed Ruthie.

For a long time they sat hand in hand, watching the searchlights silently. Upstairs, Sam heard his wife's familiar wails die away into silence. He could picture exactly what had silenced her and despite the pain her choice would bring him, he grinned maliciously.

'Over to you, old son,' he muttered savagely. 'You'll be a fine Jewish husband for a very fine Jewish wife. Sabbaths, prayers, kosher cooking and the whole perishing caboodle! Congratulations to you both. You deserve each other.'

The bitter pill was that he knew they did.

'Bloody deserving people,' he snarled to himself, getting into bed. Nursing his grievance, he fell asleep instantly and never heard Ruthie come up two hours later, fearing a scene. All she heard was Sam Saul's deep, rhythmic breathing which told her he was fast asleep. "Tomorrow then," she thought, and lay awake, listening to the pounding of her own nervous heart, dreaming with fearful excitement of a new future; a blissful future; above all, a kosher future.

'Poor Sam,' breathed Ruthie sadly.

Sam coughed in his sleep and turned over and Ruthie

eyed his back, feeling foolishly that all her sympathy was wasted.

Chapter Twenty-Six

'What I would like to know, Miss,' said Eileen one evening, having come up to April's flat on the pretext of bringing her a bit of scented soap she'd found in the back of a cupboard somewhere, 'is what you're going to do with this baby once you've had it? What are you now? Five months?'

'The antenatal and I are agreed on that.'

'Glad to hear you agree with someone occasionally.'

'Mum, if all you want is to argue, I've got things to do. I've brought some work home.'

'I don't know. A young girl like you never going out, stuck here day in day out on your own. It's not right.'

'If I was going out, you'd complain I was frivolous.'

Eileen sniffed. 'You haven't answered my question. What are you going to do with the baby?'

Resigned, April opened her door wide. 'Come on in, Mum. I'll make you a cup of tea.'

'You're being evasive, April.'

'No. I want to talk to you about the baby, only I've been putting it off.'

'Oh yes?'

April laid her little table with cups and saucers. 'It'll have to be black. I'm out of milk. I can't seem to stop drinking it.'

'That's your condition.'

'Yes. Mum.'

Eileen waited, curious.

'Do you think that Dad might go on paying David's fees if I stopped work? If I stayed at home with the baby? I could find somewhere cheap near the college or stay here, though I'd rather not. If Dad could pay the fees, we could scrape by on David's scholarship money until I could work again. Or I wondered if he might lend us the money, if he doesn't want to give it. I could pay him back later on.'

She searched Eileen's face for clues as to what the answer might be. Their eyes locked. Eileen saw with familiar pain the image of her sister when she was young. Exquisite, intense, vivid, radiant; all the hurtful words from the past, long gone compliments that had showered around April's giddy head and wounded the ugly duckling who hovered in her shadow.

When Eileen first saw her sister resurrected in her little daughter she had got books out of the library, to try to understand how genes worked; how they could play this monstrous trick on her. She grasped the scientific part, after a fashion, but to the real question there was no answer.

'Why?' she murmured.

'Pardon?' said April.

Eileen shook her head. 'I don't see your Dad being agreeable to anything like that. He's made his mind up, and you know as well as I do, there's no shifting him.'

April poured tea and her mother saw her hand was shaking.

'You should have been more careful, anyway,' said Eileen with an arch look, 'if you know what I mean.'

April blushed bright red. 'That's not your business, Mum.'

'You're making it my business, aren't you? Which is unfortunate, because your father hasn't forgiven your husband for behaving so badly. It doesn't exactly make him inclined to be generous. You don't seem to realize, you're asking a lot.'

April got up and wandered to the window. She could see George's portly back, in his old jacket with the leather patches on the elbows, leaning over what had been the deceased Lord Woolton's sty, watching his new pig gobble its afternoon scraps.

'Am I? Why does Dad have to be so harsh on everyone?' she asked, frowning. He scratched the pig's back with a bit of stick. 'Look how kind he is to the animals, but when it comes to people, sometimes I think he hates us all.'

'He was badly let down and he's neither forgotten nor forgiven,' said Eileen doggedly.

'You'd think he'd have other things to worry about, after all these years,' murmured April. She turned round and looked at her mother's grey head, with its regiment of stiffly marching waves crowned with the finest of hairnets, and wondered for the first time whether Eileen had ever been happy. 'Fancy bearing a grudge all this time. Why does he do it?'

'It's what's kept him going,' Eileen answered sourly.

April rubbed her elbows and felt her baby move, kicking under her ribs. 'It's creepy to go on hating everyone because one person did you a bad turn. I couldn't do that.'

'There was more than one.'

April was surprised.

'I thought it was the switch business that ruined him.'

'And his wife died. And the child. He could get over

the switch, that was business, but he never got over the other.'

'Well, he hasn't lost everything today. I don't know how he can be so mean,' said April crossly. 'And seeing as this is his only grandchild, I think he could be a bit more helpful. We're in the middle of a war, for goodness' sake. That's no one's fault. Without the war, there wouldn't be all these problems. Can't he make any allowances?'

'What do you want to do, then?'

'I've told you.' April heard her voice rise and fought to stay calm. 'I'd like to leave work and look after my baby, and if it's all the same to you, I'd like to live near my husband.'

'You can't afford to do any of those things.'

April tried to believe her mother had not spoken the words. She felt panicky, as though rage and frustration might at last force their way out of her in some awful way she couldn't stop. Eileen saw, and put down her cup with a tinkle of china.

'I know what he would let us do, so I came up to make you an offer.'

April glared at her suspiciously. 'I'll look after the baby for you. You can leave it with me, go back to work, and we'll carry on as if nothing's happened. What do you say to that?'

'You'll take my baby away from me.' April was appalled.

'No, I'll look after it for you. It's a generous offer. You won't find many grandmothers would take on the responsibility.' Eileen got out of her chair and put the cup in the sink. 'If you're so independent you can afford to turn down your own family, then you'll have to make do as best you can. I can't do more, I'm sure.' Eileen spoke more bitterly than she intended.

'Carry on as though nothing's happened? As if my baby hasn't been born? You want me to pretend I haven't had a baby? You're outrageous!'

'*I* had to,' said Eileen, unable to keep back the anguish that gnawed at her, casting caution to the winds with a peculiar sense of release.

'Whatever do you mean? You didn't pretend you didn't have me, did you? What are you talking about?'

'Oh no, *he* did the pretending. Has done to this day. You just ask your father who he thinks you are.' Eileen pointed accusingly at the figure down by the pigsty. 'Ask him,' she spat. 'Ask him who you are and why he won't let you go. Ask him, April.'

'Why do you hate me?' she whispered.

Eileen cackled. 'Ask him,' she shrilled stubbornly, 'who hates who in this house. Then you'll see.'

April sat leaning against the wall beneath the open window, feeling cool air softly touching her burning skin, trying to hold steady, to make sense of her mother's words. Gradually it came to her, in fragments of memory, things never understood. Mysteries.

She thought of the other April; thought of the picture over the fireplace and her own uncanny resemblance to the woman who might have been her mother and could never have been her aunt; of her father's strange angers and implacable bitterness, and she began to understand. The air in George's house suddenly became unbreathable. She scrambled to her feet, snatched a cardigan and her bag from the back of a chair and ran. At the top of the road a bus was passing. It slowed to let off an old man with a stick. The conductress helped him down the step and April, out of breath, said, 'Where are you going?'

'All the way to Regent's Park,' said the woman. 'Eventually. You all right?' she asked the pensioner.

'Thank you kindly.' He paused to arrange himself and his stick, slowly, clumsily.

'Must be rotten to be really old, like that, and on your own,' remarked the conductress sympathetically as the bus drew away. 'Ticket, love?'

'The park.'

The conductress punched her ticket and gave it to her, then wandered away to chat to two women sitting near the back. April leant her forehead on the grimy window, closed her eyes and lost herself in thought. The bus crawled its way across East London and finally drew up at Regent's Park in mid-evening. April, dazed, saw that it had been raining on the dirty window, but as she peered out, it seemed to have stopped.

'Terminus,' shouted the conductress.

April, unsure why she'd come and already anxious about how she'd get home, got off. Around her, the little crowd of passengers dispersed, leaving her standing alone on the pavement.

The bus between her and the park drew away so that she could see across the road to the green trees and grass. Further off there were vegetable patches. Ack-ack guns squatted grey and silent in their emplacements, and milling around them she saw people, heard chattering voices, music and laughter, and the tuneful jingle of a merry-go-round.

The patch of park not dug for vegetables was full of people in the early evening light; dancing, lying on the grass, strolling to and fro down shady paths between unpruned, overhanging bushes. She heard an odd, staccato voice; in a brightly coloured booth Punch and Judy appeared, Mr Punch just getting under way, waving his stick ferociously, his high, squeaky voice carrying across the open space. April walked over the grass to where a crowd sat and sprawled in a big square, around a green, impromptu dance floor.

A small brass band, sitting in a semicircle at the far end of the square, swung into the 'Palais Glide'. Legs were drawn up out of the way to give the dancers room, and whoops and whistles of excitement went up as a crowd of servicemen of many different nationalities joined hands and strung themselves out in a rowdy line, pushing and shoving, at one end of the square. Girls from offices and factories, shops and nearby homes, joined hands in a line at the other end, giggling and shrieking. With a flourish the brass finished their introduction.

'"Horsey, horsey",' bellowed the bandleader, and a cheer went up.

'"Horsey, horsey, don't you stop, just let your feet go clippety clop",' the dancers sang at the tops of their voices, hopping and ducking, weaving and skipping in a marvellous mêlée of arms and legs and faces glowing with laughter.

'"Your tail goes swish and the wheels go round, giddy up, we're homeward bound".'

Feet pounded and hands clapped, skirts flew and swirled, giving glimpses of shapely knees and thighs that drew catcalls and whistles of appreciation from the crowd. Applause broke out when the game ended and there were shouts of, 'More! More!'

'Lovely, isn't it? Real treat to see the young ones enjoying themselves. Goodness knows, they deserve it, the way they work,' remarked a woman sitting with half a dozen children and an elderly couple who might have been their grandparents. 'Wish I was young again.' She laughed wistfully and leaned back on her elbow on the grass.

April sat down near her at the edge of the crowd, and watched couples jostling, shoulder to shoulder, waiting eagerly for the next tune to strike up, toes tapping impatiently on the thin grass. She smiled at the woman, surrounded by children, and felt the baby inside her stretch and curl and sleep again. Heavy orange evening sunlight after the rain slanted through the trees behind her, casting long shadows of gun snouts across Mr Punch's booth which was rocking to the sound of his savagery.

The band twiddled and tooted and whistled, then with a one, two, three, they were away again, blowing and puffing and stomping their feet with furious enjoyment. April leant back on one elbow, wiggled her shoes off, and gave a sigh of pleasure, the pain of Eileen's words drowned out by the music. The game ended again, and the band moved smoothly, straight into a waltz.

'Ma'am, would you care to dance?'

She looked up, startled, and at her side saw a tall man in an unfamiliar uniform.

'Please?' He was bending down with hand outstretched, inviting her.

She blushed with embarrassment and pleasure.

'Oh, I . . .' she faltered. The tall American smiled courteously.

'Then would you mind if I sat down?' he asked.

'No,' April said hastily, not wanting to offend him. 'Please do.'

His rangy figure lowered itself to the grass. Looking out of the corner of her eye, April guessed he was about thirty, with thick straight brown hair, direct hazel eyes and a long, hooked nose that would have made him look severe, but for the laughter lines at his mouth and eyes.

'Would you like a cigarette?' He began to pull a packet from his breast pocket.

April shook her head. 'I don't smoke, thank you.'

'Nor do I.' He put the packet back. 'But I keep some on me, to offer them, you know. You have so many shortages, here in Britain.' His slow, deep drawl delighted her. He spoke as though every syllable mattered as much as every other, separating and emphasizing them, rolling his words in a way she'd never heard before.

'You're American?'

'Yes, ma'am. Over here to talk to your wonderful BBC.'

'Are you on the wireless?' she asked, impressed.

He laughed. 'No, I've come to discuss a programme called "Answering You". You would not have heard it. It's part of the North American service; goes out for seven and a half hours every night, but you can't pick it up here in England.'

'I never knew about that.'

'"Answering You" is a panel programme. Listeners from home send in questions about the war and a panel of British experts answers them. It's real interesting.'

'It must be. I'd love to hear what Americans ask.'

'Much the same as you would, I guess. They're curious about how you live, about what it's like to be bombed, and rationing and coupons and stuff. But mostly the questions that get discussed are more about how the war is being fought, and how it's going. It's a kind of overseas "Brains Trust".'

'I've never been abroad.'

'I hadn't until Pearl Harbor. That sure changed things around a bit and now I'm backwards and forwards all the time. I guess it won't be long before London is full of us.'

'Where do you come from in America?' asked April politely.

'Connecticut.'

'I don't even know where that is,' she confessed. 'Have you got a family there?'

He nodded and held up his hand to show a wide gold wedding band. 'My wife lives there with our little boy. He's called Teddy. She's like you,' he told her, unabashedly looking at her belly. 'She's expecting our next baby in about four months. She sometimes writes it feels more like it must be four weeks, the baby bounces so. If it's a boy, she says he's a baseball star for sure.' He grinned. 'Like to see her picture?'

April nodded. He pulled a wallet out and took a much thumbed photograph from it.

'That's her. Before the baby,' he said proudly.

April studied a fair-haired woman, about the same age as her husband, laughing into the camera. She had very white, even teeth and fresh, rosy skin.

'She's pretty. What's her name?'

'Amelia. What's yours?'

'I'm April.'

'Hey, that's a pretty name. I'm Larry. Major Larry Schwarz.'

'That's a German name, isn't it?'

'Austrian. My great-grandparents emigrated from Austria. Me, I'm as American as apple pie.'

The crowd of dancers in the square thinned as people mopped their faces and went to sit down and get their breath back. The band, inspired, burst into a fast number. The major's feet tapped.

'Hey, would you like to dance now?' he asked.

April glanced at her small bulge. The baby was quiet. She smiled. 'Why not?'

'Great.' The soldier leapt to his feet and grabbed her hand. He began to jig up and down fast, making a weaving movement with his arm and body. April recognized it from films and newsreels.

'I've never done it,' she cried, hanging back. 'I can't jitterbug.'

'Yes, you can, you just follow me and let loose. Go with me and the music and I'll show you.' He pulled her on to the grassy square and held her to him for a moment, then he flung her away, keeping tight hold of her with his big, warm hand.

'Let's go,' he whooped and April's bare feet began to skip over the grass, light as a feather, in time to the fast beat. He handled her like a doll. Other dancers stopped and drew into a circle to watch and all the onlookers began to clap in time to the music, cheering them on, faster and faster, until the band worked itself into a frenzy and suddenly, with one almighty blast, brought the dancers to a standstill and dropped their instruments, exhausted.

'You're some dancer,' remarked Larry breathlessly, 'if you ain't jitterbugged before.'

'I don't get much chance to dance since I got married,' April gasped, leaning over with a stitch in her side. The baby stirred in astonishment at all the bouncing around. They stood, side by side, at the edge of the improvised dance floor.

'Your husband's away?'

'Not in the forces. He's a medical student.'

'Don't you stay with him?'

'No. It's complicated.'

He began to apologize for being nosey, but April cut him off. 'No, it's all right. He had to go to the country to study; all the colleges moved out of London at the start of the war. I work in London, so we don't see each other very much.'

'Tough on you both.'

'No tougher than your being thousands of miles away from your wife.'

April realized she'd never thought of it quite that way before, though she'd wondered how Bridie bore the worry about Edward.

'Yes, that's true. Perhaps we could keep each other company sometimes, you know – bein' as I'm over here every month and we're kind of in the same boat?'

The invitation came so pleasantly, so casually, with beguiling innocence.

'Maybe,' April said cautiously.

Catching the air of reserve in her voice, he clapped his hand over his wide mouth. 'Ma'am, I haven't offended you, have I?'

April shook her head, embarrassed. 'I'm sorry. We do things . . . well . . . slowly in England. And with both of us being married, it wouldn't really do, I'm afraid.'

He looked downcast. 'That makes for a lot of lonely people. It's a real shame.'

'I suppose it is,' April admitted, unsure where he might be leading her.

'We're all fighting on the same side; pity we can't be friends. I didn't mean no more than that.'

They sat down to cover their confusion, separated by an unbridgeable gap.

'I'm sorry,' April said. 'It's just that – well – people would think things.'

'Sure.'

She giggled. 'And my mother and father would be scandalized. Wouldn't it be the same in America?'

'We'd be hospitable,' he said simply. 'It'd be hospitality, ma'am.'

'Oh.' April felt flustered.

'Now I've really upset you,' he said contritely. 'I've been real clumsy. It's a different outlook, that's all. We need to make allowances when we experience each other's culture. Ma'am, I promise you, it's even more confusing for me than for you, because I'm the guest and I can't go straight back home if I blunder.'

'Do we seem inhospitable?'

'Not when we get to know you. But you're more reserved than us. It takes getting used to.'

'I'd like to dance again,' she said shyly.

'It's a slow one.'

'More suitable for a lady in my condition,' she joked, trying to put him back at his ease.

He helped her to her feet. 'You sure are one hell of a pretty lady,' he observed, leading her on to the square. A couple mooched past and a French soldier winked over his partner's head at Larry, then swept off to the other side of the dance floor. Larry held April gently, never too close; they circled the square to the slow beat of Vera Lynn's favourite 'White Cliffs of Dover'.

'What do you do when you're not in the army?' asked April.

'I teach law school, like my father.'

'You're a lawyer?'

'A hot shot.' He grinned.

'I work for a lawyer. I'm a secretary.'

'Is that so? What kind of laywer would he be?'

They slid into such an easy way of talking April forgot the time. The shadows lengthened into darkness. Punch fell silent and his owner came to sit among the crowd, a glass of beer in his hand. Women shivered and put on cardigans and babies fell asleep on their laps, thumbs in mouths, eyelids fluttering. The band broke for refreshments and came back with renewed vigour. A group of West Indians, volunteer workers in munitions factories, opened a huge cask of lemonade, passing mugs of it round their part of the crowd. Night gathered under the trees and a summer moon lay on the horizon, its weak light gleaming on brass as the musicians played on for dancers still spinning in the deepening dusk. The gun crew peered at the moon and muttered, but no planes had come for a long time and they relaxed again.

'You shouldn't do too much,' said Larry, after they had danced for an hour and the moon was riding high. April pulled her cardigan round her shoulders and they strolled in the park; the music following them on the air. Still they talked, exploring the fascinating differences of their lives, acknowledging their strangeness to one another with all the confidence of old friends. Or the frankness of children.

At last April noticed the chill in the air. 'I have to go home.' The band were packing up and people drifting away. Babies were piled into ancient prams. Bigger children trailed behind, yawning and complaining and dragging tired feet.

'But I'm not sure how,' she added. 'The last bus might have gone. Oh dear, I should have noticed how late it was getting.'

'You want to go see?'

She nodded. They hurried across the road. A few cars went past, their headlights dipped, going slowly.

'I'll have to walk home if there isn't one.' April began to shiver, cold and dismayed.

'I've got an idea. Look, can you wait just over there? Will you be safe, do you think?' Larry pointed to a bench that stood under a lilac bush, not far from the bus stop.

'What are you going to do?' Her eyes were silver in the moonlight and Larry stared, enchanted.

'I may be able to borrow a bike. I'll drive you home on the back. Ever ridden pillion?'

'No.' April giggled.

'Sorry it can't be a car; I'm not allowed the petrol. You wait right here, OK?'

He walked away from her backwards, holding out his hands in appeal to do what he said. She sat down on the bench. Larry turned and ran, his long legs covering the pavement rapidly. April waited.

The last stragglers from the park were leaving when she heard someone give a shout of triumph. Two dim blue lights crawled along towards them, down the Marylebone Road. April stood up. She looked up and down the dark road. There was no sign of a motor bike, much less of Larry. She hesitated; she knew he'd come but she wasn't sure she wanted him to find her waiting. This magical evening . . . She remembered his strong arms around her, the wild grin on his face as he spun her around and around 'til she was giddy. His slow, wonderful voice and those emphatic words. Larry was dangerous magic . . . and magic, thought April nervously, is only magic; it cannot last.

The conductor rang his bell and the bus moved on. April ran for it, leaped on to the platform just as it began to draw away. As she fumbled for her fare, still out of breath, a motor bike roared past the other way and she heard the squeal of brakes as the engine raced and then died. Frozen, she listened, and maybe she heard a shout, a cry of disappointment and betrayal. Then she found a two shilling piece and the bus picked up speed.

'Where have you been?' cried Eileen, whey-faced with worry and anger.

April found her sitting on her bed, the blackout up and the light on, head covered in crocodile clips and a heavy duty hairnet. Eileen pulled her old dressing gown tighter around her wiry frame and tightened the tasselled belt 'til it pinched her.

'I've been worried to death. Whatever have you been doing?' She saw grass in April's hair and her dress was stained with crushed dandelions and dry earth. 'Where have you been?' she repeated.

'I went to a dance. People were dancing in Regent's Park.'

'Regent's Park?' squeaked Eileen. 'What were you doing there?'

'Running away.'

Her mother's mouth shut with a snap.

'I'm tired. I'd like to go to bed.' April wondered what else her mother wanted after what had already been said between them. Suddenly all the magic of the evening began to fade and April shivered, bone weary.

'I've been waiting to say I'm sorry.' Eileen's words were so unexpected April didn't hear them at first. 'I'm sorry for what I said.'

'It doesn't matter, Mum.' April took her nightdress from under her pillow and waited pointedly for her mother to go. Eileen didn't move.

'Yes, it does. What I said was true and I realized when I said it how it's been between us all these years. I took it out on you.

'Your father hurt me, April. He worshipped my sister but he's never loved me, and when you were born you were her all over again. It was startling. Even as a tiny baby you had the look of her. First I was jealous of her and then I was jealous of you. I couldn't help it, but that doesn't excuse my behaviour. I want you to know I'm sorry. That's all.' She got to her feet. 'I'll go now and let you get to bed.'

'Oh, Mum.' April saw for the first time, as if she had at last left childhood truly, shockingly behind, a lonely, unhappy woman, dry as a stick, betrayed into being unloved and unlovely. She dropped her nightdress and put her arms round her mother. 'I'm sorry, too.'

Eileen sniffed feebly and drew away, fumbling in her pocket for a handkerchief. She blew her nose defiantly.

'And I was thinking about what we said about the baby. I never really wanted to take it from you, dear.'

April drew back, looked directly into her mother's eyes and shook her head.

Eileen pleated the handkerchief corner, avoiding her daughter's gaze. 'Yes, I was jealous of that, too,' she admitted wretchedly.

'I know.'

'And your husband. He loves you and I couldn't bear it.' She bit her lip and sniffed miserably. 'I don't know what you'll ever think of me after this, April.'

'A lot. You're brave to tell me. We'll manage, Mum.'

'Do you think so?' Eileen peered at her daughter, nose quivering doubtfully.

'I didn't know Dad was that obsessed. It's horrible,

but I'm glad you've told me. So many things will make sense now that never did before. You did right to tell me.'

Eileen nodded eagerly, crocodile clips a-wobble in the thin grey hair.

'It's been a special day, today,' April said gently. 'In lots of ways.'

'Has it?' Eileen said hopefully.

April nodded.

'I suppose we'd best get to bed now.' Eileen began to shuffle uncertainly towards the door.

'Mum?'

'Yes, dear?'

'I do love you.'

Eileen gave a watery smile. 'I love you, too, dear.'

She opened the door and April kissed her cheek. 'Good night,' she whispered.

Eileen began to go down the steep stairs. Halfway down she paused. April still held the door, to light her way.

'I'll tell you what I'm going to do, tomorrow,' she said in a hoarse whisper, sounding oddly excited.

'What?'

'I'm going to take that wretched portrait down and put it in the attic. And if he doesn't like it, it's too bad. He'll have to put up with it.' The crocodile clips quivered. 'Won't he?'

'He won't like it,' April whispered back, amazed, 'so he'll just have to put up with it.'

'I should have stood up to him years ago, shouldn't I?' Eileen's sudden, radiant smile took twenty years off her, even with the ironmongery, hairnet and all, as she was dazzled by a vision of liberation far beyond her modest dreams. 'Bless you, dear.'

'Good night, Mum.'

April closed her door. 'Well, baby,' she said, 'what did you make of all that? What do you make of a day like that?'

She made herself an enormous bread and margarine sandwich, and then another one because she was famished. And then she went to bed.

'One battle doesn't win a war,' remarked Rachael doubtfully two days later, 'but it'll start the campaign, I suppose.'

'Well, it's down and there's a great patch on the wall. When George saw it had gone, he looked at me without saying anything for a bit, and then he just said, "I'll have to get someone in to see to that", so I expect he's going to put a bit of fresh paper up or something.'

'You'll be lucky to get anyone to come in and do anything. They're all still out propping houses up,' said Rachael. She regarded Eileen's animation with misgivings, feeling she might be underestimating George and riding for a nasty fall.

'I've been a real doormat all these years,' Eileen rushed on, not noticing her friend's unease. 'I shouldn't have let him get away with it so long.'

'Hmm,' murmured Rachael. 'Perhaps.'

When Eileen got home she stopped in the kitchen doorway, stared and then felt faint. The portrait was back in its place. She went over and touched its corner, wondering if she was dreaming. It was solid and as she tugged at the frame, part of her mind screaming that she'd pull it off and smash it to smithereens, she saw that it had been bolted to the wall.

'Dear God, he's nailed it down,' she muttered. 'I can't believe it. Nailed.'

She hadn't even won the battle, let alone the war.

Chapter Twenty-Seven

The summer of 1942 passed slowly, mostly rainy with a few fine days. Along with the cool damp, the threat of invasion hung in the air. April had two weeks holiday in August. As she wandered about Valentine Park, sitting by the lakeside with her feet in the water, or sat in the garden, watching George working their allotment, she felt bored, fat and aimless. The baby had taken to kicking like a little whirlwind at night, keeping her awake in her humid, airless space under the eaves.

'You should be knitting for that baby,' said Eileen, coming across her slumped in a deck chair, looking out of sorts and sickly.

'I can't knit in this weather. My hands get all sticky.'

'Sewing, then.'

'What with?' demanded April tiredly.

Eileen heaved a sigh. 'Make do and mend,' she said. 'It's time you started making do, for some baby clothes. What's that poor little mite going to wear?'

'Mum,' said April, 'the pile of woollies in your bedroom drawer is already enough to dress three babies. I can't beg any old wool or material from Rachael, because she's already given it all to you. I can't unravel any of my old things because then I won't have anything to wear. Anyway, you like making things and I don't.'

'It's a bad time to have a baby, December. I don't know how we're going to keep him warm. There's no coal for a fire in the daytime, you know.'

'I know. We'll have to do what everyone else does – manage.'

Eileen sighed. These days they were like conspirators, united by the fiasco of the portrait.

'I'll manage, you mean. But I'm looking forward to it,' she said.

'Have you told dad you're minding the baby for me?' April asked.

'Yes.'

'What did he say?'

'He's pleased.'

April pulled a sour face.

'For all the wrong reasons. But since it suits us that he's pleased, I'm not going to say another word to him about it. What he doesn't know won't hurt him, miserable old beggar.'

April grinned at her mother. 'Fighting words.'

'I hope this baby's a boy,' said Eileen seriously.

April shaded her eyes and peered under her hand at her mother's anxious expression. Then she nodded. 'So do I. I really do.'

Two days later it rained first thing in the morning, then cleared up and the sun shone. Sparkling raindrops dried in its heat and the air was fresh and sweet.

'I'm going to go and see if Lizzie Norris is in,' April told Eileen, who was sorting rubbish for salvage and the pig. She held up a chicken bone; they'd killed a chicken and eaten it with gusto. The bone was picked clean as a whistle.

'Do you really think they want this?' she asked.

'Surely you won't get much spitfire glue out of a chicken.'

'Send it anyway.'

Obediently, Eileen popped the little bone into the salvage pile. 'The things they use,' she remarked, and tied up a bundle of newspaper with a scrap of string. 'Why are you going all the way over there?'

'I feel like it. It's something to do, and I'd like to see her. She's a nurse and there's one or two things I'd like to ask her about babies.'

Eileen sniffed.

'I don't mean you don't know. She's up to date. Anyway, I like her and it would be nice to see her.'

'Well, it's a long way to go on the offchance, but if you must, you must. When will you be back?'

'I don't know. Late, I should think. If she's not in when I get there, I'll probably wait. I can always go and see Ted and Ethel.'

Eileen, whose introduction to them had been a strain for all concerned, sniffed again. 'Give them my regards.'

'I will.'

April was glad to escape. The bus bowled briskly along and by lunchtime she was in Mile End. The cinema where she had met David had received a direct hit and was damaged but still open for business, showing *One of Our Aircraft is Missing*. She and Eileen had seen it. One of the things they enjoyed was going to the pictures together. April thought her mother must be one of the most satisfying Cinema-going companions. Her usual stiff, suspicious manner gave way, under cover of darkness and the big, flickering screen, to passionate patriotism. She applauded Allied officers, who were always decent, and the men, who sometimes said 'bloody' or 'basket' but were cheeky and gallant. 'Swine,' she would mutter at German soldiers who were all oafish, and German sentries who never heard saboteurs until they were cracked over the skull. She booed unrestrainedly at German officers, monocled sadists who clicked their heels crisply in the presence of superior monocled sadists.

'Oh, I did enjoy that,' she'd cry, emerging into the blackout of an evening, her arm happily tucked under her daughter's. Last time, April had giggled.

'Remember that man with the raspberry?'

Eileen tittered.

Quick to show their feelings during newsreels, audiences clapped and cheered, whistled and stamped, if Churchill appeared; booed and hissed like a crowd of angry ganders if Hitler was shown making a speech or shaking hands with Mussolini. That evening, someone had blown the loudest raspberry they had ever heard at the end of one of Hitler's rantings and ravings. It had been an expression of utmost contempt, perfectly vulgar and perfectly timed, and the whole audience had howled with delighted laughter. April giggled every time she thought of it, and grinned at the memory now as she walked down towards Lizzie's house, not far from Bridie's, which was now all closed up, with planks nailed over the door and windows to protect them from further damage.

There was a note for Bridget pinned to Lizzie's front door and no answer to April's knock.

'Gone to Mrs MacDonald. Back after tea,' said the note. April refolded it and stuck it back on the door, then decided to find a cab and go over. She was tired, but having come so far it seemed a waste not to find Lizzie if she could.

* * *

'Good gracious, look who's here, cried Lizzie, opening the midwife's door. 'Come on in, love.'

The tiny house smelt fusty and unused.

'She's been poorly,' Lizzie explained, taking April through into the one downstairs room, with its door to the staircase standing half open, 'and I don't think she can really manage on her own. I'm worried about her. I came over because I heard she wasn't well, but I didn't except her to be as poorly as this.'

'She's getting on, isn't she?'

Lizzie closed the staircase door and lowered her voice. 'I ought to call the doctor.'

'Do you know what's the matter with her?'

'Well, I'd need the doctor to say, really, but I think she's got pneumonia. She's hot and her breathing isn't right. And she says her chest hurts her.'

'Why don't you go and leave a message for the doctor to call, then? I'll stay here and keep an eye on her.'

'Would you?' cried Lizzie. 'I was going to wait until Bridget came, but if you're sure you don't mind . . .'

'Shall I go up and see her?'

Lizzie nodded, opened the door and they climbed the narrow stairs.

'Look who's come to see you.'

The old woman lay in bed in the room in which Bridie had given birth to David over twenty years before. She was propped on pillows, her eyes closed. Lizzie had brushed and tidied her thin white hair and sponged her sunken cheeks.

'She's going downhill very fast,' whispered Lizzie. 'Someone should have realized sooner. She was fit as a fiddle two weeks ago but I don't think she's been eating; there's not a crust in the house.'

'An old lady like her shouldn't have to stand in queues and that. No wonder she doesn't eat. She probably hasn't the stamina to go shopping,' murmured April.

Mrs MacDonald opened her eyes.

'It's April, David's wife,' said Lizzie.

The old woman stared at her blankly.

'She's going to stop with you a minute while I run down and ask the doctor to come.'

'I don't want no doctor.'

'Nonsense. April's going to stay, if you need anything.'

Lizzie disappeared down the stairs and left the house. April stood awkwardly since there was no chair.

'Can I get you anything, Mrs MacDonald?' she asked, to fill the silence.

'No, dear.'

"Don't die while she's gone," thought April, suddenly apprehensive. "I wouldn't know what to do."

Suddenly she jumped in alarm. Outside in the street several guns went off. Voices shouted, barking short, sharp orders. Another volley rang out and footsteps thundered past beneath the window and retreated into a maze of bombsites a little further down the narrow street. April looked from the window to the still figure on the bed.

'Mrs MacDonald,' she hissed urgently.

There was no answer. The old midwife snored briefly, then was silent again.

More shots came from across the way. April tiptoed nervously to the window, and, standing to one side, peered out. Men in uniforms and tin hats ran like rats in and out of the bombsites, guns and bayonets held at the ready.

'Oh, my God!' yelped April.

'What?' croaked Mrs MacDonald.

'There's soldiers running down the street with guns. They must have invaded at last. Oh, dear God, what shall we do?' A thought struck her. 'And Mrs Norris is out there! Whatever should I do?'

She peered through the curtain again; this time there were more of them. April put both hands to her face in dismay.

'Germans,' she whispered to herself, and then, moved by a curiosity greater than terror, peeped out to see what the legendary monsters looked like. The fighting had receded several streets away and muffled shots tracked its progress. Up and down the road, windows flew open as people leaned out to see what was going on.

April shook with terror. Visions of Eileen and George with their hands over their heads, surrendering, passed rapidly through her head, and sinister threats repeated themselves until her heart pounded. All young women would have to have German babies . . . April clutched her belly and whimpered. Mrs MacDonald, suddenly lucid, demanded in a scratchy voice, 'When are you due?'

April jumped like a scalded cat. 'Oh, are you feeling better?' she blurted stupidly. 'I think the invasion's come.'

Mrs MacDonald began to laugh. It was a faint rasping sound. 'Home Guard. They been practising for days. They're a nuisance,' she ended petulantly, closing her eyes again.

When Lizzie came back to say the doctor would come within the hour, she found April white and trembling with relief, and Mrs MacDonald apparently with her wits about her again.

'You are coming to stay with me, soon as the doctor says you can be moved,' Lizzie told the old woman. 'And don't try and argue, because I shan't listen. What's the matter?' she added, seeing April's disarray.

'I thought it was the invasion,' she said weakly. 'All those men running about with guns.'

'Home Guard,' said Lizzie. 'Aren't they over your way?'

'I don't think so.'

'Help me sit her up.'

They propped Mrs MacDonald upright, one each side of her.

'That's better for her chest. She's taken care of women in Stepney for nearly fifty years. I think now we're going to have to take care of her. Aren't we, Mrs MacDonald?' said Lizzie loudly.

'Eh?'

'I said, we have to take care of you.'

The old woman grunted non-committally.

'Are you all right, dear?' Lizzie noticed that April had put a hand to her side. She nodded. 'Then go and put a kettle on, will you? When the doctor's been I'll give her a little washdown, make her more comfortable.'

The doctor said it was pneumonia and that the old woman couldn't be moved.

'I can't stay,' said Lizzie worriedly, when he had gone. 'I'm on duty tomorrow morning.'

April said it before she had time to think. 'I will. I've got another week of holiday, nearly.'

Lizzie looked doubtful.

'The baby's not due for another four months. I'm all right.'

'D'you know anything about nursing?'

April shook her head.

'Then I'll have to show you, and you'll have to learn fast.'

And she did.

'You're a natural,' remarked Lizzie with admiration.

Bridget went down to the baker's and the grocers's and said the old midwife was ill. She came back with a covered basket.

'Look.' She pulled the cloth back and April gaped. There were four brown eggs, a fresh loaf, a tiny pat of butter and a scrap of cheese, two tins of soup, an orange, a lemon, and a half-used pot of honey. Wrapped in newspaper, to keep it cool, was a pint of fresh milk.

'They love her,' said Bridget simply, when April found her voice and squawked in amazement. 'They'd give her the clothes off their backs if she needed them. If you're staying to look after her, you'll have a job keeping them out of here, now they know she's sick. You'll have the whole neighbourhood trying to visit.'

Bridget was right. A constant stream of callers came to the door after Lizzie and she left, promising to get a message to Eileen about where April was staying. Stirring honey and lemon into a hot drink, she stood in the doorway as three women handed her a bunch of flowers. There were field daisies and golden rod, rosebay willowherb and two roses stolen from the park, pink and yellow campion and a small sprig of sweet peas.

'Ain't much, but give her our love.' Then they walked quickly away, their faces expressionless.

Several times there was a bang on the door, and no

one there when April opened it. Looking down at the step she found tiny offerings of spare rations, a shawl knitted in many colours from several unravelled garments, a handful of clothes coupons with a terse 'get her something warm'. A man came by briefly and said gruffly that if April needed anyone, he lived over the way. A great stout woman followed soon after, garrulous about how Mrs MacDonald had delivered all eight of her children and if she needed anything, April was to let her know. She thrust a bit of paper into the girl's hands.

'That's me address,' she said, and lumbered off down the street, her slippers slip-slop-slapping against the pavement. April stared at the growing pile of gifts.

'Now I see what David meant, but I still don't know why he wants so badly to run away from them,' she said aloud to herself, and took up the lemon and honey before it got cold.

Five days later, Lizzie arrived in a cab and took the old woman away with her.

'You've been lovely, my dear,' rasped the midwife. 'I can't thank you enough.' She squeezed April's hand and pulled her down so that she could plant a kiss on her cheek. April slid her hand round the birdlike shoulders and hugged her gently.

'I remember David as a tiny boy and all his life since. He couldn't wish for a lovelier wife. He's a lucky boy.' Mrs MacDonald's faded grey eyes peered at all their faces, as if defying them to disagree.

'And that *is* an accolade, coming from her. Nothing and no one was ever good enough for her David before,' whispered Lizzie. 'Bless you for looking after her.'

They parted at the cab door.

'Sure you'll get home all right?' asked Bridget.

April nodded, wishing it wasn't over. But it was. The cab drew away and April went inside the house for the last time, took her bag and left, locking the door behind her and dropping the key in through the letterbox.

'She's getting to be one of us, isn't she?' said Bridget to Lizzie, twisting round in the seat of the cab. 'I thought she was stuck up at first, but she's really nice when you get to know her.'

'Pity David's so far away,' murmured Lizzie thoughtfully. 'She seems awfully alone.'

'We're all on our own,' said Bridget sadly. 'Her, Bridie, me . . .' Her mother gave her a sharp look, but Bridget had her face turned to the window. 'Even poor Sam Saul,' she added.

'That's a shocking business.'

'Isn't it? Fancy going off like that with a foreigner. Mrs Saul must be an odd woman.'

'I have a feeling there's more to it than that,' said Lizzie. 'That his affections have long since been engaged elsewhere. I've always felt rather sorry for his wife.'

'Bridie, do you mean?'

Mrs MacDonald woke up.

'Where's Bridie?' she asked, looking round.

'Not here, I'm afraid.' Lizzie said gently.

The old woman dozed off again.

'Has that been going on long then?' asked Bridget. It was the first time her mother had ever openly mentioned the subject.

'Ever since the day they met, I imagine,' said Lizzie dryly, 'though I think it's always been one-sided.'

'I'm quite certain it has.'

Lizzie glanced at her daughter in surprise. 'What makes you say that?'

'I never met a man who loved someone like Edward loved her.'

'Really,' said Lizzie thoughtfully, and by tacit agreement they left it at that.

Chapter Twenty-Eight

At the end of October, April gave up work. At the beginning of November, Montgomery and the Eighth Army defeated Rommel at El Alamein, turning the tide of the war in North Africa. All over London bells pealed in celebration.

'If they had rung a year ago, it would have meant the invasion had started. Perhaps now they'll open the second front in France and push those Germans right back where they belong.'

She studied the photographs, in *Picture Post*, of death and destruction strewn across the desert sand, and felt saddened.

'We're all tired of this war. I wish it could be over by the time you're born. I hate the idea of putting you in a Mickey Mouse gas mask. Goodness knows what sense you'll make of that,' April told her baby, who listened quietly, having turned cartwheels all night. 'And don't you think you could sleep at the proper time, so we could both get a good night? What with you, and being hungry and cold, it's no fun at all. I'd like to tell them what to do with their Mr Therm and their Squander Bug.'

Mr Therm demanded that everyone save as much as they could of every kind of fuel. No lighting fires and stoves just for heating rooms, ordered a Ministry of Fuel advertisement, which claimed that the saving made by each individual in a week of economizing could make enough bullets or cannon shells to supply a fighter pilot for ten seconds.

'Huh,' said April, unimpressed, but everyone economized whether they liked it or not, since there was no fuel anyway. Eileen sifted the grate each morning, to save what nuggets of coal or slate there might be left for the evening's fire, but the results were disheartening and her stock of coal fast dwindling to a pile of dust. Tensions were set to one side as the three of them shared what there was, and Eileen and April together struggled to find food and make it go round.

April was hungry. She dreamed of food day and night. Like a starving prisoner, she had fantasy feasts, orgies of gluttony that left her emptier and hungrier than ever. Guiltily she remembered the times she'd made herself sick with rage when George and Eileen tormented her, and wondered if being hungry now was a punishment. She vowed never to do it again, to see if she could bargain good intentions with God or fate or the Ministry of Food in exchange for more, but as her baby turned and settled down for the last days before it would be born, she was hungrier than ever.

George sat reading his evening paper – one folded sheet of rough newsprint full of death and defeats. Eileen had coaxed the fire alight and it began to glow, bulked out with exploding slate, tar oozing and flaring from the meagre lumps of coal.

'Do you know that ninety percent of the world's rubber resources are in enemy hands?' remarked George, shaking his paper as if it were the thick, satisfying *Times* of yesteryear. 'No wonder they're tightening up on tyres.'

'It'll make travelling even more difficult,' called

Eileen from the kitchen. The smell of horsemeat spiralled through, mingled with swede and curly kale. Eileen had resisted horsemeat until, Lord Woolton having long since been eaten and the new pig nowhere near ready, she came across April crying silently with hunger. Unseen, she tiptoed away and that evening they were astonished to be served richly savoury meat stew, full of dumplings and herbs from the garden. The new pig would fatten as fast as she could collect scraps for it, but until then she merely sniffed virtuously and fed her family whatever she could lay her hands on. The fire spat and George leant forward with the poker, releasing a dense little curl of dark grey smoke up the back of the chimney.

'How will David come?' asked Eileen, bringing in the dishes so that they could all eat huddled in the small circle of warmth around the fitful glow of the fire.

'Train, as usual. I expect they'll be crowded.'

'Everyone trying to get home for Christmas.'

'I wonder if the baby will be born on Christmas Day,' said Eileen, for the hundredth time. 'Wouldn't that be lovely.'

'Going to be the only lovely thing about it, then,' remarked George dourly, folding his paper. It wasn't clear whether he meant Christmas or his grandchild. 'Christmas,' he snapped, in response to a look from Eileen.

'Wouldn't be so lovely for the poor midwife, would it? Having to come out on Christmas Day,' answered April, helping herself to a huge plateful of potato and ladling stew on top. 'This looks wonderful, Mum.'

'It's part of their job,' said George.

'You could call the baby Noel or Noelle. That would be pretty,' said Eileen happily.

April decided to ignore her; the baby was due any day and she knew it wouldn't wait until Christmas.

'But you're to wait until your father is here,' she ordered it firmly. 'I want us at least to start off as a family, even if we do all know he has to go away again the first week in January. We can pretend, can't we – just for a bit?'

'If you're going to talk about pretending things, how about a cup of pretend coffee?' asked George.

'I'll do it.' April got to her feet with an effort and went into the cold kitchen to stew chicory, flavoured with coffee, in a jug. She piled Eileen's utility dishes into the sink and leant against its cold white rim, waiting for the coffee grounds to settle in the steaming jug. All the talk of Christmas filled her imagination with the scent of pine trees, of burning candle wax, of roasting turkey; she pictured a table groaning with mince pies, gaily decorated Christmas cake, steaming tea pot and decanter of brandy, crackers and forfeits, chocolates and marzipan. April groaned.

She heard George calling, 'Where's that coffee?' She looked into the jug of insipid liquid and called back, 'Coming.'

"I suppose it could be worse," she thought. "It might be raining bombs, and it isn't. We might have been invaded, and we haven't. And I've got David here for a whole fortnight because it's Christmas." Her back twinged painfully. "And you are nearly ready, aren't you?" she said silently to the baby as she took the coffee in.

Twinges came and went. April cleaned her flat until it shone in the cold air, scrubbing and polishing furniture and rearranging her bedroom, with its little cot and pile of baby clothes, until David fled to the library to get away from the nesting.

'It means you're due,' Eileen told her, but the days passed and still she wasn't in labour. The midwife came and said she hadn't started, but was nice about the prospect of a Christmas baby.

'There's always something special about a baby born on Christmas Day,' she said. 'Seems so right, somehow.'

'You don't mind, then?' April gasped, feeling the girl's cold hands on her belly.

'Of course not.'

She finished her examination and said, 'You call me when you want me, my dear. Baby doesn't know about Christmas and he'll come when he's ready.'

''Course, my husband's here now, so he can help. He ought to know something after all the time he spends down in that college.'

'Medical students?' The midwife raised a daintily plucked eyebrow. 'Wouldn't trust 'em with a cat having kittens.'

'I'm sure he knows more than that,' cried April indignantly.

'They're best kept out of it, in my experience. When I was doing my training we had them on the labour ward, observing. You could guarantee that if anyone was going to faint, it would be one of the medical students. No good to anyone, they weren't.'

'Oh,' said April, subdued. 'I was thinking he might deliver the baby.'

'Absolutely not,' declared the young midwife firmly.

'But that would have made it perfect,' said April wistfully, 'for us to deliver the baby together.'

'It's ideas like that that put babies at risk, Mrs Holmes.'

'Very well, we won't,' said April meekly, trying to put the cherished picture out of her head.

'I should think not. You can get up now.'

'Well, I hope it comes soon, because I feel stretched as far as I can possibly go.'

'You could try a spot of castor oil,' agreed the midwife. 'The baby is overdue.'

April's stomach heaved; castor oil was nauseating but she drank it anyway, holding her nose, because time was slipping away and soon David would have to leave.

Sam Saul conjured petrol from somewhere and arrived unexpectedly and unannounced early on Christmas Eve, his arms full of presents.

'My own nearest and dearest having taken themselves off, you are the next best thing to a family I know,' he declared, apparently unstricken by his deserted state, handing David a wooden tray of Cox's orange pippins. 'Here, hold this.'

Amazed, Eileen sidled from behind her daughter, and said, 'Well, introduce us to your friend, April.'

'Mr Saul, my mother, Mum, Mr Saul, a friend of David's, really. He took us to see Bridie when she was in hospital, remember?'

George came to the door to see what all the fuss was about.

'And my father,' said April.

'Merry Christmas,' called Sam.

'Humph,' growled George and went indoors again, rubbing his hands against the cold.

'Come on in,' cried David, sniffing the mouth-watering smell of apples.

'Can you carry things?' Sam asked.

April said of course she could.

'Then try this.'

She took the carton and peeped at the label on the top. 'Hershey bars!' she shrieked. 'Chocolate! Oh, where did you get that?'

'London'll soon be up to its neck in Hershey bars,' said Sam cheerfully. 'And Americans to go with them.'

'Chocolate,' she moaned. 'Can I have one now? Do I have to wait until tomorrow?'

Sam grinned and winked mysteriously. 'Gobble away. I've something else to go under the tree.'

April's eyes were round. 'Food?'

'Plenty of that, too.'

'Oh, my,' said Eileen faintly, all of a flutter and pink in the face. 'Do come in, Mr Saul, you're more than welcome.'

He shook his head. 'Thank you, but I thought we'd do the rounds first, seeing as I have petrol in my car. Your mother,' he went on to David, 'is still in Yorkshire, of course, but I thought we'd drop in on Ted and Ethel, and the Norrises. I can bring you back afterwards. How about it? A seasonal tour?'

'Oh, yes.' April clutched the Hershey bars to her. 'Let me get some out first though.'

'You'll come back? Spend Christmas with us? We'd be delighted. Oh, please do,' Eileen begged, mentally dividing their Christmas dinner into five and hastily deciding it would stretch.

Sam bowed and his black eyes twinkled. 'I'd be delighted,' he said graciously, 'have you somewhere cold to put the wine?'

Speechless, Eileen nodded vigorously and led him through the hall into the unused drawing room.

'Everywhere's cold,' she said simply. 'Will this do?'

'Beautifully,' said Sam Saul.

April and David and Sam squeezed into the front of the car, wrapped in overcoats and scarves and mittens.

'Something's sticking into me,' complained David. 'What have you got, April?'

She blushed. 'Hershey bars. In my pocket.'

Sam leaned out of his window to call something to Eileen. She hurried forward.

'Have you forgotten something?'

'Yes, I meant to tell you . . . if you look in the biggest box, at the bottom; you'll find a turkey. Not too big, shouldn't take too much fuel to cook.'

With a squeal of tyres he shot away from the kerb, leaving Eileen staring after him with her mouth open.

'George,' she cried dizzily, 'we've got turkey.' And scuttled guiltily indoors, bolting the door behind her in case the neighbours should have heard.

Turkey!

The visit to Lizzie was a disappointment. Banging on the door, and then a quick look round the back to see if there was anyone there oblivious to the sound, made it clear that no one was in. Sam put two parcels and something in a bottle on the back doorstep, covering it all up with an old sack.

'Ted and Ethel next,' he said, hopping back into the driver's seat.

Squeezed together warmly, they first hummed then sang aloud at the tops of their voices: 'O Little Town of Bethlehem', then the 'Rocking Carol', with special reference to the baby, and then they roared out the chorus to 'O Come, All Ye Faithful' as they drew up at Ethel's door.

'Happy Christmas,' they shouted, opening the car doors and letting in the raw air, waiting for Ted to open the door to the commotion. No one appeared.

'Go and see,' Sam said to David.

They watched from the car as he banged on the door, and banged again.

'Nothing,' he called, turning with a worried look. 'No one here.'

'You lookin' fer Eth? You're 'er David, ain't you?'

An old man appeared in the doorway of one of the few houses standing in what had once been a long street of back to backs. His gaze swept over them suspiciously, taking in the car and their flushed faces.

'Ted's took 'er down the 'ospital. She came over queer.'

'How? Where?' cried David.

The old fellow shrugged dismally. 'Dunno what's wrong wiv Eth,' he said, 'but they was took down the London.'

'Took?' demanded Sam.

'Ambulance come.'

'We'll get straight down there. Ta.'

The wizened face nodded and vanished back inside its hovel. They piled back into the car.

'Step on it,' muttered David.

Throwing the cautions of the Ministry of Supplies to the wind, Sam stepped on it.

Ted sat outside the door to the ward on a bench, his hands between his knees and his head so low he didn't see them come up until David laid a hand on his shoulder gently.

'What's happened?'

His grandfather sighed and looked suddenly so old

and worn that tears came to April's eyes.

'She was all right one minute, and the next she was sittin' there sayin' she couldn't take it no more.'

'Take what?' asked David.

'The pain. She pulls up 'er skirt and I nearly 'ad a turn meself.

'She's all ulcers, son. I never knew . . . I never see 'em. She always 'ad summat on. It's too cold 'an damp, you see . . . I never see 'em.' He shook his head slowly from side to side, as if he didn't believe his own words.

'Varicose ulcers,' muttered David.

They started as a doctor came through the swing doors.

'Mrs DuCane's family?'

'I'm her grandson,' said David.

'I'm afraid your grandmother is a bit poorly,' began the doctor, his glance taking in Ted's gnarled old hands working miserably. 'She has varicose ulcers that have been neglected for a very long time, and I'm afraid she has now developed a very painful condition.'

'Gangrene,' said David.

The elderly man blinked.

'I'm a medical student,' David explained, and the doctor broke into a smile of relief.

'Then you'll be better placed than me to explain this to your grandfather. There's advanced gangrene in the right leg. The other leg is ulcerated but treatable. I shall have to ask your permission to operate.'

'Will you have to amputate?'

'Yes. I'm sorry. Your grandmother should have seen a doctor long before this.'

'I didn't know,' Ted said, barely audible.

'Didn't you notice a smell?' asked the doctor.

'You smell all sorts round our way.'

'I expect you do,' answered the doctor, revolted.

'Can I see 'er?'

'She's had something for the pain. It's made her very sleepy, but you can look in when I've got you to sign a couple of forms.'

He turned to David. 'We've given her a largish dose of morphine.' He shook his head meaningfully and inclined his head slightly towards Ted.

'I see,' said David, understanding that Ethel was unlikely to respond to any of them.

'I'd rather not come in, if you wouldn't mind,' said April, sitting down on the bench, 'I don't think I could bear it.'

'No. Do you want to sit here?'

She thought for a moment. 'No, I'll go outside and walk around. Get some air. I'm sorry not to be a help, but my head goes round at the thought of poor Ethel like that and I don't think I could cope. But you all go in.'

Ted muttered.

'I beg your pardon?' said the doctor.

'I said, she give up when Edward died.'

'Edward?'

'Her son,' said Sam.

'An' I never see 'er undressed,' Ted continued miserably.

'I see,' said the doctor, blinking in astonishment.

'I'd like to come, if I may,' said Sam.

'Are you a relative?' asked the doctor.

'Yes,' said David, before Sam could answer.

'Very well.'

'They won't be in there long,' said the doctor kindly to April. The ward was decorated with sprigs of holly and some coloured paper chains in a brave effort to make Christmas Christmassy; April glimpsed them through the door as Ted and David and Sam followed the doctor inside and she smelled the smells that all hospitals have and her stomach heaved.

"Castor oil," she thought desperately and fumbled for a handkerchief. Hershey bars spilled on to the bench and suddenly she couldn't bear another moment of it: Ethel, lying on the narrow trolley, drugged and rotting and stinking and no longer the Ethel they'd all taken for granted for so long. The whole awfulness of the war seemed to consolidate itself in that one terrible image. April almost ran out of the hospital doors, blindly escaping from the pain of it, the waste of it, the sheer needless cruelty of it.

'Ethel,' she sobbed. 'Why Ethel? Why any of all these people dead and dying? Why?'

Down along the Whitechapel Road she half ran, half walked, burdened down by the baby. Turning into a side street she came to a bombsite that had a tiny stack of bricks to one side that someone was salvaging from the rubble of the Blitz. Overhead the sky was overcast and low, a thin, raw drizzle hanging in the air. It would be dark long before tea time. April sat on the bricks and shuddered, shock chilling her to the bone.

'Why?' she yelled furiously, looking up at the dismal sky. The drizzle turned to thin rain. Shivering, she pulled her coat tighter round the great bulge of her belly and wandered round the deserted bombsite.

Golden rod and rosebay willowherb lay rotting where they'd died, weeks earlier. Black, tangled stalks pulled at her legs, decayed leaves slippery under her feet. She scrambled on, driven by some wordless need to go somewhere – anywhere except back to the hospital. Then there was a strange feeling, as though her feet touched something softly giving, and with a tearing sound she slid, scattering Hershey bars, into the cellar that lay beneath the open bombsite, hidden by rotting beams and a thin layer of soil. April lay on her back, staring up at the small hole twenty feet above her.

'Help me,' she screamed, but only a stricken whisper came out.

When it started to get really dark, David called out the police and the ARP.

'She's going to have a baby any minute,' he shouted when they stared at him with impassive eyes and suggested he should wait a while before panicking. 'And she's had a shock. Anything could have happened to her.'

Ted stood bleakly to one side, bewildered by the speed and enormity of events.

'The sites are dangerous,' he muttered from the fringe of the group of men. 'She could've fallen. People do. She ain't the kind to go off missin' fer nothin'.'

'Can't have gone far, can she?' remarked one of the policemen. 'We'll have a look round.'

'I'll stop 'ere. Wait fer Ethel,' Ted said, staring again at the green doors through which they'd wheeled her away. 'I couldn't go away, not while she's in there.'

'Finding anything in the blackout is going to be the devil of a job,' said the other policemen. 'Perhaps we'd better get men searching straight away.'

Sam wondered furiously what had made him see sense at last, but put on his most amiable smile.

'We'll go and scout round nearby streets for a start,' he offered, 'because if anything happens to that lady or her baby . . .'

'We'll find her.'

'We'd better,' said David grimly.

The rat and April stared at each other. The rat had unblinking black eyes. Its snout, fringed with short, thick whiskers, snuffled and twitched continuously and it made little darting forays towards her, retreating again and again to the dense darkness away from the hole in their roof. She drew her legs under her as far as she could and covered them with her coat. She was too big and her feet and ankles stuck out. The rat twitched its whiskers and snuffed the warm, meaty smell of her. It watched her intently. It was well able to wait.

April looked up at the grey light filtering through the roof and then at what was probably the wall of the pit into which she'd tumbled. It was so black. She'd be safer with her back against it, but wouldn't be able to see; her mind weighed possibilities while the rest of her crawled with terror.

'Stay put,' she whispered. The rat backed off. 'And move to the wall when it's quite dark.' There was a strange sound; she looked up at the hole hopefully and went to call out but it was her own teeth chattering.

'Someone, please help me,' she called. The words fell dead against the damp walls and, bolder since nothing happened when she spoke, the rat crept forward and crouched. It stared, its vision excellent in the dark, with bright, unwinking eyes. Waiting.

With a soft slither, a fragment of roof gave way, slipping down in a shower of wet splinters and debris. The rat vanished and the tiny puddle of light seeping through brightened a little. A wad of damp paper came to rest by April's legs, falling open. Thinking it might have some use, she dragged it towards her and peered at it in the half-light, recognizing it as *Housewife* magazine. Eileen took it regularly. The rat was nowhere to be seen, perhaps scared off by the tiny landslide. April held the mildewing paper close to her face and could read the print. Despite herself, she smiled.

She saw an article written by the good lady who covered baby topics for the magazine. It was dated back in August 1940, just before the Blitz:

> The point is that however courageous you are, the actual noise of an air raid is apt to be very upsetting, and you may find yourself without milk for a few hours; then baby can have a full feed of the dried or evaporated milk to which he has become accustomed, and will return quite happily to the breast when, with returning serenity, your milk comes back.

April giggled. The rat lurched just out of sight.

> Whether you've decided to have baby at home or away, it would be a wise precaution to have all your own requirements, sanitary sheets, mackintosh, nightgowns, sanitary towels and all the small etceteras you have prepared, fitting into a large suitcase, so that if your own house, for any reason, becomes uninhabitable, you can slip over the way and have your baby in the house of some hospitable friends. You'll be surprised and gratified how completely a confinement takes your mind off 'enemy operations'.

'Well, I've slipped, all right,' said April aloud, putting

down the paper which was tearing with damp. 'But it doesn't say if a confinement takes your mind off rats. Stupid magazine!' She slapped it down on the ground and rat jumped and bared its teeth, angered by its own alarm.

The light faded fast. April's back ached savagely from sitting on the dank ground. Since the rat stayed out of sight, she crawled cautiously to the side of the cellar, expecting any moment to bring it down around her. Feeling the slimy walls, she found no way of climbing out. She was stuck, truly stuck.

When she looked back down, it seemed all of a sudden to have got dark. April shuddered, terror taking a renewed grip on her. Fear hurt her. Her whole body ached with it.

'I must not panic,' she said aloud. She began to explore her pockets. One remaining Hershey bar, a clean handkerchief, a door key; those were in her coat pocket. She sighed. Then she remembered that her grey maternity dress had pockets, and there was a box of matches she'd used to light the fire the previous evening. She almost sobbed with relief.

'If I can burn something – this rubbish and paper – it might keep you at bay,' she told the rat in what she meant to be a strong voice, but which came out a disappointing quaver. She felt the box; it was almost full. She struck a match and the rat squealed with rage, withdrawing with a fluid movement into a hole in the wall. April saw that the walls were sheer and crumbling, rafters leaning crazily, festooned with the hairy roots of golden rod and all the other weeds that grew rampant over the bombsites. One move too many, and it would come down. She crawled back and leaned against the wall, feeling the damp through her coat. Like the rat, she could only wait.

Within the hour, it was pitch black in the pit. Outside there was little more light; moon and stars were hidden behind a thick pall of cloud, and rain gusted fitfully across London. Policemen combed the ruins, but it was slow, dangerous work. An alsatian nosed in the dead willowherb, sneezing mud from its muzzle. David called until his voice was hoarse, but there was no trace of her.

'P'raps we're barking up the wrong tree altogether,' said Sam, worried.

'Where else can she have gone?' said David, exasperated by their failure.

'You're right.' Sam scanned the darkness, but it was hopeless; and you couldn't see your hand before your face. Their torches were pinpricks dancing over the ruins. 'Funny,' he said.

'What?'

'I can smell something burning, and it's been raining for hours.'

David sniffed. 'So can I.'

They began to hunt again, keeping an eye open for firelight.

The rat watched, its belly grumbling, its mouth watering with the smells coming from April. It was deterred only by her tiny fire and the billowing smoke that stung its delicate nose. The human had eaten, something with a sickly, thick smell that it couldn't recognize. She kept groaning and breathing hard. Frustrated, the rat edged forward on its belly, keeping below the smoke. Fire it hated, but not as much as the ravenous cramps in its belly. In the end, if she didn't give up first, hunger would win against its fear, the rat knew. But it had to get a little hungrier first.

April fed her smouldering heap of wet paper and bits of wood. Her eyes ran with smoke, but she could see that it billowed out at the top of the pit, and all the time she tended the fire, she prayed that someone would see it.

'Help my baby,' she prayed. 'Forgive me all the things I've done wrong, but don't punish my baby, only me.' She put her hand to the vicious ache in her back, then tore another sheet of paper into shreds and piled them slowly into the little, licking, flickering flame. Church bells pealed nearby, calling the staff of the great hospital to an early midnight mass, for those who would be on duty later. April remembered Sam's pile of presents and Eileen's turkey.

'Please, God,' she begged.

The rat crept forward another six inches. It could smell her feet inside her shoes and it mewled with longing. April turned to collect wood, to keep the centre of the fire going, and met its eyes, only a yard from her feet. She shrieked and threw the wood at it, but the rat only crouched lower this time and did not flinch.

'Oh, dear God, help me!' sobbed April, feeding the fire though her eyes streamed so, it blurred before her in the faint, flickering light. 'Please, please, please.' The pain in her back became agony and the rat came closer. From there, it could jump at her neck. It froze, calculating.

'Smoke smells stronger over here,' shouted Sam, probing in some dark undergrowth with his torch, lighting up burned earth in which worms squirmed. 'Ugh.'

'Hey!' yelled an excited voice. 'Look at that.'

David and Sam strained their eyes in the direction of the shout. 'It's like the entrance to hell,' yelled the voice. 'There's smoke coming out of the ground.'

Stumbling and cursing, they began to run. Two policemen knelt, looking down into what seemed to be a smoking hole.

'Bloody hell, it's a woman,' shouted one of them. He made to jump up but his companion grabbed him and pulled him down.

'If she's fallen through, you could too,' he said urgently.

They knelt still, then one of them put his torch through the hole and shone it over April.

'Don't move,' he said calmly. 'We'll get you out of there in a jiffy.'

The rat, sensing its meal about to disappear before its eyes, leapt.

'You've a lovely little girl,' said someone over April's head.

'Can she hear you?' came David's voice.

'She's coming round nicely. 'A cool hand felt her pulse and touched her cheek.

April opened her eyes and saw green walls and a nurse in green overalls looking directly into her face.

'Hello, Mrs Holmes.'

April blinked. Her head felt heavy and fuzzy.

'You've a beautiful little girl, Mrs Holmes. Seven pounds eight ounces. She's doing wonderfully well.'

David's face peered over the nurse's shoulder.

'He shouldn't be here,' she said with a grin, 'but seeing as he's a student, we decided to let him in.'

'Where am I?'

'In Recovery, dear. We had to give you a Caesarean

after that nasty fall you had. Baby got a bit confused by it all and tried to walk out. But she's splendid, and so will you be, once you've woken up.'

'Where is she?' April struggled to sit up but her muscles wouldn't let her.

'She's in the nursery. They'll look after her there until you're better. We'll send you up to the ward soon, and you can have a rest.'

'What happened?' asked April drowsily. She felt numb and as if she was floating.

'A policeman dived through into the cellar you'd fallen down, to save you from an enormous rat. It was a miracle the pair of you weren't buried. We've been incredibly lucky to get you back safe and sound.'

'A little girl,' said April dreamily.

'Yes,' said David.

Her eyes felt heavy. The nurse clattered a metal tray full of instruments and began to make notes on a chart which lay to one side.

'Aren't you pleased?' April whispered.

'Yes, of course I am,' said David in a low voice.

'You don't sound pleased,' she complained sleepily.

'It's all been a bit of a shock, what with you running off when we took Ethel into hospital, and now a Caesarean. I haven't had time to think whether I'm pleased.'

Ethel.

'How is she?' April's eyes snapped open. 'How is Ethel?'

The nurse shook her head warningly.

'She's still in hospital and we'll have to wait and see.'

April frowned. 'Of course she's still in hospital. Am I in the same hospital?'

'Yes.'

'Then I can take the baby to see her when I'm up, can't I?' April smiled contentedly and slid into sleep again.

'Oh dear,' said the nurse.

'Oh dear, indeed,' said David.

No one had the heart for turkey and Christmas pudding, though they ate it all the same, because to throw it away was unthinkable. April cried quietly most of the day they told her Ethel was gone, and sat for a very long time gazing at her daughter's smooth little face. A Christmas baby after all.

'I'm so sorry Ethel will never see you.' She touched the soft skin with gentle fingers; she would never tire of that softness, she thought, it was unimaginable unless you actually felt it.

Hannah stirred, screwed up her face and sneezed. Beyond the window the last days of 1942 were ending but the war went on.

'You are worth fighting for,' April said. 'In a queer kind of way, you make sense of it. I don't really know how, but with you it seems more bearable. I couldn't let you be taken by the Germans.'

The baby, she realized with chilling insight, made her truly vulnerable for the first time. She knew, now, how her mother had felt. April shivered violently, as if touched by some dreadful knowledge, and sat lost half in thought, half in a dream, until a nurse took the baby from her and brought her a cup of tea instead.

'Do you have to go back?' April said, knowing he had.

'I have to,' answered David. 'I'm terribly, terribly sorry.'

'We haven't had a single day together,' she said sadly.

'You won't be out of here for another week or two. There's really no point in my hanging around.'

'You haven't had a chance to get to know Hannah. When you next see her, she won't be new any more.'

David leant across and kissed her with a tenderness that surprised her, sitting as they were in the middle of a public ward full of women.

'I miss you, when you go,' she said tonelessly.

'I know. I miss you, too. But there's no way round it. We have to do the best we can, April. It's all we can do.' He spoke with such suppressed urgency that she stared in surprise.

'Is something wrong, David?' she asked quietly.

For one wild moment, he thought of the relief of telling her, the indescribable relief that would bring. Confession. He yearned for it, would have sold his soul for it, but he was bankrupt already, the dwarf had said.

'David, darling, you look dreadful all of a sudden. Are you ill?'

'No. Disappointed not to stay, that's all. I miss you desperately, April. You've no idea.'

She was startled. 'Do you really?'

'Yes.'

'I'm sorry, darling.'

'I know. April?'

'Yes?'

'Nothing.'

He took her hand and held it tightly. 'Look after her, won't you? I mean, really look after her.'

'Of course I will.'

'I'll say goodbye on my way out, through the nursery window.'

'Yes.' She tried to smile.

'I have to go.'

'Go quickly, then, before I hang on to your coat tails and won't let you.'

He turned to wave by the ward door then hurried out, giving the nursery a wide berth. He felt himself sweating as he emerged into the Whitechapel Road. Every time he saw her, he felt this urge, this primitive, appalling urge. He hurried, half running. Away from the hospital and Hannah. To keep her safe, there would be no end to running.

No help? A vicar perhaps?

'Forgive me, Father, for I have sold my daughter and the reproach is such I cannot bear it. I want to strangle her, Father. Help me.'

David knew now what agony was and cursed the dwarf with all the passion of the damned. But it did no good, no good at all. He walked faster and faster towards the City. Away from Hannah.

Chapter Twenty-Nine

The night he got back to college, David tossed and turned, drawing back in fitful dreams from precipices yawning at his feet, only to fall then wake with a fearful jolt, heart pounding, sweating with horror. The next morning he was hollow-eyed and drawn and found that his hands trembled and twitched as if possessed by some hyperactive demon. He shaved, cut himself, and arrived late at his first lecture, bits of tissue paper stuck all over his chin. Cutie affected not to notice, keeping her head bent over her notebooks. Inwardly, she went cold with dread.

The lecturer droned, the clock on the wall ticked heavily with each passing minute. Pens scratched across inch after inch of grey, pulpy paper, noting, drawing, labelling, as thirty medical students dutifully swallowed another dose of physiology.

' . . . and this is particularly prominent in the cerebral cortex of children,' pronounced the lecturer, turning a page in his notes and pausing to give them time to catch up.

' . . . cortex of ch—' wrote David automatically. His hand twitched and spilled a long trail of ink down the page, the pen dragging off the paper as if with a life of its own. He frowned, shook his head to clear it and gripped the pen tighter.

'Ch—' he wrote again. The pen lifted off the paper and hung suspended, then dropped heavily, bending its own gold nib. The student next to him looked at him curiously.

'Sorry. I'm tired,' he muttered, pushed his page of notes aside and started on a fresh sheet.

'Cortex in ch—' he wrote, grasping the pen determinedly. It slewed across the page, out of his fingers, and dropped to the floor with a small clatter. His neighbour picked it up, puzzled.

'Doesn't want to write, does it?' he joked.

David took the pen from him.

'You're freezing,' whispered his fellow student, frowning. 'Are you ill?'

The hand that held the pen was numb. David shook his head and looked at the inky splashes on his pages. The pen refused to write 'children'. What about 'baby'? The pen twisted itself nib upwards and dribbled ink. David sat like a statue, unaware of the lecturer starting on a fresh aspect of their topic, unconscious of covert glances from people close by. A single thought hung in his mind and a chill crept through his bones.

Hannah?

He held the pen so fast his knuckles whitened, put the nib hard against the grey paper and pushed resolutely on the downstroke of the H. The pen remained in his fingers. No spluttering or dribbling or jerking about. David sighed with relief, than gaped. The downstroke of the H had carried on round into an upward curve; the rest of the word had followed easily in his usual even script. 'Damned', it read.

Cutie knew he was behind her but she didn't turn round.

'I have to talk to you,' he begged, trying to keep up with her as she quickened her pace. 'It's urgent.'

'No.'

'I have to.'

'I don't want to hear.'

'You're in this as well,' he muttered.

She stopped, turned and faced him. Several students banged through swing doors at the far end of the corridor and then suddenly they were alone.

'Please, I have to talk to someone or I'll go mad. There isn't anyone except you. Please, Cutie.'

She looked steadily into his ice blue eyes and saw herself reflected in his glasses.

'No.'

'Why?' he begged.

Cutie shivered. 'You scare me.'

'How do I scare you? I'm the one who's scared. Look at me.' He lifted his shaking hands.

'You aren't mad,' she said in a very low voice, 'but I don't think you are quite normal, either. That's what scares me. You are creepy, David, and I want you to leave me alone.'

She turned away from him and hurried down the corridor, a chill between her shoulder blades.

'Go then,' he said after her. All of a sudden, he didn't seem to care. It just meant he couldn't do the paediatric option next year. There were always other choices.

Chapter Thirty

When Hannah was several weeks old, and April getting stronger and stronger after her birth, Mr Stephenson sent a note, asking when she was coming back to work. The sooner, it seemed to suggest, the better; she'd had plenty of time to recover from her ordeal.

'I'm sure the doctor would give you a note,' said Eileen indignantly, but April didn't want to argue.

'Mum, we both know why I've got to go back. Nothing's going to change Dad's mind. I'm well enough and I've got to go sooner or later, so I might as well get it over with. Mr Stephenson's been generous, really, to give me this long. And she's used to you, now. She'll hardly notice I'm gone.'

Hannah gurgled on her grandmother's lap and smacked her lips contentedly over the last dregs of a bottle. Eileen sat her up and rubbed her back.

'All right, dear,' she said over the baby's head, which was already showing signs of a delicate tangle of silky chestnut curls. 'Whenever you like.'

'I'll let him know I'll be in next week, then, if you're sure you can manage?'

Hannah burped and her eyelids drooped contentedly.

'We'll manage, won't we, precious? You're good as gold, aren't you?' Eileen said to the sleepy child. April sighed. Hannah was the easiest baby in the world. She hardly cried, slept all night at five weeks, smiled at six, and enchanted them so thoroughly that April worried she'd be spoiled to death when she went back to work. Even George was under her spell, mellowing into benign, grandfatherly indulgences like taking her to the park in her pram, secretly proud as could be.

'She'll soon know you better than me,' said April sadly. 'I always wanted to stay with my baby and give her everything I didn't have. I vowed I'd give her the very best, and I'm not, am I? She'll grow up like I did, thinking her mother doesn't care.'

Eileen flinched under the reproach, holding Hannah tensely. 'Nonsense.'

'It may be, but I worry about her all the time.'

'A child knows its mother.' Eileen dismissed her doubts briskly, fearing she'd not go back to work, given the smallest encouragement, making trouble for them all.

'I do hope you're right,' said April, but her heart sank.

Mr Stephenson was flattered to be asked to stand as godfather. It was not a disingenuous request, April hoping that he would let her spend more time at home if it was to look after his god-daughter. She'd have liked to ask Sam Saul, but he was Jewish. Rachael stood as godmother, because she'd love the baby to bits and would lend Eileen a hand if needed.

April wrote to David:

It's a bit cynical, really. I've chosen people because they might be useful. I'm sure that's not right, but what else can I do? I need their help. I do so wish you could be here. It seems so wrong that you can't come, but if you say they will not let you, then I suppose there's no point in arguing. Why are they so tight, all of a sudden? Anyway, Hannah sends her love, lots of wet, dribbly kisses and a bright red cheek, which I think means she's getting her first tooth.

David crumpled the letter into a ball and flung it from him. The thought of his daughter tormented him. He made feeble excuses to April and invented examinations. Cutie wouldn't come near him. He avoided other people, increasingly alone. He didn't dare go home.

Hannah learned to sit up. She lolled in her pram at the end of the garden, watching sunlight dapple the leaves of the old pear tree above her head. She rolled, wriggled, crawled, and one fine autumn day rose up on two legs and took her first unsteady steps without holding on to the furniture.

'More!' she shouted, banging her small pudgy hands on the wooden tray of her high chair, seducing George with her bright-eyed giggles.

'Trust you to learn "more" as your first word,' observed April, shovelling grey porridge and treacle into her. 'Though why you want more of this stuff I don't know. It looks revolting.'

'Dadadadada,' shrieked Hannah, spitting porridge in fits of laughter.

'Dada,' said April grimly, 'is going to have to come home, or we'll have to go and see him. I won't take any more excuses.'

George scowled. He tended to forget, these days, that David existed. They were happy just as they were; the perfect little family.

'Man's a scoundrel. Don't know why you don't just let him be,' he grumbled.

'He's Hannah's father and he ought to be coming to see her,' answered April firmly. 'And one way or another, I'm going to see he does.'

'Why don't you leave it 'til Christmas?' suggested Eileen. 'Then he could come for that and Hannah's birthday, and we could all have a nice celebration. I'm not supposed to know but I do, for a fact, that Rachael's been storing bits of rations for ages, to make a birthday cake.'

'All right.' April gave in reluctantly. 'I'll wait until Christmas. The trains are so full of soldiers anyway. It'd be dreadful trying to travel with a child.'

December came, bright and clear. They took long walks, Hannah toddling until she was tired. Then George would pick her up and put her in her pram, pushing her tirelessly, showing her the bleak wartime world as if it were a conducted tour around wonderland. For Hannah, it was.

One day they took the bus to Barking Creek and stared at the great concrete towers going up in the dry docks, like blocks of flats. 'Dangerous Talk Costs Lives' read posters plastered to every wall in sight.

'Those are what they're taking over for the invasion?' whispered Eileen, awed equally by the sight of the half-built Mulberries towering in the distance, and the thought of the danger of saying even a whispered word for fear of personally sabotaging the invasion.

'They've got a lot of Irish labour over there,' observed George, 'and the poor beggars aren't allowed to go home in case they say anything and it gets to the Germans. Fancy being stuck here.'

The whole of London was crowded and congested. Troops poured in from every corner of the world; GIs thronged the streets; white-helmeted Military Police pounded the pavements alongside the London coppers, back in their proper helmets instead of tin hats now the danger from the air seemed over. Traffic roared all day – jeeps, lorries, officers' cars – in a busy, hooting, tooting stream. Sightseers paraded in Piccadilly, up and down Coventry Street, queued to see *Gone With The Wind* at the Ritz cinema and then queued all over again to have tea for one and fourpence at the Lyons Corner House. Despite all the to-ing and fro-ing, the Automobile Association's building was silent. In one of its windows was displayed a picture of a country road in peace time – lines of family cars being given the friendly salute by an A.A. scout. Over the picture was written 'Until these days return . . .' In the next window was a picture of two Tommies in a tank turret in the Libyan desert, looking back at an A.A. scout disappearing in a cloud of dust. One Tommy said to the other, 'Trouble ahead, Bert. He didn't salute.'

GIs stood trying to figure the joke, gave up, and moved on to the Monseigneur News Cinema and Leicester Place. London buzzed with tension and excitement, and the East End guarded the secrets of its great Mulberry harbours, its laying of a huge undersea petrol pipeline, and all the fantastic preparations for the invasion of France and the final confrontation with Hitler.

'This is history in the making,' April told Hannah. 'You are too young to remember, but you have seen things that will never be seen again.'

423

''gain,' mimicked Hannah, sucking her fingers.

'No, never again,' said her mother.

Eileen and April went to the Christmas Toy Exchange, there being nothing to be had in the shops at all. April begged two cartons of Hershey bars and some scented soap from Sam Saul and asked if she could exchange them for toys, since Hannah had none as such.

'We'll take anything,' said the woman, 'especially chocolate. How many points do you think that earns her?' she asked another assistant.

Enough for a well-worn but clean teddy bear and several rag books, which they took home and wrapped in carefully hoarded brown paper.

'I hope David brings her something,' said April, sitting on her heels, cutting the paper so exactly to size there would be no waste. 'I don't know why we're doing this. She'll only try to eat it.'

'Unwrapping is most of the fun,' remarked Eileen.

'She's lucky to have something to unwrap. I hope we have a quieter time than last year. It'll be strange without any of them.'

Ted had died two months after Ethel; he just gave up without her. Bridie made rare, flying visits to see Hannah, smart in her uniform, her face filled out by enough food and newfound confidence. She'd held the tiny child for a long time on her first visit, and gazed at her intently, an oddly sad look in her eyes. Hannah had stared back, seeming fascinated.

'She's adorable. She's going to be as pretty as you,' Bridie had said, 'but I can't see much of her father in her yet. All her colouring's yours.'

'There's red in her hair. That's your family, I should think.'

Bridie had nodded. 'Maybe. Is she her Daddy's girl?' she asked, touching the baby's soft cheek, smiling. She looked up in surprise when April didn't answer. 'He comes to see her?' It was more of a statement than a question.

April looked down, playing with Hannah's fingers.

'He doesn't come?'

'Not yet,' muttered April, humiliated.

'Not at all?' Bridie was scandalized.

'Never, since she was born. He hasn't seen her.'

'Good God! Does he say why?'

'He makes excuses. Says he has to work, and the travelling is so hard with all the troop movements and things.'

It was on the tip of Bridie's tongue to say 'What rubbish', but she thought better of it.

'It isn't easy to get about, that's true. But I should have thought he could have got to London occasionally. Why don't you go there?'

'I can't get the time off work,' said April. 'I've hardly got back.'

Uncomfortable, they avoided each other's eyes.

"There is trouble here," thought Bridie, her expression giving away nothing of her thoughts, "and I don't know that it's going to help for me to go prying. Better let them sort it out themselves."

The rest of the brief visit was overshadowed by April's embarrassment at her failure to persuade David to come home, and she and her mother-in-law parted awkwardly.

'I'm very sorry you've been left alone so much. I wish I was nearer,' was all Bridie would say as she left.

Later, she told Lizzie in a letter:

I'll wring my son's neck if he hurts them. I know

he can be thoughtless – even selfish – but I can't imagine why he doesn't see that beautiful baby as often as he can. There's something wrong, but I can't ask April what. And, in any case, I don't think she knows herself, though she's much too loyal to say so. I'm worried, and there's nothing I can do.

There was a Christmas card for her, some photographs of Hannah, and a small note from April towards the end of the baby's first year.

We are both well, and Hannah is walking steadily and has lots of words. Her hair has become quite reddish and her eyes are a greenish-yellow – very striking.

I am sorry to say that David still does not visit, though we expect him for Christmas. He writes often, though, and says he is doing very well in his studies. He has once again had his scholarship extended, which I know was on his mind a lot. Perhaps he'll be able to get away more now.

Bridie held the letter in her hand, reading it again and again, trying to find something that might be a clue, but there was nothing.

'It might be none of my business, but I'm going to have to put him right,' she concluded unwillingly.

'What did you say?' asked an ATS driver, who was lounging in the back of a staff car while her passenger talked round a long table in a smoky room, planning supply lines to the invasion troops with half a dozen brass.

'I said she's gorgeous,' answered Bridie, passing over

the small, shiny collection of photographs.

'She is, too. You must be proud, though I wouldn't have thought you were a grandmother.'

Bridie nodded at the automatic compliment. 'I'm proud of them both,' she said ambiguously, and folded April's letter.

'Not easy, kids in wartime.' The younger woman stretched and yawned, 'I'm glad I haven't got any; little perishers are always hungry.'

"Perhaps it is just wartime," thought Bridie. But she felt a deep sense of unease, and it wouldn't go away.

April wrote again, two weeks later.

David came for Christmas, and we had a nice time. Hannah loved her presents. Thank you for the little beads. She tries to chew them, so I think I'll keep them for her until she's older. All the presents were for Hannah. The rest of us didn't bother. Food is an endless problem and we are hungry all the time because we can't refuse Hannah what she needs. I wish the invasion would come and that this endless war would be over. It is hard to keep Hannah warm and she has chilblains, which makes her very cross. David promised to come more often.

"Maybe my letter made him think," thought Bridie. "At least he's been. It's not natural, though, to stay away like that. Perhaps he's just not got used to being a father, having to be away like that."

She tried to reassure herself and April's letter sounded chirpy enough. But it said nothing about David and Hannah; nothing that sounded as though he cuddled her and played with her. Surely April should have said something like that.

April had been careful not to let anyone know that David, so far as she knew, had not touched Hannah. She'd watched carefully, after the first two days, thinking surely she was mistaken. He hadn't touched her once, but had gone to great pains to disguise it. April began to feel haunted by a sense of unreality as their week together dragged by; she kept looking, looking for the touch. She'd even, in desperation, gone to dump the child on his lap but he had said 'No', and clumsily leapt to his feet, saying he'd forgotten he'd promised George he'd sort scraps for the hens. April was left holding Hannah out to an empty chair.

Clinging to the hope that she was imagining it, or that David would overcome whatever it was himself, given time, she said nothing to him, but simply waited.

"But he never touched her once," she admitted bleakly to herself, after he had long gone back to the country. She stared at the spluttering little pile of coal in the grate, so meagre its warmth barely took the chill out of the room of an evening, while the raw January night seeped in through every nook and cranny of the big, draughty house. She sat every evening by the fire's small glow, holding Hannah close, the warm, plump little body tucked cosily next to hers underneath the worn overcoat April wore to keep them warm.

'I'm sorry, baby,' she whispered when Eileen and George weren't there and she couldn't hold the truth silently inside her any longer, 'but your daddy doesn't love you. And I don't know why.'

Chapter Thirty-One

Johnathan calmly dozed, ignoring the buzzing, revving, droning and fighting going on above his head. Lizzie fidgeted nervously and looked longingly at the Morrison.

'I'd forgotten what this felt like,' she said, her voice shaking.

Johnathan half opened his eyes and yawned. 'What a blasted racket,' he observed.

'Look at it!' cried Lizzie, going to the uncurtained window. 'It's more than a bit of a racket. Don't you think we should shelter?'

'It's freezing cold more than six inches from this apology for a fire.'

'There's plenty of fire out here, if it's fire you want.' Lizzie watched the display in her garden with terrified wonder. Incendiary bombs spluttered silver fire about the frozen grass and bounced around on the roofs of the house and the garden shed, trailing sparks that glittered against the frost.

'Go and see none have penetrated the roof,' she said, hearing them rolling and banging about.

Johnathan gave up. 'I'll look,' he said, leaving his small patch of warmth for the icy regions of the hall and stairs. The roof was still sound.

'All clear,' he called, rubbing his hands briskly to

keep warm. A bomb whistled down and shook the house. At the front, glass shattered inwards.

'Johnathan,' shrieked Lizzie.

'I'm all right but this isn't.' His voice came from the small hall. 'Come and look.'

She went to look. Water fell in a curtain over their front door, which leant sideways, splintered by the tearing of its hinges. The flood splashed everywhere, freezing cold.

'Where's it coming from?'

'Broken pipe,' Johnathan said. 'I'd better go out and check.'

A bomb exploded nearby with a tremendous crump.

'Johnathan . . .'

He ducked under the water and she heard him give a shout of incredulity.

'What? What's the matter?' she quavered.

'What's this?' he called. Unflappable Johnathan sounded frightened, and that scared Lizzie more than anything the Luftwaffe could do. She shot out through the water and bumped straight into him, standing staring at a hissing, smoking, glow-worm.

'Get inside,' he shouted, and they both backed through the deluge, standing dripping and shivering in the hall.

'What is it?' Lizzie's teeth chattered.

'Hello,' a shout came from the garden.

'It's all right, that's the wardens. They'll know. You go in the warm.'

'Oi,' came another shout, 'you got a phosphorus bomb in your coke shed, mate.'

'So that's what it is,' said Lizzie, dripping all over her living room floor. Johnathan went outside and stood with the wardens, looking at the long, green, glowing thing that hissed and puffed and smelt horrible.

'Got to keep the blighter wet, or it'll go up,' they said. 'Fetch some buckets, quick.'

'Come on, Lizzie, all hands to the pump,' called Johnathan, filling a bucket from the broken pipe and passing it to the wardens. 'We need to form a chain.'

Lizzie described the scene to Bridie in a letter:

> We poured water on that evil-smelling thing all night, raids and warnings and all. We kept at it and by morning we were all hysterical with laughter, watering this noxious thing in our coke shed like some ghastly flower while we clouted incendiaries about in the mud like footballs, sodden to the skin. Still, we've been lucky. The roof stayed on and all we lost was the lilac bush in the front garden; that disappeared without trace and all we could see was a huge red hole. Since then, we've been left in peace. I've heard it called the 'Baby Blitz'. I just hope it never grows up, because I don't think any of us could take anything like the last one again. We are all simply too tired.

The Baby Blitz never amounted to anything like its full-grown predecessor and in May the caissons for the mulberries were floated down the Thames on their way to the Solent. Everyone waited for D-Day with anxious anticipation. Much of the bombed out wilderness of the East End, especially Canning Town and Silvertown, became a huge transit camp for thousands upon thousands of men, waiting to embark for Normandy.

April stood watching the Thames one overcast afternoon, along with a small gathering of silent

Londoners. It was solid with shipping, its shores and docks jammed with men and equipment, and they all knew that the invasion must be very near.

Eileen, pegging out threadbare sheets, looked up, her eyes narrowed against the bright light. All day the sky had been full of planes, streaming wing tip to wing tip towards the coast. Rachael stood in the back doorway, chatting and watching Hannah play.

'Something must be up,' she concluded wisely, looking up at the roaring planes again, 'Oh, Eileen, look at that.'

'What?' Eileen scanned the sky.

'No, the sheets. Look at the sheets.'

They were black with oil and smoke from the dense formations of low-flying planes.

'Oh!' Eileen was speechless. Soap was very short. 'They'll never come out,' she said sadly, gazing at the stains. And, a permanent reminder of D-Day washday, they never did.

'Well,' remarked Sam Saul to Hannah several days later, while the Allies advanced into France, 'what was it that chap said? "We can look forward to a new year with some confidence that the last siren will sound before the last Trump?" Something like that. What have you found?'

They were sitting in George's garden on a rug, Hannah exploring his pockets thoroughly; there was always something good to eat in them, cunningly hidden for her to find, wrapped in a twist of coloured paper or a little box she had to find a way to open.

'Babies. Where in the world do you get jelly babies?' cried April, seeing the packet clutched in her daughter's hands while she gave a toothy grin of triumph.

'You can get anything you want, if you know where to look for it,' said Sam. 'Ask that old crook you work for, he could tell you.'

'He's in steel and stuff. I bet he couldn't find jelly babies.'

'Don't you believe it,' said Sam dourly. 'He's got his shifty fingers in diverse pies.'

'You don't have anything to do with him, do you?' asked April uneasily.

'Not directly, but I hear . . . this and that.'

'Well, keep it to yourself. I don't want to know. Some of the things you turn up with make me wonder what *you've* been doing during the war, I must say.'

'Must you?' he said, pained. 'I've devoted much of my time to wearing tin hats and being an exemplary air raid warden, though that's a bit redundant now. I should think Hitler's got his hands too full to bother with London any more. If I'd been a bit younger, I'd be obliged to do something military, but I'm quite glad I'm not,' he said candidly. 'I never fancied being shot at by some fellow at the business end of a bayonet. I prefer the Home Front myself.'

'What did you do in the last war? You weren't a conscientious objector, surely?'

'Fought,' said Sam briefly. 'It made me disinclined to repeat the experience.'

'Are you a pacifist?' she asked curiously.

'I would have refused to fight again, yes.'

'Even though it's a kind of Jewish war, if you believe what Hitler's supposed to have done.'

'Precisely because of that.'

'I don't understand.'

'I don't know that I do, either. It has to do with not

433

meeting violence with more and more violence; something I understood much less about in my young days, I have to admit. Your mother-in-law could tell you a tale or two on that score.'

April twinkled at him. 'Surely not.'

'Oh, yes. I was well on the way to becoming a bad lot. Then I met her and she took me in hand, and I never looked back,' said Sam cheerily. 'She reminded me I had a conscience hidden away somewhere.'

'Don't you think we have to have a conscience about Hitler, then, and fight what he stands for?'

'Of course. But I try to fight it in my own way, rather than by putting on a uniform and picking up a gun. It's a very personal thing for me.'

'I see,' said April.

'I doubt it. I hardly do myself,' said Sam dryly. 'I think it's a somewhat eccentric way of looking at things.'

She clasped her hands round her knees and gazed at him. 'I suppose it is,' she said, thinking how very much she liked this tall, middle-aged man who let Hannah ride on his shoulders to the park, where he sailed little leaf boats and always had a scrap or two for her to throw to the ducks on the lake. And who had let his wife go with wry, self-mocking good humour, speaking of her always with affection and a kind of angry respect.

'A wide boy,' grumbled George dismissively. 'I don't know why you encourage him, April.'

'You didn't turn his turkey down that Christmas, nor ask him where he got it.'

'Don't approve of black market.'

'Everyone buys bits and pieces if they can afford them,' Eileen argued. 'I don't know how we'd make do otherwise.'

April wondered what he would say to her parents' accusations.

'Do you trade on the black market?' she asked quietly, picking up a green jelly baby and licking a tiny trace of sugar from its head.

Sam eyed her thoughtfully. 'You know, my esteemed fellow Jew, Dr Freud, claims that we tend to choose people like our parents for our wives or husbands. When I look at you, I believe he may be right.'

'Why?' asked April, astonished.

'You remind me very strongly of your mother-in-law when she was younger. Forthright.'

'So you do?'

'You enjoyed the champage. You didn't think I bought it in the corner shop, did you?'

'No. I didn't mean to be critical. I was just curious. I don't think the black market is right, but I know almost everyone buys from it. And I did enjoy the champagne though I knew I shouldn't, so I can't criticize.'

'That's honest enough.'

Hannah planted herself in Sam's lap, leaning against his chest, looking out at her mother with a complacent smile. 'It should have been David,' thought April. A tiny, unripe pear fell from the tree with a small smacking sound. She jumped nervously.

'Things landing from above will never be the same again, will they?' remarked Sam, amused. He tickled Hannah's ribs slyly and she squealed with delight.

'I'm glad she won't know the kinds of things we've had to live through. Well, not remember them too much, anyway. At least she waited until after the Blitz to be born.'

'Wise child,' said Sam earnestly.

Hannah's cheek bulged with a mangled jelly baby.

April wiped her mouth and patted the little bulge. 'Now the war's nearly won, maybe there really will be peace for good. I should think we've seen the last of Hitler here. There won't be any more really bad times,' she said.

'More,' echoed Hannah prophetically, spilling all the babies on to the rug and stirring them delightedly. 'More.'

'What's that?' grumbled Lizzie. Half awake, she turned over and closed her eyes again. No trace of early morning light filtered through their blackout. Johnathan grunted in his sleep.

'How inconsiderate,' Lizzie muttered to herself, 'riding a motorbike like that.'

The noise grew. It sounded less like a motorbike and more like a powerful sawmill or a vast clockwork toy. The doodlebug, one of ten, made its way over Lizzie's roof and flew on, to the Bow Road where Bridie lost her shoe when she arrived in London many years before. Just before Bow, it veered slightly, to pass over Grove Road, and the noise stopped. It carried on as far as the bridge, to the count of twelve, and then it fell. At twenty-five past four on a beautiful summer morning, Bow woke to the sound of the shattering explosion which followed. In defiance of April's confident prediction, Hitler's secret weapon arrived with vengeance.

Chapter Thirty-Two

David held April's letter in one hand and ran his fingers through his hair with the other. It had 'Opened By The Censor' on the envelope and half of it had been obliterated. For the hundredth time, he wondered why. Why should they censor letters from London to inside Britain, especially now D-Day was well past? What was the big secret they were trying to keep? Nothing in the newspapers, nothing on the wireless. The only way to find out would be to go there and see.

A familiar dread tugged at him; less sharp than at first, but still enough to make him hesitate. He looked at the letter again. Curiosity and anxiety finally forced him to a decision. He'd try to break Mr Hubbard's hold, even though the mere thought of it brought him out in a cold sweat.

Several times he wandered down into the village and stood outside the small church at the far end. Once he watched the priest arrive on his bicycle and stood rooted to the spot, hidden by the tall, ivy-covered gateposts at the entrance to the churchyard. His need to go inside was counterbalanced by his fear of what might be said, so he waited, paralyzed, until the priest came out again and pedalled off without noticing him. Then David crept up the quiet path and, finding the door unlocked, went in, half expecting the roof or a thunderbolt, or both, to land on his head. Instead, he found cool shadows filled with flowers from village gardens and the soft cooing of a pair of doves roosting in the rafters. He looked round, embarrassed, then sidled into a pew and knelt, clasping his hands and staring straight ahead of him at the altar.

He tried to pray, remembering words from the convent school, long disused and forgotten. They came back quickly enough, rolling off his tongue, bringing memories of school: chalk dust; long, darned, itchy socks, and the pale flat eyes of the boy who used to sit next to him at their pitted wooden desk. His mind wandered and he brought his attention back with an effort.

'Forgive me, Father . . .' The words fell like sand in the desert. Dry, silent, meaningless. David began to understand. Beyond the fear and the loneliness, the guilt and despair, was nothingness.

'You are bankrupt,' the dwarf had said.

It was true. The flowers bloomed in their vases, cool, fragrant air stirred, doves in their corner cooed softly. Everyday things of comfort and peace.

"I can't feel them," thought David in sudden panic. "I can't feel them."

He concentrated hard, trying through sheer force of will to feel the redness of the roses and the greeness of their leaves. Nothing. He could see, but not experience what he saw; hear, but not experience what he heard; touch, but not feel the reality of the object. "I can only think," he thought, eerily disconnected from himself. "I can only think." And was filled with such an extreme horror that he stayed kneeling for a long time, head bowed as if in prayer, unable to get up. Thinking about thinking about thinking . . . that he might be going mad.

* * *

'I want to talk about something personal. I wondered if you could spare me a few minutes? If you wouldn't mind, that is.'

The lecturer in psychiatry looked over his glasses and said, 'Certainly, Mr Holmes. This evening suit you? In my rooms?'

'Yes. Thank you,' said David.

Funny chap to ask for a consultation, thought the psychiatrist. He asked discreetly around the senior common room during the course of the day. An excellent student. First class. Conscientious. Married, with a child. Very quiet, very reliable. Not a mixer, inclined to keep himself to himself. No problems, no, not as far as anyone knew. "Wonder what the problem is," thought Dr Fisher. "With a reference like that, can't be serious." He decided it was probably some minor marital upset, what with being separated for so long. He had ward rounds at a nearby hospital that afternoon, and put the student quite out of his mind.

David spent the afternoon at the same hospital, taking histories from women with gynaecological problems. One of them, a great overweight lump of a woman, had seven children and a tiny husband. The seven children were at school but the tiny husband sat by her bedside, nodding at her long tale of pain, bleeding and mysterious inner tremblings.

'If you'll just excuse me a minute, I'd like to examine your wife.' David tried to warm his cold hands, waiting for the nurse to pull the curtains close and for the small man to finish being apologetic and leave. He sat on a chair outside the ward, his mouth clamped shut in a straight line, his red-veined, farmworker's face immobile with anxiety.

David eyed the great mound of flesh on the bed and wondered how he'd find anything. He began to feel the woman's warm, rolling body, prodding and exploring carefully, trying to map with his fingers the picture he had in his mind of the female pelvis. He forgot about seeing old Fisher.

'What a nice young doctor,' whispered the patient loudly to the nurse, as he washed his hands.

'He is rather, isn't he?' whispered back the nurse, rolling her eyes.

'If I was young and pretty like you . . .' The fat woman winked merrily and ran her hand down her mountainous belly. 'But I've seen better days, my dear. Shame, isn't it?'

The nurse pulled her gown down and helped her sit up.

David wrote up his notes in the office, while the houseman examined her again, watching the busy ward through a glass partition.

'Have you nothing better to do than get in my way?' demanded Sister, bustling in. 'I've got report in fifteen minutes; you can't hang around here.'

David collected his papers and stethoscope. Still he lingered. There was nowhere else to go except back to the college, and he was in no hurry.

'Is there something you want, young man?' asked Sister impatiently.

'No, thank you.' David wandered out, longing for the day when they would treat him with some respect. Young man! She was hardly older than he was. Fed up, he went home and spent the rest of the afternoon trying to bone up on ovaries. He found it depressingly hard going.

* * *

Dr Fisher got out a glass decanter and held it up to the light. It twinkled, half full of brandy.

'Ah, still plenty there. Hard to get, these days. Like a drop?'

'Please,' said David, nervously pulling at his trouser knees and running a hand through his hair. He took the brandy and sniffed its strong, throat-catching fumes. Fisher took the armchair opposite and took off his glasses, leaving them lying loosely in his hand as he sipped at his glass.

'Well, I've asked about and everyone gives you a glowing report,' he began. 'Wish I'd had reports like that when I was a student.' He folded his spectacles up with one hand and looked vaguely round for their case. 'Never know where I've put it,' he grumbled.

David reached over to a small table and handed the case to the psychiatrist.

'Thank you. Helpful, observant, nice way with the patients. I found myself wondering what kind of problem you could possibly have. Want to tell me?'

'It isn't my work.'

'I'd rather assumed it couldn't be.'

'It's a personal thing.'

Fisher nodded.

'I'm afraid I don't know how to begin.' David began to sweat and his hand around the delicate stem of the glass was unsteady.

'Try the beginning.'

David sat in miserable silence. If he started at the beginning, they'd throw him out. He couldn't confess to the false birth certificate. But he had already realized that only the beginning was important, that the first capitulation was all that mattered. Already, he knew it was hopeless.

'There was once something I wanted very badly.' His voice sounded squeaky to his own ears, as though it was just breaking.

'What sort of something?'

'An ambition.'

'Ah.'

'And I . . . there was a block. It seemed that nothing could be done about it, and then it sort of turned out that there was a possible way round.' David's heart thudded painfully. 'So I took the opportunity and I did get round the problem.' His throat was dry.

'You got round the problem,' said Dr Fisher.

'Yes.'

'Did getting round the problem land you with another one?'

David stared at him gratefully. 'Yes. An even worse one, and I can't find a way out of it this time.'

'Want to tell me what it is?'

'No.'

'Hard for me to help, then.'

'I didn't mean I wouldn't. I meant I don't want to. I feel so terrible about what I've done. It haunts me.'

'Guilty feelings, eh?'

'Yes.'

'We all have them. Sometimes they get inflated . . . get things out of proportion, you know? Think no one else ever did something so bad, when it turns out half the population have been there.'

'It's not like that.' David began to lose hope.

'You'd better tell me, then.'

'I sold my soul.'

It came out as a comical squeak.

'Did you indeed? That sounds like a matter for a

priest rather than a psychiatrist, if you're serious.' Dr Fisher smiled deprecatingly, discounting what the student was saying. He sipped at his brandy and regarded the serious young man opposite him, wondering whether overwork and the war were precipitating a breakdown in him. It happened. Students who couldn't take the isolation and homesickness. There had been a few.

'I am serious.'

Dr Fisher crossed his legs and rubbed his chin thoughtfully.

'Sleep all right?'

'Mostly, yes.'

'Dream?'

'I don't usually remember them.'

'D'you get depressed. Miss your wife, Child?'

'Yes, of course, but . . .' He couldn't explain to this man that this was the complicated crux of the matter.

'It's natural, you know. All this separation from home, tucked away here in this godforsaken spot, it gets on people's nerves. We all feel it. And when you get low like that, it's easy to start thinking that things are worse than they are. Why don't you get out a bit more? I hear you're a bit of a loner; tricky, with a wife back in London, but all work makes Jack a dull boy. Go down to the village pub and have a beer with the rest. Get your wife up here for a week. You'll soon dispel notions of selling your soul over some matter when you were young. It's pressure, you know. Does terrible things; the mind starts harbouring all manner of strange thoughts and delusions.'

'You think I'm deluded?'

"Psychotic? No, no sign of it," thought Dr Fisher. He beamed broadly and held up the decanter.

'Not at all. I think you are a young man under great strain, and inclined to dramatize a tiny bit over something long past. A hook to hang your guilt feelings on, probably to do with leaving your wife alone so long. Quite irrational, you see, since you really can't help it, not unless you want to abandon a most promising career?'

'No.' Helplessly David shook his head.

'Loosen up a bit,' said the psychaitrist heartily. 'Enjoy life. Once this confounded war's over, you've got everything ahead of you. What with Beveridge and what have you, it's exciting times ahead for the likes of us. Cheers.'

David put down his glass, giddy with despair and disappointment. 'I'm sorry, sir,' he muttered. 'I don't think brandy agrees with me. Would you forgive me if I go? I'm sorry to have wasted your time like this; I'm sure you're right. I'll try to take your advice.'

Fisher smiled contentedly. 'Not at all. Any time I can help. Lots of people feel the same way. Nothing to apologize for. Trying times, you know, trying times.' He shook his big head mournfully.

'Thank you, sir,' David said desperately.

Fisher put a hand on his shoulder, seeing him to the door.

'Go and live it up a little. Have fun.'

'Thank you,' said David, frantic.

'Good night, then.'

'Good night, sir.'

The door closed. David stared at it, his eyes burning like live coals in his head. A vice closed on his mind, tightening the circle of his thoughts to screaming pitch.

"I have to confess," his mind screamed. "I want release from this dreadful thing. I want to confess."

"Confess all you like – go ahead," said a cold voice, cutting through the feverish turmoil. "Speak freely, my dear fellow. Try, by all means. You see, no one will believe you. Confess, David, confess—" the words thundered in his ears with insane mockery – "go ahead, old chap, confess away. We shan't hold it against you."

David clattered down stone steps, almost falling in his panic. Howls of demonic laughter followed, until he clapped his hands to his ears in agony.

'No,' it was only a whisper, but he thought he heard it echo across the courtyard of the great house and up to the evening sky, the stars just visible in the darkening blue. Laughter pealed, bouncing insanely off high stone walls. David fled.

Chapter Thirty-Three

'There's been thirty-seven gone over so far as I've counted today.'

Eileen met April when she got home from work, standing in the hallway with Hannah in her arms. 'And I didn't catch them all,' she went on, her voice rising with strain.

April took Hannah. The little girl clung so tightly round her neck she had to loosen the small arms, to breathe.

'It's been bad everywhere,' she told Eileen. 'An office block near us got a direct hit just before I got in this morning. There were some killed, but it was before half-past nine, so there weren't too many people in.' She coughed. 'It's as bad as the Blitz. They make an awful lot of smoke.'

Eileen's face was shrunken and drawn. 'There's streams of them coming over,' she said dully. 'They don't stop. Fast as one goes "buzz buzz buzz", and stops, and you wait to see if it's you it's going to fall on top of, and you hear it drop and you think, "Thank God that's not dropped here" . . . you hear another one coming. The warning goes so often you can't remember if there's another alert or whether it's still the one before. In the Blitz you knew where you were, but this lot – you can't tell any more.

'We haven't got a chance, April. I thought we'd nearly won. What's the Army doing, not stopping them? They're in France, aren't they? Why don't they stop them?' Eileen cried like a bewildered child.

April shifted Hannah on to her hip and put her arm round her mother's shoulders.

'Come on. We haven't been hit yet.'

'Yet!' yelped Eileen. 'That's just it. It's yet. It's coming.' She looked imploringly at April, as if she had the answer.

'Why don't we all go down a shelter?'

'George says they're no good. The bombs get into them. Nothing is any use against them. I don't want to get buried alive down a shelter.' Eileen's voice rose hysterically. Hannah began to wail and her hands grasped painfully at April's hair.

'That child is terrified,' babbled Eileen. 'Every time an alert goes, she screams and tries to run to the Anderson, and your father tells her to come back in, and shouts at her, which makes her cry, and it's pandemonium. I can't bear it. I can't look after her, April. Hitler won't let me.'

April smiled weakly at her mother's childishness. 'You're going to let him stop you?'

Eileen sobbed into a corner of her frayed and threadbare pinafore. 'I'm so frightened I don't know whether I'm coming or going,' she wept. 'And your father's no use. He just shouts. I know it's because he's frightened too, and doesn't know what to do. He's used to being in control of everything, and there's no control at all, now. It's all gone, April.'

She picked Hannah's fingers out of her hair and bit her lip. Flying bombs had passed constantly overhead all day. Sirens had screamed, people had screamed, and Mr Stephenson had worked on relentlessly through the screaming. Now her mother was screaming.

'Stop it!' she yelled. 'Shut up, Mum.'

Eileen sniffed incredulously. Then she stopped crying. She mopped her eyes with the pinafore, which frayed a lot more with the treatment it was getting.

'Give me that child, while you go upstairs and have five minutes peace. If those stupid doodlebugs let you.' Eileen snatched Hannah and covered her face with kisses. 'Silly old grandma,' she cried, 'getting in a state. Come on, precious, let's get your mummy's tea.'

She vanished into the kitchen, promising extra national orange juice as a treat, and a spoon of radio malt. Hannah adored radio malt and would be quiet for it. It tasted like toffee; soft, runny toffee. April ate some, sometimes, when her longing for sweets overcame her and Sam Saul hadn't delivered Hershey bars in a long time.

'Stealing food out of your own child's mouth,' Eileen had hissed, when she found April with the spoon in her mouth one day.

'Hitler is who's stealing my child's food,' April hissed back savagely, and Eileen had been silenced.

On this appalling evening, the radio malt silenced Hannah, who was as good as gold with a spoonful to lick.

'There you are, not as bad as all that, is it?' Eileen stood, arms akimbo, watching them pull towards them plates of food that she had made superhuman efforts to come by.

'This looks tasty,' said George bravely, mixing whalemeat sausage with swede into a nauseating mix. 'Isn't Hannah having some?'

'She won't eat it and I haven't got anything else,'

answered Eileen, her little moment of happiness rudely destroyed.

'Look, Hannah, yum, yum.' George stirred his horrid plateful and courageously put a spoonful in his mouth. 'You have some?'

Hannah, undeceived, hid her face in April's dress.

'She's hungry, but she won't eat it,' said Eileen hopelessly. 'And who can blame her.'

The food depressed them all.

Hannah cried and wouldn't sleep.

'She's hungry,' said Eileen. 'I told you, she won't eat, but it's all I can get.'

'I know, Mum. I'm very grateful. You do your best.'

April's head ached. Her stomach ached because she, too, was hungry. The incessant alerts, punctuated by the sound of collapsing buildings and screaming, wounded, buried people, tore at her nerves. Coming home, she'd passed ARP and other rescue workers, paddling through glass, helping people red from head to foot into ambulances. Others were bagging ghastly remains – whole bodies, parts of bodies – ignoring the 'buzz buzz buzz' of more bombs overhead. A baby's hand lay on the pavement; April saw it just in time. Up in her little flat, alone with Hannah, she tried to blot out the grisly memories.

The child whined and thrashed and grizzled.

'I know you're tired and hungry and scared,' burst out April, 'but, for heaven's sake, so am I!'

Hannah howled, seeing her mother cross.

'Stop it!' April slapped her with terrifying suddenness. 'Stop it.'

Hannah hiccoughed desperately, trying to hold her breath. April stared at her white, pinched little face, looking so frightened and so lost. Huge tears rolled down her cheeks, unstoppable now they had started.

'I'm sorry, baby. I'm sorry. I wouldn't hurt you for the world, Hannah, but we're so tired, aren't we, and so frightened and so by ourselves that I don't know what to do.' She covered Hannah's face with kisses, clutching the child fiercely to her, rocking and rocking, trying to comfort them both.

After a long while, Hannah fell asleep and April, drained beyond exhaustion, looked down at her. The small face was streaked with dirt and tears. The distant sound of a doodlebug cut through the night air. Sirens wailed and April held her breath. The engine cut out well before it reached Ilford and she heard the explosion some way away. A great column of smoke rose into the night, and inside it people screamed and screamed and screamed. These days, it seemed, only the dead were silent.

'Why don't we leave? said April. 'What about the Chislehurst Caves? I could even get to work from there. People did in the Blitz.'

'I'm not leaving here,' said George stubbornly. The war had made him a very old man. The jacket with leather patches, worn to nothing since the days of Lord Woolton, hung loose on his shrunken frame. Wispy grey hair straggled across his head, above faded eyes. He had taken to blinking in quick, irregular bursts and then staring vacantly around him, as though he didn't quite know where he was.

'Mum?'

Eileen looked at her husband and April saw that she was hopelessly resigned.

'I couldn't leave him.'

'The government's telling people to go. They'll pay.

You don't have to go to an official billet; we could go as aided evacuees and they'd pay our train fares and an allowance every week. Let's go, Mum, and get away somewhere safe, before we either go mad or get killed.'

'No,' said George mulishly. 'If I'm going to die, I'll die in my own home. I'm too old to go living in someone else's, who doesn't want you there and who makes your life a misery. I've heard about it. I'll end my days here.'

'And take Mum with you, I suppose?' said April scathingly.

'She can go if she wants. It's up to her,' the old man said fretfully.

'You know she won't,' April began angrily, but Eileen shook her head.

'Don't . . .'

'What about Hannah? Don't you care about her?' April tried, but it was no use.

'You should take her away. You go,' said Eileen.

Their tired grey faces, the lines of worry and want, their dreadful passive resignation, their terror and their clinging and their hopeless dignity, defeated her. She knew they had again trapped her, and how futile were her struggles.

'If Hannah gets killed, it'll be your fault,' she screamed at George.

He looked up, mildly surprised. April fought an impulse to slap him, to force something from him, some kind of recognition. 'I can't go and leave you here alone, you know I can't. You're making me keep Hannah here and she'll get killed. She's going to die, Dad, because you're too selfish, and too narrow-minded, and too sunk inside yourself to care. You don't care!' April yelled. 'You never cared about anyone except bloody April.' She flew at the fireplace and tugged viciously at the portrait.

'I'm getting rid of it,' she gasped, pulling at the heavy frame. 'I hate it and I hate you and I hate what you do to me and Hannah and Mum and David . . .' The picture began to come away from the wall with a crack.

Eileen darted forward, her hands outstretched in warning. 'April!'

The picture lurched to one side and then toppled onto the fireplace with a crash of broken glass.

'Good riddance,' whooped April, beside herself.

'April,' bleated Eileen. 'April . . . your father!'

George had gone puce. His eyes bulged and he made an odd noise in his throat.

'I don't care. I wish I'd done it when you nailed it up,' April shouted. 'When you nailed it up, although you knew Mum hated it. You horrible old man!'

A shudder went through him.

'I'm going to write to David and make him come home, and we're going to go away and find somewhere to live, and if you don't like it, you can stay here and wait for a doodlebug for all I care.'

George spoke with difficulty, his voice choking. 'You will stop.'

April, colour draining from her face, stood in the wreckage of the portrait and stared at him.

'I'm sorry,' she whispered.

He leaned forwards, out of his chair, and crept towards the shattered picture. He fingered the broken frame wonderingly.

'You've destroyed her,' he muttered.

'No, Dad. She died years ago. I haven't destroyed her, just broken an old portrait that needed getting rid of.'

George's head bent over the canvas. April's painted eyes, torn by a shard of glass, looked back crookedly. His back shook and April realized with horror that he was crying. Eileen backed away from him, a strange twist to her mouth.

'You've been crying over her since the day I came and found you upstairs like an animal. It's time you stopped.'

George groaned and shook his head.

'Let her go, for God's sake, Dad.'

He raised his head and looked up at her. 'I loved you,' he said bleakly.

'You loved her,' said April calmly. 'Not me. Because I look like her.'

'No,' George groaned. 'You've never understood.'

'I understood when Mum said you made her call me April.'

George knelt and carefully picked glass out of the frame. 'It can be mended,' he muttered.

'No,' said Eileen. To their surprise her voice was firm. 'I'm going to sweep that mess up and put the glass in the dustbin. The frame will do nicely for lighting the fire. The picture's ruined, George. We'll burn it.'

He looked up at April again, pleading. She shook her head. 'Mum's right.'

He wiped the back of his hand across his eyes.

'Come on, Dad,' April put her hands under his elbows, 'before you cut yourself on that glass.'

He clutched her arms and she felt the great heavy weight of him bearing her down again.

'Get up,' she snapped.

George struggled to his feet. Eileen knelt and began putting bits of glass into a sheet of newspaper. George watched, dazed.

'Shouldn't have done that, girl.'

'No, perhaps not, but what's done is done. It can't be put back now.'

'Never seen you in a temper like that before.'

'I've never lived through a war before. Or had a starving child before. Or a husband I never see before. It's changed us all, Dad. And you, like the rest of us.'

George looked vaguely round the bare kitchen, as if searching for something.

'It's all gone, hasn't it?' he whimpered.

'What has?'

'Everything.'

'Not everything, Dad. But a lot. The way we were.'

'Get your husband. He should be looking after you. Tell him I can't do it any more. Tell him to be a man and come and do his duty,' George ordered querulously. 'I can't do it for him any more.'

'David will come and help me decide what to do, but he has to go back again. He has to finish his training. I've given up too much for him to stop now.'

George peered at her. 'You've changed,' he mumbled. 'Don't know you any more.'

'She's growing up,' muttered Eileen from the grate.

The door opened and Hannah stood before them, rubbing her eyes, her nightdress soaked.

'Wet.'

April picked her up. 'Sodden. You don't wet the bed, darling. Why are you wet?'

'One, two, three . . . bang,' recited Hannah miserably.

'She's terrified of the bombs,' Eileen said. 'I told you. It's on her mind. I'm not surprised she's wetting the bed.'

'Let's change you,' said April. 'And your cot. I have

455

to do something about this.' She pulled the soaked nightdress over Hannah's head and Eileen took it from her. 'David has to come home and help me.'

Eileen nodded and they all looked fearfully at the ceiling.

'One, two, three, four, five . . .'

On the count of twelve the bomb landed.

Chapter Thirty-Four

'I want to give up,' David announced.

'You can't,' said April flatly. 'I've been thinking about that and I couldn't bear you to give up now. I thought that was what you wanted, and I suppose I did for a long time, but we've gone through too much. I don't want it all to have been for nothing, David.'

Hannah sucked radio malt off a spoon between them, sitting on Lizzie's front room floor, where they were supposed to be able to talk in private.

'I don't think any of us can exactly go on.'

'Rachael's looking after Mum. I can stay here for a bit.'

'Who will look after Hannah? Your mum won't be in a state to do anything for a long time. She certainly can't have Hannah any more, even if Rachael didn't mind.'

'No,' April sighed.

David pinched his lip and worried. She looked ill and thin and near the end of her tether. The beautiful curls he loved so much were dull and lank. The jagged cut on her neck from flying glass was healing but it could easily have taken her head off, and David knew it gave her nightmares. Hannah was unscathed, since when the bomb hit she'd been in April's arms and had fallen beneath her, shielded from the rain of glass and blast and the howling whirlwind of bricks and mortar that had engulfed them. George had died instantly and Eileen had lain next to him, trapped beneath fallen beams, his dead eyes fixed on her until after several hours rescue came, patient hands, digging and digging until they were free. Eileen had been rigid with shock and pain and April still wasn't sure that she'd fully taken in that George was gone. It seemed to be the house she mourned most.

'We can get it rebuilt after the war,' April had told her, over and over again, but her mother's dull eyes didn't respond; somehow they'd retreated right inside her head above the sunken cheeks and she would not be comforted. In the end, it had been Lizzie who came and took April and Hannah away. Rachael said they should go; she'd take care of Eileen, always supposing there wasn't a doodlebug coming with her own address on it. In which case, she pointed out resignedly, they'd just have to see.

'My house seems to have a charmed life,' observed Lizzie. 'And you are welcome to stay as long as you like.'

But it didn't solve all the problems.

'I can give up,' urged David. 'Come here and help you.'

Hannah got to her feet and brought the spoon over to him. He was holding the malt jar. She leaned on his knee and proffered the sticky spoon.

'More,' she commanded.

April saw the colour leave his face as Hannah began to clamber on to his knee, eagerly watching as he unscrewed the jar. He seemed to suffer in some way. He hung his head for a moment, as if concentrating on something.

'More,' insisted Hannah.

David raised his head and there was some faint colour in his skin.

'Are you all right? You've gone quite white,' asked April.

'Yes.'

"I have to learn to live with it. It is getting fainter," he thought, holding Hannah on his knee as she stuck the spoon into the jar. He took her small fist and guided her hand. The agony of the first few moments of closeness had shrunk to an occasional piercing stab. He'd get used to it.

'You can't leave,' repeated April, trying to sound coolly practical. 'I won't let you. I've sacrificed so much to your career that I'm not going to let you give up now.'

David looked haunted.

'I really want to. It is costing too much, in every sense.'

'No.'

'April, I don't want to go on. It's been a mistake; there are things I can't explain. I'll find something else.'

'If you give up now, when you're so nearly qualified, and deprive me and Hannah of any point to all the things we've given up, I'll never forgive you. We've gone this far and you're not going to let us down.' April heard herself starting to shout. Hannah's face closed. April saw it with a searing pang of guilt but she couldn't help herself.

'You can't do it. I'll never forgive you if you do,' she said more quietly.

'Maybe you'll never forgive me if I don't,' he said even more quietly.

'What's that supposed to mean?'

'Couldn't you trust me to do the right thing?'

'I can't trust anything,' shrieked April, losing her nerve. 'I can't even trust that I'm going to live through tomorrow. Or even that any of us will live through today. I can't trust that I'll have enough to give Hannah to eat, or that I'll ever see my mother again, or that Hitler isn't going to win the war. We thought we'd won, and now we're practically back where we started. Don't ask me for trust any more,' she finished despairingly, 'because I can't. I just get by thinking about afterwards, when you'll be a doctor, and we can afford to get away from London and find somewhere peaceful and be safe.' She burst into frantic tears. 'And you can't take that away from us. Not after all we've gone through. You can't!'

David saw that he could not take away her hope. It was hers, or his. One had to go. It was the moment of choice and he made it. Dr Fisher would have been proud of him, he thought grimly.

'If it's what you want, I'll go back and finish,' he told her drearily.

'It is.'

'Then we won't discuss it again. What are you going to do? If I have to finish, I'm afraid we'll still need money. Now your father has gone, we'll depend on what you earn even more.'

April looked steadily at him, her face hard with determination. 'I'll send Hannah away. Up North, where she'll be safe.'

David looked at her with pure disbelief. 'You won't go with her?'

'No. I'll take her and come back. So long as she's safe with decent people, I'll be able to manage here.'

'Have you found someone already?'

'There's a Salvation Army family near York who will be glad to have her. I've talked to them over the telephone.'

'It was all arranged before I came, then?'

'I can't see what else there is. I've thought and thought about it. It's the only way.'

'Then there's nothing to discuss.'

'No.'

'Then I might as well go back.'

Hannah put her fingers inside the jar and scooped malt into her mouth. Her parents stared at each other, frightened of each other and of the place they had reached without knowing how.

'You'd better get on with it, then. The sooner she's safe, the better.'

'I'll take her as soon as I get my travel warrant.'

'You're sure you'll be able to leave her?'

'She's got no future if I don't.'

David gave a bark of derisive laughter. April regarded him steadily. 'They get paid, don't they, for having her.'

'The government pay.'

He considered. 'But that's not the only paying, is it?'

He saw in her eyes that she knew what he meant.

'No,' she said slowly, 'there is a price and I don't even know what it will be. Maybe she'll hate me for it. Forget me.'

"Maybe I'll die inside and not be able to love her."

'Those are awful risks to take with our child.'

'Perhaps. But I'm prepared to take them, to make sure she lives.'

'And with my feelings, too?'

'What feelings? You can hardly bear to touch her. I tell you, there's no choice.'

'There was,' said David bleakly.

April stood up and took the jar from Hannah. 'Not a real choice. Not this time.'

'Maybe it simply came too late,' he murmured.

'What did?'

He didn't try to answer.

The journey to York seemed interminable. Hannah first watched out of the window and then quickly got bored, fidgeting and whining and grizzling until April walked her up and down the crowded corridor, past compartments full of women and children, all fleeing London.

April avoided their eyes, her expression stony. They'd be staying; she was coming back.

'Want to go wee wee,' cried Hannah as they drew into the outskirts of the city.

'You'll have to wait.' April looked at the passing houses and felt intense surprise, a kind of disorientation, because they stood in orderly rows; it was like a picture book. There had been bombing, the Baedecker raids, but York still stood, not greatly changed.

"I had forgotten," thought April, struggling hastily along the corridor again with the insistent Hannah, "that London isn't everywhere. It's like serving a life sentence, only to be suddenly let out and you can't cope with the ordinariness of it. How very strange."

There was a queue for the lavatory. Hannah crossed her legs threateningly and five minutes later a small puddle appeared.

'Oh, for heaven's sake,' snapped April, dragging her back again to change her knickers. They drew into York and she hastily stuffed the wet ones into her handbag.

'Don't want the Downses thinking you're not potty trained,' she muttered, straightening Hannah's dress. Hannah headed for the door gleefully, delighted to be getting off at last. April stood stock still in the middle of the carriage, appalled by the pain that welled up and threatened to crush her. Her legs were leaden. Women with suitcases and bundles pushed impatiently round her, calling to children, carrying little ones and babies, fetching prams from the guard's van at the far end of the train. The engine blew off steam with a huge roar, filling the air with white wisps and tendrils that curled into nostrils and made people sneeze. April still stood, dazed.

'This yours?' asked a tall woman, holding Hannah by the wrist and looking in at the compartment.

'Yes.'

'Well, you'd best keep an eye on her, then. She's all over the platform and she could get hurt.'

"Incompetent mother," her eyes said.

'Thank you.' April reached out her hand to Hannah. 'Come on.'

It was time for the leaving.

The Salvation Army couple had suggested meeting in the cafeteria because their house was twenty miles away and there was no petrol to make a double trip, to fetch April and take her back to the station. She dragged Hannah through the ticket gate and said, 'Stand still a moment, while I look . . . Where it is.' They struggled across the busy concourse towards the wide open doors of the station café. Inside, the Captain and his wife were easy to find, with their blue uniforms. They all stood, awkward and unsure, round the little table marked with rings of cold tea.

'This is Hannah,' said April stiffly.

The young woman smiled. She had cropped auburn hair underneath her bonnet, and twinkling brown eyes.

'Hello, Hannah.'

Hannah put her fingers in her mouth and clutched April's skirt.

'She doesn't know,' stammered April, at a terrible loss how she was going to manage the next few moments. 'She's too young to explain to.'

'Hannah, my name is Ida. I've got something for you.'

April felt Hannah burrowing inside her skirt, hiding. 'Oh, it's chocolate!' she exclaimed.

Hannah peeked.

'Look, Hannah, Ida has chocolate. She adores sweet things, but she doesn't often get them,' she said apologetically to the Captain.

Ida put the bar on the table and tapped it. 'Shall I open it?'

Hannah clung round April's knees and turned her face away. 'Mummy,' she begged, holding up her arms, 'carry me.'

'I'm sorry,' April said desperately, 'I don't think she's going to make this easy.'

'We've got time,' said the Captain.

April felt as though she wouldn't be able to breathe if this went on. 'No, I don't think so. I think you should take her, please, and go.'

Ida slid the chocolate into her pocket 'Do you think . . .?' she began uncertainly.

'Yes,' answered April, frantic. 'I won't be able to leave her unless you do it quickly. I have to, you see, but I won't be able to. Just take her, quick.'

'It won't do her any good to be grabbed,' said Ida.

'It won't do her any good to come back to London. You don't know what it's like. You can't do. She can't come back or she'll die. Will you take her, please?'

'If you feel that bad, why don't you stay?' asked Ida.

April looked at her fresh face, full of pink good health, and saw that she was condemned.

'I can't,' she said numbly.

Ida shook her head pityingly. 'Well, we'll look after her for you, though she needs her mother, really. We can't be you for her.'

"If you preach one more word I'll grab her and run," thought April, hating her so savagely her fingers twitched to smack that judgmental young face. Her eyes pleaded with the Captain to help her. He nodded slowly.

'Come along,' he said to his wife. He swung Hannah into his arms with an easy movement. 'And you too, poppet. You come along with us.'

Hannah looked startled and twisted round to look for April. 'Mummy, Mummy!' she screamed, struggling frantically to get down.

'I'll let you know . . .' said the Captain breathlessly, holding on to her kicking legs.

April nodded dumbly.

He took his wife's unwilling arm and marched out of the cafeteria. April heard Hannah scream wildly. People stopped talking to turn and stare. The screams echoed in April's head long after Captain and Ida Downs had hauled a thrashing bundle into their little car and set off for home.

Hannah screamed herself into a stupor and then fell asleep on the back seat of the car, hiccoughing, while Ida watched apprehensively, wondering whether this

465

arrangement could possibly work after such a disastrous start.

'She'll get used to us after a bit, love,' said her husband, understanding.

'I do hope so, poor little mite. For my sake as well as hers,' she added.

'Give her time,' he said.

April walked in a daze, in and out of the station, round and round the concourse, until the announcer said in half-intelligible words that the train for London was standing at platform five. It was two hours before she left York. She sat in a corner seat, her forehead pressed against the window, apparently watching the countryside slide past in the evening light. She saw nothing and hardly moved. Other passengers gazed at her curiously but she took no notice.

Only when she went to pick up her handbag from her lap, as they slowed down in the London suburbs, did she notice what they had been staring at. Blood seeped from beneath her finger nails and stained her worn grey skirt; there were four wounds on the palm of each hand. Painfully she opened her fingers and looked at them with surprise.

"I've done it," she thought.

Then the inexorable sequel.

"What is it I have done?"

Lizzie had called Sam Saul.

'We're going to need you,' she said, 'and I'd be glad if you could find a bottle of something.'

'Be over in a jiffy.'

They helped April out of her coat and sat her by a fire Lizzie had made specially.

'Here,' ordered Sam.

Whisky made her splutter and cough but she swallowed it obediently.

'I've put a hot water bottle in your bed,' said Lizzie, 'and I'm going to settle you in then bring you up a hot toddy, if Sam will spare the whisky. It'll make you sleep.'

'Yes,' whispered April.

'You'd better keep the bottle. Might need it,' said Sam seriously when Lizzie came down again. 'This is a very bad business.'

'It's the best they could work out between them,' answered Lizzie. Sam still looked unconvinced.

'Don't start blaming,' she said wearily. 'You and Ruthie. April and David. Bridget and . . . well, Bridget. The war has changed all of us. We'll never go back to the way we were, so we may as well go forwards. April's done what she thought was right, and it's not for you or me to judge her. She'll do that, and harshly enough, for herself.'

'It's a crying shame, though.'

'Yes,' Lizzie said, 'and I've no doubt there'll be plenty of crying before it's all over. Would you like a toddy before you go? Johnathan will be in soon and I expect he'd enjoy a bit of a treat.'

Sam stretched his long legs in front of the tiny fire and nodded. 'Plenty of crying,' he reflected sadly. 'Oh, yes, in our land of rations and shortages, there's always plenty of that.'

Chapter Thirty-Five

'They're dancing in the streets out there,' called Lizzie, coming in puffed with carrying a heavy shopping bag. 'You been home long?'

'Ten minutes,' answered April, 'I've seen them. It's almost as good as the war being over, isn't it? For London, anyway.'

Lizzie's careworn face brightened, her eyes crinkling happily. 'Fifth of September and no more bombs for London. What a day to remember. Shall we go and see?'

The two women grinned at each other, suddenly not tired any more. 'Come on, then,' cried Lizzie. 'Let's go and wave a flag with the rest.'

The next day Herbert Morrison made it official by ending the London evacuation. Mr Duncan Sandys went further and announced to a press conference that 'except possibly for a last few shots, the Battle of London is over'.

Excited and relieved, evacuated Londoners grabbed their goods and their children and came flooding back without delay.

'It's over!' they yelled to each other. 'We can go home. We've as good as won. The war's as good as won.'

They cheered and sang and rollicked home in their

thousands. London was safe as houses now, they said.

With the number of houses demolished, and many of the rest very far from safe, they should have known better. The era of the flying gas main introduced itself with gigantic, mysterious explosions in Chiswick and Epping. Censorship was total, so for two months no one knew what caused the immense explosions that demolished huge areas of London several times a day.

'I'm thinking of going to fetch Hannah. It seems the bombs have stopped,' remarked April in the second week of September. 'I can probably get her into a nursery while I'm at work.'

'What do you reckon those big bangs are?' asked Lizzie thoughtfully, peeling potatoes. 'There seem to be ever such a lot of them. Surely all our gas mains can't be going up, just like that?'

'Someone in the office said they thought it was German paratroopers blowing up key installations, but that doesn't sound right. If we'd got German spies, surely the government would have warned us. Anyway, what key installations are in Epping and Peckham? That's where two of the bangs came from.'

'They make a double bang. It's very odd,' said Lizzie.

'Not doodlebugs,' remarked Johnathan from behind his paper, 'and there's not a word in here about them.'

'Definitely not doodlebugs,' said Lizzie, popping the last potato into her pan.

'Then I wonder what they are,' April said, 'I thought we'd had the last of the bangs, but it looks as if perhaps we haven't. Have you heard they're lifting the black-out? We've got dim out instead.' She laughed.

'We'll get fewer broken legs and bumped heads in casualty,' remarked Johnathan. 'They're standing the Home Guard down, too. In November.'

Lizzie turned, potato peeler in hand, astonished.

'Something nasty is going on in London, and they're not telling us what. Seems a queer time to take the Home Guard away. Doesn't seem right to me. What do we do if it really is Germans? There won't be anyone on the streets to protect us.'

Johnathan shrugged uneasily. 'I don't know, love.'

Then Churchill told them. Rockets, he said, launched from Holland at twice the speed of sound, to rise sixty miles into the air in a huge parabola, before landing in London with a destructive power that made doodlebugs look like toys. They were assembled deep in the Harz mountains, Mr Churchill explained, by armies of slaves from concentration camps, and had been so well hidden that the Allies had not even suspected their presence. It was the last straw.

'We don't even have a sporting chance,' cried Johnathan, shaken out of his usual calm by the horrific numbers of horribly injured people flooding his hospital. 'You can't hear them, and they come at you so fast you can't do a thing. There's no warning, no sirens, nothing can stop them. We've got no chance at all.'

'They're unnatural,' said Lizzie, shivering. 'Things from outer space. Hitler's monstrous to send them at us. They don't do anything except kill people and knock down houses. They aren't even aimed at anything.'

'Nor was the Blitz,' interrupted April.

Lizzie's friendly face twisted in a scowl. 'Yes it was, up to a point. They got the docks and factories and things. This is different,' she insisted. 'There's something inhuman about it. Outer space, I ask you! This isn't war, it's science fiction.'

'There are women in the streets, praying for them to stop the war,' Johnathan told them, 'and that's something I never saw before, not even when the Blitz was at its worst.'

'We wanted to fight, then,' Lizzie broke in angrily, 'and now all everyone wants to do is stop it. People have changed. They've had enough. I know I have. Do you know what I heard somewhere?' she went on indignantly. 'That Hitler and Göring spend hours and hours with a map. Drawing squares to work out how many people their rockets can kill per square mile. It's the most disgraceful thing I ever heard.'

'That reminds me,' said April, 'when I went to see Mum, Rachael told me they've all been sending letters to Churchill, saying if the rockets were landing on Westminster, they'd be quick enough to stop them, but Ilford doesn't count. They're very bitter there because they've had more than anyone else.'

'The old togetherness has gone.' Lizzie mashed potato with margarine and peered at the swede she was boiling in another pan. 'It's all me, me, me, now. Us and them.'

'It tends to be "Us" who haven't got anywhere to live,' remarked Johnathan. 'You can't blame people for being angry. "They" always seem better off. Do you know, more than half the houses in London have been destroyed or are beyond repair. They've got a frightful problem, even with the new prefabs.'

'Is it really as bad as that?' April started to lay the table, thinking of her own house, flattened into a crater, and the streets and streets of houses gone on either side. She supposed, thinking about it, that it must be.

'You know something?' remarked Lizzie. 'When this war is over I'm never going to touch another swede again.'

It got worse. Rockets came more often as autumn passed and dragged into a bitter, freezing winter that brought Arctic winds, sleet and snow, to all alike.

'Homes for heroes,' snorted Johnathan one evening, coaxing a bit of flame out of a pile of slag in the grate. It spat and crackled, refusing to catch. 'Fat chance!' He sounded unusually bitter.

'We're lucky. We've not been damaged,' Lizzie pointed out from the kitchen. He rubbed deep frown lines from his forehead and said that wasn't the point.

'I know,' answered Lizzie sharply, 'but there's no point making yourself miserable either. There's enough of it around without you adding to it.'

He came over, put his long arms round her and rested his head on top of hers. 'I know, love,' he said tiredly, 'and I'm sorry. I just wish it was over.' He sighed deeply and kissed her hair. 'I want it over, more than anything else. Just for it to be over. I've had enough.'

Lizzie reached up and touched his face. 'Yes,' she said gently. 'We all have. Please God, it'll finish soon, or we'll all start hating each other.'

'Not while we've got the Germans to hate,' put in April.

The invariable swede frothed and boiled over. Lizzie banged pans noisily. 'Drat!' she said crossly. 'Haven't you hated them all along?'

'No, I hated Hitler and the Nazis, but I always thought that German people probably loathed the war just as much as we did. Now, with the concentration camps and space rocket things, I'm not so sure. Perhaps they are evil. Germans, I mean, not just Nazis.'

'This swede's as tough as old boots,' grumbled Lizzie. 'I could shoot a German for every mouthful of disgusting food I've had to eat for six years.'

'Do you really want to punish them?' asked Johnathan, listening quietly.

'Yes.'

'I think people do, now. It makes me wonder where this madness will end,' he sighed.

'How do you forgive anyone for making you cook carrot Christmas pudding?' demanded Lizzie. 'Carrot cake, carrot jam, carrot marmalade, carrot pie, and now carrot Christmas pudding! A "one boil" pudding, they call it; saves five hours of fuel.' She banged a carrot down on the table and glared at it in disgust.

'There's not even Hershey bars without all the GIs,' mourned April.

'Not the same as proper Cadbury's,' snapped Lizzie.

'It was something. There isn't much else, considering it's nearly Christmas.'

April wanted to visit Hannah for Christmas but the weather was so bad, and fuel so short, and travelling so difficult, she didn't go. Ida sent a photograph, taken on Christmas Day. Hannah, round-faced and bonny, rode on the black furry back of a toy Scottie dog, holding its ears and laughing.

'At least she's having a good time,' said Lizzie, looking at it over April's shoulder. 'Better than she'd have here. She looks ever so well cared for.'

'It's not the carrots I mind so much, it's being apart at times like this.' April didn't want to be comforted. 'We're all over the place, aren't we?'

'No worse than anyone else.'

'Stop it, Lizzie. I want to be miserable. I can't think of any single reason not to be.'

'Try this,' snapped Lizzie without sympathy. 'You're alive. And so is she. And so is David.' She dug her darning needle into one of Johnathan's socks with a vicious jab. 'If you want to dramatize, April, think that you and Hannah could be dead and see how much misery you can wring out of that.'

'I'm sorry,' muttered April. 'Don't shout.'

'I shan't shout if you don't whine.'

'I won't.'

The bombardment of London petered out after the Allied destruction of Dresden.

'You've got your punishment now,' observed Johnathan. 'They think a hundred thousand people burned to death in Dresden. That settle the score?'

Lizzie paled. 'I never meant anything like that.'

'Tit for tat.'

'No. This is as terrible as the rockets.'

'We're just slugging it out for vengeance on each other,' Johnathan stated. 'It's not war any more, there's no meaning to any of it.'

'Then perhaps they'll soon stop it?' suggested April wistfully.

'They'll have mutiny on their hands if they don't,' he said darkly. 'And I'll be in the front line. I'm sick of it.'

'Have a carrot,' crowed Lizzie, and burst into hysterical laughter. 'Go to war on a carrot and see the world in blackout.' She held her sides, laughing until tears came to her eyes. Then the laughing stopped and there were just tears.

'Those poor people.' She turned to Johnathan. 'Whatever are we doing?'

'Winning, I suppose.'

In Mr Stephenson's office April answered the phone and put the call through to him. His door was open and she heard him pick up the receiver.

'Yes? Is it? Leave off now? I see . . . yes. Goodbye.'

She heard the ping as the receiver went down.

He came to his door and stood looking thoughtfully at the floor. 'It's over,' he said. 'If you want to, you can go home.'

May sunlight lit the courtyard outside and streamed through the window behind him.

'It's a beautiful day. Go home,' he repeated, then turned and walked back into his office, shutting the door behind him.

April stood for a long time, leaning against a tree in the yard, gazing up at its fresh green leaves, dappled in sun against a clear blue sky. VE Day, she thought. At last, it's over. Birds hopped at her feet, hoping for crumbs. She closed her eyes and weariness washed over her as though a source of bitter pain had lifted, leaving a tired peace in its wake.

Trafalgar Square and Whitehall were packed with people. A deep hush fell as Big Ben struck three. April held her breath and then there was his voice, relayed to the silent crowd, saying what they had waited so long to hear.

'The evil doers now lie prostrate before us . . .'

The crowd gasped.

'A fine turn of phrase to the end,' muttered a man behind April. 'Good old Winnie.'

'Advance Britannia,' shouted Churchill in jubilation, and then the 'Last Post' led straight into 'God Save the King', which they roared out at the tops of their voices. All of London was in the streets and April strolled with the crowds to Buckingham Palace to cheer the King and Queen. And then Mr Churchill joined them, and such a roar went up she found herself shouting though unable to hear her own voice. She waited to see them come back on to the balcony three times, then threaded her way through the crowds to St James's Park. She sat on the grass in the warmth of the sun, remembering the night she danced in Regent's Park, in the shadow of guns, then walked arm in arm with her American under the moonlight. She wondered if he had survived, gone home to the pretty woman and his children, and if he ever remembered her. Dreaming, she dozed, then woke again to the sound of bagpipes. A lone, kilted Scotsman marched up and down, earnestly puffing and pumping, his chest thrown out with pride.

'We won!' he suddenly yelled, leaping in the air with a swirl of the kilt and a huge shout of triumph. 'We won.' Everyone laughed. April brushed grass from her skirt and watched him adjust his bagpipes, then caught his eyes. He leaped again until he landed beside her and, throwing one arm wide, grabbed her to him and kissed her soundly.

'That's for winning,' he shouted, and there was a chorus of clapping and laughter. Then the bagpipes swirled again, and she heard them go right down to the other end of the park then veer off towards the palace where the King and Queen still came to the balcony to wave to the cheering crowds.

As dusk fell, London glittered. Every window and door shone, bonfires were lit in parks, and garden and steet lamps shone bright. Traffic lights winked unshaded. Cars and buses hooted and honked with headlamps ablaze. Fairy lights strung from trees twinkled and winked in the night breeze and above the city the sky darkened slowly, empty, quiet and peaceful.

David sat in the glow from the door of the village pub, watching the great string of bonfires that twinkled across the Downs. On the green, the village burned an effigy of Hitler, ate meat paste sandwiches and drank beer until the pub ran dry. The publican dusted off his piano, hauled it close to the doorway, parked a row of pints on top, rolled up his sleeves and began the dancing with a thunderous rendition of 'Knees Up, Mother Brown'.

'Want to dance?' a voice said in his ear. David started and looked up.

Cutie held out her hand. 'Let bygones be bygones?' she asked quietly, under cover of the piano's thumping rhythm.

He looked away, into the darkness. Children ran in and out of the firelight, holding burning sticks that showered sparks like fireworks. He got to his feet and took her hand as she led him to the edge of the green, among the dancers.

'I didn't think you'd forgive me,' he said in her ear as she moved close to him.

'It's easier to forgive and forget when it's over,' she said, pulling away to look at him. 'We'll see each other in London but it won't be the same. I wanted to put an end to this.' She gestured at the surrounding night. 'To close the door on something.'

'A goodbye.'

'Yes. I'm sorry it was the way it was, David.'

'So am I.'

The music stopped as the sweating publican reached for a long swallow of beer.

'David?' He put his arm round her shoulders and they strolled close to the fire, its red flames reflected in their eyes.

'Yes?'

'Put whatever it was behind you. Try and start afresh when you go home to April. I don't know what it was that tormented you, or what you did when . . . you know. I don't even really know that you did anything. Maybe I got it wrong and it was a coincidence. I don't want to know. But I'd love to see you happy, and now the war's over we've all got a second chance. It can be a new beginning, if you make it one.' She kissed his cheek and stood back from him.

'Thank you,' he said, barely audibly.

She squeezed his hand and then she was gone, into the ring of darkness beyond the fire.

'I'll do it,' he said to the leaping flames. 'I'll go home and I'll damn well do it!'

He wandered off, beyond the firelight, away from voices and laughter, and found a small wooden bench beneath two great old rhododrendron bushes.

'Well,' he added, already backtracking dismally, 'I'll damn well do it if I can.'

He sat down, elbows on his knees, his chin in his hands. 'If I can,' he repeated resignedly, knowing the futility of good intentions. He stared at the ground. The long grass brushed at his legs, shedding unripe seed pods and invisible insects. Two bats swooped low, gobbling moths dancing above the glow of the fire and the open pub doors. He sighed, dispirited.

'That sounds bad,' observed a quiet voice from the bushes. Surprised, David turned to peer behind him. Shadows moved.

'Everyone's having a high old time, yet you sigh like your heart's breaking.' The voice was like a sigh itself, papery and hoarse. David recognized it from long afternoons bent over test tubes, stained laboratory benches, worn eyepieces in old microscopes. A patch of darkness moved out of the rhododendron bush to David's left and stood by the end of the bench.

'May I?' asked the spare, elderly figure of his pathology tutor, his head inclined towards David, poised to sit down.

'I suppose so,' answered David gracelessly, resenting the intrusion.

The doctor settled down and looked at the distant light of the dying bonfire, then up at the sky. 'Beautiful night, eh?'

He bent very slightly towards his student, as if waiting for an answer, but David sat rigid, irritated, hoping he'd go away.

'Very well,' observed the tutor in an undertone, pulling his coat more closely around him, 'we'll just wait.' The doctor bowed his head, folded his hands in his lap, and, without the least sign of it, began silently and steadily to pray.

David had shut his ears to his teacher's words. "Last thing I want just now," he thought dejectedly, "is a blasted gossiping grandad."

'I'll be off then,' he said. 'Back to the jollities.'

The tutor remained motionless, his face hidden, tucked down into the worn collar of his coat.

'You'll excuse me?' David began to feel uneasy.

What if the old chap was wandering; shouldn't be out alone? Senile, even.

'Can I take you back to the village, Mr Cornhill?' he asked, annoyed at the unwanted responsibility. 'It's so dark you can hardly see where you're going. Would you like a hand back?'

The doctor appeared to breathe deeply, meditatively, for a moment, then he raised his head and turned, holding his face close to David's. Startled, he shrank back, seeing in the gloom two deep-set eyes fixed piercingly upon his. They held each other's gaze for several moments and David frowned uneasily, feeling the weight of some unspoken exchange. Something rustled in the bushes and he looked away, confused.

'So,' said the pathologist, as if taking up again a conversation recently abandoned. He regarded David's downcast face steadily.

Nearby an owl drifted on wide wings, watching while a mouse bustled about noisily in last year's dead leaves. The white barn owl hooted, gliding low and unexpected through the trees.

'Ah, look at that! Beautiful. One of the loveliest of our English predators. A true creature of the night. Do you like the night, David? The dark?'

'What?' asked David, after a long pause. 'It's only a bird.'

'So much death,' the thin voice said reflectively. 'The owl is far more civilized than we are. It never slaughters for pleasure.'

'I suppose not.'

'Nor betrays for profit,' Mr Cornhill remarked thoughtfully.

'The slaughter's over,' said David defiantly, trying to

ignore the dry words. "Betrayal for what profit?" he thought bitterly.

Mr Cornhill sat back on the bench and lifted his thin, ascetic face to the black sky. His voice sounded lighter and stronger.

'For now, yes. We have exhausted ourselves once more,' he said sadly to the tops of the trees, his gaze wandering over their dark shapes. 'Collectively, I suppose, one would call it a victory this time.'

'What are you talking about?' asked David, edging away along the bench, anxiety sending prickles up his neck.

'National Socialism is defeated.'

'I know that,' David said, not bothering to hide his impatience.

'And what about you?'

'Pardon?'

'You seem defeated. I see things . . .' He let the unfinished statement trail between them.

David felt sweat bead on his skin. Out of the corner of his eye he saw his teacher lean closer.

'Pens that jump from your hand, for instance. Odd things in my laboratory. Very odd. Miss Cuthell is frightened of you, and I think to myself, how odd,' said the papery voice reflectively. 'And then I see a young man who should be looking forward to going home and a splendid career, skulking in the bushes. I see despair, David. Why?'

He shook his head, numb.

'What have you done?' persisted the old doctor, his face close to David's in the grey light of night.

'Can't say.' David's voice was muffled as he bent his head, tucking his face down to his chest as if something crushed him.

'You think no one else could know or understand.' The tutor made a vague gesture with one hand, then laid it limply back on the bench.

'They wouldn't. I am on my own.'

'You think you are, I know.'

'How do you know?' David whispered.

'That you have done something evil?' asked Cornhill matter-of-factly. 'For anyone with eyes to see these things, it's not hard to tell.'

The moon rode high and fast across the sky. Cornhill, praying silently, watched it in the long pauses in their exchange.

'How?' demanded David at last.

'I have seen it before. You think you are the first person the devil ever tempted? It's one of his tricks, making people think they're special. Divide and rule, that's all.' The elderly man made a joke of it, dismissing the devil with a wave of one thin hand.

'What?'

David sat up suddenly in sheer astonishment.

'Oh, yes. Plays on one's pride, you see. What was his particular bargain with you? Not that one should call it a bargain, because he always cheats.'

'Ambition,' gasped David.

The aging doctor's gaze was suddenly steely. He bent forward and grasped David's forearms, thin fingers biting as he dragged the younger man round to face him. The heavy lidded eyes probed David's, glittering in shadow. 'What did you give?'

David heard the dwarf's mocking laugh, tinged strangely with fear.

'No,' he whimpered.

'What?' insisted the quiet voice.

'I can't,' moaned David. 'You know I can't.'

'You can.'

'Why are you tormenting me?' yelled David, losing control, spittle flying into the night air.

'Are you not in torment?' his inquisitor demanded remorselessly. 'He doesn't let go easily,' he went on compassionately. 'But I can hold it for you, if you will let me.'

'Hold what?'

The words came out like gunfire, very loud and sharp, too big for David's mouth.

'The pain,' Cornhill whispered urgently, 'and the fear. I can hold them for you if you want to break this bargain of yours. You have given your soul, haven't you? They always do. But it belongs to you. You can break the promise, David. Break it!'

David rocked back and forth under the old man's hands, fighting for breath.

'Do you repent the bargain, David? You only have to repent and the bargain is severed. David?' Mr Cornhill shook him none too gently, peering urgently into his averted face. 'David?'

At his name, David's head shot up, his teeth bared. 'I can't.' The words fell dull and hopeless, like spent shot.

'Ask God to forgive you.'

'I am unforgivable.'

'You are that arrogant?'

The whites of David's eyes rolled up, shining.

'Unforgivable.'

Cornhill held him and laughed aloud. The sound stilled the small animal rustlings around them and the owl, watchful in a nearby tree, shifted uneasily, its big head swivelling anxiously. David tensed expectantly.

'That's truly the devil talking,' the elderly man

cried contemptuously. 'Be gone! Out with you.'

'By whose authority?' demanded David's voice. But the other man stilled warily, knowing it was not David who spoke.

'Jesus Christ. I tell you, be gone in the name of Christ.'

David lurched forwards. 'Heart attack,' he grated.

'No. It is leaving you.'

David's eyes flew open.

'Are you sorry?' asked the old man simply.

'Yes.' The word was a dry cough of pain.

'That is enough. In the name of Jesus, I command you to leave this person. Evil Spirit, depart.' Cornhill began to make the sign of the cross, his hand trembling with exhaustion. Behind David's closed eyes the dwarf's face shivered as it had in the mirror and the image began to splinter.

'Dear God, help me,' David muttered.

'Pray with me,' murmured his tutor.

'Our Father . . .'

Their voices were as soft and dry as the rustling leaves. The moon was setting and darkness deepened, heralding the bright early summer dawn. The village, silent for the short hours since the celebrations ceased, would stir soon and the yawning publican emerge into the early light to stir the bonfire, still smouldering and cooling in front of his pub. The church clock chimed the half hour, the sound drifting over fields and woods at peace for the first time in nearly six years.

'We shall meet again, but we shall not speak of this,' sighed the pathologist, ordained many years ago as a young man, who had chosen to follow his calling as exorcist in the dingy corridors of a great teaching hospital rather than in the church itself. 'It is finished. Go, and sin no more.'

David sat silently, his head in his hands.

'There's still something.'

'Yes?'

'My daughter,' he said drearily. 'It wasn't just me. I promised her, too. Can I save my daughter?'

The old man closed his eyes; he seemed weary to the bone. 'Then she is compromised.' He sounded drained and sad. 'Your knowing that will help her when the time comes. She is not yet lost. That is the most comfort I can give you.'

'I can't . . .?'

'No. It is for her to do.'

David stared into the night. 'I'm so sorry. God forgive me, I'd do anything to undo it for her.'

'This will be part of your penance,' said Mr Cornhill sternly. 'So pray for your soul and hers and sin no more.'

A strange incident was reported in the *Hackney Gazette* later that week. The little optician who had had premises in Mare Street for thirty years was digging his garden when his spade struck an unexploded bomb, apparently buried without trace in his cabbage patch. His obituary was fulsome.

> He will be greatly missed for he was something of a legend around these parts. A friend of the poor and needy, he would always find a way to help a person in trouble. He fixed spectacles for many hundreds of Hackney people, some of whom could not afford to pay him. He liked to fix things

for people. Our Optical Fixer, we'll miss seeing you.

David put down the paper, which April had sent him, and couldn't stop shivering for a long, long time.

Chapter Thirty-Six

Doors banged open down the length of the train and passengers poured out in a dense, jostling throng, making for the barrier. A little crowd waited on the other side, watching expectantly.

'Can you see them?' asked April, scanning the arrivals. 'Can you see up the platform?'

'A bit,' answered David, craning his neck. 'There they are!'

Captain Downs turned back to the compartment and helped Ida lift down two cases. Then she appeared at the top of the steps, holding Hannah by the hand. 'Careful, pet.'

Her husband took the child and swung her up on to his shoulders, away from the scurrying people with their heavy bags and trailing children. 'You go up there, lass, and you'll not get bumped.'

Hannah clutched his thick, wavy hair and looked round smugly. With one hand he grasped her legs to steady her, picked up her case with the other, and said 'Ready?' to Ida, who pulled a long face.

'No, I'll never be ready. But we might as well get it over with.' He nodded.

They walked up the long platform slowly, Ida dragging her steps, Hannah holding on tight, looking all round with a beaming face, surveying the station with an air of superiority.

'She's so happy with us.' John Downs heard the muffled cry and his heart sank. He stopped and looked back. Ida stood mutinously, several feet away.

'We knew when she came that she wouldn't stay. It isn't possible, pet, she doesn't belong to us.'

'She could. What kind of mother leaves a child like that, for all this time?'

'Ida, love, we've been over and over this.'

She came towards him, reached up and touched Hannah's dress. 'I know. I know really.'

'Then let's give her back with joy. For her sake.'

'All right, I'll try.'

Hannah drummed her hands on his head to make him go.

'Hey, you do that and this horse will put you down,' he called up to her. She laughed and did it some more.

They were through the barrier and looked around when John said, 'Over there.'

April came forward, staring at Hannah. 'She's grown. She's so big!' she exclaimed, truly astonished.

'Children do,' remarked Ida acidly. Her husband glanced at her quickly and she said no more.

David waited in the background, uncertain. He took in Hannah's pink, cheerful little face, her easy confidence in her high perch, and he was afraid. She could be Downs's child, a Salvation Army child, he thought guardedly. She has that air of belonging.

Hannah bent forward on John Downs's shoulder and whispered something in his ear, her eyes sliding slyly over April.

'Do you remember your mummy?' he asked, trying to twist his head to look up at her. Hannah instantly looked round for Ida.

'No,' she said bravely. 'I'm Ida. There's your mummy.'

Hannah squeezed her eyes shut and put her face in the Captain's hair.

They all stood uneasily, wondering what to say or do.

'Let's end as we began, over a cup of tea,' said John.

'I haven't introduced my husband,' said April, remembering they'd never met him. David held out his hand and shook the Captain's warm, strong fingers.

They straggled to the cafeteria. A group of soldiers stood up, collecting bags, their train announced over the noise of the station.

'There,' said John, lifting Hannah down. 'We'll get four teas.' He nudged Ida to come with him.

Hannah looked round, suddenly alert.

'Hannah, come and say hullo to Mummy,' said April, catching her hand.

She snatched it away and began to clamber past the crowded chairs, looking for Ida.

'Hannah, come on . . .' April stood and caught her clumsily. 'Don't you remember me?'

David watched.

'Please, Hannah.'

She fought to get loose, her eyes round with panic, her breath coming faster and faster until she let out a tremendous shriek. Ida spun round and four cups of tea were hurled to the floor. The counter woman clucked, outraged.

'Can't get crockery for love nor money,' she snapped. 'I'll have to charge you for them.'

Ida stared across the crowded place, holding up the queue, not caring. She saw April drag Hannah on to her lap where the child lay kicking wildly, screaming at the top of her voice. People stopped talking to turn and stare, as they had in York.

'Help me,' hissed April.

David moved to the chair beside her and picked up his daughter, looking into her red, puckered face, its mouth opening and closing in rhythmic yells.

'Quiet,' he ordered calmly, 'Hannah, be quiet a minute. Look what mummy's got.'

April remembered the chocolate. 'Look,' she said, pulling it from her handbag and putting it near Hannah on the table.

'Are you goin' or what?' demanded the counter woman. 'Or do you want those teas again?'

Ida tore her eyes away.

'The teas again.' John apologized for the broken cups and the brown puddle on the floor and, mollified, the woman poured fresh cups while Ida held the tray. The screams stopped.

'It's real chocolate. I've had it several weeks and the number of times I've nearly eaten it . . .' April chattered with relief, Hannah sidled round to Ida, holding the chocolate, leaning against her knee and staring suspiciously up through her lashes at April.

'She's got a sweet tooth a mile long, hasn't she, pet?' cried John. Ida nodded.

'She gets that from me,' said April.

They sipped tea in awkward silence.

'We're staying a week,' said John Downs, 'Ida here has never been to London before, so we thought we'd make a proper outing of it. See the sights.'

'There's not many left,' muttered April.

'Well, such as there are.' John was imperturbable.

'Where are you staying?' asked David.

'I've an aunt in Hammersmith.'

'Oh.'

'Were they bombed at all, your house?' asked Ida, trying very hard.

'Me? Our house is a hole in the ground. I've been living with friends for almost as long as you've had Hannah. Don't you remember?'

'Oh.' Ida was nonplussed, not knowing how to go on.

'We're going to live with my mother until we can get a place of our own,' David told them. 'There's such a shortage of housing, that'll probably be a while. Unless we leave London.'

'David still has to finish his medical training,' April put in. 'He's got another two years. Then we could move right out.'

Hannah listened, looking from one to the other as they spoke, feeling the strange tension between them.

'My mother was bombed, too, but the house is nearly repaired, thanks to an old friend. She's been in the ATS but she's home again. Hardly knows what to do with herself, I expect. It'll be nice for her to have Hannah.' David felt he was doing well.

Ida tensed. 'Won't you be looking after her yourself, now?' She did her best to sound friendly but she knew she sounded resentful instead. April looked at Hannah and shook her head.

'I have to earn, for David to finish his studies. We can't make ends meet without. It's a shame, because I think the best person to look after my child is me. But it really and truly can't be helped, and she'll be very well cared for by my mother-in-law.'

Ida's mouth drew into a thin line. 'She needs a proper mother,' she began. 'A child that's been passed pillar to post isn't secure. I don't know how you can leave her.'

'Ida!' thundered her husband.

She glared at April and stopped with a little snap of her jaws, as if biting off even angrier words.

'It's time we went.' John pushed back his chair and found their case. Hannah got up to go too.

'No, my pet, you stay here with your mummy and daddy. Say bye bye, now, like a good girl.'

Hannah didn't care two pins about being a good girl. She fought and screeched and howled as John Downs and Ida hurried across the concourse and out of the nearest exit, out of her sight. She threw herself on the floor and screamed. People watched and commented and April's face burned.

'Just pick her up and bring her,' she told David desperately.

Clenching his teeth, he picked his daughter up off the floor, filthy and scarlet, tears running making tracks down her chocolatey cheeks. He planted her on her feet. Hannah promptly sat down again and began to kick.

'What shall we do with her?' cried April helplessly. 'Pick her up, do. I'll take the case.'

'She's scared of us,' said David, Hannah's fear somehow diminishing his own.

'She's forgotten me. I was afraid she would,' said April sadly.

Their eyes met across Hannah's head.

'Can we try again? Start properly this time?' asked David softly.

'Like it might have been?' whispered April.

'Yes. I want to try.'

'She's having to start all over again, poor little mite, isn't she?'

April touched Hannah's tousled curls, just like her own. Hannah looked up, desolate.

'She'll need us, then, won't she?' said David.

'I need you, too.'

'I'll be here, this time.'

'You're sure you want to? Shall we let bygones be bygones?'

A strange look passed over David's face.

'Will you?'

'Yes,' said April. 'Let's take her home.'

Hiccoughing, Hannah let David pick her up and set her on her feet. 'Take your mummy's hand,' he said gently. Hannah looked up at April. Her small hand reached out obediently and April clasped it firmly. David picked up her suitcase and took her other hand in his.

'We're going home,' he said to them both.

They walked across the concourse, swallowed up in the crowds, then emerged from under an archway, out of the gloom into soft sunlight. Hand in hand, they turned and set off for the house by the canal, at the edge of the park, where Bridie waited to welcome them home.

Chapter Thirty-Seven

The house was full of hammering. Damaged roof timbers had already been replaced and the side wall rebuilt, but the top floor needed a lot of work before it would be useable and materials, despite Sam's magic, were nearly impossible to get. She listened to the workmen, hoping they'd be gone before David and April brought Hannah home.

Sam had given it a lot of thought, Hannah's home-coming. The evening before, he sat down at the polished dining table in his big deserted house in Golders Green and laid out several small heaps. One contained jelly babies, the same as those he'd once had in his pocket in April's garden. Squares of Cadbury's chocolate lay in a tidy pile in another. A third held a little string of blue glass beads that had belonged to Ruthie, left behind, unwanted. A fourth was a liquorice stick. He frowned, uncertain that she'd like it. A fifth was made of white sugar lumps and the last was a pair of white cotton socks, edged with pink, from America. Carefully, he wrapped and tied each small pile with bright paper and ribbon. Then he leaned back and surveyed the results thoughtfully.

'That just might do the trick,' he said aloud to

himself, and retired to his solitary bed in a cheerful mood.

Bridie heard their voices before the knock at the door and flew down the stairs into a hallway crowded with departing workmen.

'Goodnight, goodnight,' she said impatiently, pushing them out of the front door at the same time as welcoming the others in.

'Come in, come on in!' she cried, kissing David's cheek and hugging April. She looked at Hannah. The child looked exhausted and frightened.

'She's very tired,' said April, seeing her mother-in-law's expression.

'I'm not surprised,' said Bridie. 'All the way she's come today, and everything.'

'She didn't want to leave Ida.' April put a battered case to the side of the hall and picked Hannah up. 'Come upstairs and see if Granny's got you some tea.'

'Downstairs, in the kitchen,' called Bridie.

April turned and came down again.

'We've only got the downstairs, the ground floor and one room above, at the front. The rest won't be ready for a while, but we'll manage,' Bridie explained.

'It's more room than we had at Lizzie's,' said April, coming into the basement kitchen. 'Oh, you shouldn't have.'

The table was laid with assorted crockery and cups and saucers that didn't match. But Bridie's silver gleamed against a white cloth, and sandwiches lay piled invitingly, side by side with fairy cakes and a pot of real strawberry jam.

'Sam,' said Bridie, following April's gaze.

'Who else?' April laughed and put Hannah down.

A kettle whistled and Bridie emptied the warming teapot, spooning in generous heaps of tea.

'Sit down. I've put a cushion on that chair for Hannah.'

April slid the child's legs under the table and pushed in the chair. Hannah's nose was on a level with the tabletop, big hazel eyes visible above her plate.

'There!' Bridie brought the steaming pot to the table.

They all sat down. Hannah stared past the rim of her plate at the sandwich April gave her.

'Eat up, sweetheart, you must be hungry,' she said.

Hannah's eyes looked up and around the table. They all talked at once, reaching for sandwiches, lifting teacups to thirsty mouths, eagerly talking, talking. They talked about Ida, and John, and something called Hammersmith.

'Eat up, darling,' said April, seeing Hannah's food untouched.

'She's too tired,' said the person they called Granny.

'I'll put her to bed when we've finished,' said April, holding out her cup for more tea.

Tears gathered slowly in Hannah's eyes, dripped unseen past her nose and blurred the untouched sandwich so close to her gaze.

'Oh dear.' Bridie noticed her distress after several minutes of silent weeping, 'April, she does look unhappy.' Bridie wanted to pick her up and cuddle her, but was afraid to interfere.

'Everything's new and she'll miss the Downses to start with,' David remarked, looking across at Hannah, wondering what they'd do with her if she moped.

Hannah slowly slid under the table, until all they could see was the very top of her chestnut head.

'I think I'd better put her to bed.' April went to get up and there was a knock at the door.

'It'll be Sam,' said Bridie. 'Would you let him in?'

Hannah, hearing another voice, disappeared altogether.

'Where is she?' demanded a deep voice. Sam came into the room and stood looking round. His gaze settled speculatively on an empty chair. April nodded.

Underneath the tablecloth, Hannah's ears pricked up.

'I've come to see Hannah,' said the deep voice. 'My pockets have come to see Hannah, too.'

Hannah listened attentively.

''course,' Sam remarked, after nothing stirred, 'she might be too old and too grown up to look for sweeties in pockets any more. Or pretty beads. Or white socks with pink lace round the edge that would just fit someone's feet who is – ah – about – oh, very grown up. About three years old. But I don't suppose she's interested in liquorice sticks, either. And the chocolate will melt, isn't that a pity?'

He walked round the end of the table, pulled up a chair and sat down. 'I'll have a cup of tea, please Bridie,' he said, taking no notice of the crown of a small head, appearing under the edge of the tablecloth. April grinned and pretended not to notice, either. David felt rather than saw his small daughter climb down from her chair, scuttle round the other side of the tea table and slip her hand into Sam Saul's trouser pocket. Sam affected to feel nothing.

'I have some jelly babies in the trouser pocket, you know. April, do you like jelly babies? I know Hannah does, because she gobbled all the ones I brought to Eileen's garden. That was when she was a baby. Do you remember? She found them in my pocket.'

A fragment of paper crackled and a small shower of babies fell into Sam's lap.

'Well, my goodness me. Look what's here,' he exclaimed, drawing his chair back with astonishment. 'It's my friend. It's Hannah. And, oh my word, look, she's found jelly babies.'

Hannah's eyes, bruised-looking, met his.

Sam winked cheerily.

'Coming up?' he asked, holding out his hands.

She let herself be lifted on to his knees.

'Try in here,' suggested Sam, sliding her small hand into the warmth of his breast pocket. 'Is there anything there?'

They all watched silently as Hannah unwrapped her socks. She held them, uncertain.

'Tell you what,' whispered Sam against her ear, tickling, 'do you want to put them on your feet?'

Hannah nodded.

'I'm no good at that. Why don't you let your mummy put them on for you, then you come back here and we'll find which pocket the chocolate is in. Yes?'

Hannah looked across the table at April.

'Shall we put them on?' asked her mother, crossing her fingers like a child, hoping Sam's ruse would work.

Hannah slid down from Sam's knee, clutching his trousers.

'Go on, then we'll hunt in all the other pockets. I've lots. Look.' He opened his jacket and showed her.

Hannah hurried round the table and held out the socks.

'Put them on, Mummy,' she said.

Tears rose in April's eyes and she blinked them away. She lifted Hannah on to her lap, undid her sandals and together they pulled on the new socks.

'Aren't they pretty?' cried April. 'You do look

501

pretty, Hannah. Show Daddy and Granny.'

Solemnly she stood in front of each of them, her feet pressed tight together.

Bridie bent down and kissed the serious little face. 'They're lovely,' she said. 'Just lovely.'

'Pockets?' asked Sam.

'Chocolate,' answered Hannah, and came round the table again, back on to his knee.

'Give your mummy some,' he whispered again, when she'd found it.

Obediently Hannah made the trip round to April again. 'For Mummy.' She held out the square of chocolate, then went back to Sam.

'Some for Granny,' she demanded.

'And for Daddy,' she said next.

Then she found the beads. Sam fastened them round her neck and fussed them straight.

'Here's the other presents,' he told her, producing them from the tiniest pocket inside his jacket. 'Why don't you keep those to open in bed?'

Hannah clutched the doll-sized packages and Sam winked at April.

'Come on, let's take you to bed.' April held out her arms to Hannah.

'Beddybyes, beddybyes,' chirped Hannah, as Ida always did.

'Beddybyes, then,' agreed April, lifting her up. 'Say night night to your daddy, and your granny, and Uncle Sam.'

'Sam,' he growled. 'Otherwise I sound like a continent.'

'Say night night to Sam.'

Hannah wriggled and April put her down again, sighing.

The child went up to Sam and raised her face. 'Kiss,' she ordered.

He grinned and kissed her cheek gently.

'Kiss,' said Hannah to Bridie.

'Kiss,' she demanded, raising her face to David.

'Beddybyes,' she said, holding her arms up to April.

'Sam Saul, you are the most wonderful man I ever met. God bless you,' said Bridie, when they'd disappeared upstairs with not a tear or a tantrum. 'They'll be all right together now.'

'You've got a way with her, right enough,' said David, reluctantly admitting to himself that he was beginning really to respect his mother's old friend.

Sam raised a sardonic eyebrow and grinned. He lifted his teacup, half mocking, half serious.

'Here's to Hannah and homecoming,' he announced, 'and all our happiness in wherever we go from here.'

They raised their cups in response.

'Amen,' breathed Bridie. 'Let's drink to that.'

And they did.

A selection of bestsellers from Headline

FICTION

THE DIETER	Susan Sussman	£3.99 □
TIES OF BLOOD	Gillian Slovo	£4.99 □
THE MILLIONAIRE	Philip Boast	£4.50 □
BACK TO THE FUTURE III	Craig Shaw Gardner	£2.99 □
DARKNESS COMES	Dean R Koontz	£3.99 □

NON-FICTION

THE WHITELAW MEMOIRS	William Whitelaw	£4.99 □
THE CHINESE SECRET SERVICE	Faligot & Kauffer Translated by Christine Donougher	£5.99 □

SCIENCE FICTION AND FANTASY

MAD MOON OF DREAMS	Brian Lumley	£3.50 □
BRIDE OF THE SLIME MONSTER Cineverse Cycle Book 2	Craig Shaw Gardner	£3.50 □
THE WILD SEA Bard III	Keith Taylor	£3.50 □

All Headline books are available at your local bookshop or newsagent, or can be ordered direct from the publisher. Just tick the titles you want and fill in the form below. Prices and availability subject to change without notice.

Headline Book Publishing PLC, Cash Sales Department, PO Box 11, Falmouth, Cornwall TR10 9EN, England.

Please enclose a cheque or postal order to the value of the cover price and allow the following for postage and packing:
UK: 80p for the first book and 20p for each additional book ordered up to a maximum charge of £2.00
BFPO: 80p for the first book and 20p for each additional book
OVERSEAS & EIRE: £1.50 for the first book, £1.00 for the second book and 30p for each subsequent book.

Name ....

Address ....

....

....